TRAVEL
FUC*
LOVE

A True American Love Story

J GATZ

Two Bridges Press

TRAVEL FUCK LOVE, US. Copyright © 2020 by J Gatz | Jerry M. All rights reserved.

Cover designed by Jerry M.

Two Bridges Press
TwoBridgesPress.com

ISBN 978-1-7350569-9-9 (paperback)
ISBN 978-17350569-7-5 (ebook)

Library of Congress Control Number: 2020913508

This book may be purchased in bulk for promotional or business use through your local bookseller or distributor.

Two Bridges Press, First Edition: September 2020

if you are expecting the ordinary
please **turn back** NOW
for you *will be* greatly disappointed

However, if your mind is open to *new*
adventures, perspectives,
and possibilities...
please continue

She Made Me This Way

Part 1:
Before Her

Some may never live,
but the crazy never die.

—— Hunter S. Thompson

CHAPTER 1
It's Just Me, Max

I'VE RECENTLY COME TO SEE—that no matter who you are or how you live—people will always disappoint you. Not letting it surprise you is really the only thing you can do. I've also come to see—through months of happy-hour fueled self-reflection—that I've failed to live up to my full potential, and that I'm a full-blown psychopath. Not the scary kind, no danger to anyone, besides maybe to myself, but rather, a self-aggrandizing, manipulative son of a bitch. Basically, the way every woman describes her ex.

The Tom Bradley International Terminal is buzzing as I find a seat. I've got a beer in hand, and though I'm pretty sure you're not supposed to leave the bar with a beverage, I tipped the bartender a twenty on top of my three overpriced pints—so he let it slide. Nobody has said anything, so I sit here sipping.

In my other hand, I've got a folded *USA Today*, which I paid $2.75 for at the snack shop next to the Starbucks. When I inquired how a paper that's clearly priced at two dollars—could cost $2.75, a tiny Chinese woman in a yellow visor yelled at me, "Dis is California, we do what we want!" I was too tired to argue, so I paid her in exact change and a Pan Am smile.

On my lap sits a now crumpled flyer that was handed to me by a heavily caffeinated hipster as I exited my Uber. It's information for some online Osho seminar, and for whatever reason, I didn't throw it away; even through security, I tossed it in the bin. On the front is a black-and-white photo of some bearded Bengali guru, laughing next to a beautiful woman looking up at him in total admiration. The neon pink and purple title reads: *You Love Me and I Love You.*

I stared at that stupid slogan for most of my walk through the terminal, through my two beers at the bar, and now as I sit here in silence, thinking of the last time I said *I love you* to a woman. It was actually just a few months ago, and I may have even meant it. But now, once again, I see love for what it is; a path to misplaced promises and unrealistic expectations; a fallacy, a manmade myth meant to keep us miserable.

Thus far, you could say I've lived a pretty laissez-faire lifestyle; where women come and go with the ease of a toast or a text, and the words *I never do this*, always lead to sex; a lifestyle where every pilgrimage in my passport is more important than a new Porsche or a park view.

I sit at the gate rubbing my fingers through the four-day unshaven shadow swallowing my chin, savoring the last sips of my Sam Seasonal, and staring at those words for what must've been a while; for when I glance up to a fresh whiff of wintergreen, my eyes are met by a striking blonde. We both look up at nearly the same time, and for a second, we get stuck in each other's stare. I hold my eye contact for that extra moment, and surprisingly, she holds hers. Before I know it, it seems as though we're entangled in some sort of staring competition to see who will look away first. My smirk is growing into a smile, and I almost let out a simple *hello*; but I'm not much in the mood for conversation, so I keep my mouth shut, turn my head and lose.

She has a pretty face, not super beautiful or anything, but plain and pretty. She's fair-skinned and skinny, with her hair pulled into pigtails. She's in her twenties, and judging by the perfectly crisp passport she has in her hands, she hasn't been out of the country much, if at all. And after taking a second to solidify an opinion of her, I'd confidently wager this is her first overseas trip, at least alone; and that if I wanted her, I could have her. Sure, that's somewhat of an arrogant assumption, but it's just how it is. I don't presume to be recklessly smug, but over the years, through extensive trial and error, a fair amount of failure, and a shitload of success; I've come to recognize—with an uncanny certainty—whether or not I could sleep with a woman; typically within moments of making eye contact. Malcolm Gladwell refers to this type of tightly tuned intuition as "thin-slicing"; it's definitely not an exact science, but I'm nearly never wrong. Sure, I wouldn't be able to knock her out right here at the airport; I'm no Mötley Crüe member or anything. But, according to the Cathay Pacific ticket bookmarking her passport, she's on my flight. If I struck up a conversation, listened to her tell me why she's going to Asia, and how she *just loves to travel.* Then throw in a few seemingly random stories I've acquired in the fifty or so countries I've seen thus far, there's a better than not chance she'd wake up in my bed after that first night in Hong Kong. In reality, she most likely doesn't stand a chance not to. But for some reason, I'm not really up for it right now. Don't get me wrong, I can tell she'd be a blast in the sack, and I can sense she's hoping I say something, as her eyes keep trying to catch mine. She's dying to tell someone her story, and in an effort to make this journey she's on as memorable as possible, she most likely wants to share her body with someone as interesting and free-spirited as she sees herself. At least that's how it usually goes. But, if I've learned anything in this life, it's that she's probably sitting there, thinking to herself—that she could have me too.

We travel, some of us forever,
to seek other states, other lives, other souls.

— Anaïs Nin

CHAPTER 2
The Heartland

THIS GIRL gets me thinking about my morning, and then all the events leading up to my airport arrival.

As I glance up again to her not-so-subtle stare, my mind begins to wander as my fleeing eyes fall heavy.

It was only four days ago; I was in Chicago handing over the keys to my West Loop loft. "It's a fine apartment, Max. I bet a handsome man like yourself has had some wild times here," said the fifties-and-flirty ferret-faced landlady.

"It didn't suck," I said. Eyes sore, voice raspy, still recovering from the farewell festivities.

"I haven't seen that girlfriend of yours in a while, bet she's sad to see you go."

"I think she'll be alright."

I had spent the last few months on the Don Draper diet of strong drinks and bad decisions. So, I decided to drive to Los Angeles instead of fly. It was a bit of a last-minute move, but I needed some time to myself. And I find that there's no better way to unwind and let your mind wander than a solo cross-country cruise. However, to say that self-reflection was my only motive would be misleading, as my mind was rarely free for long, and my body certainly stayed busy.

My first stop was St. Louis. Her name is Andrea, and her apartment overlooks the arch. She's an overworked pharmacist with an out-of-state fiancé.

It'd only been a month since we met, but in that time, she'd become my weekly forty-six-minute flight escape, and I, her escape from whatever demons she was dealing with. And

✈

that night, we escaped over seemingly every square inch of her Pine Street apartment and passed out in each other's arms.

I woke a few hours later, showered, and was on the road as the sun rose.

Denver was the day's destination. And after five hours on a rainy Route 70, silently praying as I'd pass spraying semis. I stopped for an early lunch at the barbeque joint Jack Stack. Somehow, in the two-dozen or so times I made that drive, it'd become a tradition of sorts. I'm not sure if it's something in the sauce or the fact you're nearly starved by the time you reach that isolated metro oasis called Kansas City, but their stuff always hits the spot.

Sitting there, alone, in a midday shadow of that rustic restaurant, a bottle of Boulevard in hand and sauce on my face, I started thinking of the last time I was there.

It was a little less than a year ago, and I was with her. I had told her over the phone that *it wouldn't work*, and that *we couldn't see each other anymore*, and then she asked where I was, and I slipped.

It wasn't six hours later that I got her text. She'd taken the first flight out of LaGuardia and asked *where we could meet?* And like all the times before, I caved.

She met me there at Jack's. It wasn't the first time she had found me, but it ended up being the last time she needed to.

She didn't care for the food; to her, anything outside of Manhattan was insignificant and not worth a shit. That was except for me. It seemed as though she'd do anything for me, anything to get close to me. And no matter how many times I told her to *take care*, she kept showing up. It didn't matter how much distance I put between us, she never let up, not even once, until I was hers.

Her name is Nadja, she's a French Canadian model from Montreal, who I met two winters ago when her Jimmy Choo got stuck in a slushy SoHo sewer-grate, and I came to the rescue. She lives in Hell's Kitchen but spent most of this year with me. Nadja isn't a household name in the modeling world. However, you've certainly seen her face in the stores you most frequently shop. Her long amber hair is eye-catching, yet hardly noticed past everything else. Every time we'd walk into a room together, people would stare. Hell, they'd slap me on the back and buy me a beer. But every time she was away, she'd be high on pills and powder, partying in some exclusive penthouse, or on a private plane with "important people," I didn't know.

These last few months haven't been my finest, but it's my own fault, really; I know better than to trust anybody who believes they're better than you.

After decades of endless fields, shape-shifting darkness, and a discernible temperature dip, I could finally see the city lights swelling ahead. Following a stop for essentials, I pulled into a modern stone-and-steel estate just south of downtown Denver.

It had been more than a year since I had Suzanne, a twice-divorced snow bunny I'd see whenever I'd pass through. She said *hello* with her devilish stare; we skipped the formalities and headed straight to the same position where I'd seen her last. Somewhere between all the slapping and screaming, I ended up losing count of who came more, but I imagine it was close.

I woke before sunrise, showered, and slipped out.

✈

CHAPTER 3

Rocky Mountain High

THE RISING RED SUN set ablaze the mountain range as the running engine melted the overnight frost. I pulled out the two peanut butter cookies I had picked up upon arrival. It's not a typical thing, but I'll partake in a little treat to myself whenever I pass through these parts. The kid who sold me the stuff said, "they're strong." He recommended I *start with* half a cookie, wait an hour, and then *decide* if I want the other half. I thought about it as I text my friend, James, confirming my upcoming arrival. Obviously still up, he responded, a selfie of his face resting upon a cartoonish set of silicone breasts, with the caption: *We're ready for ya baby.*

I scarfed down both cookies and pulled away, looking forward to the day, as everything from here to the Silver State is deep-cut canyons and mile-high mountains.

After my Silverchair CD ran out of songs, I stopped at a snowy gas station to fill-up. The cookies had fully kicked in, as the corners of my lips involuntarily curved into a smirking smile. The muscles throughout my back were warm and relaxed, my chest light, and every breath somewhat pleasurable.

I was back in my car, checking The Weather Channel app, chewing on an extraordinarily satisfying breakfast burrito, when—*Boom! Boom! Boom!* There was a loud knock at my driver's window. It would have normally startled me, but in my chemically altered state, I wasn't fazed. Instead, I slowly turned, wide-eyed, with a stoned stare. It was a tramp—a homeless man, in desperate need of a shave, a shower, and a heavier jacket. He had what looked like a car's serpentine belt in hand and was signaling for me to roll down my window. As I obliged, I caught a gulp of his body odor, a pungent combination of gin and piss.

✈

"Excuse me, sir. I understand you're busy, and I hate to bother you so early in the morning, but I'm on my way to Denver to see my brother and his little baby girl. And my car broke down. It's the red one right over there, and well, it appears that I've left my wallet back in Vail. I'm just wondering if you had anything you could spare, so I could give my brother a call and get a lift."

I held up a finger as I dug into my pocket and fetched out a ten-spot, handed it to him, saying nothing, just a smile.

"Thank you, sir. Thank you so much." And my window went up.

I usually don't give to homeless guys, had an incident, and stopped some years back. But I had to respect this guy's hustle. He wasn't sitting on the ground, holding a sign or begging. He came up with a story, a somewhat elaborate plot, with characters and props, and delivered his spiel with such passion, that if I hadn't seen a woman getting into the car he had just told me was his, I might have even believed him. Anyhow, he was polite. I figured that ten would get him a couple beers and make him happy for a few hours.

Back on the road, cruising through Colorado, the Switzerland of the states, full of fourteeners and fine women. My high was now in full effect, and my mind kept drifting beyond the boundaries of weird.

Just as some scientist on *The Joe Rogan Experience* had me sufficiently freaked about the future, I speculated how the future might see Joe. Today, historians rely on murals, memoirs, and monuments to paint a picture of a man. But whatever studies us will have videos of a guy making coliseums full of people crack-up on command. A guy who gets into cages with modern-day gladiators. A guy who has his face tattooed on his followers. A guy who for years, told people to eat cockroaches and drink donkey-spunk, and they happily slurped that shit down. I surmised that future historians might see Joe as a spiritual leader, a king, or a sorcerer of sorts.

Tracing the Colorado River, Route 70 slices through miles of magnificent mountains, lush forests, and early December snows.

I tried to imagine what it must be like to live in every cliffside cabin I'd pass. I kept thinking; *it's got to be so goddamn beautiful up there.* I couldn't conceive why every person on earth doesn't live on one of those ridges.

Then hours later, while winding through the red-ribboned gorges of central Utah, I briefly believed I was driving on the surface of a far off moon, a mix between Mars and the Mojave, where rust-red rock runs to a horizon of snow-capped mountains and baby-blue skies.

At this moment, I was feeling glorious, the best I had in months, and though it wasn't thirty degrees on that high-desert highway: I had the windows down, the heat up, and *Free Bird* on blast. I felt like Hunter S. Thompson himself, steaming towards the bright light city, and my soul was already on fire. This right here is the real reason I decided to drive. Sure, I may have gotten a few kicks on route. But the freedom you have while driving fast and alone in the middle of nowhere is the reason songs like this are sung. Life was good, and for the moment, my worries and woes were in the rearview mirror.

However, no matter how perfect the moment was, how high I was, how red those rocks, or how sweet that song, I just couldn't shake her. She kept creeping into my thoughts, a constant distraction I couldn't avoid. Nadja would never take no for an answer. Not only in real life but now also in my mind.

She had relentlessly pursued me, not just for a couple weeks or months, but for a whole goddamn year that girl chased me, before I gave in, collapsing like a gazelle with a big cat on its back. She refused to quit, and I admired that about her. I've always kept my heart casually cool, but through unwavering persistence, and never before seen resilience, she found her way in. Where others saw her steadfast pursuit of me as strange or even scary, I thought it to be endearing. Definitely not at first, but over time, she wore me down. She indoctrinated me into

✈

believing that love was her singular motive, and all she wanted was me.

CHAPTER 4
Sin City

PULLING ONTO THE VEGAS STRIP, traffic was its typical terrible. My high had faded, only a tallboy between my legs to keep me easy. People were everywhere, and you could feel the raw energy in the air that only this four-mile fluorescent fantasyland can supply.

Though I was staying at CityCenter, I exited at Sahara. I like to drive down the once upon a time soul of the strip by Circus Circus, where, as a kid, I'd stay at the Stardust with my grandparents and collect nudie-flyers for my friends back home. I couldn't tell you why, but whenever I find myself between Treasure Island and The Stratosphere, I get some sort of sooth-ing nostalgic feeling, a reminder of simpler times, I suppose.

When I finally arrived, I valeted my car and text James. He got right back to me, saying he'd be *right down*.

I've known him and his roommate Sam since freshman year. They grew up on the same street, and I lived across the hall. We got along because we didn't belong. Like me, they were worlds away from that place—wild and free—put there by pushy parents with big pocketbooks. But unlike me—they've never swayed from their Lebowski mindset, mastering Manson's *Subtle Art*, and I envied the shit out of them for it.

It had been over a year since my last visit to Vegas. I usually made it every few months, but I didn't dare come while dating Nadja. Didn't want to deal with the doubt it'd of caused. Of course, I would never tell James that. He met her once, and after ten minutes, turned to me and said, "Too young, too emo-tional."

The elevator opened, and we slapped each other on the backs like old buddies do.

No matter where you live in this town, the valley, or the hills, a strip view means you made it, and damn he has a good one. James lives the lifestyle rappers rap about. He drives hundred thousand dollar cars, always pops bottles, and fucks models; the Bilzerian type—the epitome of contemporary success—who lives hard and always seems to be having more fun than everyone else.

He's a tall, well-built Italian guy, sporting his signature black-on-black with his hair slicked back, and Sergey Shanko arm-sleeves. If the guy could sing, they'd throw him on the cover of *Rolling Stone*. For lack of a better adjective, James is cool. He's definitely cooler than me. Hell, he's cooler than Johnny Cash.

As the condo door opened, Sam bear-hugged me and heaved me over his shoulder. "Where you been hiding you motherfucker!" he shouted, two-rotations into a helicopter spin.

Sam is a guy's guy, the kind who mentally never checked out of college, the guy you'll see on *Barstool Sports* chugging beers and chanting *Saturdays are for the boys*. Though he's smart as shit, he loves to get fucked-up, and always has the most ridiculous stories of stupid stunts he's pulled.

"Max, I thought you were gonna be here at like seven, man, what the fuck?" he said, returning my feet to the floor, and promptly placing a cold-one in my hand. You could see he had started early.

"I hit snow near Zion," I said, suggestively exaggerating the severity of the storm. I didn't tell them I had been high all day. Or that I got distracted feeding chips to some squirrels just past Grand Junction. Or those lonely moments I spent staring down into Devils Canyon, questioning *who would miss me?* Or how at dinner, I got caught in a lecture by this old redneck in camo-everything, warning me of the *evil virus* coming.

"Yeah, it's a beautiful drive," I said to Sam.

"Same ole, Max," he slurred back. He was definitely blitzed, his eyes empty and unfocused. Nearly assuring another "epic tale" being told tomorrow.

James chimed in. "If you're gonna shower, you should get in now, the girls will be here soon."

Obviously, girls were on their way, why would I think otherwise? With James, it was always a party, a buffet of booze, blow, and babes. Before every painful flight home, I'd always promise myself I wasn't going back for at least a year; this just happened to be the only time I kept it.

"And you know who's gonna be here, don't yous," Sam slurred. I knew who he was talking about the second he said it.

It seems like forever ago, but Vegas is one of the several cities I've lived in my adult life. The "who" is a girl named Lexi. A few years back, she and I dated a few months. I ended it two days after she said she *loved* me, then confirmed the relationship dead when I moved back to Chicago weeks later. Before Nadja, Lexi lasted longer than any girlfriend I ever had. I'd still see her from time to time when I came out west, but we hadn't spoken in over a year, and I obviously wasn't the one who told her I was here.

Freshly showered, I walked out to the now noisy room full of girls, and two random dudes I didn't know: both in skinny shirts, tatted sleeves, and too many muscles; a similarity that's standard in this city and not exclusive to any sex.

The ten or so girls were all pretty much clones of each other. Likely all from different parts of the globe, they move to the desert, and the longer they stay, the more they end up looking alike. They all had tight bodies, big tits, fake lips, designer bags, and squeezed into the shortest skirts they could find. The only differentiating factor being: the length and color of their hair, the shade of their tan, and types of tattoos covering their skin. I caught a few of their names as James went around introducing me, or rather, using me as a tool to refresh them for himself. There was Candy, Lacy, Stacy, Sasha, and I believe a Tiffany or two.

"Hey, I know you. Aren't you the guy from Chicago? The one who dated Lexi?" asked one of the platinum clones. I think her name was Heather.

"Maybe, what Lexi?" I said, with self-evident sarcasm.

"Um, she's like really tall, with super-shiny hair, perfect teeth, and like um, really huge boobs."

Heather obviously didn't catch the quip. "Yeah, that may have been me." Now smiling to myself, suddenly reminded how bubbly West Coast Barbies can be.

"Oh my God, she's like, so like... still totally obsessed with you."

"Really?" I said, genuinely surprised.

"Ugh yeah, and she like... like just text me. She's gonna be here like any minute."

I wasn't planning on seeing Lexi on this layover, but it was a satisfying surprise. And though she's definitely not meant for me, she reminds me of a good time in my life. I was happy that last summer in Sin City, and she was a part of that.

Lexi may look like these girls, who are so into themselves, they'd never care about anyone else. But to me, she was always so different. She grew up here; under the bright shade of The Strip, and in her all-exclusive world, she's living the luxurious lifestyle considered success. Sure, she's a stripper who's slept with more men than Madonna, and she parties harder than Elvis, but that's who she is, and she isn't ashamed of it. I'd take that any day over the common counterfeit virtue. At least Lexi doesn't pretend to be anything she isn't. And we had good times together. We laughed a lot, fucked a lot, and really enjoyed each other's company.

She took over the room in her barely-there disco-ball skirt, said hi to some girls, but as soon as our eyes met—she screamed and sprinted towards me. "Max! You came." Leaping into my arms as though I had just returned from war.

"You know I can't stay away."

"And you weren't even gonna tell me you were in town. You're such an asshole."

"I didn't know till three days ago, I swear." My eyes go to Sam, the obvious source of the leak. Raising his palms, he comically pouted his lower lip and shrugged.

I could see Lexi was genuinely happy, and so was I. We split a bottle of sparkling wine and threw back a few tequilas. The party picked up, and before we knew it, we were laughing like old times. In all, about forty people crowded the condo, which stunk of Skunkweed and Coco Chanel, set to the sounds of G-Eazy and Post Malone. Where every slightly significant second seemed to be documented by an overwhelming on-slaught of staged selfies, as Millions of followers in combined *Instagram* fame snorted substantial amounts of uncut cocaine. And though it's not my thing, *I'm not one to judge*, I thought to myself as I tossed back another tequila. Everyone was partying, laughing, smoking, and having a great time.

Lexi and I pretty much stuck together. She would occa-sionally bring a friend over, and to my surprise, they knew quite a bit about me.

"So, Max, I hear you're a traveler. Where are you going, where have you been?" asked Sasha, one of the original clones, in a thick British accent: ass-length platinum extensions, leopard print sleeve, and perfect teeth.

"I've seen a few things," I said. "Not too sure on the near future."

"Where you heading after here?" asked Lexi.

"Los Angeles." Factually true, yet still a lie by omission. I have my reasons.

"I heard you're an Ivy Leaguer?" said Sasha in her sophisticated cadence.

Pointing at Sam and James, I said, "And so are they." Failing to mention that I dropped out after freshman year.

"Aces for sure, Max. So, you and your mates are like super smart?"

"They are, I just cheated a lot."

"Ah, a cheeky bastard, eh?"

✈

I smiled, recalling the words of an old mentor. "That admiration for attending a selective school is an exclusive trait of the truly uneducated and the truly uninteresting."

"I'm fuckin smart," Sam blurted out of nowhere, then stumbled over and put his arm around Sasha. "Do we have a sapiosexual in the house?" he asked.

She shrugged him off, rolling her eyes, as I assume she considered without conclusion if he had insulted her or not.

"So what you fellas do for work?" she asked.

"This fucking guy," Sam slurred. He was definitely on a different level, and then, for seemingly no reason, he lifted his shirt, revealing the black pistol he had tucked into his belt.

"Whoa, what have you got that for, mate?" said Sasha.

"Because I'm a fucking agent," Sam whisper-mumbled back, wide-eyed and wasted.

"You work for the government, do ya?" she questioned.

"I am the fucking government," he confidently claimed, as Sasha's eyes searched mine for confirmation.

"He's a federal agent. US customs," I affirmed.

Mouthing me the words, she asked, "Are we ok?"

"He's harmless," I said, smiling.

"Vegas is a little different from Liverpool, hey, baby?" Sam said.

"How'd you know I'm from Liverpool?" she promptly responded, seemingly suspect of his insight.

Sam stood there, strangely silent as he creepily gazed with his glassy eyes. Several seconds passed before he slurred, "With an ass like that, you can call me an anglophile."

My eyes jumped to hers, anticipating anger. Instead, she appeared perplexed. I imagine she was waiting for a punch line, or possibly an explanation. Despite the fancy accent, she definitely didn't come off as the quickest in the conversation, and I suppose strippers grow accustomed to ass complements, so no offense seemed to be taken.

"Seriously, how'd you know I'm from Liverpool?" she asked again.

✈

"You's got that, that fuckin, what do they call it. That fuckin Merseyside dialect," Sam mumbled.

"Ah, a clever bloke. Quite pissed, I'd say, but spot on."

"Let me know if you want some fuckin crumpets, baby." He leaned in like he was going to kiss her, stopped himself, then dramatically turned on a dime, mimicking a palace guard as he marched off.

Her eyes rolled before she turned her attention back to Lexi and me.

"Your friend's delightful," she said, with an exaggerated toothy smile.

"It's early," I replied.

"Can't wait."

"Don't worry about him, he just likes to go hard sometimes. He's harmless," I re-affirmed.

"And what about you, Max?" she asked.

"What about me?"

"Do you like to go hard?" Her plump lips pouted.

"Nah, I'm just old and boring."

"I don't believe it."

"I promise you."

"And what is it you do, Mr. Max?"

"Oh, it's not that interesting."

"No? I doubt that."

"He won't tell you about his work," Lexi blurted out. Possibly to suppress the unsubtle sexual undertones bouncing between us.

"And why is that? Keeping secrets, are we?"

"No secrets, just nothing too exciting," I said.

"Are you CIA? A federal agent like your loose legged friend over there?" she pressed.

"Believe me, he won't tell you," said Lexi.

"I don't understand."

"He won't tell you what he does, because he lives a secret double life."

"Double life," Sasha exclaimed. "Sounds mysterious."

"Hardly," I said, before Lexi jumped back in.

✈

"Yeah, he'll go to Asia for a couple weeks and come back with a twenty thousand dollar check that he doesn't rush to cash, but he won't tell you anything about it. I promise you, he's not gonna say a thing." Lexi, obviously a little loose-lipped and tipsy herself, was referring to the time she went snooping through my room a few years back, and found, then googled the name on a check.

"So you are CIA," Sasha said with a wink.

"More like, C-I-Actually just fuck old women with big bank accounts," Lexi said, in her best impersonation of me.

"Like, as in you're an escort?" Tiffany, another nearby clone, chimed in.

"No," I said.

"Because being an escort doesn't necessarily mean you have to sleep with anyone," she justified, for whatever reason.

"It's not that... really, it's nothing too exciting."

"Come on, Max, you can't leave us like this, no secrets here. Tell us," Sasha pressed.

"All right, if you really want to know," I said, squinting my eyes, appearing sincere. "I'm a strength and conditioning coach." I scanned their reactions. "See, nothing notable."

"Like a personal trainer?"

"Exactly, but—" I started to say before Lexi cut me off.

"Coach my ass. More like a hard dick for hire." She was the only one laughing among our growing group of onlookers. "And then one day, he'll just disappear, and never answer your calls again, isn't that right, Max? Tell 'em how it is." Nobody said a word, but their eyes stayed affixed as Lexi's half-serious, half-smiling rant rolled on. "Is it because I don't give you twenty grand to fuck me? Is that what it is? I'm half her age. Don't I get some sort of dick discount?" Her smile had subsided as the steam from her stored-up hostility hissed.

Sasha, seemingly to minimize the awkwardness of the moment, turned to James and spoke loud. "So, what is it that you do?" she asked.

James, who was hitting the hookah, and probably not paying attention, paused, and after a long exhalation of thick cinnamon-scented smoke. "Uh yeah, I do the same thing."

"That's cool," Sasha said, but everyone in the know—including Lexi—just snickered to themselves. See, James doesn't actually have a job, at least not the nine-to-five kind. And when asked, he always has a tale to tell. Over the years, I've heard them all, from plastic surgeon to fighter pilot, or whatever came to his mind at that moment, but hell, he pulls it off. In reality, James is a salesman, commodities mostly; the kind that gets you time. The crazy thing is, Sam—his roommate and best friend for life—really is a high-ranked US customs agent. I'm not sure how the whole racket works, as I've never actually asked.

"Let's get out of here and go to the fucking club!" James shouted, the crowd cheered, and the condo quickly emptied.

Sam, myself, Lexi, Sasha, and four of the other clones piled in James' Escalade for the fifteen-minute traffic jam to the MGM.

After the required hike through the casino, its typical synthetic sparkle, full of working girls and shattered dreams. We're greeted by a sharp-suited VIP host, who whisked us past the insufferable maze of ropes herding the masses.

Lexi grabbed ahold of my hand as we're escorted to our private table, an oversized curved leather sofa that sat center of the main stage. I've been to nightclubs all over the world, but the attention to detail and over-the-top showmanship behind these walls is second to none, a mind-blowing madhouse, yet as luxurious as it gets. Velvet and leather everything, with bottle service girls—plucked from the pages of *Playboy*.

Within a song of being sat, we were all popping bottles of Ace of Spades Rosé and jumping to the soaring sounds of The Chainsmokers.

In Hakkasan, you don't just hear the music; you feel it pulsating through your plasma as powerful explosions of green flame and glitter shoot into a downpour of confetti. Laser lights dance in delirium, as seizure-inducing strobes distort the senses.

✈

If not for the acrobats swinging from the chandeliers, it'd be difficult to determine the difference between down and up—a perfect combination of class and commotion; controlled chaos at its finest.

James had our table as crazy as a Kirill party, where top-shelf tits were soaked in a small fortune of fine champagne.

I had been dancing between Lexi and her girlfriends, passing around a bottle of 1942; when out of nowhere, I started thinking of Nadja. Through all the lights, the noise, and raw sex pouring through this place, there she was, I couldn't help myself. It was as if I had stepped into a quiet bubble, just me and my misery. She was always in a place like this. *Was she out tonight? Was she having a good time? Was she thinking of me? Did she ever think of me?* But before I could go into further reflection—Lexi grabbed my face and pulled me in. "Let's get out of here, babe."

"Sure," I said. And like that, my bubble burst.

"Sasha's staying with me too," she said, grabbing her friend's hand.

After a quick cab ride, we were on the 28th floor of Panorama Towers. I hadn't been in a while, but it was just as I remembered; a large open space of pink pillows and floor to ceiling windows overlooking The Strip.

Lexi threw on some Springsteen, then walked straight into kissing me. It was a hard passionate kiss, the kind you could tell had been building for a while. She was moaning and murmuring under her breath, "Baby, please don't leave again." She pulled me in closer and kissed me harder. "I miss you so much. I'll do anything you want. Just stay this time."

It's here I realized that Lexi, my girlfriend of four months, a few years back, likely still loved me. Maybe she never stopped. And then, without influence on my part, she confirmed her stated willingness to do anything. "Sasha, come over here," she said, signaling her friend with a single—come here finger. Sasha stood and strutted towards us; a catwalk type intensity, long confident steps, and unwavering eye contact. She put her arm around Lexi and gleamed sinfully into my eyes.

"You think Max is hot, right?" Lexi asked.

"He's quite a man." She replied in her posh accent.

"And you want to kiss Max, right?"

"I'm all for it if you won't get mad at me."

"His lips are perfect, give them a taste."

"With pleasure," Sasha said before her tongue slid into my mouth.

I suddenly jumped back, not physically, but in my mind. *What am I doing,* I thought. *How the fuck did I even get into this!* I shouted inside myself. *Do I even want this shit anymore?* But my weak-will didn't stand a chance as they tasted like champagne and smelled of seduction.

Lexi slipped behind me and whispered into my ear, "I'm gonna make you so fucking happy, baby." Her hands clawed across my chest as Sasha slid her tongue back into my mouth. But before I could take them, before I could spread Lexi's legs or bend Sasha over, my world started to spin, a violent storm of excess. Beyond being sick of myself—I was sick, sick-sick. I pulled my lips from Sasha's, snapped my head to the side, and *Woohaatt!* A stinging tequila-scented stew of Ace of Spades and stomach acid sloshed onto the floor.

"Well, that was fun," Sasha cracked.

"Oh babe, are you alright?" Lexi patted my back as I heaved again, *Woohaatt!*

"I'm sorry," I murmured. "I'm really sorry." And just like her vomit-topped tile, my life, a pathetic fucking mess.

After a shower, some mouthwash, and a Sprite for my stomach, I threw on a robe and sat back in Lexi's California King as the girls smoked a bowl.

After a few laughs, several handfuls of Sour Patch Kids, and some well-deserved teasing, Sasha kissed both of us good-night. She smiled as she said how "marvelous" I was, and how she'd "never forget me." Then turned, tucked herself under the sheets, and slipped into a snoring sleep.

✈

Lexi and I sat up and talked for some time. She asked if I could "ever see us together again?" A question one doesn't foresee from someone who just picked up his puke.

I learned a long time ago not to lie to women, lead them on, or make them promises I can't keep. So, I didn't. I told her I was glad we spent the night together, that I think of her, and would always wish her the best. I said I'd call her when I got back in town, but that I didn't know when that'd be. Then we fell asleep in each other's arms.

I woke before sunrise, walked to James' for my stuff, another shower, and again was on the road.

I did not tell half of what I saw, for
no one would have believed me.

— Marco Polo

✈

CHAPTER 5

A Dead Dream

I JUMP AWAKE. Startled, my arms flailing as I franticly look around. Forgetting where I am, I instinctively snap my head to see if the plane is still here. The girl with pigtails is laughing.

"Did you have a nightmare?" she asks.

"No, maybe," I mumble, stupefied, and somewhat embarrassed as I wipe the drool dribbling down my chin.

"You were out cold for about ten minutes, but they haven't started boarding yet," she informs me.

"Great," I say, one eye still half-shut.

"I would've woke you if they did." She smiles.

"I appreciate that."

I toss my head back and stretch my arms to the sky. I'm completely spent. What was supposed to be a spiritual soul-searching cross-country cruise; somehow slipped into six hours of total sleep, an innumerable number of orgasms, and a hangover I still haven't shaken.

Yet, despite my current condition, I had a decently productive day. Not only did I make the daunting desert drive across California: but also satisfied my In-N-Out fix, sold my Subaru, threw down a few *hair of the dogs*, and arrived early enough to catch some scores. Sure, I got taken on the car a bit, could have gotten a few grand more if I didn't sell to a dealer, but *oh well.* I still have my old pickup parked at my dad's.

They announce the boarding of first-class passengers. I don't waste time getting to my feet. I'm tired and anticipating slipping into a pair of provided pajamas, throwing down a glass of champagne and whatever amuse-bouche bullshit they give you, and passing out.

Even though I'm flying at the front of the plane, I'm really a pretty simple guy who could live on cheese sandwiches, hell, has lived on cheese sandwiches, and would be perfectly happy in coach, but I'm not paying for it, never do, so why the hell not. "Thanks for not laughing at me," I say to pigtails as I toss my bag over my shoulder.

"No problem... I hope I run into you in Hong Kong," she says, giving me one of those hesitant half-waves, where you don't actually wave.

I get to my seat, where I'm greeted with a flute of bubbly and a bowl of fresh fruit. I pull out an Ambien and empty the glass. I typically don't take pills on a plane. I like to stay up and enjoy the movies, the food, the booze, and the international air travel experience. No matter how many times I've done it. But I'm weary and want for nothing more than to slip into a substance-induced slumber.

The seats up here are large and luxurious. You don't have your own room, but it's basically your own cubical—all equipped with a touch screen TV and a seat that folds flat into a bed. The attendant brings me my toiletry bag and sleepwear, so I make my way to the bathroom to change.

I emerge from the john in a two-piece grandpa style getup with matching slippers, looking overanxious as most passengers are still yet to board. But I don't care. I just want to be comfortable and crash.

Knowing I can't recline till takeoff, I pull out my phone and read through my messages.

The first is from Suzanne in Denver: *You're Amazing! Let's do that again soon!*

I respond: *Definitely!*

The second is from Andrea in St. Louis: *When will I see you again?*

Just as I reply, three suits walk into the first-class cabin laughing up a storm. "And I told them to take that Singapore bidding contract and shove it up their ass!" the oldest of three roared. The other two are dying, laughing like fucking hyenas.

I quickly order a Johnnie Walker and a Heineken from the passing stewardess. And lucky for me, they're in the three cubicles closest to mine and continue as though they're in a busy bar. Usually, I'd welcome this. I'd probably order us all shots and shoot the shit, but I'm spent and seeking silence.

As the stewardess delivers my medicine, the youngest at around thirty-five, and best looking of the bunch, pokes his big grin out from his cubical and loudly whispers to the other two. "I'm calling up Pinkerton in the morning and telling that rat bastard if his client reneges on this fucking deal, that I have no other move than to bang his wife!" They all roll in hysteria, and I smile as I sip my whisky.

After listening to them for a few minutes while I fuss with my headphones, I come to see they're bankers, working on some multi-billion-dollar deal. They're not spinning the roulette wheel of Wall Street, slinging subprime loans, or shorting Tesla. These guys build things; they contribute to the world and add value to the lives of people they've never met. It's pretty inspiring, really. And again, it gets me thinking about my life. Not about how typical my last few nights have become, but rather my life from a decade ago, and how it almost ended up so differently.

I try not to live in the past, or let the woulda, coulda, shoulda's affect my present. But as I sit here, in this oversized first-class seat—listening to these guys snicker, I can't help but let my mind wander, imagining what my life would be like now, had my uncle never gone out for groceries that day.

It was just a few months after graduation. And even though I had no job, and barely any bread, I had been traveling the world—chasing memories—living cheap. My parents were just happy I graduated, having spent the last couple of years worried I wouldn't. Not only did I transfer out of their top university—the only thing they ever agreed on—but then I dropped out to move to Hawaii for a semester, which turned into two, and then twelve-months. But eventually, after growing tired of dodging their calls, I did it; I went back to Illinois and got my degree. But after months adrift on a post-graduate pilgrimage, my bank account had run dry, and my parents weren't jumping at the chance to further sponsor my escapades. I had absolutely no idea what I wanted to do, few prospects, and even fewer funds.

I was visiting my dad in Louisville, Kentucky, a two-day layover before heading home. Before that night, I never really knew my uncle Chuck. He was more of a myth than a man. Sure, I'd see him at Christmas parties and the occasional family function, but I definitely didn't know him.

From what I'd been told, he was rich as hell, owned a half-dozen homes around the world, sat on the boards of banks, and was considered by many *a pioneer* of western investments in Asia. But most of this info came from my grandfather, who often confused me with my dad. So, in reality, I didn't really know my uncle Chuck. However, that all came to change on that chilly Kentucky night.

After dinner, he asked me to join him for bourbon on his big old southern porch. We got to talking about school, and traveling, and how—at my age—he also had no clue what he wanted out of life. Then he went on about his investment group in Korea, and that if I went back to school, and got an MBA, or Masters in finance, that he'd hire me the day I graduated. He told me I'd *work my ass off for five years, but after that, I'd make more money than I could spend*. He told me I'd be able to *travel the world*, and that in ten years, I'd have *two homes* bigger than the one we were at that night.

I was fucking pumped. I had found my path and instantly committed myself to do whatever it'd take to accomplish my new dream.

It was mid-March; most business school's applications were due in the next few weeks. If I wanted in, I had to take the GMAT entrance exam, write essays, and schedule interviews.

I signed up to take the test just eight days after our talk. Most study for a few months—if not longer—but I didn't have that kind of time. I'm good at math and had bullshitted my way through most of life.

I set up shop in Chicago, where I spent the next seven days locked in the 24-hour Starbucks on North and Wells, with a stack of thick books and yellow legal pads. Fueled by a few hundred dollars in Adderall and Iced coffee, I wrote one essay every morning, then studied through the night.

I took the GMAT on an hour's sleep and scored in the top 96th percentile. I got into three of the five schools I applied to. I chose Indiana because it was close to my dad and because Mark Cuban went to Indiana, and look at him.

Staying in constant contact with my uncle, who by that time had become my mentor, I killed it that first semester. By nearly never partying and living on less sex than an unmarried Mormon, I had straight A's going into finals week. I was proud of how consumed I'd become by the process. In just sixteen short months, I'd have my MBA and be on my way to Seoul to stack stacks. My future was pretty much mapped out; become an investment banker, stick with it ten—maybe fifteen years, retire a millionaire, and then travel the world. I thought about it every damn day, and it was a strong enough motivator to stay away from women, drinking, drugs, or anything that typically sidetracks an ambitious twenty-three-year-old. And then I got that call.

My uncle had been taking a culinary class in his spare time. On a warm Tuesday at his West Texas ranch, he wanted to try a new recipe but didn't have fresh tomatoes. The sun was shining, so he and his wife hopped on his motorbike and headed into town. Ten miles down the road, a drunk driver ran a red light. My uncle never got to try that recipe.

I didn't return to school after Christmas break; I lost my drive and dropped out. But to this day, whenever I'm down on myself, I always try to remember how inspired I was on that one cool Kentucky night, and it keeps me going.

See, I'm nobody special, a simple guy really. Everything I have has been given to me or obtained by some old-fashioned luck. I once thought I had something, but came to see I was mistaken. I have no special talents. I've created nothing noteworthy or built anything worthwhile. The only success I've ever attained is with women, a skill set of diminishing returns. And though I've never

✈

actually failed at anything, I've also never really tried. Yet despite this, I still retain a childlike sense of wonder, where I curiously pursue knowledge for no other reason than procuring it. I read religiously and always over-analyze everything in an effort to see the unseen. I wander freely, yet the future frightens me. Living your life in constant pursuit of pleasure leaves little time for structure or stability. I'm not old, but old enough to remember when we made memories for ourselves—instead of strangers. Sometimes I experience pain, but it's usually dulled by disappointment. Everyone says I'm running from something, I say—only from standing still. I don't know where I'll be in a year, or even a month from now, but I'm sure it won't be too bad.

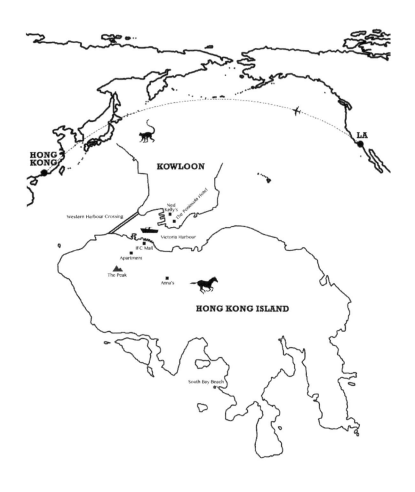

When I lived in Hong Kong,
I felt that Hong Kong is my family.

— Jet Li

CHAPTER 6
Anna

I WAKE UPON LANDING. I hadn't been to Hong Kong in over a year, which is weird, as I've been coming here nearly every month for most of the last decade. At one point, I owned piles of first-class pajamas—a collection that could rival The Points Guy's.

I turn on my phone. A year ago, I would have landed to a dozen messages, but in my Nadja induced solitude, I fell out of touch with a few friends and a fair amount of lovers. I have new *follow* requests from a few of the clones, and a text from Sam: *You missed it man! I banged this hot midget wrestler on a bet with James!* I don't respond.

I have no checked bags as I tossed or donated nearly everything I owned before I left. I don't really have a plan, but I know I'm not going back for a while. Most of my remaining possessions are in the small Tumi duffle on my shoulder and need a wash. I take a mental inventory as I make my way to customs: I have my MacBook, two pairs of jeans, a few T-shirts, my favorite Banana Republic button-down, a worn-out copy of *The Spy Who Came in from the Cold*, a couple pair of Calvin Kleins, some workout gear, the boots on my feet, the clothes on my back, and the Ray-Bans on my eyes is pretty much everything I own.

I quickly clear customs with my express pass, and as expected, I find a suited driver waiting for me, but he isn't Chan, Anna's driver for years.

"Hey, I'm Max," I say to the shiny-faced Chinese man holding a sign with my name. "Where's Chan?"

"You, Max?" he replies in a heavy Cantonese accent.

✈

"Yeah, I'm Max, but where's Chan? I was expecting Chan."

"No, no, no. No Chan. I Lee, you, Max." He obviously doesn't speak English. A *Napoleon Dynamite* kind of character, so awkward and odd, he seems somewhat synthetic.

"Good to meet you, Lee." I turn towards the limo-lot a little bummed; Chan was a good drinking buddy, the kind I could use about now.

I stretch out in the back of that slate-gray Bentley limousine with the all-white leather interior, open a cold bottle of considerately stocked San Miguel.

I'm looking forward to the forty-minute ride to Anna's, then again, for seemingly no reason, my mind goes straight to Nadja. Like Vegas, she's why I hadn't been to Hong Kong in a year, or do much of anything. I spent my entire adult life living fast, doing whatever the fuck I wanted, hell, I was everywhere. But as soon as I committed myself to her last New Year, I never went anywhere. She didn't ask me not to, I just didn't. I'm very aware of my own fallibility, so I purposely eliminated all possible temptations. I hate men who cheat, so I stayed put. Thinking about it now, it must have been strange for her. She had gotten to know me through infrequent layovers from exotic destinations, living with a catch me if you can attitude. And then suddenly, I stopped. I know she couldn't see that I stayed home for her. Even though I was fairly honest about my past, I don't think she ever truly understood the depths to my depravity; therefore, she could never fully appreciate the effort I was making.

We emerge from the Western Harbour Crossing tunnel and are now downtown. Hong Kong is just as it always is—the mythical Queen Mother—both beautiful and intimidating. I rush to lower the windows, so I can hear the sounds and smell the smells. Immediately I taste a variety of tropical curries, diesel fuel, and fresh seafood in the air. This city is unlike any in the world. It's clean, but not too clean. It's run by the Chinese but heavily influenced by a fading English colonial sophistication.

There's an endless array of billion-dollar skyscrapers, surrounded by fish markets, and rundown medicine shops—selling dried shark fins and hundred-dollar-an-ounce ginseng. It's the historic financial capital of Asia, built by the British Empire and ever-expanding skyward. It's basically New York City if Manhattan had ten-million-more Asians and was in the middle of a fucking jungle.

I know we're getting close as we emerge from the chaotic city and begin climbing the hill. High concrete walls replace the ornate shops. Thirty and forty million-dollar homes become abundant, housing the island's most prestigious residents. These are the streets where Hong Kong's super-rich and morally bankrupt sleep.

The car slows as the towering wrought-iron gates swing open. Revealing the sunlit side of the seven thousand square-foot, all white, modern box of a building. Then crawl along the curved stone driveway, meant to remind you that money doesn't matter.

Anna's husband is an executive at one of the world's largest banks, which recently relocated its Asia headquarters from Hong Kong to Singapore. He makes millions a year, but only works because he wants to, as he's already fabulously wealthy. As an heir to a substantial family fortune, Teddy inherited several million pounds when he was seventeen and has since multiplied it many times. Some men come from money, and some make their own; because he's bread from both, Teddy demands the best of everything because he demands the best from himself. Yet despite his exceptionally high standards, he's become a great friend of mine.

Anna is outside, waiting for me as we pull up. The driver stops so that my door opens just in front of her. "Hello, sunshine," I say, with the biggest smile my face has felt in forever. "Are you expecting someone?"

"Now, don't tell me, no, it can't be," she says in her sweet southern style. "Yes, yes, I do believe it is, Mister Max

Malovice himself, gracing me with his presence, for I didn't think he remembered where I lived, or even who I was."

"Oh, is this your place?" I say, looking around as she gleams at me. "It's alright, I guess." I peel off my shades. "Hell of a hike from the airport, though."

"Oh, Max, darlin', come and give me some shugah."

Her arms open, and I pick her off the ground. She smells of opulent roses, and we both revel in the reunion.

Upon her feet returning to the grass, she gathers herself and turns to the driver. "Lee, I'll be taking Mister Malovice to the apartment in about an hour, so if you could come back then, I'd appreciate it." But the driver responds with a blank stare. You can see he has no idea what she said. "*Yī xiaoshi hou huilai*," she says, in the most Americanized sounding Chinese accent you've ever heard.

"Ah ok-ok, I go," Lee says, before getting back in the Bentley and pulling away.

"When the hell did you learn Cantonese?" I ask. I've been coming here for ten years, and I've never once heard her even attempt a word in the local tongue.

"Well, I hope I told him to come back in an hour, and not go home, or go to hell or something." We laugh. "Oh, Max, that damn driver has got me studying Chinese just so I can get around town, it's positively awful."

"What happened to Chan?"

"Teddy fired him. Says he caught him staring at my behind or something silly like that. You know how absolutely barmy he can be, always thinking everyone's trying to shag me."

Anna is from a small swamp town in East Texas, where the locals speak in a slow southern slang, something similar to Forrest Gump's momma. However, with Teddy being English, you'll sometimes hear her slipping in some unnatural quasi-British lingo. I swear it's the strangest goddamn thing you've ever heard.

"Do you need help with your bags, Mister Malovice?" She's eyeing my duffel. "Is that really all you brought with you?"

"You know it is."

✈

"Aren't you staying longer than tonight?"

"That's the plan."

"Well, that's just fine. We'll go into town tomorrow and get you some new clothes."

"I think I'm good, I'll do some laundry later."

"Now I'm not gonna hear it. We're gonna get you some new clothes because I guarantee that dingy little bag is holding nothing but smelly old T-shirts and dirty socks."

"We'll figure it out." I smile, knowing she nailed it.

"All right, sounds like a plan. We'll go tomorrow. Now come on, you must be awfully exhausted after that flight, let's get inside and get you a proper drink."

"I actually slept pretty well on the plane, but I could go for that drink."

"Well, shugah, you are in luck. Last month, Teddy and I won a private bartending class at some charity auction. We took it just last weekend, and I positively do believe that I now make the best martini in all of Hong Kong." I try, but fail to conceal my thoughts. "Why are you laughing at me?"

"No, I'm not laughing. I swear," I say, but she knows I'm full of shit. "I'm just wondering, though. How much did this private bartending class end up costing you?"

"Oh, I don't know, it was for charity."

I had missed the fun of her over the top frivolousness. "Come on, I'm just curious. What was the final bid?"

"Oh, I don't know, I think we paid around a hundred thousand Hong Kong."

"So, about thirteen thousand US dollars," I say.

"Shugah, you know I don't pay attention to those kinda things, you know that."

"Sounds like a good deal on such a useful skill." I smile.

"You know that I only buy useless stuff, useful stuff is so damn unfulfilling. Besides, it was for charity."

"And what charitable cause did this once in a lifetime opportunity aid?"

"Oh, I don't remember, maybe cancer, or sick African child, or something like that. You're gonna stop laughing when you taste just how delicious my martini is, you'll see."

I sit at the white marble bar in her colossal restaurant-grade kitchen: twenty-foot ceilings, matching marble floors, and stainless everything. White and clean, the theme throughout the entire home. Besides an Alec Monopoly painting, I helped pick out—everything is white on white—with no color in sight.

I find myself staring at her, thinking of all the memories I've made with this woman.

She looks up at me with an endearing eye as she recklessly pours the Grey Goose into the silver shaker tin with two hands. "Stop laughing at me, it's gonna be delicious, you'll see."

I smile, but stay silent. It's been so long, I almost forgot how beautiful she is. It took me nearly two years before I finally got her age out of her. Let's see, *fifteen years older than me*, so she'd be, *wow,* forty-seven. I swear you would never know. And if Hollywood ever made a movie about my life, there is no doubt Anna would be played by Charlize Theron. Even strangers say it all the time. The only difference being that Anna's blonde hair is always shoulder length. And then there's those eyes, a vivid blue with a ring of gray around the irises that somehow make you feel special with just the slightest gaze. At 5'8, she's slim, but not bony. She has curves on her hips and an ass most twenty-five-year-olds would kill for. I can't imagine the amount of lotion she uses, as her skin is the creamiest yet firmest you've ever felt. She shaves nothing. Every unwanted hair has been laser removed, and her nails always have a fresh French-finish. But those eyes, I swear they're something a young Elton John would sing songs about.

"What are you lookin at, shugah?"

"Nothing... I'm just excited to try the best damn martini in Hong Kong."

"Well, your wait is over... here ya are." She carefully hands me the oversized, overflowing, crystal martini glass.

"It looks good," I say, and it does look the part: the vodka and vermouth mixture is shaken extra cold, with a few rapidly liquefying ice chips, the color—a perfect shade of dirty, with two plump olives on a chopstick pick.

I toss the martini back and an approving "*Mmm Mmm,*" gulping. "*Mmmmmm,*" I moan again as it's halfway back.

"Now you're just being silly," she says.

"*Mmm Mmm Mmm,*" I finish the entire icy cocktail in one solid swig, then eat the olives while staring into her eyes.

"Oh, you are such a jerk to me." She playfully pushes my chest.

"What, it was so good. I couldn't stop if I wanted to."

"It was terrible, wasn't it?" she says. "I promise it wasn't my best. Your handsome face got me all nervous."

"I don't know what you're talking about, it was good... I don't know if it was thirteen thousand dollars good, but it was definitely the best damn martini I've ever had in Hong Kong."

"You are such a jerk, I swear to God." She looks into my eyes. The seconds seem to slow as our smiles subside. The room quiets, our eyes linger. "Oh, come here." She leans in and pulls her lips to mine.

I haven't kissed her in what feels like forever. My breath skips as she slides her tongue across my bottom lip. She moans to herself, and I'm reminded of just how much this woman cares for me. She would literally do anything for me, and without expecting anything in return. She kisses me harder, but I pull away.

"It was a long flight. I need a shower."

"Oh, you silly man, I nearly forgot about your ceaseless fear of body odor. Go on now, you know where it is."

I grab my bag and head back to the master bathroom.

A steamy shower is something I've always enjoyed. It's where I go to relax, recover, or even catch a nap. But at the size of a standard bedroom, this all-marble masterpiece, with multiple faucets, a waterfall, and a bench that could double as a bed, is a shower lover's dream, and I'm living it.

I strip down and turn the two overhead spouts on extra hot. The waterfall flows, and the glass quickly steams. I grab a bar of Irish Spring and start with my chest. Working my way down, I hear her sweet southern voice call out. "Do you need a hand with your back?" I turn to see her standing there, her clothes gone, and her hands on her hips. She stares at me through the steam, and any remaining morals I may have had—get sucked down the drain.

"Sure," I say, and she steps in.

"You don't even know how I've missed you. That face, and oh, those eyes."

I hand her the soap and turn away. She starts with my shoulders, sensually sliding her hands over my skin, squeezing whenever she finds a muscle she wants to feel. Once my chest and shoulders are sufficiently lathered. Her French-tips trace down to my hips, to the inside of my thighs, where she confidently takes ahold of my cock. I can feel her heartbeat flutter as she squeezes it in her hand. "Oh God, where have you been?" she murmurs.

I turn, pulling her in tight, her body against mine, my lips to her ear, I whisper a dramatic conspiratorial whisper, "It's your turn." I smirk, spin her, and snatch the soap.

"You're such a jerk to me."

I start by kneading her smooth, ageless skin, with steady, measured pressure. Relentless, her fervid fingers reach back and grab my cock. And despite my short-lived second-rate effort, I cave. I can't control myself around her; she makes me feel like a real man, important and powerful, she always has. And she's so fucking sexy; I have to have her. So, I slide my hands to her hips and pull her towards my now throbbing self.

"Oh, Max," she moans.

"You got me so fucking hot," I whisper. Her hips roll, and somehow I get even harder. My hands explore her perfect tits, her tight toned stomach, and the inside of her thighs. I crave to be inside of her, but I want her to want it so badly, she begs for it.

Her chin shoots skyward as I slide my fingers across her clit. Even with the water, I feel how wet she is. Just then, the bathroom door squeaks open. Startled, my head snaps, my eyes

✈

dart to the door, my mind races to Teddy. I search for words, an excuse, an explanation, something better than I'm sorry.

"It's just Muskrat," she says. And I look down to spot her seldom seen, all-white, cotton ball of a cat creep in.

She pulls my focus back to her. "Max, I can't wait any longer. I need you right now."

I lift her against the white marble wall, and she swallows me with her legs. Her eyes clench tight as my entire rock-hard self slides inside of her. The rhythm builds, my body colliding into hers, the salty burn of sweat blurring my vision, her nails digging deep into my back. I thrust my hips upwards, pulling her into me, rolling—an effort to hit her spot. My sole purpose becomes her pleasure. "Oh, fuck me, Max," she screams. I fuck her deeper and harder, grabbing ahold of her hair and looking into her. I can see the pains of pleasure upon her face: her mouth agape, her eyes unfocused, her lips quivering. Our torsos tango in a violently harmonious rhythm, her clit clenches on the cusp of euphoria. "Cum for me, Max, cum for me, baby." I'm on the tips of my toes, an attempt to bury every bit of my dick deeper inside of her. "Cum for me, cum for me, Max." Her panting morphs into cries as she bites down on my shoulder to muffle her moans. Her spread legs squirm. "I'm cumming! Fuck I'm cumming!"

"Ah, shit," I shout. Shaking, on the edge of an orgasm, my cock about to explode. "Ahh, fuck!"

"Cum inside of me!" she cries as her climax culminates, my cock contracts, and I release what feels like every drop of my body into hers. It takes everything I have not to fall to the floor—not to collapse from the pleasure.

Still inside of her, I hold her there, pressed against the wall—while we work to catch our breaths.

"You're a fucking god," she whispers. "That was the best orgasm I've ever had." Her head falls to my shoulder.

"You say that every time."

"And it's the truth every time. I swear it is."

I pick her off of me and slide out.

We both stand there in the steam, strangers of a year, lovers for ten, admiring one another. Her top teeth covering her bottom lip, her eyes holding mine. "I love you, Max."

My lips purse, I lean in and give her a soft kiss on the crown of her head, and again move my mouth to her ear and whisper, "Should we have another martini?"

"You're such a jerk to me. I swear to God." We smile. "What time is it?"

Tapping my Seiko, I say, "Needs a new battery, but it's probably been about an hour."

"I'm sure Lee is back by now. Let's get you home."

CHAPTER 7
It Happened in Hawaii

ANNA is put together in less than ten minutes. Her wet hair is pulled into a ponytail, and she's covered head to toe in navy Lululemon. "Do you need to follow us, or do you remember the way?" she asks sarcastically, fastening her gold Bvlgari earring.

"I thought Lee was driving us?"

"Now, shugah—don't play games with me this time."

"No games, just—"

"Max, I don't even know how I'd tell that Chinese man to pick ya up, and drop you off every day, and you're gonna need to get around. You're taking the damn car, and I'm not gonna hear it any other way."

"It's just... I haven't driven it in a while. But if that's what you want."

"Good, I'm glad that's settled. Now let's get going."

"Should we stop and have a drink on the way?"

"Oh, shugah, I'm not riding with you."

"How you getting there then?"

"Lee, of course."

"Why?"

"How else am I gonna get back here, you silly goof? And you know I hate riding in that thing, you nearly scare me half to death every time I do." She tosses me the keys.

"What if I just want to ride with you?"

"Shugah, it's your car, you're gonna keep it at the apartment while you're here in town, and that's the end of it."

Anna and Teddy have a fairly decent collection of cars. There's the Bentley limo that takes Anna everywhere. Then there's the Maybach, the Range, the restored 57' Jag that I've never actually seen out of the garage, Teddy's Porsche 911, and my personal favorite, the Ferrari 458 Italia Spider Convertible in Silverstone metallic gray, with a tan leather interior. I helped them pick it out a few years back, and they've never stopped insisting they bought it for me. That it's mine to do whatever I want with, even if I want to ship it back to the US. Of course, I could never accept a gift like this, so I always give Anna a hard time. She thinks it's pride, but honestly, no matter how much I enjoy driving the damn thing, I know I don't deserve it.

"All right, shugah, I'll see you soon. But please, do be careful. That thing is awfully dangerous."

I hop in and instantly recall how cool I felt that first time I took it for a spin, as cool as Ricky Ricardo. So that's what I call it. I press the *Start Engine* button to fire him up, pull onto the road, and rip away. His throaty-scream and torque off the line is a sweetness everyone should experience.

I'm heading just across town, through mostly crowded city streets, so I keep him quiet. It's been a while; I almost forgot how many eyes Ricky garners. Sure, exotic cars are plentiful on this island built into the heavens by bankers and businessmen. But it doesn't matter where you are in this world; a Ferrari is always a head-turner.

I'm to meet Anna at an apartment building she owns in SoHo, the city's epicenter of high-end entertainment, brimming with chic bars and bougie restaurants. It's a contemporary four-story building, composed of a dozen executive apartments, all occupied by professional expatriates. Teddy bought it for her some years back to keep her busy—decorating and whatnot, and it worked for a while. But you can only make something so white.

I park Ricky in the underground lot, meet Anna at the elevator, and ride up together.

"Just as you left it," she says as the elevator opens to the inside of the apartment.

"You haven't had any renters?"

"No, silly, I've told you a hundred times, this is your place." Saying it as though I should know better.

With three bedrooms, a dramatic loft-style living room, and a chef-inspired kitchen, the penthouse apartment is, well, white. The walls are white, the marble floor and matching countertops, the furniture, picture frames, and even the Persian rug. The place is so goddamn white and clean, you're almost afraid to fart.

"And you said that you're staying a month, right?"

"Yeah, probably."

"Well then, here you are." She hands me a crisp check, autographed with her big swooping signature.

"Anna I—" but she cuts me off.

"Take it, and I don't want to hear another word of it."

"Thank you," I say, folding it in my hand.

"Now you let me know if that's enough. It is still five thousand a week, right?"

"Sure."

Obviously, I see how this could appear as some sort of quid pro quo arrangement, but it's not like that. I mean sure, I don't run around telling people how I make my money or anything, not even my good friends. But I know she loves me. I'm certain of that. Besides, it's Teddy who pays me; Anna just signs the checks.

"Don't act like I'm giving that to you, I'm putting you to work while you're here. I need to tighten up this old body of mine. And Teddy is coming to town this weekend. He's awfully excited about you being here, and you know he's gonna want to get in a few sessions himself."

"That's not a problem," I say, suddenly flashing back to the first time I ever saw Anna.

I was twenty-one and living in Hawaii. A time when everything I knew about women came from college keggers and Carrie Bradshaw. Combine that with a freakish libido and no fear of rejection, I was pulling girls out of bars two at a time. And then

I met her, and she was unlike anything I had-yet or have-yet to experience.

I was at Duke's, one of the best beach bars on the planet. Just thinking of it now, I can smell the coconut oil and coconut cocktails. My buddy Mark and I were sipping Mai Tai's, talking about nothing. The tropical sun was sliding into the Pacific when I looked over to see this beautiful woman staring at me. Our eyes met, and she smiled.

She said nothing, just stood there, so I slid over and said *hello*. We chatted while she waited for her drinks. The conversation wasn't much, seashells or snorkeling, or something like that, and then her piña coladas came, I blinked, and she was gone.

Mark, who had been sitting there silently, "What the hell happened, man, I thought you were in?"

My eyes searched the bar but didn't see her. "I don't know," I said, "but she was fucking hot, though, huh?"

"Man, she was a perfect ten—no—she a twelve, maybe a fifteen." But she was nowhere to be seen.

Some time had passed; the early moonlight rolled in with the nighttime waves as the Hawaiian breeze blew. We had finished our drinks and were about to take off when she reappeared. She grabbed my arm and whispered into my ear, "come with me, handsome." I didn't ask questions or say anything to Mark. I just got up and left with the lady.

She guided me to some *employee only* marked door, and down a well-lit corridor till we reached some small turnout, a silverware wrapping station—I think.

She turned to me, pulled me in, and kissed me. It was like something out of a movie, and before I knew it, she was bent over. I pulled her pink Hawaiian print dress up and her panties down. I fucked her right there in that hallway. She came within a minute, and I moments later.

She straightened herself as I zipped, took ahold of my hand, and led me back the way we came. Once we were in the bar, she turned to me and said, "See ya later, shugah." And slipped into the crowd.

I rushed back to Mark and told him everything. I didn't think he'd believe me, but he did.

"I fucking knew it, man. I knew you were banging her," he cried.

It was crazy; I had slept a lot of women that summer, but nothing like that. "Where is she?" he asked, but I didn't know. I had lost her the second we split. "Come on, let's find her. Maybe she has friends." He handed me a fresh Mai Tai.

Tiki torches and Tanya Stephens' *It's A Pity* electrified the sandy oceanside patio. Scouring through the smiling herd of tan tourists in Hawaiian shirts, we spotted her. She was at a table with a few people and saw me as we approached. But before Mark or myself could say anything. "Honey, these are the gentlemen I was talking about. The ones from the bar," she said to the good-looking guy next to her.

The man stood to shake my hand. "Ah, the personal trainer I've been hearing about since we arrived. It's good to meet you, chaps. I'm Teddy, and you've already met my wife, Anna, and these are our friends..."

I had stopped listening as soon as he said, *wife*. I looked over at her; she gave me one of those bite-your-bottom-lip—*oh, by the way*—sort of smiles as she shrugged her shoulders.

I glanced over at Mark, who was tight-lipped and wide-eyed, trying his hardest to not laugh in the guy's face.

"I'd like to get a session in tomorrow morning if you're available, mate?" Teddy asked me.

The strange thing was—at that time—I had never been a personal trainer. In our brief conversation at the bar or our back-room rendezvous, I never told Anna I was. And until that moment, I had never once even thought about it. But for whatever reason, that's what she told Teddy. And for God knows why—I agreed to train him.

Mark and I joined their table for a round, which turned into a few, and we ended up having a hell of a time.

I trained both of them the next day, and for the next two weeks while they were on the island. I'd train Teddy in the mornings, then fuck Anna in the afternoon while he golfed.

I'm not sure what it was, but Teddy and I just clicked. As an avid fitness nut, he said I was the best trainer he'd ever worked with. He told me that if I ever came out to *Hong Kong*, that he'd make it *worth my while*.

Before she left Hawaii, Anna confessed to me—*it was love at first sight.* That she couldn't explain what came over her that night, but that she knew that she had to have me—*right then and there.* And that she'd always love me—*till the day she dies.*

To this day, she tells me she'd give up everything, that she'd leave Teddy the moment I ask her to, I just never have.

Feeling wealthy with my twenty-thousand-dollar-check in hand.

"Let me take you out to dinner."

"Why, because I look so lovely in my beautiful dress." She glances down at her spandex suit.

"We don't have to go anywhere fancy."

"Shugah, you know I'd love to go out with you, but I look absolutely dreadful. Let's get you settled in tonight, and we'll rain check it for tomorrow, and we'll have a big ole day."

"Ok," I say. I haven't been here in a while and was hoping to take in the night.

She senses my dissatisfaction and suddenly changes her tune. "Do you wanna go grab a beer at that old dingy place you like so much?"

"Ned Kelly's?"

"Yeah, that's the one." And my smile spreads to hers.

"Duh," I reply. "Are you sure? I don't want to put you out or anything."

"Don't be silly, you know I wanna spend time with you. And you're right, we haven't seen one other in the longest while, why wouldn't we go have ourselves a drink." Now I didn't actually say it out loud. But she knew.

I pick her up—postnuptial style—and carry her across the room and into the elevator.

After a quick ride across the harbor, we roll into one of my favorite little watering holes in all of Asia. It's dark and rustic, a wood shack of a bar that's stood here for decades: walls filled with faded maps and antique photos, the Jazz is lively, and the beer ice-cold. A spot where Anna's pompous social circle would never be seen, so her hair comes down, and we get wild.

She's easygoing once you get to know her, definitely not what you'd expect. Sure, she has her supercilious moments, but she's unlike any woman I've ever met, and I wouldn't change a thing about her. In fact, she's the only woman I've ever been completely comfortable around.

Our one beer turns into too many, and my face grows sore from smiling.

Several hours and an untold number of spiced rum shots later, they're dropping me off at the apartment. She reminds me of our workout in the morning, and I say, "farewell." Actually, I say it in a gravelly Jack Sparrow pirate's voice. "Farewell mi wench, don't che dare lose dat booty." For some reason, we started talking like pirates and cracking up every time we did. I blamed it on the booze, saying, "It's hard not to talk like a pirate when you drown yourself in Caribbean rum."

CHAPTER 8
Real Men Wear Chanel

I WAKE with a horrendous headache, which I remedy with Gatorade and gummy worms. I couldn't tell you why, but gummy worms always seem to help. I'm typically not a particular pain in the ass when it comes to food—I'll eat almost anything—but with hangovers, they have to be gummy worms; the bears just don't do it for me. I'm not brand loyal, but over the years, I've become a connoisseur of sorts. I usually go for the sour ones with the grainy texture, unless I'm really hurting, and require the plain. This morning is a plain gummy worm type of torture, and I got two bags.

I sprawl out on the shower floor and let the hot water and worms work their magic. I hate myself at the moment, but I'm sure Anna hates me more.

An hour of near-scalding steam and another half-hour curled on the couch eases my misery before I make my way to her place.

Unlike yesterday, where Ricky and I welcomed onlookers, I'm loathing every pedestrian gawking our way. Smells of past-prime fish and sour rubbish make me wish I'd made better decisions.

I open the gate with my remote and knock before I let myself in. "Are you ready to sweat?" I say.

"I hate you," she cries out, with a noticeable discomfort in her voice. I turn the corner to find her flat on the couch, in a bra and an ice-mask.

"C'mon maté, it's time to sweat, or I'll make ye walk the plank," I say it in the same pirate's voice responsible for her current state.

"Fuck you," she says listlessly. I laugh it off and make her a mango smoothie. After another half hour of suffering, I get her up and into the gym.

She has a full fitness studio with every piece of equipment one could need, and we actually have a halfway decent workout, then we shower—separately—and head into town together.

Lee drops us off at Sevva, a haughty eatery in the center of the city. Despite my double dose of worms, today's hangover is still lingering. So, I borrow Anthony Bourdain's advice: I pop an aspirin, wash it down with a Jack and Coke, and order the spiciest thing on the menu. She does the same.

Sipping my whiskey while massaging my still sore smile, I'm reminded of just how much I care for this woman. Sure, it may not be the same as she cares for me, but it's definitely real, and I truly value it.

"Now Max, I don't give a damn what you say, we're going shopping after we finish here." I knew she insisted on this restaurant for a reason. Coincidentally close to Hong Kong's high street.

"Come on," I say. "Let's just go to The Peak and grab another drink."

"And we can do that after we take you shopping. Max, you're a gorgeous man, but you're wearing a faded five-dollar T-shirt, and a pair of worn-out jeans I gave you six Christmases ago." I glance down for a quick self-assessment; *she's not wrong.* "Come on, you know I love to shop, and I already have two of everything. Please, let me get you something."

"I'm pretty sure faded is back in fashion," I say.

"Max, please... don't make me beg-ya."

"Fine," I exhale. "But nothing too crazy. Just something for dinner tonight."

"Sure, shugah, whatever you say."

Our first stop is Dolce & Gabbana, where we're greeted by a tall, thin, well-groomed, better dressed, fully flamboyant French salesman. "Madam Hammond, welcome-welcome. It has been much too long. You missed our anniversary party. I nearly rang the police, as I had grown concerned." His haughty French accent pompously amplified.

"Well, I'm just fine, honey. Been spending a little time at the Dolce Singapore, but I do appreciate your concern."

"While I am sorry to hear that you've been cheating on me, I am much relieved to see that you are ok," the salesman quips.

"Oh, honey, you're so funny." He shrugs. "Leo, this is my good friend, Max. He's visiting Mister Hammond and myself for a few weeks, and we need to get him some things."

"Bonjour, Monsieur Max."

"How do you do?" I say, and we shake hands.

He eyes me up and down in a glance, pauses mid-shake, and turns to Anna. "We have a fine canvas to work with, no?"

"He doesn't think he needs anything, but I want to make sure that whatever we do here today, that you're gonna personally cut-up and dispose of that smelly old T-shirt he's got on."

"I will do it with pleasure," Leo says, then theatrically snaps his fingers three times. "And what is it we are we looking for today, Monsieur Max?"

"He's looking for a couple shirts, and maybe some slacks. Yes, definitely some slacks," answers Anna.

"Parfait," says Leo, before he calls back to one of the sales girls, but in Italian. "Loretta, porta un po' di champagne per favore."

"Just something basic, nothing too trendy," I say.

"Ok, pas de problem. I see you are a rugged man, and I promise I will do you no disservice."

"Don't worry, shugah, Leo's gonna fix you up just fine."

"Ciao, would you care for some champagne?" asks a malnourished, fair-skinned girl, holding a bottle of Moët and two flutes.

"Please," I reply.

Two glasses of bubbly a piece, three shirts, a pair of navy slacks, which I wear out with a logo sweatshirt, and $3,500 US dollars later, we're heading to Gucci for a belt. Two belts, a pair of black leather brogue boots, three pairs of socks, and $2,300 later, we're on our way to Louis Vuitton for a wallet. A pair of loafers, a new Neo Eole carry-on bag with matching wallet, and $5,500 later, we're on to the next. Anna, who wears nothing off-the-rack—is having a blast. She gets excited every time she picks something out that I like, and bubbles over in bliss whenever her Black Amex gets swiped. I try to say no, not really wanting or needing any of this shit, but seeing her so happy—makes me happy.

Somewhere around our second bottle of champagne, I overcome my initial uneasiness. Our stop at Prada is $4,500, then $3,800 at Valentino, $2,500 at Ermenegildo Zegna for a cashmere bomber, another $1,800 on an Armani blazer. And then there's the Chanel tie that I just "have to have" because, according to Anna, "All real men wear Chanel."

She drops another $1,400 at Burberry before ending the day with the pièce de résistance, a stainless Cartier dive watch for $7,900. I really do try to refuse, but she casually dismisses my resistance. "Such a beautiful man should have a beautiful timepiece." Plus, they threw in some complimentary cufflinks. She says she'll give them to Teddy when he comes into town on Thursday.

Lee has been following us, packing the Bentley throughout our extravaganza. When we finally finish the four-hour champagne buffet, half the cabin is crammed with luxury bags of all shapes and sizes. It looks like a housewife's wet dream.

"Oh God, wasn't that the most fun you've ever had in your entire life?" She throws herself back in her seat, satisfaction smeared across her face.

"I had a great time, thank you," I say, "but damn." I lift the new Cartier on my wrist.

"Oh, shugah, money doesn't matter."

"Sure... but we just spent like forty grand."

"Max, look at all the beautiful stuff we got. I spend that on myself and get two tiny little bags. Look at us, we won." She signals to the stack of luxury goods. "And I had a wonderful time, and I'm happy. Aren't you happy, Max?"

"Sure..." I say, suddenly imagining her back in Texas, wondering if she'd even recognize herself now.

Raised in a trailer in *the tough part of town*, she relied on her looks to get by. She met Teddy when she was just twenty-two. He took her from working happy hour at Hooters to Grand Cru and caviar.

"Sure, I'm happy," I say.

"Good," she replies, rolling down the partition. "Lee, would you mind driving us around the island before we head home?" He just stares at her through the rearview mirror; you can tell he didn't catch a word. Anna pulls up a map of Hong Kong Island on her phone and makes a circular motion with her finger. Again, nothing.

"*Zai daoshang kaiche*," I say. A shoddy attempt at one of the twenty or so phrases I've picked up over the years.

"Ahh, drive around. Ok, no problem." Lee is now in the know, and Anna closes the partition.

"Thanks, shugah. Although I'd hate to know how you learned that," she says, fumbling with a concealed cooler, before pulling out a bottle of Dom Pérignon and two flutes.

"Will you do the honors?" She hands me the bottle; I pop it, pour it, and we tap glasses in a toast. "To love and to lovers," she says.

"May we never run out of either," I add.

"Oh, you're so bad." She slaps my arm, and the corners of her lips curve into a scandalous smile.

"I love you, Max, I really do. So much."

"I know. Not a day goes by where I don't."

She reaches over and rubs my earlobe between her forefinger and thumb. "No, I really, really love you, and I'm not afraid to tell anyone."

"You're really drunk, that's what you are," I smirk.

"But I ain't lying."

For whatever reason, Anna's words flash me back to the last thing Nadja said to me. "*I love you, but if you loved me—*"

"Shugah."

"Yeah?" I snap to.

"Where did you just go?" she asks.

"I'm right here."

"You sure?"

"I'm sure," I say. Refocusing, I gaze into her glassed over eyes. "What are you thinking about?"

"Oh, I don't know. Just that it takes over an hour to drive around this island, and well, there's a drunk woman sitting next to you. And in my opinion, she ain't that bad lookin. Can you, by any chance, think of anything that could kill an hour?"

My eyes sharpen as I sip my champagne. Watching her smile all day did get me hot. Hell, I nearly bent her over in the back room at Burberry, and I know that shopping gets her *Fifty Shades* freaky. So, I put my glass down, pull her on to me, tear-off her clothes, and take her right there.

My sinful-indulgence sighs as I spread her legs and pull myself into her. Our bodies effortlessly fuse into a finely tuned rolling-rhythm as I fuck her the way she likes to get fucked. Squirming, panting, and pushing me away, I know she's close, but I don't want her there yet. So, I reach into the Gucci bag for a belt that's yet to be worn on a waist. "You're so naughty," she says, before I bind her wrists taught, bend her over, and bury myself back into her. Her locked body flushes crimson as I fuck the shit out of her. "Oh, Max, oh, Max... I'm cumming, I'm cumming. Fuck, I'm cumming!" But I don't stop, and with her wrists tied, she can't do anything but take the pleasure.

"You're being a bad girl," I whisper, grabbing a handful of hair as I bury my dick deeper inside.

"You're fucking insane," she cries as my pleasure peaks, and everything I have empties into her.

I throw myself back into my seat and breathe. *Life isn't that bad.* I'm in the back of a Bentley limousine; the sinking sun has the sky ablaze a powerful pink, the ocean a deep blue, and the orgasms intense. I have a pile of designer digs stacked in front of me, and I just fucked a beautiful woman who loves me. *This is about as good as it gets*. But for whatever reason, I'm not enjoying it as I once did. Something inside me feels invalid, uneasy, and even in her inebriated, post-orgasmic state; I know she can sense it.

After our island tour, we return to the house. She has Lee pack the goods in Ricky's hood and sends him home. I ask her if she wants to go to The Peak with me, a tradition of sorts. She says, "I think I'll have a martini for dinner and call it an early night," and that "tomorrow" we'll go.

I'm a little disappointed, but I know had she stayed in last night like she wanted, we'd probably be at The Peak now.

She asks me to join her for a drink before I leave, and though I probably don't need another, *what the hell.*

Sitting comfortable on her oversized couch, in her all-white oversized home, sipping oversized martinis. She asks me the question I know has been hanging over her head since I arrived. "Max, what the hell is going on with you?" I had expected a slightly subtler approach, but she's tipsy, and I had just fucked her, so I guess this is how it goes.

"What's that?" I ask, knowing perfectly well what she means.

"Stop playing games with me. You know exactly what I'm talking about. You've been coming here ten times a year for ten years, and then suddenly, I can't even get a text back from you for weeks, hell, even months at a time. I know you were dating that crazy French girl, who I warned you about. Remember? But I know you've dated girls before, and I don't know, you show up here, and you're all sad. I see you're trying to hide it, but I know you, Max, you can't hide from me. Please tell me what's the mater, shugah. I hate to see you like this."

Well, she laid it all out there. I have no other choice but to tell her what's going on. So, I do.

I start by reminding her of Nadja and how she had chased me for a year. "Oh, I remember it, shugah. There was a time when Teddy and I thought for sure she'd show up here looking for you." We smile. Then I tell her about the day I woke up and asked myself, *why am I running from this beautiful girl who hasn't stopped chasing me?* So, that's what I did. I stopped running. I cut off all communication with girls I was sleeping with, girls I had slept with, even girls that were attractive and I'd probably sleep with. Instead of traveling, I turned my attention to her. And I focused on building a business I had been working on.

"That little website you emailed me?" she asks.

"Yeah, that's it."

"Oh, it's lovely, it'll make you a fortune someday. I know it will."

I tell her how Nadja would come to Chicago whenever she was free, and how I would fly out to New York about once a month to spend the weekend with her. How everything seemed to be going great and how I may have even loved her.

Then I go on to explain how it all crumbled. I tell her about the summer and how Nadja suddenly stopped coming to see me between shoots like she always had. How in August, she said, "She'd ruin my life if I ever left her," some crazy *Gone Girl* shit, but then canceled two trips to see me that month. How she wouldn't answer my calls on a Friday or Saturday night, then surprise me on Sunday, and search my apartment. And that in September, she called to say, "If I loved her, I'd be there with her." Then she hung up, blocked me, and that I haven't heard from her since.

"Oh, shugah, I'm so sorry, that's awful... I can't stand to see you so sad."

"I mean, I'm ok, it's just that, well, it's been a couple months, and I don't know; I can't get it out of my mind. What the hell is wrong with me?"

"Oh, nothing's wrong with you, shugah. It's just how it goes. Breakups are bad, but it'll get better."

"I just don't get it is all."

"What don't you get?"

"I mean, I don't know... was I just not good enough for her?"

"Oh, shugah, that's not it at all. You're wonderful."

"Well, what then? Was I a tremendous disappointment? I mean this girl chased me for a year, a whole goddamn year, and when she finally catches me, she gets bored with me before the end of the summer?"

"You're definitely not a disappointment, and you're not boring. That's for sure."

"Then what the hell is it? I don't get it. Was she fucking someone else?"

"No shugah, I'm sure that's not it either."

"Then what? I'm completely lost. You know this is new to me. What the hell did I do?"

"Ok, we're gonna sit here, and we're going to sort this out right now."

"We don't have to," I say.

"No, believe me, we do... I can't handle you moping around like this all month. But before we go any further, I'm just wondering. Why the hell are you even concerned about a girl who's threatened to ruin your life?"

"I don't know," I say despairingly. "I don't even know how to explain it. It's not that I want her back per se, because I don't think I do. I just need to know why. Why did she leave? What turned her off so much that she went from chasing me to hating me in eight months? What did I do to her? Where did it all go wrong? Where did I go wrong?"

I know she wants to say, *you were wrong by dating a crazy kid who'd show up at your place uninvited and threaten you if she didn't get her way*, but she doesn't.

"Ok, let's see here." Her fingers tap her lips. "She said that if you loved her, you would be with her, right?"

"That's right."

"Well, if you loved her, why didn't you visit her in New York more?"

"I went, I told you. I went nearly every month."

"Yeah, but once a month isn't a lot, especially if you don't have a job."

"I mean... I wasn't just sitting around. I was working on that business. That website."

"Sure, I know. But, well, you know what I'm talking about, a regular job. Now I'm not disparaging whatever it is you're doing, I'm just sayin... ya had plenty of time, and I know you had the money."

"I mean, sure, it wasn't a nine to five, but I was busy. I really thought I had something."

"Max, you say this girl was coming to Chicago to see you every chance she got, right?"

"She came almost every week and stay a day or two. What was I supposed to do, fly back to New York, and sit around her tiny apartment while she was working?"

"Well, did she ever ask you to move to New York?"

"Sure, all the time."

"And why didn't you?"

"I don't know, because we'd only been dating for six or seven months before things started going bad."

"Ah, that's it right there."

"What is?" I ask. Unable to believe that Anna, a woman who spends her days' shopping, and paying people to paint shit white, could diagnose a problem in seconds that I've sat on since the summer.

"You see, shugah, in your eyes, the two of you had been seeing each other for only six months, but to her, the two of you were together since the day you met. And if you're with some- one for that long, more than a year, and you love them, then you should've been with her in New York."

"I did love her," I say.

"Well, a minute ago, you said 'I think' I loved her. So, did ya or didn't ya?"

"Yeah, I did. I'm sure I did."

"Well, the fact is, you said, 'I think' I did."

"Ok, sure whatever, I misspoke. What does it matter?"

"Believe me, shugah. It matters. It does, it really does.

"Well, yeah, I did. I mean—sure—she was a pain in the ass, but yeah, I did. I'm sure I did."

"Well, ya either did, or ya didn't, and if ya have to think about it, then I'm sorry, but it doesn't sound much like love to me. And even if it is, or was, you certainly didn't love her the way she needed you to."

"But I told her I loved her all the time."

"But you didn't move to New York."

"Because it had only been six or seven months!"

"No, Max, you just don't get it, do you. See, you get a lot of girls, I know you do, you can probably have nearly any girl you want, and it's not because of your looks, or that sharp jaw, it's because of the way you look at a woman. Believe me— I've seen it—I've felt it. From the moment you meet, your eyes are just full of love, and women are just drawn to it, they can't help themselves. This poor girl probably fell for you from that very first hello, and a year-and-a-half later, you weren't even sure if you loved her or not."

"But what the hell does that have to do with anything? I'm talking about her leaving? I mean, was she fucking someone else?"

"You just don't get it, shugah. She wasn't sleeping with another man."

"How do you know?"

"Because I know, believe me, I know."

"Why did she give up? Why did she leave?"

"She left because she finally saw that you weren't ready. She'd been in love with you for so long, chasing you around the world and all, and you didn't even know if you were ready to move to New York—to be with her. I'm sure she grew tired of trying to make you care for her the way she did for you. She didn't leave because you weren't enough for her, or because you disappointed her, or because she was seeing someone else. She left because she saw that you weren't ready to commit to her, and that you weren't gonna be ready anytime soon. She left because she had to protect herself, and to stop questioning and doubting herself as to why you didn't love her, the same way she loved you."

"How am I not ready? I'm thirty-two years old. My brother's kids are nearly in high school."

"But that's him, that's not you, shugah. Believe me, Max, I love you more than anybody, but you're still just a child. A child wanting to run around and fuck every good-looking girl you talk to. And that's ok, you're a beautiful man, and you make it look easy. Ninety-nine out of a hundred guys would kill to have your life, but you're just not ready for a serious girl yet."

"But what if I am?"

"Shugah, look at who you's talking to. I know your heart is full of so much love, and you have so much to offer a woman, but you're just not ready. I'm sorry that this girl left you, but you gotta stop worrying about it because it ain't gonna fix anything. Believe me, your day will come. One day you'll wake up, and you won't have to be scared anymore."

"Scared? Scared of what?"

"It's ok, shugah, it's nothing to be ashamed of."

"Ashamed? What are you even talking about?"

"Oh, you know that's not what I mean, come here," she says, her hands on my thigh, tugging me towards her. "I don't mean to upset you. It's just how I see it."

I look into her eyes as I take another healthy swig from my martini.

"Max, if you want my honest opinion, I think the only reason that you're even upset is because this is the first girl that's ever dumped you, and you just don't know how to handle it."

"I was a good boyfriend," I say, borderline emotional. "I didn't do anything to make her act this way."

"I'm sure you were, shugah. I don't doubt it for even a second. But being a good boyfriend doesn't mean you love somebody."

"So, you think she left because I didn't love her enough? Or love her quick enough? That's what you think? Really?" I say it somewhat disdainfully. "That doesn't even make sense."

"What I'm saying is that she left because she finally saw that she wasn't the one for you, and you can't change that. And now, you're acting like a goddamn child about it." She says it curtly, not yelling, but her tone cuts deep. I've never heard her talk to me like this.

"You know nothing about it." I stand.

"Oh, Max, please sit down. I don't mean anything by it."

"Nah, I think it's about time to head back."

"C'mon now, don't throw a temper tantrum."

I say nothing as I swig my martini and feel for my keys.

"Max, you know I hate to see ya like this is all. Just stay and have another drink with me. Please."

"Thank you for today, I had a wonderful time, but I'm gonna get outta here." I lean down and give her a small kiss on her cheek.

"Oh, Max, please call me tomorrow when you wake up. I'm sorry if I upset you. I just hate seeing you so sad is all."

"You didn't upset me, I'm fine. Everything is fine. Good night, Anna." I place my empty glass on the table and walk out.

I don't even know why I'm angry, but I am. It felt like the walls were coming in on me in there. So I start Ricky and shoot up into the hills.

CHAPTER 9

The Reunion

RICKY'S ENGINE ROARS up the dark, winding, mansion-lined mountain pass that is Peak Road. I'm not sure why, but I can't calm myself after that conversation. *Not ready, what the fuck does that even mean?* I push him harder, accelerating through the turn; the G-force pulls me into my seat. *Scared, I'm not fucking scared! What the fuck is she talking about?* This is What You Came For pumps through the speakers as all the fun times, fast times, and bad times with Nadja—the fuel to my fury—flash through my thoughts. The road dips, my stomach sinks, the engine screams, and the tires squeal as I push him harder. On a straightaway, I glance down to see I'm doing 160kph in a 60, but I don't let up. Instead, I continue tearing my way up the hillside in that glorious beast of an automobile, boiling over in self-imposed sorrow.

Upon reaching The Peak, I park and quickly exit. Excessively anxious, I'm nearly running up to the Sky Terrace, knowing somehow it's all I need right now.

There it is, the surreal early evening Hong Kong skyline from above. The vast array of colors, the skyscrapers that seem to shoot up out of the jungle floor, the city lights reflecting off the low moist air—making it twice as bright as it'd be in any other climate. It's like being in a movie—set in the future—where you're almost expecting a ship to fly by, and you have to pinch yourself just to make sure you haven't fallen into a dream.

I'm here in search of something, something intangible; what it is, exactly—I'm still unsure. Perhaps some miraculous metaphysical manifestation, I don't know. But if I'm to find it anywhere, it's here. *It's got to be here.*

✈

And as that high harbor breeze beats against my body, my mind empties, easing me into a seductively soothing state. My soul engulfed by an inexplicable calmness: a meditative-mindlessness, a dance on the edge of truth, a Cartesian clarity, an arcane cosmic consciousness. The grief and anxiety I'd been struggling with since the summer suddenly seems weightless, lifted away on this warm winter night as though it's somehow being absorbed by the radiating neon lights of this powerful city. And in this serenely introspective moment, I once again feel free.

This unrestricted serotonin secretion lasts for some time, but like any powerful drug, its effects finite; cut short when a group of drunk English kids start chanting football fight songs and I come to.

I make my way down the escalator to the bar in Bubba Gumps. Sure, it's a cookie-cutter chain, but the views can't be beat. And it's a tradition of mine to grab a beer whenever I'm here. I order a tall twenty-ounce Stella draft; it's ice-cold and hits the spot. I sit there, staring into the orgy of intricacies only seen when looking down upon a sparkling city from above. It's been a long day, and I tell myself *just this one* while slipping again into self-assessment.

Nadja really wasn't that great to me, at least not near the end. She'd repeatedly use the information I confided in her—insecurities within myself—against me. She'd constantly compare me to other people: pointing out qualities, clout, and assets I didn't possess. But what hurt most—was that she never believed in anything I did. To her, that website was a waste of time, and any personal passion, a waste of talent.

A woman's voice calls for "two glasses of champagne," in a soothing Australian accent.

I pray I'd look over to see two sweet seventy-year-old grannies standing there, but God is playing games.

"Is this seat free?" Asks one of them. I don't say a thing or even glance up as I gesture with my hand. *Go home, Max, finish your beer and go home*, I say to myself, eyeing the half-full glass in front of me, contemplating if I should walk out, or stay put, and pray I have the willpower to wake up in my own bed. But before I commit. "Where are you from?" The one sitting closest to me asks.

I turn to her, my lips lag from the booze. "Chicago," I say slowly. *Shit, this girl is something. Just get up and walk away, Max, you've had a long day, go home, rub one out, and get some sleep.*

But it's too late. "Ah, Chicago, we were just there a few weeks back. Great city," says the further one. I reach my head forward to see that she's even better looking than her friend.

"How about you two, you're Chinese?" I ask.

"No, we're Australian."

"No way," I say. They both laugh, likely wondering if I'm sarcastic or stupid.

"Have you been?" asks the further one. She's sitting, but I can tell she's tall. She has long brown hair, dark eyes, and a deep golden tan.

"Sure," I say, without saying that I've actually been down under at least a dozen times. Often when you tell people a truth that's not typical, they perceive you as a storyteller, so I stay coy. "I've been a few times."

"Aw cool, whereabouts?" asks the further one again.

But what am I supposed to say here? Well, you see here, miss pretty brown eyes that I just met. I actually had a girlfriend down in Brisbane that I'd fly out and fuck every few months. Or that two-winters ago, which is the Aussie summer, I spent six-weeks road-tripping with a free-spirited fitness instructor, and that we drove up and down, and across the entire continent in her old El Camino. That we explored the reefs just off of Cairns, that we surfed our way from the Sunshine Coast down to Sydney, that we camped under the nighttime shadow of Ayers Rock, beneath a blanket of a billion stars, and that we fucked a minimum of twice a day in nearly every state on the continent. I mean, I don't even know how to answer that question.

"I've been to all the states besides Tasmania, and most major cities," I say.

"Noice, you've been to more places than me," says the close one, with golden hair and a cute button nose.

I try to change the subject off of myself. "Why are you two in Hong Kong?"

"Oh, it's not that interesting." *Hey, that's my line.* And for a moment, I question if I've already met these girls, and they're giving me shit for not remembering. But after chewing on it a second, I hadn't.

"Ok, not that interesting. So, I'm guessing you two are Mormons, and you're here to spread the word of Jesus Christ of the Latter-day Saints."

"You're funny," says the closer one. "Are you in Hong Kong for business or pleasure?"

"Strictly for pleasure," I reply.

"Oh, we've got an honest one," says the girl with the golden hair.

"Guilty," I say.

"What is it you do?" questions the further one.

"For what? For work or fun?"

"For your job," she says. I actually hate it when girls ask me this. Perhaps it's because I don't really know how to answer them, never have, some latent insecurity in the question itself. Or maybe it's just boring and basic, and it makes me think less of them.

"Oh, I don't have a job. I just sleep with rich-old-white-women for money."

"How old do you have to be?" quips the close one, then introduces herself. "I'm Sara." And I give her mine.

"And I'm Sammy."

"Listen, Sammy—Sara." I turn my full attention to them, my confidence casual as I slip into my comfort zone. "I know this great little place downtown where we can get you two some proper champagne, and well, I won't have to worry about driving down that winding road after another one of these big beers. What do you say?"

"You drove here?" asks Sammy.

"Sure."

"So, you live here?"

"No, but I keep an apartment."

They look at each other, a conversation of glances before answering in unison. "We're in."

"Perfect," I say, sliding the barkeep my empty glass and a handsome tip. "I'm just outside."

Approaching Ricky, his metallic paint sparkling under the silver moon, his tan leather interior so inviting, I can see them hoping he's mine. Appeasing their anticipation, I remotely flicker the lights and open the passenger door.

"This is your car?" asks Sara.

"No, you're helping me steal it, so act cool."

At about a hundred pounds apiece, they both pile in the passenger seat.

I pull away, and we began our descent into the heart of the spirited city I stood over just a short beer ago.

I take them to Armani Prive, an upscale lounge with an elegant rooftop terrace. And it's walking distance from the apartment, in case driving isn't desirable.

I valet, and we're escorted to the elevator. I recognize the doorman from a bar I frequented a few years back. I took care of him, so he seats us at a prime table under the stars. I order the girls each one of their famous Lychee Mojito's, myself a Heineken, and a bottle of Ruinart Rosé for the table.

"So, Mister Max, tell us about yourself," says Sara.

"What do you want to know?"

"Where'd you go to uni?"

"What makes you think I did?"

"Just a hunch."

"A small school. Probably never heard of it," I say.

"What d'you study?"

I hold up my Heineken. "Mostly imports." They laugh.

"What's your biggest fear?"

"Fascism... no, wait... shark attacks."

"More than one?"

"Sure, one shark doesn't scare me." I wink.

"What's your favorite color?"

"That's a little personal."

"Only if it's pink," says Sammy.

"Zero-zero-nine-nine-nine-B," I say without thinking.

"What the bloody hell is that?" asks Sara.

"You asked for my favorite color."

"How is that a color?"

"Is it the color of your eyes?" asks Sammy.

"No," I say.

"Then what is it?"

"It's the digital color-code for the water of my favorite lake. It's deep in the Canadian Rockies." My head tilts as my eyes search for an invisible nothing in the sky. "Whenever I'm there, all my problems seem to dissolve by the brilliance of that blue almost green water." Sure, it's shameless pre-rehearsed—Strauss's *The Game* sort of bullshit. But it works. It always works.

"I don't imagine you having too many problems," says Sara.

"Now, that's personal." I give her another wink.

"Well, my favorite color is purple," says Sammy. "Not purple 557-something, just purple."

"I like purple," I say.

"What's your surname?" asks Sara.

"Are you gonna google me?"

Sammy jumps in, "In case we kidnap you, we need to know where to send the ransom letter."

"You won't get much," I say.

"Oh, I doubt that."

"Malovice." They both look doubtfully at one another. "My name, its Malovice."

"Malovice? As in your name is Max Malovice?" Sara asks skeptically. "Hmm, sounds a bit made up."

"Sounds like a comic book character to me."

"Or perhaps a supervillain," says Sara. Her chin lifts, and her lips pout. "Are you sure it's really Malovice?"

"Sure, I'm sure." Knowing the most common side effect of being pretty is being lied to all the time. "I don't know what to say, it's my name."

"Then, what's your superpower?"

"Mindreading."

"What am I thinking?" Sammy asks.

I look at her, lean in and whisper. "I can't say it out loud, we'd probably get kicked out." They both laugh.

"Is it European?" asks Sara.

"No, Tatooinen."

"What's that?"

"Yeah, I've never heard of Tata-Tootian or whatever you just said. Where is it?" Sammy questions, both earnest in anticipation.

"It's where my father is from."

"Is it an island?" asks Sara.

"No, it's in the Outer Rim, quite far from here."

They both give one other a: *what the hell is he talking about?* eye. "My father, his name is Anakin, overlord of the dark side, and infamous supervillain. Maybe you've heard of him." I say it with a dead straight face.

They both look back at each other and once again sync thoughts. "Vader," they say in unison, and both laugh.

I'm glad they got it as I don't suppose most super-fine girls are too into Sci-Fi, but these two are cracking-up at all the crap coming out of my mouth, and I know I'm not that funny.

"God, you're so funny," Sammy squeezes my leg.

"But seriously, is it your real name?" asks Sara.

"It seriously is," I say, handing her my phone. "Here, you can call my mom if you'd like."

"Oh, I didn't realize we were that close."

"You kidding me? This the longest relationship I've ever had."

"I bet it is," she says.

"You're so mysterious, Mister Malovice," Sara says, leaning in as she looks into my eyes, and I wonder if she can see how truly sad I am inside.

✈

"I'm just a normal guy," I say.

"I'm not so sure about that." She bites her lip.

"And why would you say that?" I ask.

"Well, let's see, a normal guy who drives a sick car, dresses head-to-toe in Dior, keeps a flat in Hong Kong, travels the world, or at least extensively through Straya, and has captivated my attention in the time it typically takes a bloke to say hello. Well, I guess I just don't meet normal guys too often."

"You should get out more," I say, and the conversation continues like this for some time, great banter and lots of laughs.

These girls are fun, smart, and fucking hot. I come to find out they're here doing promos for Hong Kong's Fashion Week.

I'm about to order a second bottle of champagne when Sammy pulls me in for a kiss. It's nice, her lips are soft and satisfying, and I could stay here all night. But as the carefree kiss concludes, and I sit back in my seat, still looking into her eyes, a hand touches my chin and turns me.

"Hey, what about me," says Sara, sliding her tongue into my mouth.

I feel myself smiling as she does until Anna's words flash through my thoughts. *Not ready, scared, still a child wanting to fuck every good-looking girl I talk to,* kick me in my guts. Dead-fish and flushed, I pull back. "Listen, I've gotta go," I say, standing.

"Whoa, whoa, what do you mean you've got to go?" says Sammy.

"Seriously, it was great meeting you two, but I have to get home. You girls have a safe night." I pull a handful of loose cash from my pocket, at least a few hundred American, and toss it on the table for the tab. Turn and walk away.

"Max, where are you going? What the heck?" I hear over my shoulder, but I don't look back.

Now at street level, I stand on the edge of drunkenness, assured it was me who sucked down most of the champagne. So I leave Ricky and walk the ten blocks back to the apartment.

✈

Reflecting on my rooftop freak-out, I laugh to myself, trying to imagine what those two must be thinking. I conclude it can only be one of four things: They think I'm gay, married, already came in my pants, or just fucking weird. I suspect they'll lean towards the latter. I mean, *what the fuck is wrong with me? How the hell did I ever let a girl get to me like this?* A girl that, according to Anna, I apparently never even loved.

I look up about a block from my ménage à trois retreat, at the crest of self-contempt, and feel the shimmer of a friendly face shining down on me; a neon Budweiser sign burns brightly in the window of a dingy bar. It reminds me of my own *Cheers* back in Chicago, so I give it a shot.

The place is small and smoky, dark and dangerous, smells of stale vomit and urinal cakes, with fluorescent reds reflecting off the random assortment of shiny-skinned strangers. Everything you look for in a Hong Kong hole in the wall. There's a few tough-looking fellas bellied up at the bar, a mama-san singing karaoke in the corner, and two Asian suits shooting pool.

"Hey, how you doing?" I say to the guy two stools down from mine as I swig my fresh bottle of Bud.

"You an American?" he asks. He's a good-looking kid, the Twan Kuyper type, clean-cut and cool.

"Sure am," I say. "The great-great-great-grandson of Sam Adams himself." It's bullshit, but I love saying it.

"Who ye thinks gonna win the Super Bowl this year?"

"Why does an Irish guy care about the Super Bowl?"

"How'd ye know I'm Irish?"

"You aren't French, that's for sure." He laughs.

"No, I'm certainly not. I'm Paul."

"Saints," I say.

"He?"

"Saints, I think it's their year to win the Super Bowl. And I'm Max."

"Good to meet ya, Max." And we shake hands.

"But you still didn't say why an Irish guy cares about the Super Bowl."

"I'm an American football fan. Go Lions."

"And how's that?" I ask.

"Long story."

"I've got nowhere to be."

"Well, it was after college. Me and a gang of me mates made our way out to San Diego."

"J-1?"

"Ye, familiar with J-1'ers?"

"Yeah, I've been out in PB when all you Irish kids roll into town thirsty and ready to fuck shit up."

"Ah, well boy, that's the Irish for ya, always out on the tear." We both raise our drinks and take a swig. "Anyhow, while I was out there in California. I got hired on with this massive marketing group that works with the NFL. And the job, it was in Detroit, so—"

"Hold on." I cut him off and signal the bartender. "Excuse me, can I please get another one of these, and one of whatever my friend here's drinking. The poor guy has lived in Detroit."

Paul and I sit there and shoot the shit for five rounds. He buys the next, then I the one after, and so on. I never bring up Nadja, or how I believe it's bullshit when girls say they want *the fairy-tale*; romanticizing Ryan Gosling saying, "I wrote you every day for a year," yet in real life, it's *crazy* when you text her six times to say you're sorry. Besides, guys look lame when they talk about old girlfriends with other guys, hell, even with good friends. I tell him of pleasurable times I've had in Dublin, and he tells me strangely similar stories about Detroit.

I could sit here bullshitting with Paul all night, until I stand to piss and realize one more drink would drown me.

We exchange numbers, saying that *we'd catch a game or something*, and I head for the door.

I'm only a few blocks from my place, dumb-drunk and walking fast. My head is heavy and hanging as I turn the corner. *Ugh!* I run square into someone, nearly knocking them off their feet.

"Oh, shit, I'm sorry," I say, scrambling, struggling to keep them from falling.

"I'm ok, I'm ok, thank you," says the voice of the small girl I just collided with. "Hey, it's you," she says, looking up at me, her eyes wide.

And even though I'm well past polluted, I immediately recognize this person. "Look who it is," I slur, swaying above the pretty blonde with pigtails from the airport.

"I had hoped I'd run into you," she murmurs.

"Well... it looks like your wish came true." My lips curve to a smile, mostly because I'm hammered, but also appreciating the timely coincidence.

"I guess it did."

Standing there, I think about my night, a terrifyingly typical catalog of sexual opportunities and out-of-control consumption. *Ah fuck it*, I say to myself. *I am a goddamn child, and I just want to play with my goddamn toys.*

"Do you want to grab a beer with me?" I ask pigtails.

"I'd love a beer." And her smile somehow grows.

We walk a block till we come across the first random shithole bar we see. The beers are cold, and our conversation blah. She tells me she's a waitress, that she's twenty-four, from Columbus, and other than a family trip to Florida, she's never been outside of Ohio. I'm not really listening, though, mostly focusing on not falling over. An obvious deviation from the Flynn effect, she rambles on about wanting to come to Hong Kong because of some *Transformers* movie she saw with an old boyfriend. She makes it a point to tell me how *important* he is at some food processing plant. "Wow," I slur, unsure what the fuck she's even talking about, and barely holding my shit together. She goes on-and-on about how she got hundreds of *likes* on an *Instagram* pic she posted from The Peak. And asks if I'd ever been. I tell her, "No," but that, "one day I'm gonna go." She asks if we could take a selfie, so I oblige. I look drunk and sloppy, but she says I look "sexy," and she posts it to her *Snap*. A few seconds later, she shows me a friend's comment: *Yes, definitely*, with a tongue-wagging emoji. And I notice she has her tongue pierced, which I like because it makes her look even sluttier. But I keep that to myself. I tell her a couple pre-packaged travel stories that put an awe-expression on her face, and after a few beers and a couple shots of shit tequila, I ask if she wants to come to my place. She kisses me and accepts with a wide-eyed grin.

It's no secret I'm beyond bombed, and she probably only says yes because of her friend's emoji. Either way, I pay the tab, and we head home hand in hand.

She appears to be a fan of the apartment. "Holy moly, do the Kardashians live here?"

I toss the keys on the counter and say nothing. "This is really your place?" she asks, her mouth open and head on a swivel.

"I just stay here when I'm in town," I mutter, but I don't want to talk anymore. I pull her in close and peel off her clothes. I take her into the bedroom and fuck the shit out of her. She's tiny and light, so I toss her around in a few different positions, mostly doggy, while I pull on her pigtails. I don't kiss her neck or whisper into her ear. I just fuck her like a little doll. When I'm about to cum, I tell her to *stick out* her tongue, so I can see her piercing. I'm not sure if she cums or not, I think she does as she seems to enjoy herself, but I'm not sure.

I wake early. My eyes ache, and my head feels like I've been hit by a fucking truck. I tell pigtails *I have to go to work* so she'd leave. I tell her, "I'll text you," and that we'd "get together again" before she goes. But it's all bullshit. Because in reality, I hope I never run into her again.

CHAPTER 10
December 6th

EVENTUALLY, I cajole myself to crawl out of bed and make my way to the corner store for my morning essentials: Gatorade and gummy worms. I keep my shower under an hour, and though I'm hanging hard, I tell myself not to sit inside all day, so I head downstairs and hail a taxi to take me to Ricky.

The bright red taxi is extra clean, smelling of sanitizer and stale cigarettes. Behind the seat, I find a folded tourist map. Inside, there's an advertisement for the ferry. *I haven't been on the water in a while*, so I make an impromptu change of plans and have the driver drop me at the Central Star Station.

Being too nauseous to focus, I've ignored my phone all morning, but now, walking onto the ferry, the fresh air has me feeling fine. I have two texts from Anna. The first at 10:15: *Hey, could we get in a session around noon?* That doesn't look likely, as it's 12:20. The second, sent at 11:57: *Are you still mad at me?*

I don't feel like dealing with it, so I don't. Instead, I turn my ringer volume to vibrate and take in the sights. The sky is free of clouds. The December sun warms my skin, and for whatever reason, I'm reminded of the dirty south back in the states, Memphis or maybe Mobile: an aromatic mixture of moist mucky-water, spicy fried-fish, and spilled gasoline. The dull daytime moon appears smudged, faint, and fluctuating through the thick wavy fuel-fumes and tropical South China smog.

I still have a headache, but it's a beautiful afternoon, and I'm on a boat in Victoria Harbour, while most people are stuck in their offices, worried about quotas, or if their kids are fucking up in school.

✈

Leaning against the railing, I watch that grand skyline grow more impressive the further we pull from shore. I'm not sure what it is exactly: maybe the comforting breeze at my back, the rhythmic rumbling of the backwash hitting the hull, or the sight of seabirds soaring effortlessly just out of arm's reach—restlessly petitioning tourists for scraps, but I decide right then, that *I'm fucking finished with this, I'm fine*. I'm done being worried about a woman who walked away. A worry—that had become a festering infection in my mind, an exhausting sickness I couldn't control. But now, somehow, someway, I know it's over. I can finally see that I was the greener-grass, a desire due to distance, but disappointing once walked upon, and I'm ok with it. I get it. I can't change anything about it. And looking back on it now, I doubt I would. I guess that's how breakups go; you're bad, then you're better. And for some intangible reason, I know there'd be no more bullshit, doubts, moping, soul-soothing quests, or self-aggrandizing sexual indulgences. She had successfully sucked the spirit from me, reduced me to an arrogant shadow of myself, rock bottom and barely recognizable. But when I look around, my life isn't too bad, and it's time to stop feeling sorry for myself. Sure, I'm not wealthy, but I have money. I'm not particularly successful, but I'm optimistic. I have people who care for me. And excluding this hangover, I'm healthy as hell. Life is pretty fucking decent when I think about it. And though I may never be the same, I'm not upset anymore. It's just gone.

Having had to piss since we pulled out of port, I head inside. With this weather, the cabin is open and eerily empty, except for one person—a woman—sitting alone at the far front. It's strange, and I want to say something, but I have priorities.

Once relieved, my curiosity gets the best of me. It's something out of a creepy seen in a scary movie. There are a dozen rows of forward-facing benches—split by an isle—like a church. The entire cabin is abandoned, besides this woman. She's sitting silent and still, and I can't walk away without in-quiring.

With her back to me, she faces a fogged-over opaque window. So I don't know if she's sixteen or sixty. She's sitting straight, her blond hair hanging over the back of the bench.

I make a point to be noisy as I approach, dragging my feet and tapping the top of each bench, but she doesn't turn or react in any way, so I sit next to her. Not in her personal space, but close enough to smell the Chanel.

"Great view," I say facing forward, eyes on the foggy-glass, fighting the natural urge to turn towards her

"It suits me," she says, I believe her eyes stay straight as well.

"I mean, it's really something." With all the fog, it might as well be a white wall. "I see why you picked this spot."

"It's the best," she says, with what I perceive to be a Russian accent.

"Yeah, there's way too much fresh air out there," I say, still looking straight.

"I prefer it here."

"You're not missing much: just sunshine, skyline views, a beautiful breeze, and dolphins."

"There are dolphins?" she asks, with the slightest hint of enthusiasm.

"No. But there could be," I say. "Don't worry, I'm sure we'll see them from here." I'm not sure if she's smiling, but I imagine so as a short silence slides between us. Still having yet to see her face, I press down on the wooden bench below me with both hands. "I get it now; it's the benches. They're much more comfortable than the metal ones outside. Comfort, that's what you're after." Searching the corners of my eyes, I look for some sort of reaction, anything.

"You figured me out," she says, turning towards me, and I turn to her. *Holy hell, this girl is spectacular*—bone-white skin with slight shadows under her exotic blue eyes. She's in a black Philipp Plein tee, dark jeans, and in need of nothing else, an Anna Kournikova kind of obvious beauty.

"It wasn't easy," I say, now glancing around the room, almost waiting for someone to tackle me—for talking to her.

"You are not nervous?" she asks.

"Should I be?"

"No."

"Maybe I should be, you're kind of strange," I say.

"I'm strange?" she asks, her eyes on mine, ice-cold with the confidence of a cage fighter.

"Yes."

"Yes, I'm strange?"

"That's right," I say.

"That's not very nice."

"Strange isn't a bad thing. I'm sure there's a perfectly good reason you, me, and the captain are the only ones sitting inside on what's maybe the most beautiful December day in Hong Kong's history."

"Maybe I'm not the best swimmer," she says.

"Yeah, I heard if a boat sinks, it's best to sit inside."

"Stop it... you know what I mean."

"I'm sure you're not that bad."

"No, I can't swim. I know I should know, but I don't."

"Have you tried?"

"Yes, I tried before when I was young, but it didn't work."

"Maybe you had a lousy teacher."

"No, I think he was good."

"Maybe it wasn't your time."

"My time?"

"We all learn different things at different times in our lives. Maybe you should try again."

"Maybe I will."

"Hopefully not today," I say.

"Don't even say that." She smiles.

"Have you ever been to Hawaii?"

"No, why do you ask?" Her near-perfect lips pout.

"Well, in Hawaii, on the island of Oahu, there's this magnificent hotel. It's called the Kahala. And at this hotel, you can actually swim with the dolphins. Now, I haven't done it myself, been saving it for a special occasion... but, if this boat we're on doesn't sink today, and somehow you and I ever end up in Hawaii at the same time. I'm going to take you there, I'm going to teach you how to swim, and you and I will swim with those goddamn dolphins. What do you say?"

"I say that you are the strange one."

"And I'm ok with that."

"You are very confident, aren't you?" She looks into my eyes as she says it, but already has her mind made up.

"I'm just a normal guy," I say.

She sits back, squinting as she sizes me up. "No, you are not."

"That's not very nice."

"It's not a bad thing." She smirks.

"Good."

"My name is Natasha."

"Get out of here..."

"Why—what?"

"My dad, he just got a new dog, a puppy actually. She's a beautiful Belgium Tervuren. Her name is Natasha, too. She's very sweet."

"I promise you, I don't have fleas."

"Me either," I say, theatrically scratching the fake-fleas in my hair. "I'm Max."

"Max is a dog's name, too, no?"

I say nothing; instead, I show my teeth and growl, *Grrrr!*

"Ah, don't bite me, beast." And I growl again.

"You are a kind of crazy, no?"

"Maybe," I smile.

"What do your friends call you, Max?"

"They call me Max."

"And what about your enemies?"

"Who cares."

"Ah, I like that," she says. "And why are you going to Kowloon today, Max?"

"Because I'm too hungover to do anything else."

"Ah, you are too honest with me. I like that too."

"A man I knew once said, 'lies are the tools of the less intelligent.'"

"Sounds like a great man." Her Caribbean blue eyes take ahold of mine.

"He was," I say, now helplessly stuck in her stare.

"Your eyes, they're so intense," she tells me. "They're almost dangerous."

"I'm sorry," I say, "I'll try to be careful." I cross them as I say it.

"Ah, you are silly."

"Damn," I say. "For a second there, I thought maybe I was handsome."

"No, you are handsome," she says. "But, you know that you are, so it doesn't count."

"Nah, this old thing." I tap the bottom of my chin with the top of my hand.

"You know who you look like, Max?"

"Who's that?" I ask. Expecting her to say *a young Baldwin brother,* having heard it since I was seven.

"You look like Jon Kortajarena."

"I do not."

"You know who he is?"

"Yeah, sure, he's pretty famous." *And way better looking than me at my best.*

"And you don't think you look like him?"

"No, not particularly," I say. But if I was honest, and we weren't face-to-face with a foggy—lusterless window, I'd likely be searching my reflection for similarities. But it's strange, I suddenly sense her watching me, studying me, factoring in every nostril flare, and documenting any deferment in eye contact; almost as if it was a test, a test to gauge my vanity. And once recognized, I'm glad the window is watery.

"You really think I look like him?" I ask skeptically.

"No, you don't." She says it with a serious face and a restrained smile.

"Then why'd you say it?"

"Because you're getting too confident." She smirks, and I laugh.

"That was kind of mean."

"You called me a dog."

"Wrong... she's a puppy. And she's one of a kind." This puts a smile on her face.

Natasha is intelligent, outrageously sexy, and can keep you on your toes. She has a cool, almost mechanical presence to her, and a hell of a wit.

"Why are you going to Kowloon today, Natasha?"

"I can't tell you."

"It's a secret?"

"No, not a secret."

"Then why can't you tell me?"

"Because you will laugh at me."

"I won't."

"But you might."

"I promise you I won't."

"Let me see your hands," she says, so I hold up a hand. "No, both of them," she insists.

"And why am I doing this?"

"I want to make sure that your fingers aren't crossed."

My lips curve skyward, and I hold up both of my hands, palms flat, fingers spread. "I promise and I swear that I won't laugh at you. And if I do, I'll jump overboard and drown myself."

"No, don't say that that's terrible... and you know I can't save you."

"Well, I won't laugh."

"Ok, I tell you." She squints, studying me. "I'm coming to Kowloon today to get my fortune told by an old Chinese fortune teller." I see her analyzing my reaction.

"So you really are strange," I say, straight-faced.

She pushes me. "Don't be cruel."

"Hey, I didn't laugh. There's no need for violence."

"But you wanted to, I know it."

"You kidding, that's not even weird. I'm here to get my fortune told too."

"You are?" Her eyes widen.

"Nah," I shake my head. "But I'm definitely probably going to get a fortune cookie after lunch."

"Ha-ha, you are mister funny man." She's blushing. "I tell you about me, now you tell me something about you."

"What do you want to know?" I ask.

"I don't know. Anything. Something not many people know."

"Hmm," I think about it for a second or so. "Ok, I got something."

"What is it?"

"Well, just this morning—"

"You had a hangover."

"Yeah, that too. But I also remembered that, well, that I left Chicago without paying my library late fees. I'm sure I owe at least five, maybe ten dollars."

"Hopefully they don't come for us." Her smile mirrors mine as the docking ferry bumps the pier.

"Natasha, now I'm no expert or anything. But I'm pretty sure I read somewhere, I think maybe it was in *The New Yorker* or possibly *Psychic News Magazine*. I'm really not too sure on the source, but I believe I remember it saying something about fortunes being like sixty-to-seventy percent more accurate on a full stomach. So, I'm thinking that it's probably a good idea, for you at least, if the two of us were to grab lunch together first. What do you say?"

"Hmm." A single finger taps her top lip. "I think you might be right. But only for the sake of the fortune."

"Of course. No gimmicks here."

As we stand to exit, I finally get a good look at her: five-nine, with long legs, and subtle curves everywhere you'd want them, a woman who'd stand out anywhere in the world.

We both agree on something low-key, a place only a local would eat. We walk the brick-lined sidewalks past blocks of western retail stores and chain restaurants. We keep a brisk pace for twenty minutes until we find ourselves canopied by countless lines of brightly-colored clothes that hang between endless rows of monochromatic-buildings covered in shabby satellite dishes and rickety window-mounted air-conditioners. We're off the tourist beat where the real Cantonese-flavor lives.

She's adventurous and never complains about the long walk, strange smells, or pushy salesman. Our time together is full of carefree smiles and jovial jokes.

We pick a hole-in-the-wall noodle shop on Woosung because of its neon sign and swords in the window.

We don't ask many questions about one another—which I like. Too often, when people first meet, they never truly get to live in the moment, like real friends do. It's nice that she can enjoy the walk, the sights, the smells, the flavors, the energy, without knowing how many brothers I have, where I went to school, or what I do for a living. It's refreshing to spend time with someone who, in a matter of an hour, feels like an old friend—with inside jokes, instead of an interrogating interview, where under heavy questioning, I divulge every damn thing I know about myself. Besides, we're always just telling different people the same six stories and judging them on how they react.

She tells me how she wants to move to Paris. And her desire to sip creamy coffees at smart street-side cafés, where she'd watch tourists take selfies, and spend her summer on the Seine, sipping champagne and listening to foreigners trying to pronounce fancy French foods.

Full of dumplings and *beef chow fun*, we walk down Woosung to Austin. She knows exactly where we're heading. A friend from Moscow had been in Hong Kong some five-years ago, and everything this woman told her had apparently come true. "What if she tells you you're to become filthy-rich, and six months from now—you do? Wouldn't I get some sort of commission for coming with you?"

"What if she tells me I need to push myself to the max?"

"You think she'll say that if I tip her?"

This psychic has apparently been here forever, giving readings on a strict in-the-know basis. As she can't be found in any print or online publications, and isn't at the night markets, like all the other prominent Kowloon fortunetellers.

And after countless blocks of fast-moving motorbikes, potent smells, and relentless spitting, we arrive at the address.

Like the rest of the neighborhood, it's a dilapidated old building barely holding on. We stand below a daunting red metal door, with a buzzer and a well worn, heavily taped cardboard sign that reads: *Your Future*, scratched in English, and I assume the same in Chinese.

"Are you ready to learn everything about *your future*?" I ask dramatically. She has a noticeable worry in her eyes before they wander over to the bar across the way. "You want to grab a quick one?" I ask.

A single finger unfolds. "One shot," she says. So I grab her hand and pull her across the street.

We walk into the smoky six-seat bar, with ten bottles of visible booze and a one-armed bartender.

"*Wǒmen lái hējiǔ,*" I call out.

"You know Cantonese?" she asks.

"No, that's all I know."

"What did you say?"

"Not sure, but he doesn't look happy."

The man has a half-smoked cigarette hanging from his hardened face and greets us with indeterminate mumbling.

"Hello, friend," I say, pushing away a pile of stale cigarette butts atop a tiny ashtray. "We'll have two shots of..." And I turn to her to finish the order.

"Gin."

"You sure?" I grimace.

"You don't like gin?"

✈

"Hey, it's your future," I say, and turn back to the bartender. "Two gin shots, please."

You can see that she's genuinely nervous, believing in this whole fortuneteller folklore. I had been cracking jokes, but she's truly troubled over what this total stranger is about to tell her. I find it amusing, but I obviously keep it to myself. It makes her seem sweet and vulnerable, something I rarely find beautiful women to be.

The bartender pours our shots, and I pay him. We tap glasses, and I make a toast.

"To good fortune. Hopefully." She scowls, and we shoot our shots.

Slamming her hand atop the bar. "Let's do it," she proclaims, before leading me back to the red door.

With her new gin-fueled confidence, she presses the buzzer. Five long seconds later, there's an obnoxious *Ehhhhh* sound, and I pull the heavy door open.

This takes us to a small foyer with a shoddy staircase. It smells like there should be flies, but I see none. I hold out my hand, and we climb the steps together. There's another red door at the top, I go to knock, but before I do, an old woman's voice calls out, "Enter children."

I'm not sure if I was expecting a crystal ball and a warted witch. But what I see is a thin, gray-haired Chinese woman in a purple-sweatsuit and pink fanny-pack. Her delicate papery skin melts into a well-worn ducked-taped Lazy-Boy recliner, facing a portable television—with rabbit ears—atop a yellowed TV tray. A foldable card table and foldable chairs fill the rest of the otherwise empty room.

"It's quaint," I cough.

On the table, there's a glass tank holding a small box turtle. And on the wall, an old paper calendar and a few photos.

"Have a seat," says the woman in a smoker's voice. She looks at Natasha. "So, you are here to learn of your future."

Natasha's eyes widen. "I am."

✈

"One-hundred Hong Kong dollars for your fortune. Two-hundred Hong Kong dollars for your future."

Natasha pulls out two hundred and places it on the table with purpose.

The old woman smiles, her teeth are terribly brown, but as straight as a Crest commercial. She rocks herself free from the chair's grip, and struggles to stand, but before I can move to help her. "Sit child," she hisses, as if she anticipated me doing so.

She hobbles to the table; she's tall, with little weight to her. Up close, I can see that she must be at least ninety, maybe a hundred. She's wrinkled, and sun spotted, with faint European features. Yet, somehow, through her considerable age, I can see she was once attractive.

She reaches across the table with her shaky hands, picks up the money, and places it in her fanny-pack. As she's zipping the waist-worn pouch, her head involuntarily jerks to the side. She ignores this, and as the spasm passes, she reaches into the glass enclosure with both hands to pick up the turtle. Struggling with the five-inch reptile as though it weighs sixty-pounds, she places it on the table in front of her. "Give me your hand, sweet child," she says to Natasha.

I feel my phone vibrate in my pocket. The old woman turns to me, "No phones!"

"Sorry," I say, taking it out and turn it off, wondering how she even heard it.

She starts her sorcery by grasping Natasha's hand with her frail fingers, telling her things I suppose would be tough to guess, like: "Your winters are long and cold, and there's no sea."

But as she's doing so, I turn my attention to the wall where there's an old Coca-Cola calendar from 1961, and the date, December 6th, is circled in black marker. I look down at my new Cartier and confirm that today's date is December 6th, and it gives me the fucking willies, like something out of *Great Expectations*. Is this a strange coincidence? Or does she have a closet full of these backdated calendars to creep customers out?

I glance over to see the woman scratching her fingernail across the top of the turtle's shell and chanting something in mixed Chinese. I want to watch, never having witnessed a psychic at work, but I can't keep my eyes off that goddamn calendar; it's the most peculiar thing I've ever seen. I want to ask about it, but dare not disturb.

My eye moves over to a black-and-white golden-framed photo. It's of a man with a mustache embracing a Chinese woman. And after a second or so, I realize that I recognize this man. He's distinguished-looking and handsome with a nice haircut. I just can't place him. The Chinese woman is young and beautiful. She's slim, with a pleasant smile and European features, almost as if... *ahh*. I see it now. I look over at the old woman, then back at the picture. Matching the small mole on her right cheek. The photo is of her. Wow, this has to be sixty or seventy years old, and it hits me, the guy is fucking Ernest Hemingway, and the building they're standing in front of is The Peninsula Hotel, just down the road. This picture must have been taken before the Japanese invaded Hong Kong. *Wow*, I say to myself, that's definitely something you don't see every day.

I stare at the old woman. I'm so interested in her now. I want to know more, but I stay silent and study the two artifacts adorning the well-stained wall.

"A great fortune of fantasy awaits you," she chants, now nearly shouting in an over the top finale. "For it may leave quicker than it came, but don't give in, for your light will shine forever." The small room falls silent.

"Wow," I hear Natasha whisper to herself. I assume it's over when the old woman releases her hand, leaving her with a dumbfound stare upon her face.

After a second, she snaps out of it and turns to me. "What do you think?" she asks, but I'm locked on the old woman.

"Great," I murmur.

"You have many questions, young man," the woman says. "Would you like to know your future?"

"No, I'm good," I say, somewhat freaked out. I really just want to get the fuck out of here, but curiosity can be a bitch. "How did you know Ernest Hemingway?" I ask.

"Ahh, you like my picture?"

"Yeah, it's great," I say. "How do you know him?"

Once upon a time, I was hooked on Hemingway. It was he—at least in part—who initially inspired me to see the world. I remember being a teenager: wanting to travel, wanting to sip champagne with women I barely knew, and fall in and out of love.

"Ernest was a—" Her head jerks again, and she gurgles a bit, but ignores it. "A friend of mine," she says.

"What kind of friend?"

"Oh, child, don't be silly."

"I mean, how were you, friends? How did you meet?"

"I worked as a barmaid many-many years ago. He was a customer, a good customer, and a great man."

"Did you love him?" I ask. I don't even know why I said it; it just slipped out.

"I did," she replies promptly with a warm wrinkly smile.

"Did he love you?"

"I'm not sure. And I suppose I'll never know."

"And what about December 6th being circled on that calendar there? Why do you still have a calendar from 1961?"

"You don't like my calendar?"

"No, I do... it's nice... or it's fine... it's just that, well, today is December 6th. It's a strange coincidence, don't you think?"

"That is strange," Natasha says to herself.

"Oh, think little of it, child. That was a day for me, a long-long time ago, in another life. It's merely chance for you."

"Why do you keep it?" I ask.

"Take some free advice from a very old woman. Don't live in the past. Live your life for now, how it's meant to be lived. And if you believe in something, you are never to second-guess yourself... for fear is temporary, but love is forever."

"Ok," I murmur, a dumbfound stare upon my face.

✈

"Now, you kids go; go and live well this day."

Natasha and I stand, thank the woman, then exit down the same stairwell, and out the same red door.

When we reach the road, we stop and stare at each other, wide-eyed, with our mouths open. I struggle to find my words, so theatrically, I scratch at my chest and arms. "Goddamn that was spooky," I say.

"That was incredible, wasn't it incredible?"

"Yeah, it was definitely something."

"How do you feel?"

"How do I feel? I got the freaking heebie-jeebies, that's how I feel."

"It was great, right?" She's excited as hell.

"That definitely was a memorable experience, I'll give ya that." And *dammit*, it's the truth. "Is it always like that?" I ask.

"Is what always like what?"

"Fortune-telling, or fortunetellers, what we just did. Is it always that spooky?"

"No, I've experienced anything like that in my life. She knew everything about me. It was crazy. Oh, Max, it must be true, I'm so glad I went, and I'm so happy you were there with me."

"I'm glad I got to see it," I say.

"Seriously, thank you so much for coming with me. It was everything I wanted it to be." She looks into me, squinting, seemingly waiting for me to say something.

"So, what do you think?" she asks.

"About what?"

"About my future."

"What do you mean?"

"You heard her. Did you like what she said?"

"Um, well..." I search for an excuse. "I hate to say this, but that calendar sort of threw me for a loop. I mean, I wasn't really paying too close of attention. I'm sorry."

"What did you hear?"

"Not much."

✈

"Did you hear anything?"

"Maybe the beginning... but no, not really."

"Then, I think it was meant to be that way." She smiles.

"What do you mean? What did she say?"

"Maybe you'll find out."

"Now I can't know?"

"If you tell a wish, it won't come true."

"I thought it was your future, not a wish?"

"It is a wish if you want it to come true."

"So, it's a good thing?"

"Maybe, we'll see."

"Come on, now I have to know."

"Maybe sometime... in the future."

"Ok, but I'm going to hold you to that, maybe. And don't for a second think I'll forget about that commission check when you hit the lottery either." She laughs, and then locks back into my eyes.

"Seriously, thank you for coming with me today."

"You're welcome," I say as she leans in and gives me a small peck on the cheek. "We can go back if you want." I turn towards the red door. She pushes me, and her face warms.

Now walking towards the ferry, I remember my phone is still off, so I power it up. I have two new messages, both from Anna. The first: *Max, come to the races with me tonight, please!! It's some type of championship, and everyone will be there. I'll be so bored without you. Please, please, please! It's the usual box and starts at 7:15.*

The second: *Max, Teddy just came home early and surprised me. Said he'd like to see you. We're still going to the races. Meet us there if you want. Let me know.*

I text her back as soon as I read it: *See you at seven.*

"Natasha, some of my friends just invited me to the horse track tonight, some championship or something. Is there any chance you'd want to go?"

"A boat ride, a psychic reading, and now a horse race. If we ever get married, this would be a great story to tell our grandkids." She gives me a wink.

"So, that's a yes?"

"Yes, it's a yes."

"Well, good," I say. "And while we're checking boxes, I think we should add, had a drink at the world-famous Peninsula Hotel to that prenuptial list." And I wink back.

The hotel is close to the ferry and on our way. I was hoping to stop by after seeing that photo of the old woman. Guess I've always been one of those nerds who wish they grew up in a different era, and this is the perfect place for those kinds of people.

Historically the finest hotel in all of Hong Kong, The Peninsula, opened in the 1920s, with its still preserved original colonial design. I remember reading they built it here as the final stop of the famed Trans-Siberian Railway, which imported wealthy travelers from Europe. It stands today as an ornate time capsule to a more sophisticated, more romantic era, when jazz was on the radio and revolution was in the air.

We make our way to the bar on the first floor. It's busy, but not packed. We find two stools and are greeted by an older Asian gentleman in a white suit, who introduces himself as Johnny. I order myself a martini—extra dirty, and she selects champagne. The room is elegant. It's dimly lit, with dark hardwood and generous touches of gold. The type of place Hemingway's characters, with their regal titles and squandered fortunes, would sip Asti and apéritifs and talk about how drunk they all are.

"When I get married, I want it to be in a place like this," she says.

"So you do want to get married?" I wink again.

"Doesn't every woman want to get married?"

"Perhaps."

"You don't want to?"

"No, I suppose I do. I just don't think about it too much is all."

"I don't think about it too much either. But I do dream about it sometimes, and I hope that one day I do."

✈

Our drinks come fast. "To our future," I say, and we raise a glass.

"And to good luck at the track tonight," she adds.

"Ah, yes, and to my commission when you win." We laugh.

I take a sip, turn to the bartender, and say, "Johnny, this is the best damn martini I've ever had in Hong Kong."

CHAPTER 11
Happy Valley

BY THE TIME I PICK UP RICKY from the night before, I only have twenty minutes to get ready. After two shower-beers and a fresh shave, I toss on my new white Valentino button-up, tuck it into my new navy slacks and brown Gucci belt, part my hair JFK style, and chug a Red Bull before I bounce.

Natasha is waiting as I pull into the circular drive of the Four Seasons. She's stunning in her all-white, high cut, backless dress with long sleeves and matching red bottoms. Her long blonde hair is down and curled at the ends. She's wearing almost no makeup, other than a light lip stain. But despite her glamorous outfit and regal beauty, those bright aqua eyes stand out above all else.

"I don't even know what to say, you look incredible."

"Thank you. You clean up well yourself." And she delivers a small kiss on my cheek. "Nice car."

"Thanks, it's a loaner," I say. And it feels good to be honest with her. Typically, I'd just say *thanks* and leave it to the imagination. "It's my friends."

"Nice friends," she says.

"The best." And with that, we pull away.

It's precisely seven o'clock as we enter the elevator to take us to the sixth-floor private box suite. Natasha squeezes my hand and smiles with her eyes as we climb.

As I reach to open the door, she grabs me by my shirt, thanks me for inviting her, and pulls me in for a kiss—a real kiss.

"I'm glad you're here," I say, slightly flushed as I turn the knob.

"Hold on," she wipes away what I assume to be lipstick from my top-lip.

"There's the man of the hour." Teddy broadcasts across the room as he rushes to shake my hand and embrace me in a brotherly hug. "By God, it's good to see you, mate."

He has a powerful presence, a natural vigor for life, a contagious Gary Vee type gusto, and an encouraging—almost spellbinding smile. His accent and finely tailored suit tell you he's British, while his gold-tipped cowboy boots say he's spent time in Texas.

"It's good to see you too, Teddy," I say, turning to introduce Natasha, but he beats me to it.

"Natasha, what a lovely surprise, I hadn't been made aware you'd be joining us this evening."

"Good to see you, Mister Hammond," Natasha says and extends her hand. Teddy takes ahold of it, bows slightly, and gives it a small gentleman's kiss.

"You look positively lovely this evening, my dear."

"Thank you, Mister Hammond."

"Please, we're at a racetrack, call me Teddy, or perhaps Theodore, if it better suits you."

"Ok, Teddy," she says.

"How do you two know each other?" I ask.

"You mean... you don't know?" Teddy says, seemingly surprised.

I look over at Natasha, who looks back at me, eyes cold, lips pressed. "No, tell me," I say.

"Well, isn't this quite serendipitous," Teddy says. "As it so happens, mate. Natasha here is the daughter of our chairman and my boss. So, I suggest you be on your best behavior, young man." He pretends to punch my stomach.

Looking at her, I try to minimize any visible reaction to this revelation. Yet, at the same time, she appears to be studying me, for what I can only assume signs of unease.

"I only tease, this is a good man right here, Natasha, the finest," Teddy says with both of his hands now firmly grasping and squeezing my shoulders. "Had I only known you were in town, I would have invited you myself."

"Well, it all worked itself out," she says, still eying me.

"Max, Natasha, what a wonderful surprise," says Anna, sauntering in from the balcony, wide-eyed with a painted smile. "Please, make yourselves comfortable."

"By Jove, Max, my boy, you look fantastic. Doesn't he look fantastic, Anna?"

Ignoring Teddy. "Natasha darlin', you look so pretty. I'm so glad you're here, but I wasn't expecting you."

"Max didn't tell you he was bringing someone?"

"Oh no, Max never tells me much of anything," Anna says with a dismissive wave. She's looking sexy herself in a low-cut lace dress and a pearl necklace.

"It's been far too long, my boy. Anna, doesn't Max look fantastic? Just positively fantastic." Teddy says it twice, till Anna finally turns to me.

"Max, you look fantastic. I really like that belt." And turns away.

"I can't get over it, my boy; you're a thoroughbred you are. And seeing the two of you together, you make a damn fine couple, damn fine."

Teddy is a hopeless romantic who's always rooting for love, and like Clooney—he keeps getting better looking with age. I mean, the man could have any woman he wants; that's if he didn't love Anna so damn much.

I remember a few years back—he had to go to Tokyo on business and didn't want to go alone. Anna wasn't up for it, so he took me. We stayed at the Ritz and got rowdy. There were beautiful women all over us that weekend. But he never broke, bent, or even came close. He loves Anna like crazy and would do nothing to disrespect her. I admire that about him. Most men with that money and those looks wouldn't be so true to their wives.

"Come on, Max, I want to introduce you to some friends and colleagues of mine." At a quick glance, they all look his typical mahogany and tweed type, overeducated and overpaid: a look back in time to when men sat in smoky offices, sipping Scotch, and screwing their secretaries. "This chap here is our North America CFO, Daniel Stevenson, and his wife, Jane."

"How do you do," I say as we all shake hands, making sure my posture and inquisitive eye contact provide a patina of purpose.

"It's a pleasure to meet you, Max. Teddy always has the nicest things to say about you."

"He's a big liar, don't believe a word of it," I say. Morphing into my well-cultivated Dale Carnegie chameleon of a character.

"And Daniel, Jane, you know Natasha, of course."

"Pleasure to see you again, Miss Cameron."

"Same to you Mister Stevenson, Misses Stevenson."

"And Max, you already know Dr. Webber and his wife, Kerry." Both gray-haired and round-faced. Him, a thick mustache and tan suit, her a sensible schoolteacher style.

"Good to see you again, Dr. Webber, Miss Webber."

"And this is my old chap, Jim Thompson."

"Good to meet you, sir," I say as I shake his hand. He's the distinguished Ivy League type, puffing on a tobacco pipe.

"I'm surprised we haven't yet met, Theodore here has told me books-worth about you," says Jim Thompson.

"Good things, I hope?"

"Just that you're a hell of a trainer and a great friend."

"Teddy's too kind, more like mediocre at both."

"Oh, I doubt that..."

"This is my friend Natasha," I say to Jim.

"Pleasure to meet you," Natasha says as she extends her hand.

"The pleasure is all mine, Miss Cameron." He takes her hand. "I've actually had the opportunity to converse with your father on a multitude of occasions."

"That's very nice, what a small world," she says. I was thinking the same thing, but she said it.

"Yes, isn't it," replies Jim Thompson. "The most recent rendezvous was in Palo Alto, about a year ago. We split a bottle of Screaming Eagle and enjoyed an enlightening conversation on informatics and San Francisco in the sixties. A wonderful man, your father is."

"I'll tell him you send regards."

"I'd appreciate that very much."

Teddy turns us. "And this bloke is my attorney, Peter Pinkerton. He only attends these pro bono functions because I personally put a new wing on his house every other year."

"And after this Deutschland merger, I'm buying my goddamn neighbor's house too. I can't take any more of those late-night pool parties," proclaims Peter Pinkerton, and I shake the man's hand.

"I keep reminding the chaps back in London that you're bound to pull it off," says Teddy.

"You bet your ass, I'll pull it off. By next week, those fuck-heads will be begging you to take their money."

Teddy turns to the woman next to Peter. "And despite my attorney's primitive vocabulary, this lovely lady here is his wife, Doctor Stacey Pinkerton."

"Pleasure to meet you both," I say as I reach to shake her hand. Peter Pinkerton is middle-aged, well-worn, with thinning hair, porous skin, and a stained smile. And his wife, well, she isn't. No, Stacey Pinkerton is a platinum blonde of indeterminate age. Her face is fixed like most women with money, she has big lips, and is very attractive in that hot cougar kind of way.

"Please, call me Stacey." She says it with a slight lisp and a sultry smile. And I suddenly realize that I've already met Stacey Pinkerton.

It was over a year ago, here in Hong Kong. I don't remember ever getting her last name, but I do remember the small butterfly tattoo on her lower back—that I discovered when I bent her over in her hotel room. I remember saving her number in my phone as *Hong Kong Cougar XXX*, and that she had texted me as recently as August, but that I never wrote back.

"Will do," I say. Carefully controlling the curvature of my lips.

"Max, Teddy tells me you were a Bulldog, that you studied economics," says Daniel Stevenson, holding a plate of pungent cheese and a pile of beluga caviar. He's a jovial older gentleman, with phosphorescent teeth and a houndstooth suit.

"Yes, sir, that's correct... I was, and I did. Seems like a lifetime ago."

Teddy knows damn well that I graduated from a state school, but you might as well say trade school to this crowd. I didn't leave Yale because my grades were bad; they were fine, I just didn't fit in, or at least that's what I'd say to myself whenever I'd socialize with those prep-school polished tea-sipping snobs, who could come up with fifty things they'd rather do than watch a football game. If it weren't for James and Sam, I wouldn't have lasted a month; because at that time—barely eighteen—I didn't yet possess the humility to fake it as I do now.

"Well, Max, we all went to school a long time ago, some of us much longer than others." He chuckles reminiscently before continuing. "You know I've spent a bit of time in Connecticut myself—"

"And my brother, he's a Yalie," interjects his wife Jane, in that old-money type of way. "It's such a wonderful school."

It's funny; people always say that to me, *what a great school it is*. The truth is, of all the prestigious universities my parents pressured me into, I picked Yale—because the cafeteria reminded me of Hogwarts.

"Maybe I knew him," I say.

"Oh, I doubt that..." Her laugh, a phony Katharine Hepburn, "Ha-Ha-Ha."

"Did you spend some time at the OC?" I ask Daniel Stevenson.

"No, Max, I'm a Princeton man myself, class of 67'. But I was born and raised on the coast and always drove up to New Haven for the pizza."

"Ah yes, the apizza. Where was your spot?" I ask.

"Oh, I don't know, Max. Showing your hand on your favorite apizza spot can be more divisive than politics. You'd have to promise me you won't hold a grudge."

"Oh, I know it," I say, laughing. "I've seen relationships sour over apizza sputes, but you have my word." And though it's bullshit, we both know it's probably happened at some point.

"Well, Max, I'm a man of tradition. I like to keep things simple—"

"Frank Pepe's," I call out.

"You got it, Max."

"What do you get?" I ask.

"What else, the white—"

But I cut him off again, "white clam," I say. "I'm a Pepe's man myself."

"Max, I knew I was talking to a rational person. Teddy, you got a wicked good man here."

"I had said you two would get along famously. Didn't I?"

"I could eat white clams every day," I say. "But I'm not going to lie to you, Mister Stevenson."

"Max, please, call me Daniel." I can't decide if he keeps saying my name to commit it to memory, or if it's just the way he is, but I decide to start saying his back, in case he's keeping count—I'm determined to win.

"I won't lie to you, Daniel, once in a while, I'd switch it up and get the white spinach and mushroom."

"Because you love the mootz, right, Max?"

"Exactly, Daniel."

"Oh, I understand, Max, I'm a mootz man myself. Every time I'm in New Haven, I get a white clam to eat there, and take a white mushroom or fresh tomato to go, because of that damn mootz." He kisses his fingers.

"But Daniel, fresh tomato—only in the summer," I say.

"And that there, Max, is why Jane and I only summer in Connecticut. Damn, it's good to have a Constitution man here in the flesh. These people just don't get it, they don't know good pizza."

"Where did you grow up, Daniel?" I ask.

"Bridgeport," he says.

"Ah, I spent a few nights in St. Vincent," I say.

"Nothing serious, I hope?"

"I'm here, aren't I?"

"Max, you know my mother was a nurse at St. Vincent when I was growing up. Now that was a lifetime ago."

"It's a small world, Daniel." I smile over at Natasha for stealing her line, then glance back at Stacey Pinkerton.

"Are you Catholic?" asks Jane Stevenson.

"I am," I say.

"He's a damn fine Catholic too," says Anna, randomly, raising a flute of champagne to herself as she says it.

"Oh, that's wonderful. Daniel and I have belonged to Holy Trinity on 82nd for the longest time. What a fine church," says Jane Stevenson. "Don't you just love the churches on the east coast? So elegant, so European."

"Sure," I say.

"I also enjoy St. Paul's on Columbus and 60th, but even those darn Episcopals, like Grace on Broadway, in Manhattan, they're truly something. Or those Presbyterians, I tell you. There's this one darling little church near Washington Square, it's just breathtaking, I mean absolutely majestic, like something out of a medieval storybook; almost makes me believe I could be a Presbyterian. That's if they weren't so damn democratic."

"Well, I've had my fill of religion for the evening," says Teddy, apparently tired of the topic. "Especially as we're all drinking and about to start gambling."

"Hear, hear!" says Anna, again, toasting herself.

"Natasha, did I hear correctly, is your father to be attending our little award shindig this year?" asks Teddy.

"Well, yes, that's the reason I'm in town. It was a last-minute decision. He is to arrive on Saturday."

"Marvelous, I hadn't known it to be confirmed." He turns to me. "Max, my boy, if you don't yet have plans, you should join us as well. It will be a brilliant time."

"Sure, why not," I say.

"Do you have your dinner jacket, pardon, your tuxedo here?" he asks.

"No, I didn't bring it."

"Of course not, why would you? It's not a problem. I'll have my suit guy come by the apartment tomorrow, he'll take care of you."

"Sure," I say.

"He's the best in Asia, maybe the best in the world. They're damn fine suits they are. Terribly expensive, but worth every penny."

"Sounds great," I say, smiling at Teddy's profound opposition to anything ordinary. Everything has to be fine or marvelous, handmade, and expensive as hell.

"Here, I have one of his jackets now. Isn't it fine? Go on, give it a feel." And he has me touch it.

"It's very nice."

"Max, I don't want to see you in any of that bottom of the barrel designer rubbish Anna is always carrying on about. I'm paying for your dinner jacket."

"You don't have to Teddy, I'll get the tux," I say.

"I'm afraid I can't let you do that, my boy. You're my guest, I've just invited you, and it's money you would have not otherwise spent. It will be my pleasure. It will be the finest tuxedo you've ever seen, Max, the finest."

"Sure," I say.

"Ay, it will be a grand time, with plenty of drinking and dancing. It will be a marvelous evening."

"I could use a drink right now," I say.

"Indeed, of course you could."

"Teddy, you're talking the boy's ear off. He's been here fifteen-minutes and hasn't had a moment between your jabber to get himself or his date a proper drink," Anna says, with subtle hints of a faux British accent occasionally overriding her deep southern drawl. It's the strangest goddamn thing, I swear. But, I guess that's how it is for people who have traveled everywhere, and seen everything, and lived all over the world. Teddy himself is a perfect example of a mixed-hybrid accent. Raised by a well-to-do family in London, he believes he speaks the Queen's English—the kind you find on the BBC, and for the most part, he does. But like everyone, he's a non-consenting sponge of his surroundings. Teddy left England just after Oxford and has spent the majority of his life abroad. So, sometimes, especially when he's had a few, you'll hear the twelve years he spent in Houston seep through. I'd imagine anyone who's lived in Texas that long would leave with a little drawl in their jaw. Then there are the years in Dublin, Mumbai, Johannesburg, and Sydney. Now that truly is the strangest thing you've ever heard. When He's all drunk and excited, and within a sentence or two, he'll say something southern with an English accent, and then throw in some indistinguishable Irish slang while shaking his head side to side. If you didn't know any better, you'd think he's being some sort of a fancy-ass jerk.

"He's not a boy, he's a goddamn man. He's capable of getting himself a drink anytime he damn pleases. Max, what are you drinking, mate?" Teddy asks.

"What do you suggest?"

"Well, my boy, you know what I always say. We drink according to the wind, and by God, it's picking up out there." He raises his glass of whiskey as he says it.

"I'll have one of those," I tell the bartender.

The box suite is about the size of a two-car garage. The walls are a deep burgundy and covered in gold-framed horse paintings. The floors—dark mahogany, and there's a large flat-screen TV that streams the races. Along the back wall is a table with a vast array of decadent foods, and a bar stocked with an exquisite selection of premium liquors.

The bartender hands me my Woodford and Natasha a flute of champagne.

The 6th-floor balcony has a row of eight stadium-style seats that look out to an exceptionally bright-green egg-shaped all-grass track that's exquisitely maintained. The entire visual of the track at night, under the stadium lights, engulfed by the towering high-rise buildings of metropolitan Hong Kong, is an empowering experience in itself.

J Gatz

"So, your father is the chairman of one of the world's largest banks," I say privately to Natasha as we enjoy our drinks.

"Is that a problem for you?"

"No, but I was wondering how a woman in her twenties could afford to stay at the Four Seasons while vacationing in Hong Kong."

"And before learning of my father, what conclusions had you come to?"

"I only had one."

"And that was?"

"That you were a model."

"You lie," she whispers through her smile.

"I... thought I remember Teddy telling me his boss was Scottish."

"Yes, my father is Scottish, and my mother, Russian. My parents are no longer together."

"Ah, that makes sense. Mine either, since I was eight," I say.

"Ten for me..."

A strange, almost awkward silence slides between us. It's not long, only a few seconds or so, but it feels like forever.

"...I think I figured out who loaned you the Ferrari," she says, breaking the silence.

"Yeah, the bartender and I go way back."

"Thank you for being honest with me."

"About what?" Knowing perfectly well what she means.

"Things," she says.

"Always," I reply.

"The race is about to start, does everyone have their bets in?" announces Stacey Pinkerton in her *Clueless* California cadence.

"I'm afraid I never bet on the first race. It's bloody bad luck to bet on the first race, isn't that right, Max?" says Teddy.

"That's right," I say, suddenly recalling the day Teddy stopped betting on the first race.

He and I were in Singapore; it was horribly humid, so we had a few drinks. I don't know if it was the heat or the hooch, but Teddy got it in his mind that he would bet a million dollars on the first race. "It's the sport of kings, my boy," he'd say. "If you want to win like a king, you must bet like a king." He kept repeating that over and over, likely trying to convince himself.

He put a million on a horse named Brandy Alexander with some high-stakes bookie, at a four-to-one payout, and told me he'd give me a half-million if we won.

Brandy Alexander was in front, going into the final turn and running fast until his leg got tangled with the horse behind him, and they both fell. A horse named Bon Appetite, with twenty-to-one odds ended up taking it.

That night we ate at some fancy-ass restaurant, Baroque art on the walls, and stuffy people in the seats. As the waiter went through the specials, he informed us that their cocktail of the evening was their famous "Brandy Alexander." I saw Teddy grimace, but he stayed cool. Then, our food arrived, our plates placed before us—something with a shitload of shallots—the waiter said, "bon appétite." I thought Teddy might hit the man, but he just smiled and shook his head, and we ended up having a good laugh over it.

I honestly believe that he was never even mad about losing the money; he just stopped betting on the first race.

"So, Natasha... do tell... how did you two eva-meet?" asks Anna.

"We met on the ferry to Kowloon this afternoon."

"Just this afternoon, hmm, well, isn't that wonderful."

"Darling, the race is about to start. Why don't y'all bring yourselves out here." Teddy hollers from the balcony.

"Oh sweetie, can't we just watch it on the television. I mean, if we're not betting on it or anything," Anna says.

"I say, darling, we could have just stayed home if you wanted to watch it on the telly. Come on now," Teddy insists.

This is the first time Anna has ever actually seen me with another woman. Teddy has seen me with girls before and told her about it. And I've told her about dating other girls, but she's never seen it through her own eyes. And as we head out to the balcony, I can sense she isn't enjoying it much.

The gates swing open as the race starts. The spirited roar of some sixty thousand spectators is amplified as cheers reverberate off the surrounding city. The shouting only intensifies as the thousand-pound thoroughbreds round the first turn. Big money is at stake. And particularly enthusiastic-hollers stand out over the cacophony of cheers and chants. "Come on, McArthur!" One man shouts. "Let's go number nine, you got this nine!" says another.

My eyes move to the jumbotron as they fly around the far turn. The synchronized strength and stamina of the seven thoroughbreds isn't immediately perceived as real. It's more like a scene in the cinema, as tiny-men clench atop those majestic masses of muscle, moving at nearly forty-miles-per-hour.

"Number seven, there ya go numba seven!"

"*Lái ba dà biān! Lái ba dà biān!*"

Everyone in the place is on their feet as they approach the final furlong of the nearly mile-long track. The action is now directly below our 6th-floor balcony, giving us a brief, up-close, overhead view of those magnificent creatures as they scream by at fifty-feet-per-second.

You can see and hear the disappointment spread as half the crowd comes to realize they have no chance. However, those that do, grow exponentially louder. "Come on, Big Ed! Stay fast, stay strong!" Dr. Webber hollers while pumping his fist. Big Ed—a white horse with brown spots, pulls in front with only thirty-meters remaining. "Stay fast! Stay strong!" he shouts. Everyone in our suite gets behind Big Ed, as he surges across the finish line a half-length ahead of number seven. "Yes! I knew he had it tonight," shouts Dr. Webber. Hugs and high-fives go viral throughout our suite as though we all had money on Big Ed.

"Theodore, what do you think about that bad luck right there? Big Ed just made me three-hundred-thousand Hong Kong."

✈

"I say, good for you, Prescott, I'm truly happy for you, mate," Teddy says, and he shakes Dr. Webber's hand. And you can see he's genuinely thrilled for his friend's good fortune.

"What do you think?" I ask Natasha, who had been squeezing my arm since the second turn.

"Oh, that was wonderful. Can we bet on the next one?"

"Of course," I say.

"Indeed, we're all gonna bet on the second race. It's sac-religious not to bet on the second race." Anna says. She yells back to Teddy. "Isn't that right, sweetie?"

"That's right, darling. We all have to bet on the second race," says Teddy.

"See, it's agreed upon. Everyone's gonna be betting." And she takes another big swig of champagne.

"Ok, good," says Natasha.

"Come on," I say. "Let's go see what we're dealing with tonight." I take Natasha's hand and head to the nearest betting window. Sure, you can bet electronically from inside the suite, but Teddy always says that's bad luck too, and I'm not up for a lecture.

I end up putting a thousand Hong Kong dollars on a horse named Hawthorne *to win* at eight-to-one, and a thousand on Eleanor *to place* at a two-to-one since it was my grand-mother's name. And after I tell Natasha of my connection to Eleanor, she puts two thousand dollars on the filly to win at six-to-one. She tells me that "fate brought all this together," and she knows, "it's Eleanor's night."

With nearly twenty-minutes till the next race, we grab another drink and continue mingling with the other members of our party.

"So, Max, Theodore tells me you ran an Ironman last year?" asks Jim Thompson.

"Yes, Sir, I did."

"Max here is a goddamn machine." Teddy jumps in.

"Well... it was actually almost two years ago now. I don't believe I have one in me at the moment."

✈

"Nonsense, the boy is just being modest. He can do anything he wants," Teddy says.

I remember signing up for that damn race because Teddy started passing me on our long runs. I needed some sort of carrot to keep myself motivated.

"Teddy's pretty fast himself, I bet he could run one tonight if he wanted to," I say to Jim Thompson.

"And I haven't let up on my conditioning a bit, my boy, I'll show you tomorrow. That's if we could get in a session in the morning. Are you available?"

"Sure," I say, taking a sip of my bourbon. I can say no to Anna and anyone else, but for some reason, I can never say no to him; a binding obedience I can't break. And I'm definitely not looking forward to it, as he's in incredible shape. A man who demands the best of everything, his body is no exception. Teddy trains for vitality over vanity, a perpetual pursuit of pinnacle performance. He's nearly sixty, yet can run more than a dozen miles at a sub-seven-minute pace, and still want to lift weights.

"I'm a bit of a runner myself, but I don't believe I could pull off such a feat," says Peter Pinkerton.

"With a little time, anyone could," I say. "It's mostly mental."

"So what exactly is an Ironman? It's a run, a bike ride, then a swim?" asks Daniel Stevenson.

"No," says Teddy. "You swim, cycle, then you finish it with a run; because, if you finished with the swim, everyone in the bloody race would drown. Isn't that so?" He looks at me.

"Some probably would," I say.

"Go on, Max, tell them the distances," he insists.

He's grinning as I speak. "It's a 2.4-mile swim, then a 112-mile bike ride, followed by a 26-mile marathon run."

"You did all that?" Natasha asks.

"Damn right he did, and he did it in a hell of a good time too. Go on, Max, tell them your time," Teddy urges.

"It's really not that impressive," I say.

"Nonsense, it's fantastic for a first go. Come on, don't bundle up on us now, boy."

"Well, the professionals do it in about eight hours, and I finished about five-hours behind the fastest man."

"That's wonderful," says Natasha. "Where was this?"

"New Zealand."

"I hear New Zealand is just breathtaking," says Stacey Pinkerton.

"It's definitely different," I say.

"Your stamina must be out of this world," says Peter Pinkerton.

"It is," says his wife Stacey, with what I believe to be a Freudian slip. Thankfully, one that went unnoticed.

"Oh, Max is always running around in the hills by our house. He'll go up there for two hours at a time and come back wetter than if he had just jumped in a swimming pool. Isn't that right, Max?" says Anna. Now, staring at Stacey Pinkerton.

"I've been slacking a bit," I say.

"We'll give that a test tomorrow now—won't we, boy? By God, it's good to have you back, mate. It's been too long, too damn long," says Teddy.

"Too long," I say, feeling somewhat apathetic about tomorrow. Knowing my drinking has far out-paced my running these past few months, but I can't say no to the man.

"I say—I've just come up with the most marvelous idea. It just popped into my head out of thin air," cries Teddy.

"What is it, darlin'?" asks Anna.

"What if the three of us take in Macau tomorrow? Max, you'd be up for a little adventure, wouldn't you?"

"Sure, why not."

"Oh yes, darlin', that's a wonderful idea," says Anna.

"Isn't it brilliant?" You can see he's proud of himself for coming up with it.

"We haven't been to Macau in ages," says Anna.

"It'll be superb," Teddy continues.

"Oh, God, I'm so excited."

"What about the workout and the tux-guy?" I ask. Not trying to dampen the idea, but rather hoping he'd cancel the workout.

Teddy pauses, bites his knuckle, and ponders over it momentarily. "Not a problem, mate. I'll have my man come by in the morning and take your measurements before we train; he only needs to take them once you know, he's that good. Then we'll have lunch, and we'll all head out around four. Who's up for Macau tomorrow?" Teddy calls out so that everyone can hear, but nobody jumps at the invitation. "Natasha, would you care to join us? It's awfully nice having you here this evening. Macau would be ten-times a hoot with you there." I glance over at Anna to see her wanting to scream out a big no, but she catches herself.

"I'd like that very much. If Max doesn't mind," she replies.

"Lovely, dear. Surely he doesn't mind. I've known the boy for ten years, and he's never brought another girl around us. He's obviously smitten with you." Teddy slaps me on my back, and Natasha waits for a response.

"Should be a good time," I say.

"It's to be a grand time. Top-notch everything."

"Ok, I'm in." Natasha smiles.

I look over at Anna again. The joy that filled her face only moments earlier is flushed, and she's flustered. But unable to stop it, she stays silent.

"We'll go too," says Stacey Pinkerton.

"Marvelous," cries Teddy. "Anyone else?" You can see that Mr. and Mrs. Pinkerton hadn't discussed this prior to her blurting it out. But like Anna, Peter can't say anything now himself.

"Jim, Prescott, Daniel, what do you chaps say? Are you up for some good old fashion fun tomorrow?" He pitches the remaining members of the party.

"I would, but as you know, I volunteered to head the awards committee on Saturday. I'll be busy with that for the next few days," says Daniel Stevenson.

"Teddy, don't you have to help prepare for this awards thingamajig as well?" asks Anna, a blatant attempt to keep this impromptu idea from materializing.

"Nonsense darling, I came home a day early so we could do something. Daniel, I'll be back early Friday afternoon if you need a hand." He turns to Dr. Webber, "Prescott, what do ya say? Are you in, old sport?" Teddy only breaks out his Gatsby when he's truly excited about something.

"Sorry, Theodore, I have a board meeting tomorrow," says Dr. Webber.

"And I'm leaving for Kyoto in the afternoon," says Jim Thompson.

"Well, that's alright, the six of us will manage without you chaps. I'll have my assistant reserve us a wing at the Ritz. It'll be grand, top-notch everything, a truly marvelous time. You chaps are really missing out."

"Teddy, the boat is still in Singapore, how are we gonna get there?" Anna says, a transparent last-ditch effort to stop this getaway from getting off the ground.

"Not a problem, darling, we'll take the helicopter."

"You have a helicopter?" asks Stacey Pinkerton.

"By God no, those things are bloody money pits. I use a charter service. It's all top-notch. I'll give my assistant a ring, he'll sort all the details."

"I'm so excited," says Natasha.

"Young lady, it will be a grand time, a real hoot. They really take care of me at the Macau Ritz. We'll have the finest of everything. The finest rooms, the finest food, the finest service. What do ya say, Max?"

"Sounds real fine, Teddy."

"Ah, he's quite a cheeky bastard, isn't he?" Teddy turns to Natasha.

"Yes, he's very clever," she says.

"This boy right here is one of the most intelligent men I ever met, and I think of him as if he was my own son—I do."

"I can see that," she says.

"Barkeep, please pop us a couple bottles of champagne and fix everyone a glass." Teddy says, and we all toast to "friendship," and how "fine" our trip is to be.

"Oh, Teddy darlin', the race is about to start. Won't you join me on the terrace?" Anna says as she steps outside.

"Indeed, darling, come on all. Let's make our way to the terrace."

Since we all have money on it, the second race is even more exciting than the first. The crowd roars even louder, and the finish draws an entire football game's worth of jumping and high-fives. My horse loses, but because Eleanor won, I break even. Natasha's ticket pays out twelve thousand Hong Kong dollars, and from her enthusiasm, you'd think she'd never won a thing in her life.

Throughout the night, Anna continues coming up with random reasons why we should postpone tomorrow, but Teddy keeps dismissing them, going on about how much *fun* we'll have, and how *fine* everything will be.

We end up staying all seven races and don't leave till around eleven o'clock. Almost everyone in our group wins, a few lose, but nobody leaves disappointed.

I drive Natasha back to the Four Seasons and park far enough away to keep the valet from running over. Our conversation, which had been filled with laughs recalling the evening's events, suddenly switches to a more intimate tone.

"Max, I had such a wonderful night. Thank you for making me talk to you on the ferry today."

"Making you?" I smile.

"Yes, you made me." And she smiles back. "But I'm glad you did."

"I'd still be kicking myself if I didn't."

"Isn't tomorrow going to be—"

"Grand, fine, marvelous..." I impersonate Teddy with my terrible attempt at a British accent, and we both laugh.

"Max, can I ask you something?"

"Sure, anything."

"But it might come off as, oh—I don't know, jealous, or maybe even strange?"

"I'm sure it won't."

"Please, be honest with me," her Russian accent is the heaviest I've heard it.

"Of course."

"Have you ever been more to Miss Hammond than just a friend?"

"Why would you think that?" I ask. The muscles in my face strain to stay relaxed.

"I don't know, I just got a strange feeling from her, like she was mad at me for being there with you tonight. I've met her many times before, and I've never felt that way. It seemed obvious to me, but maybe it was my imagination."

"I didn't see it," I say. She studies my face.

"No, I feel like it was only directed at me. And the way she would look at you. I saw her staring at you several times."

"Well, that's because I looked positively fantastic," I say, again in the same crummy accent.

"Max, I'm not kidding. Please, tell me I'm foolish."

"You have to understand; Teddy, Anna, and myself have been friends for a very long time, a decade at least, and in that time, they've never seen me with another girl. Just like Teddy said, I don't bring them around. If you noticed any territorialism coming from Anna, I assure you, it was more like that of a mother looking out for the wellbeing of her child than that of a secret lover."

"Yes, you're right, that makes sense... I'm sorry I said anything."

"No need to be sorry," I say, knowing I just lied to her face. But what choice did I have?

"Oh, you must think I'm so jealous, I'm embarrassed."

"It's alright, I'm glad you asked."

"Why is that?" she questions.

"Because... now I know you kind of like me."

"Ah, don't be too sure of yourself, you are, ah... ok." She teeters her hand and smirks. "But just one more thing."

✈

"What's that?"

"You just said, 'I don't bring them around.' So I am wondering... how many girls are we talking about here?" Her face stiffens to serious. I stare at her, unsure how to answer, then, "Come on... I kid you." Her smile resurfaces. "Can't a girl make a joke?" And we both laugh. She pulls my shirt. "Come here, you handsome man," and kisses me. It's short, yet insanely sensual. Her lips are soft and moist, and she moans under her breath. "Good night, Max."

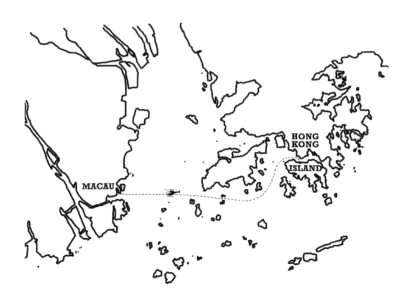

Everything's a gamble, love most of all.

— Tess Gerritsen

J Gatz

CHAPTER 12
The Vegas of Asia

WE BOARD THE HELICOPTER from Sky Shuttle's water-front terminal. Macau, known by most foreigners as The Vegas of Asia, is only a fifteen-minute flight.

Natasha, Anna, and Stacey Pinkerton are all dressed in white. I'm not sure if it's some sort of chopper tradition that I'm ignorant of—like green for St. Patty's—or if it's a coincidence, but they all look spectacular.

Upon takeoff, Teddy insists on explaining to everyone the value of a charter over ownership, because apparently, it's important. "This AgustaWestland-AW139 comes with an eight-million-pound price tag. Now mind you, that's not including crew, petrol, storage, or maintenance..." says the man with Mayweather money. He goes on like this, but I zone him out, my eyes affixed on the fading Hong Kong skyline and the scattered islands of coastal Southern China.

I purposely sat in front of Anna, an attempt to avoid any unnecessary eye contact. I'm not mad at her anymore; don't even know why I was. She did nothing to me, other than tell me how it is. I guess I couldn't take it.

Checking in, Teddy informs Natasha that his assistant *mistakenly* booked *only three* Carlton Club Suites. He tells her that even though they're two-bedrooms apiece, he'd gladly get her a separate private suite if it'd make her more comfortable.

"I appreciate that, Teddy, but I believe Max here will behave himself."

I slash an X over my heart and show her both of my wide-open hands. "So you know my fingers aren't crossed."

We follow the bellhop to our 50th-floor suite. It's large and luxurious: two bedrooms, with soaring views of the Cotai Strip. Both rooms feature their own marble-everything bathrooms, with large soaking tubs. One has an enormous plush King bed, and the other—two tiny twins.

"I want the room with the small beds," I say.

"Ok, I'll take the big bed all to myself," she replies. "But I'm curious. Why do you want the small beds? I mean... you are much bigger than me."

"Damn... I mean sure, I've put on a few pounds since we met, but ouch."

"Stop it, you know what I mean."

"Well, the truth is, or at least the way I see it. Since Macau is haunted and all, with all sorts of strange happenings in the night, you're probably going to want to come bunk with me anyways. So, I might as well have a spare bed ready for you."

"Is Macau really haunted?" she turns to the bellhop, her eyes nervous. I look at him with the straightest face I can and nod *yes*.

"Miss, I think he is... how do you say... pulling your leg." His high voice and heavy accent crack my straight face.

"There goes your tip."

"Max, you're such a jerk."

"Ok, so... I just want the little beds."

"But why? You really do?" I know she's confused by my insistent suggestion of separate rooms.

"Ok-ok, the truth is, it's so I can jump back and forth, and do tricks," I say as I leap onto the small bed, hop over to the other, and then bounce back again, before free-falling onto my back and almost bouncing myself onto the floor.

I can see the bellhop isn't overly enthused with my pre-teen antics, but he knows he already has one strike and has yet to receive his tip, so he stays silent.

I hadn't yet had an opportunity to convert any money to Macanese patacas, so I hand him five hundred Hong Kong dollars and tell him, "thanks." He appears pleased and tells me to "ring for anything." Then shows himself out.

✈

"This is so exciting, I never get to do anything like this in Moscow. What shall we do first?"

"Hmm, let's see. We're meeting everyone for dinner in about an hour, and we have absolutely nothing to do, so hmm." I move towards her, staring into her eyes as the anticipation builds with each step. And just as I reach her, so close, her breath heavy on my neck. I throw my arm around her, pick up the telephone she's standing in front of, and dial zero. "Hello, room service, please." She steps aside and gives me the biggest *oh you smart-ass* smirk of them yet. I shrug my shoulders. "Hi, do you guys, by chance, have Delirium Tremens? No. Ok... then could you please send up six Heinekens, and a bottle of Cristal? Oh yeah, Natasha, did you want anything?"

"Yes, I need ten beers," she says jokingly.

"Sir, yes, could you please add ten more beers to that. Sure, that'll be it. Just charge it to the room. And if you could, please, try to send the same bellhop who just brought up our bags. Ok, thanks." And I hang up.

"Max! I was kidding about the beers."

"You can't kid about beer," I say, again with the same serious face as the haunted hotel story. "I mean, you ordered it, so now you'll have to drink them."

"Never will I drink ten beers, call them and cancel."

"Sorry, it's too late. You have to drink them all."

"Come on, you're kidding me, right?"

"Sorry." I shake my head.

"Max?"

"All right, but I'm not the one who has to think about all those poor kids out there without beers," I say it with a wink. "And don't worry... they won't go to waste. I promise." Again, I hold up my uncrossed fingers.

I really do want her, but I'm enjoying myself. She has a great personality, and we're having fun, or at least I am. I'm not sure what it is about beautiful women, and my desire to drive them crazy. I believe I imagine it as some small victory, an untallied win for torturing us men.

"Max, you are always making jokes. I have a hard time deciding if you are kidding with me or not."

"I can be serious if you prefer," I say, switching to a deep, highly robotic, James Earl Jones voice. "Natasha, don't worry, I'm just me being serious." She laughs.

"No, I want you to be you," she says. "I like that you are so fun and happy all the time. You have the spirit of a child, and I envy your gaiety."

Still speaking in the same reverberating tone, "Natasha, I'm actually a little boy, please don't tell my mommy I drink beer." This keeps the smile on her face and reveals a yet to be seen softness in her eyes. But as she said, *spirit of a child*, it brings me back to the other night.

Anna was right. She was right about everything; I am a goddamn child. And when I step outside of myself, it's an amazingly accurate way to describe my life. Sure, I've seen the world, but what is that? I've never held a job of any merit, I've created nothing I'm proud of, and outside of chasing women and seeing things rarely seen, I've accomplished nothing noteworthy. Yeah, I've made a little money here and there, but I've never taken any project too far past profitability. Like reading Ulysses, or the New Testament, I'd start out strong then stumble at some point, allowing my ambition to slip away. At thirty-two, I still depend on Teddy's stipend, an employee still spinning the wheel, and I'm too old to lie to myself and pretend I see things changing anytime soon. Sure, he's offered me better gigs, but I don't want that life anymore. That ship has sailed, a distant memory, a dead dream.

And now, I sit here with yet another beautiful woman, a girl who—for all I know—could be perfect for me. A soul I can hold close, or hurt with little consequence. I only see two options. One, I can do as I've always done; act like a child, keep it casual, and mentally make myself unavailable. Or, I can give a shit. I can give it an honest shot and see what happens. See if she's the one for me and see if I'm enough for her. "Natasha, I want to tell you something," I say.

"What is it?"

✈

—*Boom! Boom! Boom!* There's a knock at the door. I stop mid-sentence and jog over. It's the same bellman from before. He's pushing a silver rolling cart, which holds two silver buckets, one full of ice and Heinekens, and the other, champagne. "That was fast," I say.

"Yes, sir." He's sweating a bit.

"Please, just put it over there." I slip him another five hundred Hong Kong for his hustle. I take care of him, knowing I won't spend anything on this trip. And because it never hurts to have a local who's got your back, because you never know.

"Thank you, sir, anything you need, just let me know." And he shuts the door.

I pop the champagne and pour two glasses. The toasts are getting cheesy, but I'm having fun. I want to say something special, some line that will seal this moment in her mind. But everything worth saying suddenly seemed already said. So, I steal something from Oscar Wilde. "Live the wonderful life that is in you! Let nothing be lost upon you. Be always searching for new sensations. Be afraid of nothing." We take a sip before I pull her into me. Our lips slide over another's as our rhythm effortlessly aligns. The tender texture of her tongue, and the taste of champagne, is all so satisfying. But I pull away. "We should probably get ready," I say.

"Are you sure?"

"Natasha, if I kiss you just one more second, we might miss dinner."

"You're probably right." She straightens herself. "Can I ask you something?"

"Anything."

"What were you going to say just before the champagne came?"

"That we should get ready."

"No, that's not it."

"Swear," I say, showing my uncrossed fingers to a disappointed smile.

We only have thirty minutes until we're to meet everyone. And once she realizes this, she gets motivated.

It's convenient having separate bathrooms. I don't have to navigate around the minimum twenty-seven things that all women put on the sink, and she doesn't have to pretend not to be grossed out by all the ball scratching and snot-rockets included in my shower routine.

In the time it takes me to clean up, I throw down three Heinekens and that glass of champagne.

I'm wearing the navy Armani Anna got me, along with a light blue button-down. I tie it together with a brown belt and matching Louie loafers.

I sit in the living room, pour another glass of Cristal, and prepare to wait a while, but surprisingly, she's ready only moments later. She looks ravishing in a red Jessica Rabbit style dress that's slit to her hip. She's sporting red Louboutins and an over-the-top diamond necklace. The goddamn thing must have a thousand stones. "Is it too much?" she asks, reaching her hand to her neck.

"No, you look wonderful."

"It was a gift from my father. I've only worn it once, at my brother's wedding. I brought it for Saturday, as I know it will please him. But on the flight to Hong Kong, I decided against it. I told myself that I won't wear it again until... oh, never mind."

"Never mind what?" I ask.

"Nothing, it's nothing." She blushes.

"You sure?"

"Really, it's nothing. I'm sorry. I'm just being stupid..."

It's this moment—in her nervous nonsense—that I see she's falling for me. I mean sure, this whole thing does feel like some sort of modern fairy-tale, chance encounter, love story— that old movies are made of. Even for a beautiful Soviet socialite, this can't be common. Hell, it doesn't even happen in the movies anymore.

"Come here," I say, extending my hand. She takes ahold of it, and I pull her lips to mine.

✈

We all meet at Lai Heen, a contemporary Cantonese restaurant on the 51st-floor, specializing in Chinese haute cuisine. Spicy ginger and soy sauce fills the air, and Kaskade bumps through the speakers.

Teddy arranged a private dining room, and Chef Bill greets our table, embracing Teddy like family and promising beta samples of his latest creations.

"Now you see that right there? That's called loyalty. Everyone's talking about that new posh place, THE 13. Say it will be the greatest hotel ever built; it's already the most expensive, that's for sure. But will they have their executive chef come meet me at my table? Are they going to move everything around, so that a simple banker and his friends can get three of their best suites at the last minute? Perhaps. Perhaps I'm getting ahead of myself, but by Jove, you know me, I'm staying loyal to the Ritz till the end."

"They say it cost a billion dollars to build that hotel," says Anna.

"I heard a billion and a half," says Peter Pinkerton.

"Indeed, every bit of a billion and a half. They say each room will cost seven million apiece. Can you imagine that? Max, what are your thoughts on the matter?" Teddy's attempt to get me involved in an economic conversation on a subject I could give a damn about is a transparent ploy to make me look good in front of Natasha. But I don't play along.

"That's more than I have, Teddy."

"Natasha, dear, don't let the boys disinterest in the finer things concern you. He's a fine chap. It's not his fault he's a bloody yank and won't allow himself to indulge in all of life's luxuries. We certainly can't hold that against him, can we? She's the same, this one." He thumbs at Anna. "But instead, she requires two of everything."

"Oh, shut it." Anna slaps his arm.

"But honestly, Max here is one of the brightest chaps I know, and if only he'd accept the position, I'd hire him at the bank tomorrow. The goddamn boy can do anything he wants."

"I can see that," she says.

Teddy typically talks me up to all his friends, but in the seven minutes since we sat, he hasn't let up in the slightest. His plan to push Natasha and me together is so obvious, hell, even the hostess who sat us could see it. And Anna certainly doesn't look pleased. Sitting tall in a tight bright-orange dress, with her eyes smoky, and her hair pulled back, looking beautiful as ever.

"Max darlin', I believe you need a haircut," she says. I bite down on my back teeth before I glance up at her grin.

"You're always getting on the boy for his hair. He looks fine, darling," says Teddy. Unaware that *you need a haircut* is actually a secret code for *I love you* when she can't say I love you. I don't remember exactly when it started, but it's been in place for some time.

"I just think he needs a haircut is all, I'm sure he's not mad about it." She squints her eyes and stares into me.

"I like the longer look," says Stacey Pinkerton, in her show as much cleavage as you can dress, and matching pink lipstick. Both men in bespoke suits and Rolex watches.

Our private table sits in a small swanky room adorned with gold everything. There's gold on the walls, gold in the art, and a large golden chandelier shimmering above us. A bottle of Dom Perignon is poured, and Teddy makes a toast. "To a long and luxurious ride through life with superb company."

"Hear, hear!" Everyone cheers, and we all tap glasses.

During the toast, I noticed the eyes of Natasha, Anna, and Stacey Pinkerton. They're all looking at me, and all in the most obvious way you can look at someone without being obvious.

A waiter delivers a round of cocktails, mostly martinis. I sip my Singapore Sling as I empathetically eye Anna. I imagine she hates this, but it's not like coming here was my idea. And who knows, Natasha is definitely something special, and maybe I could see myself with her. As a friend, Anna should be happy for me. It's not like I'm rubbing some hundred-dollar whore in her face.

✈

"Max, my boy, you wouldn't believe how stiff I am from our session this morning; you really earned that damn dinner jacket," says Teddy.

"Yeah, I'm a little sore myself."

"I bet I know who else is sore," says Stacey Pinkerton, peering at Natasha.

"Stacey!" scolds Peter Pinkerton. "That's none of your goddamn business!" A look of disappointment shrouds his face.

"What? We're all adults here. I mean, they are staying in the same room," says Stacey.

I watch Natasha's face flush blush. "Stacey, I hate to break it to you, but Natasha and are I simply new friends, just getting to know each other." Her hand grabs mine under the table—secretly—like we're eleven. And I had just defended her honor.

"I didn't mean to make anyone uncomfortable," says Stacey. "I just assumed."

"No, you're fine. You're a Doctor, right?" I ask.

"That's right, a Ph.D.," she says.

"And what's your field?" I already know the answer, recalling it from our chance encounter at the hotel last year. I'm just trying to lower the pulse of Peter Pinkerton, who's feverishly flushed and flustered, noticeably huffing and puffing between giant gulps of Beefeater gin.

"I'm a sex therapist," she says.

"You see, now there's no need to be upset, she was just doing her job," I say in good humor to her husband.

"She's not working now. She doesn't need to be butting into other people's business," says Peter. By the frustration in his voice, I gather their marriage isn't going so swell. I imagine I'm not the first or the last random stranger Stacey Pinkerton has privately counseled in her hotel room.

"So, what does a sex therapist do?" asks Teddy, now a few drinks deep and oblivious to the tension.

"Teddy!" Anna scowls.

"What, it's her profession. She can ask me anything she wants about asset management or the bond market if it pleases her."

"She doesn't want to ask you about banking, ya old-fool. Nobody does." Anna shakes her head and sips her drink.

Teddy turns back to Stacey Pinkerton, "If you care to, Stacey, please enlighten us all on what exactly a professional sex therapist does."

"Here we go." Peter Pinkerton sits back and mumbles under his breath.

"Ok, well, if you're really interested."

"Oh, we are. Please speak freely," insists Teddy.

"All right, well, I typically work with couples. I, well we, talk about their sex lives and like, well... we work together to try and like... you know, we try to figure out what does and doesn't work for them."

"Erectile dysfunction," Teddy calls out.

"Well, that does come up," she says.

"Or it doesn't," he quips.

"Right... but that's not usually what I deal with. It's usually like—um that one or both partners just aren't, like... completely satisfied with their current sexual experiences. And um... I... well, we... try to figure out what's wrong. And I help them. Because good sex is important in a relationship."

"So you deal with a bunch of bloody wankers who can't please their wives," says Teddy.

"No, not exactly," says Stacey.

"Sounds a bit like Dr. Laura Berman," I say.

"Yes, she's my idol. It's funny you say that; I was just listening to her right before we all met; she's influenced me in so many ways. Like when I started my *Sex With Stacey* podcast last year. I mean, I don't have anywhere near her following, at least not yet, but I'm already getting around six-thousand downloads per episode."

"Lovely, isn't that lovely darling?" Says Teddy to Anna, who's staring at Stacey Pinkerton with her mouth agape.

"Oh yeah, that's just lovely," says Anna.

"Sure, except she left out the part about her flying out to Los Angeles twice a month to work one-on-one with athletes and movie stars that look like Max over there," snarls Peter.

"It's private counseling, and I get to charge three-times my normal rate," replies Stacey.

"Yeah, and I bet they're getting their money's worth," says Peter Pinkerton, just as a team of waiters carries in another round of martinis and appetizers. "Thank God," he murmurs, nearly slamming his empty glass on the table.

"Natasha, that is just the prettiest necklace I've ever seen," says Anna, assumingly an attempt to steer the topic away from unfaithfulness.

"Thank you. My father gave it to me for my twenty-fourth birthday."

"And when was that, darlin'?"

"This past February."

"Oh God, to be young again," she says, followed by a healthy swig of champagne. "It is the twenty-four-carat Harry Winston Sunflower, is it not?"

"I'm not sure. I know it's Harry Winston because of the box, but I'm not sure about the carats," replies Natasha.

"Oh, darlin' believe me it is, and it's truly something. In fact, I was admiring it just the other day. It is a fine piece of work it is. But what can I say, it looks like you've beaten me to it."

"You can try it on if you'd like," says Natasha.

"Oh no, darlin', I've already tried it on plenty of times, and I assure you, it's absolutely wonderful. There's no doubt about that."

"I haven't really worn it yet."

A subversive smile slides over Anna's face. "Believe me, darlin', in time you'll come to love it, appreciate it, and realize there's nothing else quite like it. And it's gonna come to feel so good every time you wear it, that you'll never want to take it off. I promise you that."

"Ok..." says Natasha.

"Enough of this frivolous conversation, I feel like a shot. Natasha, perhaps you'd care to escape the pettiness of all these Americans for a moment and join me for a proper drink at the bar?" Asks Teddy in a dramatically playful tone. The poor guy probably thinks Anna is jealous of the damn necklace, and this is his attempt to lighten the mood. Being the superlative husband that he is, he'll likely have something special made for her by the end of the week. Probably an exclusive piece designed by Harry Winston's goddamn great-grandson himself.

"A shot sounds nice," Natasha says.

"I beg of you all, do behave yourselves." Teddy stands, assists Natasha out of her chair and out of the golden room.

"I need some fresh air myself. I'm going for a smoke," says Peter Pinkerton, following them out.

"And then there were three," says Anna, as I find myself alone, sandwiched a seat apart between both her and Stacey.

"Her necklace is really pretty," says Stacey Pinkerton, who's swiping through her phone.

"You've got to cool that shit," I hiss to Anna.

"Oh relax, shugah, nobody caught that. Yes, it's a lovely necklace, dear," she says to Stacey, then turns back to me. "See." Just then, I feel her foot rub up against my right leg. "Are you enjoying your evening, shugah?"

"Oh yeah, a real hoot," I say with an exaggerated smile.

"I'm having a great time too," says Stacey, sitting a seat over on my left, and is now off her phone. "Don't worry about Peter, he always gets upset when we go out. I guess he's just stressed with work or something. And I don't know if you could tell." She leans in. "But he gets a little jealous sometimes."

"You don't say," says Anna.

"Yeah, he thinks that since I started my practice, that I'm trying to sleep with every man that looks at me." Stacy's foot slides up against my left leg. *Fuck,* I say to myself, spreading my feet so theirs won't touch. Which apparently indicates I'm into it, as they both become even friendlier. Now, digging their toes into my shoes and trying to wrap their legs around mine.

✈

"So, Stacey, six-thousand downloads per episode, that's pretty good," I say, an attempt to distract her from the footsies.

"Yeah, it's growing so fast. So much faster than I thought it would when I started it last summer." She smiles at me. "It's funny, it was more than a year ago, but I remember it like it was yesterday. A group of my girlfriends threw me this little launch party at Ozone; it's the bar on top of the Ritz in Hong Kong. Have you ever been, Max?" she asks, knowing perfectly well that I have.

"Oh shugah, you know it, you and I went there last year. Remember, I had to leave early because Teddy and I were flying out to Greece that next morning. It's a lovely place."

"Greece is nice, huh?" I say, unable to concentrate, her toes now crawling towards my crotch.

"No, I'm talking about the bar on the roof of the Ritz, silly." And I flash back to that night last summer.

Stacey approached me at the bar, and she asked me if I was "fucking the woman who just left?" When I asked her, "why she cared?" She told me she could "fuck me better than that blue-ribbon bitch ever could."

"Who knows, maybe we were all there on the same night," says Stacey, a big smart-ass smirk on her face.

"Ya never know, it's a small island," says Anna. "And Stacey, I do believe you and I met just a few weeks after that. Yes, I had just returned from Greece, and we were at Jim or Jack something's fundraiser, the one for the panda, or whateva that little critter was."

"Yes, oh my God, you were so tan. I remember I was so jealous of you being in Europe, while I was stuck in the house, because Peter was working on some 'big merger,' and said he 'didn't want to worry about me.' That's what he always says. He still won't let me go anywhere, at least not without throwing a hissy fit. I'm surprised we're even here tonight, I'm sure I'll pay for it later," she says, looking back at the door before leaning in with a lowered voice. "If you want to know the truth, that's why

I work in LA all the time. I just need a break from him, always getting so angry with me."

Thankfully, just at that moment, Teddy and Natasha return, followed by a team of waiters with the food and fresh drinks, then Peter Pinkerton, and the footsies finally conclude.

"Look at what we brought," talking about the food, or maybe the fresh bottle of Cristal in hand.

"How were the shots?" I ask.

"The shots were real fine. Weren't they just brilliant, Natasha?"

"Yes, they were very nice. Thank you again, Teddy."

"What did you have?" I ask.

"Um, a Scottish-Bomb, isn't that right, Teddy?" Teddy pops the bottle of Rosé, points at Natasha, and then turns it into a thumbs-up. He's in a fine shape, having rounded tipsy and now sliding into sauced.

"I haven't done a Car Bomb since St. Patty's," I say.

"I'm afraid we didn't do your American-Irish bombs, my boy. Like chasing women and wearing blue jeans; my car-bombing days are behind me."

"Don't try and act cool in front of Max; you know you never chased women," says Anna.

"Oh, don't mind the ole chain over there." Teddy winks. "Anyhow, I had the barkeep switch the Jameson for Johnnie Walker Blue, then add just a dash of Drambuie. We dropped them into a pint of cider and drank to Natasha's father coming to town."

"Scottish-Bombs, that's pretty clever. Did you hear that somewhere, or did you just come up with it?" I ask.

"I say it's a bloody brilliant idea. I have no idea who came up with it. I just ordered it, we drank it, and it was mighty fine. Isn't that right, Natasha?"

"That's right, it was very nice. I finished it all."

"Am I going to need to carry you up to the room?" I whisper to her.

"I'm Russian, remember... the English can't drink for shit," she whispers back. There's a warm glow to her typically cool face. And I can tell she's a tad tipsy herself.

"Natasha, my dear, would it be a bother if we all shifted down a bit? I'd like to get in a quick word with my mate if you don't mind," Teddy says, and everyone rearranges themselves accordingly.

With all the chaos, you would never know dinner had just been served. But it's family-style, so it doesn't really matter where you sit. The bright assortment of artfully arranged plates provides a smorgasbord of superb smells: cinnamon, chilies, and tangy sours, an immensely satisfying Foodgod fantasy of a spread. Everything I taste is delicious. And everyone appears to have miraculously morphed into better spirits, all conversing and laughing, seemingly forgetting the short-lived stretch of hostility and jealous undertones of ten minutes prior. Even Peter Pinkerton appears to be enjoying himself.

"Max, my boy. I did a bit of investigating," Teddy says under his breath, and not too quietly, but with all the jabber, nobody who isn't listening closely can hear.

"What do you mean, investigating?" I ask.

"I say, my boy, I'm talking about Natasha. What else would I mean?"

"You don't have to do that, bud, I think I got it." I say. Now a bit tipsy myself, but positive I appear stone sober sitting next to Teddy.

"Nonsense, you're my mate. I've got to look out for my mate, my shipmate."

"Ok, and what did your investigation uncover?" I ask.

"By Jove, she's keen on you, mate. Arse over tits into you, I'm dead serious." You can see his excitement as he says it.

"Oh, yeah?" I say, having already figured this much out for myself, I humor him, let him feel as though he's my wingman. "What did she say?"

"She's planning on introducing you to her father on Saturday at the awards ceremony."

"All right, Teddy, you have my attention. What else did you uncover?" I ask, glancing over at Natasha.

"I know her father quite well, mate, better than most," mutters Teddy. "I video-conference with the man every week and meet with him in London every quarter, usually more. He speaks of his daughter often. And over the years, I've never once heard him mention her introducing him to anyone."

"Really?" I say.

"Indeed, my boy, and here's a little inside information." He glances around, making sure nobody is eavesdropping, then leans in and speaks quieter than before, now nearly whispering. "I personally manage a few of her father's private funds, I'm talking heaps mate, one of which is for Natasha. And well, the bastard has it arranged so that on the day of her wedding, she's to inherit nearly a hundred million US dollars."

"Oh, is that it?" I say.

"No, what's it—is that she fancies you, mate, big time. And I'm quite keen on seeing the two of you together." I see him looking at me the same way a proud father looks at his firstborn son when he does something truly substantial. As if I just took my first step or hit my first home run.

"I like her too. We'll see how it goes," I say.

"See how it goes? This is not one of those, we'll see how it goes, see what happens—slappers, you've been wasting your time on. This is a true mint here, mate, the kind that'll leave you kicking yourself for a lifetime if you let slip by."

"I'll do my best," I say.

"Do your best? Max, I've known you for a long time. Hell, you're my best friend. But I've got to be honest with ya, my boy, my mate, my shipmate. I think you'd be a damn fool if you don't go for this one and stick it out."

"What if she doesn't get married?" I ask.

"Pardon?"

"I'm just curious because you said 'on the day of her wedding.' So, what happens to that money if she doesn't get married?"

"Nothing, it just sits there and collects interest."

Friday, June 18

Kayce is a weirdo.

♡

Tiffany

squish
squish

Tiffany

Tiffany

✈

"She never gets it?"

"No, not until her father dies."

"Isn't that kind of fucked-up of her father? I mean, that's a lot of pressure to put on a woman. Isn't it? Get married or stay poor."

"Believe me, mate, she's not hurting for much."

"Yeah, I know, but you get what I mean."

"It's a bunch of rubbish. To be honest with you, the guy's a bastard. But that's how he operates. Everything is a zero-sum game." Just then, Natasha comes over and sits on my lap.

"And here's the lovely lady now," Teddy says.

"What are you two talking about?"

"I was just telling Teddy that I wanted to try a Scottish-Bomb." She looks into my eyes with a hint of disappointment, as though she'd hoped we'd be discussing the intent she had passed to Teddy, and that I would have said something more. So, I lean in and whisper, "and that I think you're really something." She smiles and kisses my cheek.

We all continue to eat, drink, and laugh, the dinner, a complete success. We even shoot a round of Scottish-Bombs.

The bill comes, and without looking, Teddy signs and tells the waiter to add ten thousand patacas gratuity.

"Come on, Max, let's win some bloody money."

We stroll out of the restaurant, a rambunctious group of well-dressed misfits, each fucked up in our own sensational way. I'm not sure if it's the audacious amount of cocktails consumed, the striking Russian heiress on my arm, or the Venetian casino's carefully calculated exuberance. But I feel phenomenal, the best I have in years.

With casino gambling, Teddy doesn't fuck around. Especially when he's loose like he is. As expected, we head straight for the craps table, where he says he does *the most damage*. And though I'm not much of a gambler, he's always called me his *lucky mate*.

At the table, he initially buys two million Macanese patacas, roughly a quarter-million US dollars.

"New shooter, big new shooter," calls out the dealer, pushing Teddy the dice.

"Max, Anna, blow on these," Teddy says, holding the dice high, before sliding a half-million patacas onto the *Pass Line*.

"New shooter—coming out," calls the dealer.

"Come on seven, seven—yo-leven," Teddy calls out, hoping for a seven or eleven, winding his arm back before releasing his roll. The dice dance the fourteen feet down that felt-topped table and bounce off that bumpy back-wall before coming to a decision.

"Seven," the dealer hollers, and we all cheer as he just doubled his bet.

"Let's press it," Teddy says. This combines his winnings with the original bet, all to be wagered on the next roll. Making this a million patacas bet.

"Coming out," says the dealer, establishing that *the point* (any number besides two, three, seven, eleven, or twelve) has not yet been rolled. At this stage of the game: a two, three, or twelve is called *craps* and would lose. Seven or eleven wins and any other number becomes the point.

Teddy has us blow on the dice again before he tosses them.

"Yo-leven!" the dealer shouts, after the dice dance to five and six. Teddy wins again; and again, doubles his money.

"By Jove!" He pumps his fist, and we all exchange high-fives. The energy at our table contagiously spreads, and several other high rollers gravitate towards us.

"What do you say, Max? Press it again?" He's asking if he should double-down again, putting two million patacas on the next roll, or about a quarter of a million US dollars. Every roll has the same 2/9 odds, or about a 22% chance of rolling a seven or eleven, which, if hit, would double his money again. He only has about an 11% chance of rolling a craps and losing. And any other number simply becomes the point. This is one of the few times in a casino that a player has the edge over the house.

✈

"Why not," I say, and Teddy presses the bet.

"Coming out," calls the dealer.

Anna and I blow on the dice again. "Come on seven, seven—yo-leven!" He gives them a couple shakes in his hand before his big dramatic release.

"Hard ten!" yells the dealer. "Ladies' favorite numba."

This pair of fives doesn't mean Teddy loses, but now all his money is on number ten, and he must roll a ten before he rolls another seven. If he rolls a seven now, he loses it all.

"Place your bets, place your bets, our point is ten, tens your friend. Place your bets," calls the dealer.

Teddy looks somewhat discouraged as the dice rattle in his hand. "Big-ten, big-ten, come on ten," he says as he tosses them across the table, and we all watch them crawl to a five and a four.

"Nine!" shouts the dealer. "Big nine—just like mine."

"Damn," Teddy shouts to himself, clenching his fist. But he hasn't lost, not until he rolls a seven.

"Almost another hard ten," I say nonchalantly.

He turns to me, his eyes on mine, a deep dramatic gaze. "You know you're quite right on that one, mate." His eyes widen as he says it. "Max, what is it that I always say?"

"I'm not sure," I say, thinking to myself, *you say a lot of things*. "What about?" I ask.

"Winning, mate. I'm talking about winning here. What is it that I always say?"

I pause for a second, then smile as I say, "If you want to win like a king, you must bet like a king."

"Precisely, my boy." He looks down at his chips, takes a breath, and pushes out the entire stack. "One-point-five million on hard ten," he says to the dealer.

"Mill-and-a-half on hard ten," the dealer calls out, in an attempt to lure more money from onlookers. "Place your bets, place your bets, the point is ten, the shooters hot, big money on the table, let's see whatcha got."

Teddy picks up the dice. He just put about a hundred and ninety thousand US dollars on an unlikely long shot—*hard way*—with a big payout. To win, he must roll a pair of fives before he rolls a seven or an *easy ten* (any ten besides two fives). However, if he does roll a regular ten, he still wins his first bet but loses here. Any other number still means nothing, and any seven loses. Basically, he needs a ten, and if he does it with two fives, he wins big.

He has Anna and me blow again before he winds up and releases the dice down the table.

"Eight!" the dealer calls. "Not bad, but not great, place your bets before it's too late." He slides the dice back to Teddy and continues his pitch. "The point is ten, our shooters hot, big money on the table, who's got the rocks?"

"You got this, Teddy," I say, seeing the drunkenness from earlier out of his eyes, replaced by a fiery confidence. He grabs ahold of the dice, looking down at them in his hand. He says something to himself that sounds like a prayer before he lifts them for us to blow. He kisses his clenched fist, winds back, and heaves them hard down the table. They dance off the back wall, split apart from one another, racing fast in opposite directions before they settle. I look at the first to see a five, and then over at the other. Goddammit, he fucking did it, he defied the variance, they're both fives.

"Hard ten!" shouts the dealer. "Winner-winner tiger dinner!"

Our table erupts as Teddy's arms shoot skyward. Fists-pumps, hugs, kisses, and high-fives flow freely between us. "By God, that was Brilliant, mate." He embraces me in a hard hug, then turns to kiss his wife.

When he turns back, he tosses me a chip, and then a few more. "For my shipmate and his crew," he says, before he hands one to Natasha, one to Stacey, and a small stack to Anna. He turns to Peter Pinkerton and says, "I already make you enough money, mate." Then flips him a single chip. "But what's a little more."

"Teddy, I can't take this," I say, trying to hand it back. Natasha does the same.

"Nonsense, my boy, you know how I roll. When I win, I share with my mates."

"Yeah, but these chips are worth like twenty grand apiece." *And I'm talking greenbacks.*

"Max, my boy, I doubt I'd of bet that hard ten without you in my corner, in fact, I know I wouldn't have even thought of it, not a chance. So the way I see it, I'm still up big. Plus, it's awful nice to have ya back, mate. Please, don't even think of it for another second, take it, and spend it on something you truly desire."

"Thank you," I say, and I put the chips in my pocket. Natasha and Stacey do the same. Even with sharing, he's still walking away with a candy bar shy of one-point-five million US dollars, so I'm sure he's happy.

We head to the bar and pop another thousand-dollar bottle of champagne, which I gladly pay for. And the next hour is filled with laughter, which brings actual cramps to my cheeks. Especially when Anna tells old stories of Teddy in Texas and his former obsession with silk. She goes on about how *embarrassed* she'd be whenever he'd wear his *silk PJ's* to the gas station or grocery store. And how all her friends used to call him *Mr. Smooth*, and how he thought it was a compliment.

After some time, the group scatters. The Pinkertons get into some type of tiff and storm off, and I believe Anna went back to her room.

I'm at the blackjack table with Teddy when Natasha pulls me aside. She says she's heading to bed, but that I should *be a good friend and stay*. She tells me not to worry about rushing back, but that she *can't wait* to see me in the morning. I give her a small kiss and say good night.

After Teddy goes up another ten grand, we seize the moment and get a table at the exclusive China Rouge, where we pop a magnum of Moët, pass out shots of Grand Marnier, and dance to electronic music with six-foot Asian girls. The night is a complete success. But after I catch myself stumbling more than once, I call it. I look over at him before I take off. He's throwing back shooters with some bankers from Beijing, so I know he's good.

I stumble back across the street, to our hotel, and into the elevator. I'm smiling to myself about the night I just had. The door is sliding shut, but at the absolute last second—an arm reaches through and stops the door. It's Stacey Pinkerton's arm. "Well, hello there, handsome," she hungrily grins. "Got room for one more?"

"Why not," I say, slurring and stupefied.

"And how was your night?"

"Can't complain."

"Are you just getting back now?"

"Yep."

"And where's Natasha?"

"Sleeping," I slur. I'm in a hell of a shape.

"Oh?" Her wanting eyes widen as her lips curve. "Then why not stay out for a little longer?"

As wasted as I am, I can still sense that the woman's in heat, but unlike Anna, any man warmer than her husband will do. "I'm done for the night," I say, leaning against the wall, so I don't fall.

"That's a shame, I was thinking about having a little fun," she says, moving closer.

"Not me, I'm tired."

"Max, can I ask you something?"

"What?"

"Why didn't you ever write me back?" She pushes herself closer and is now nearly purring. I want to get off the elevator, but we're only on the 19th floor.

"I was seeing someone," I slur.

"Well, are you seeing anyone now?"

"No, but—" And without warning, she kisses me.

I snap my head to the side. "What are you doing?"

"Come on, Max. Don't you want this?"

"No, I don't," I say, sliding myself out from between her and the wall. "But you did before."

"Things change," I say.

Then she does something I don't foresee. She reaches back and slides her flat hand across all the elevator buttons. Ensuring a long ride to the top. "What the hell are you doing?" I shout, but my disinterest in the scandal seems to make her want it more.

She moves towards me, her knee slides between my legs. "Come on, I'll get us a room across the street. Just for a dance or two. Let's have a little fun."

"Are you crazy, you're married. And your husband is here in this goddamn hotel." But these obstacles don't seem to discourage her as she again pins me to the wall.

"I'm not asking you to marry me," she whispers into my ear. "Just come fuck me. You don't have to stay."

"Have you lost your goddamn mind?" I say.

But she grabs at my dick and does her best to pull my mouth to hers. "Come on. Come and fuck the shit out of me, nobody will know." The door opens on the 35th floor, the first of many scheduled stops.

I squirm from her grasp and step out of the elevator. "Good night, Stacey," I say without looking back. She says nothing, and I hear the door close behind me. I don't want any part of that fucking mess, and to avoid another chance encounter, I walk to the far end of the hall and take the stairs.

I struggle up the remaining fifteen flights until I reach the 50th floor, where I slip off my shoes, quietly strip down to my skivvies, and crawl into the big bed.

I jolt awake to Natasha's tongue, tickling my nipple. "I thought you would never get up," she grins as she continues kissing her way down my stomach.

"Good morning," I say. "This definitely isn't a terrible way to wake up."

"Just wait," she says, sliding down my Calvins and putting my already wide-awake self into her mouth.

"Oh God," I murmur as she takes all of me.

After only a minute, I'm nearly there and don't want to be selfish. But as I reach for her, she pulls away. "This is for you," she says, then continues choking herself until my eyes roll high into my head, and I release into the back of hers.

We lay there together for some time as she traces her fingers along the lines of my torso.

I order room service. She picks the poached eggs and toast, and I ask if it's possible to get gummy worms. Twenty minutes later, there's a knock at the door. Natasha gets her eggs, I get my worms, and the guy gets a good tip.

The chopper ride back to Hong Kong isn't as awkward as anticipated. Teddy feels like shit and stays silent. Anna reads, and I avoid any unnecessary eye contact with the Pinkertons.

After the car drops us off, I carry Natasha's bag to her Four Seasons suite. We're naked within a minute, and fuck nearly a dozen times, all day, and deep into the night. In fact, the only time our sweaty bodies aren't grinding against each other is the half-hour on the roof to watch the sunset, the in-room couple's massage, and the room service we order to refuel.

She tells me she could "feel herself falling" for me, and that she's "never experienced anything like this." She tells me I make her feel "like a princess" and that her "fortune, no, her wish," appears to be coming true.

I like her. In fact, I like her quite a bit. We looked good together, our personalities mesh, and we're highly compatible in every attempted sexual position. Sure, we've only known one another a few days, but stranger things have happened. She's an amazing woman, everything any guy would want. *Right?*

CHAPTER 13
Never Be The Same

I LEAVE NATASHA'S an hour before her father is due to land and head to Anna's for my tux's final fitting. After an intense 20k run with Teddy, I head back to the apartment.

With nearly nine-hours till the party, I do my absolute favorite thing to do when I have absolutely nothing to do: I sit on my ass and watch Kurt Russell kick ass in *Big Trouble in Little China*, kill a couple boxes of Koala Yummies, eat Slim Jims, and drink beer. The ones I told Natasha wouldn't go to waste. I brought them back in my bag, and to lighten the load, I passed a few out to some homeless fellas. I'm sure those didn't go to waste either.

After dozing off a few times, I flip through a stack of old books and magazines, mostly *Men's Journal* and *Esquire*. I thumb through *The Letters of Vincent Van Gogh*. I never much cared for his work, but his story is inspiring as shit.

After a successful day of lounging and gluttony, I arrive at the Four Seasons Grand Ballroom a few minutes behind schedule. Natasha is standing out front, waiting for me. She's stunning in her sleeveless white evening gown. Her hair is down, long, and curled at the ends. She's not wearing her diamond necklace, but has on another that's nearly as impressive.

"That's a fine tuxedo there, Mister Malovice."

"The finest," I say, and our lips meet.

"Max, you're the handsomest man I've ever seen."

"And you're the biggest liar I've ever met." I hold out my arm and escort her inside.

The ballroom is exceedingly elegant, something straight out of a Tolstoy novel. Several rows of elaborate chandeliers light the tall ceilings. The walls are marble, with high-windows and harbor views. There must be eighty tables and six hundred people.

The check-in line is a chaotic cluster of cummerbunds and evening gowns. And seeing that Natasha already has her nametag, I skip it.

We pass satin-covered tables stacked with top-shelf hors d'oeuvres and head straight to the bar, where we run into Anna and Teddy.

"That's a fine couple right there," Teddy says more than twice.

"I love your dress," Natasha tells Anna.

"Oh, this old thing, I got it last week."

We shoot the bull, talk about the night's turnout, our run, and the quality of my tux before the stage lights flicker, and we head to our seats. "Good luck, mate." I hear Teddy whisper-shout over my shoulder.

Natasha wastes no time in introducing me to her father.

"Daddy, I would like you to meet Max."

He holds out his hand, and I shake it. He has a massive grip and sandpaper palms as though he digs ditches for a living.

"Douglas William Cameron. Good to meet you, young man." He's an ordinary-looking fellow, nothing too intimidating about him: my height, a little overweight, fair-skinned, and thinning hair. They say everyone looks better in a tux, but for the life of me, I can't find a hint of resemblance to Natasha. Her mother must have had an affair with the kid who cleaned the pool. Anyways, he introduced himself in the douchiest way possible. So, I do the same.

"Maxwell Procházka Malovice the second," I say. "It's a pleasure to meet you, sir."

"Maxwell Procházka Malovice the second," he echoes. "Now that's a powerful sounding name if I've ever heard one."

Amping-up the highbrow bullshit. "Yes sir, my father enjoys saying he's 'always worked a little harder than anyone else because people expect more from a Malovice.'"

✈

"I imagine your father and I would get on famously."
He says it as serious as a man can say something. "And with a
name like that, it sounds like you should be running a country,
or at least a large corporation someday."

"You never know, sir," I say.

"You'd know if you had a plan." He turns up his chin,
looking intensely into my eyes. "Natasha tells me you attended
an Ivy League college, and hold a degree in economics?"

"That's correct, sir."

"I'm an Oxford man myself."

"I've read their book," I say. "A bit wordy for my taste."

"Ay, comedian as well, he."

"Sometimes, sir."

"Well, do you have a plan, Mr. Malovice?"

"Sure," I say without thinking about it. But instead of
moving on, he leers into me, seemingly waiting for the details.
"Would you like to hear it right now?" I ask.

"No, that won't be necessary. Just knowing you do is
enough for the time being. Are you by any chance a hunter,
Maxwell?"

"I am... or... I have—here-and-there, but I wouldn't call
myself a hunter per se. My father is, though."

"Of course he is. But you have fired a gun, yes?"

"I am an American, sir." He almost smiles but stops
himself. "My father would enter my brothers and me in shooting competitions when we were children. I still shoot when I
visit him, but I don't particularly hunt anything."

"Well, that's encouraging. I believe every man should
know how to handle a firearm."

"Then yes, sir, I'm well versed."

"Excellent." He takes a sip of his wine. "You know
when my daughter mentioned you this afternoon, I recalled
already having heard your name."

"Is that right?"

"Yes, Theodore Hammond has praised you on multiple
occasions. Tells me you're a jet setting renaissance man with
top-tier potential."

"That's kind of him. Theodore is a hell of a man."

"Well, apparently, you must be something of a mover yourself, Mister Malovice, because, until this moment, you are the first man my daughter has ever introduced me to. And I raised her to only find value in the finest of everything."

"I'm just a regular guy," I say.

"Never let me hear you say that again," he snaps, lifting his chin higher and looking down at me. "You're not a regular man and never lower yourself into thinking you are."

"Of course, sir."

"Mr. Malovice, I've recently been made aware of a probable vacancy in our Paris office. The position is for senior vice president of our European wealth management team. Now, I don't much care for the city myself, too many rodents, but Natasha tells me she's quite taken with it. Would you be interested in an opportunity like this, if it were to say, suddenly come available?"

"Sure... I imagine that I would."

"Mister Malovice, your response or lack thereof, isn't assuring me you're serious about the possibilities of your future. Are you a serious man? Or am I wasting my time here?"

"Daddy," cries Natasha.

"Not now, sweetheart, men are speaking." He turns back to me. "So, Mister Malovice, are you interested in an opportunity of this manner?"

"Yes, sir, I believe I am."

"Excellent." A smug sociopath smirk slides across his face. "Mr. Malovice, I'm heading back to London tonight. But in the coming weeks, I'd like to have you out to my club, where we can shoot, and have a proper discussion on your future."

"I'll be looking forward to it, sir."

He nods his head, his face holding on to that same smug smile. "Now, Maxwell, the event is about to begin. Why don't you run along and find yourself a name badge like myself, and everyone else in this room."

"That's a good idea, sir. I'll go take care of that."

"In case we don't get the chance to chat anymore, it was a pleasure meeting you, young man. I'll be looking forward to our discussion." He extends his hand, and I shake it.

"Same here, sir," I say, impulsively pushing in my chair, "Would either of you care for another drink while I'm up?"

"No, Mr. Malovice, they have waiters for that," he says dismissively.

"Right," I say, then turn towards the door and start walking. *Holy fuck, what the fuck was that? Did he just Jedi fucking mind fuck me?* My eyes are wide, and my feet can't move any faster.

Our table is closest to the stage and furthest from the door. I spot Teddy beelining it to intercept me. I'm sure he was watching the whole thing and wants details.

"*Pssst*, how'd it go, mate?"

"How'd it go? That guy's a fucking lunatic."

"What happened? Was he nice to you?"

"Sure, he was nice, nice enough."

"Cameron isn't nice to anybody, so that's a win right there. What did you talk about?"

"Well... he definitely didn't beat around the bush. Got right to it."

"The bastard is incapable of bullshit. What did he say?"

"Well... I'm pretty sure I've just loosely agreed to an arranged marriage with his daughter, and possibly an invitation to join the Illuminati."

"Tell me word for word."

"Ok, well, he pretty much offered me a vice president position in Paris, where Natasha apparently has some well-known desire to live. But first, I'm to hang out with him at some club in London, where I'm positive he's gonna point a fucking gun at me."

"By Jove, that's fantastic news.

"Fantastic?"

"I worked for the bastard for five years before he invited me to that club. I'm proud of you, mate. Here, pull over, let's raise a glass to your good fortune."

✈

"Good idea," I say, and we park at the bar just before the main entrance. You can see that Teddy is proud of me; it's all over his face.

"What are we drinking?" Teddy asks.

"It feels like a storm is kicking up," I say.

"Two whiskeys," he calls out to the bartender. "Do you realize what this means, mate?"

"No, tell me."

"It means the old bastard approved of you. And if he invited you to the club, then he likes you. And believe me, he has no reservations about being a fucking knob head. If off-ered you a job, then he was impressed. And if Natasha is as smitten with you as I gather, then you're set, my boy. You're to be a minted mate, that's for sure." Our whiskeys arrive, and we throw them back.

"Press it," I say.

"Two more," Teddy tosses down two hundred Hong Kong. The drinks are free, but he wants them fast.

"Don't you think it's kind of crazy?" I ask him.

"What's that?"

"I don't know; that I met this girl four days ago, then speak with her father for five minutes, and with his blessing and a nepotistic wave of his hand, my life changes overnight."

"This is how these things are done, mate. You go to bed a commoner, and you wake up a king. Isn't that the American dream?"

"Maybe, I don't know. Something about it just doesn't feel right." Our shots are poured, and we put them back.

"Press it," I say.

"Two more," Teddy calls out, throwing down another hundred. "Max, what about that story, the one you told me about your savvy uncle, and how that opportunity came from nowhere? Perhaps lightning strikes twice. I mean, look at what you're stressing over, mate; you have a beautiful girl who adores you, and if it all works out, you catapult to the top of the food chain and become wealthy beyond your wildest dreams. Oh, Max, my boy, I can hear them weeping for you now."

✈

"That thing with my uncle wasn't anything like this. We're talking about love here, and a life-altering proposal from a man who's known me for less time than it takes to smoke a cigarette."

"You don't think you could love Natasha?"

"I've known her for four days."

"It's not as if you'd have to marry her straight away."

"Yeah, not until we get to that club, where he'll surely point a shotgun at me, and we'll set a date." Our shots arrive, and we take them.

"Another?" Teddy Asks.

"A quick one," I say. "I got to get back." Teddy fetches another bill from his pocket and tosses it atop the bar.

"Barkeep, two more on the double." Two more Jacks are promptly poured, and we raise our glass. "To your future," he says, and takes it down.

"I'm glad you're enjoying this."

"Listen, Max, you're a good mate. And I hate to see you so worked up, especially over something this great. But I think you're being too hard on yourself. Natasha is a beautiful, intelligent, well-traveled, well-spoken young lady... everything any man would want in a woman. The finest. Now, I know you're not about the money, mate. Hell, that's one of the things I love about you. But with no worries about money, you could live the way you want and truly enjoy your time together, a pleasurable stroll on the lighter side of life. I mean, look at Anna and me, and how happy we are." I nod but say nothing. "Listen, I know Natasha's father quite well. And the man is positively incapable of small talk. Hell, in seventeen years, I've never once heard him tell a joke. So, perhaps, maybe, you misunderstood him, and his intentions. Maybe he's just talking about a job. Hell, I talk you up all the time, been doing it for years. I'm sure after meeting you, he simply saw what I've been saying. I wouldn't sweat it too much, mate. Just enjoy the evening."

"Yeah, you're probably right. Maybe I did take it the wrong way. Thank you, Teddy, you're a good friend." And we shake hands.

"Just promise me one thing, mate."

"What's that?"

"Promise that when you're my boss, you won't make me call you Guvnor." He winks, and we make plans to meet up afterward. "Give me a holler if you need anything, you can find me back in the cheap seats."

The front check-in table is nearly vacant compared to the chaos of earlier. I get in the short line behind a woman with long, shiny, full-bodied brown hair, with the volume of a mature lion's mane, which momentarily distracts me from that megalomaniac's mind-fuck.

My first instinct is to tap her on the shoulder and ask *what kind of vitamins she feeds that thing*. But after playing those whiskey-words back in my mind, I decide to skip any needless flirting and stay silent.

Her face a mystery, and her skin is olive. She's thin, and unlike the rest of the room, she's not in a dress. Rather, a black semi-sheer pantsuit that hugs her all the way down to the belled-bottoms.

As she steps forward to take her turn, I overhear the check-in lady confirm *Raffaella Bellini*. And then suddenly, in what seems like the slowest of slow motions, she begins to turn. A true to life shampoo commercial unfolding in front of me, and *damn, she's worth it*.

Her catlike coffee-bean brown eyes, and classic Monica Bellucci beauty, easily make her the most exciting thing I've ever seen. I try to think of something to say as she moves my way—but my knees buckle as my mind goes beyond blank—and as she passes, I'm barely able to breathe, let alone get out a sentence, or even a smile.

The lights drop, the ballroom goes black, total darkness. The crowd cheers, and before I can catch my wits, she slips into the shadows.

"Sir, sir, what's your name, sir?" The check-in lady calls to me.

"Oh, yeah, sorry it's um, Max. My name is Max."

✈

"And your last name, sir?" But my mind is somewhere else, somewhere it's never been, and I honestly don't even know what I said to her, as I believe I blacked out; because as I come to, I'm nearly halfway back to my seat, and am on the other side of the room.

I feel strange, not sick, but nauseous. The back-to-back shots come to mind as my chest heavies, and my head spins. My heart is fluttering, and my blood feels hot as if it's boiling inside my body. Perspiring profusely, I loosen my bowtie and grab a glass of ice water from a passing waiter.

Standing there, spinning, surrounded by penguin suits and prime cut filets, this random article I once read—reads back to me. It claimed that men are capable of falling in love, in something like 8.2 seconds. Well, I don't know where they got their science, but I'd swear on anything, it took a fraction of that—to fall as I've never fallen—for Raffaella Bellini.

I make it back to my table. Natasha turns to me, and concern comes to her face. "Max, are you alright?"

"Yeah, I'm fine."

"But, you're sweating, and you're really white."

"Yeah, I don't know. I just got dizzy all of a sudden."

"What can I do? Do you need some water?"

"I've got some," I say, bringing that cold water back to my lips, an attempt to cool myself from the inside.

I've never experienced anything like this. I'm definitely sick, there's no doubt about that, but I'm not ill. It's more of a mental-mania, panic attack, with a decent possibility of passing out and pissing myself. So I try my best to appear put-together.

"I was starting to think you weren't coming back. What took you so long?"

"I stopped and talked with Teddy. You know how that goes." She shakes her head.

"Is the water helping?"

"Yeah, I think so."

"Good. You already look better, but you scared me."

"Yeah, I scared myself," I say. "And speaking of that, where's your father?"

"He's backstage preparing for his speech. He says he's leaving for London immediately afterward." *Thank God*, I think. At least I won't have to mingle with that maniac anymore tonight. "You made a great impression on him. He liked you, he told me so. And he doesn't like anyone." *No shit*, I say to myself. She grabs ahold of my hand, "Max, your hands, they're so hot and clammy. Do you need more water?"

"No, I'm fine, thanks," I say. "And I'm glad to hear that. That he likes me and all."

"You know what else you may be glad to hear?"

"What's that?"

"I now know that my fortune is coming true." And she squeezes my hand. I can physically feel my skin blanch white as the sweat on my back dries to chills.

Her father takes the stage to a symphony of applause. I sit back and search the shadows, hoping to spot a silhouette of Raffaella Bellini. Instead, I see Teddy two tables back, giving me a thumbs-up and a goofy grin.

Another round of applause echoes as Natasha's father finishes. The individual awards are next. I order a beer and again sit back, but my head stays on a swivel.

While sipping my fourth or fifth Stella and shaking my head autonomously at something Natasha says, my luck turns. *And the award for Southern Europe's analyst of the year goes to Mister Mario Bellini*, announces the host. My slouch straightens as my eyes scour the darkness. But I don't find Mr. Bellini till he's nearly on stage.

Glass trophy in hand, he delivers his short speech in broken-English and takes a bow before a round of applause sends him back into the dark sea of spectators. My eyes stay affixed until he finds his table. It's in the back, the way back, where the room is completely black. But there she is, a barely recognizable dark dot of perfection.

I know I need to say something, do something, take action, but nothing comes to mind. So again, I sit back, sipping

✈

my Stella, keeping her in the corner of my eye. I try not to stare, I really do, I fight it but fail. I'm drawn to her, and I'm not sure what to do with myself.

"Max, are you ok?" Natasha asks again.

"Yeah, sure, I'm fine."

"You look worried about something. Are you sure that you're feeling better?"

"I'm ok, no worries," I say, but she isn't stupid.

"Are you drunk?"

"No... well, maybe a little." I glance back to see the shadow that is Raffaella Bellini stand and head towards the exit. *No, she can't leave!* "Your right, I'm actually feeling kind of sick," I say to Natasha. "I have to use the restroom."

"Do you want me to come with you?"

"No, I'll be ok. I'll be right back," I say as I stand, then hastily make my way through the ballroom.

Outside, the night is cool, but the fresh air does nothing for my overwhelming anxiety. She's standing there, alone, fifty feet from me, smoking a cigarette and staring into the sky.

There's this awkward sensation when you take a step, but the surface you anticipate isn't there. Instead, it's empty space, and for a split-second, your stomach sinks, and your arms flail. Believing you're about to bite-it, you brace for impact. But in reality, that step is only an inch or so lower than expected, and you easily, yet awkwardly catch yourself. Afterward, you jump straight, hoping nobody witnessed your half-second of self-inflicted silliness. Well, that's exactly how that first step towards her feels, and then the next twenty-six, until I finally find myself standing in front of her, sweating, as fear pours from my pits. I can't get a goddamn word to come out of my mouth. I say nothing, literally nothing. Words of any worth elude my lips, while a lifetime of pre-scripted charisma sloshes around in my mind, but nothing escapes, so I stand there, staring at her—in silence.

"Hello," she says, surely to ease the awkwardness of our encounter.

✈

"Hi. How's your cigarette?" I stutter.

"You want cigarette?" she asks in a thick Italian accent.

"No, I was asking how your cigarette is." The witless-words flounder from my lips.

"Ah, is not so good. It is a cheap Chinese cigarette." She takes a long seductive drag. "You don't smoke?"

"No," I say.

"Why not?"

"I don't know, I just never started."

"That's good. I don't smoke either," she says.

"But you're smoking now."

"Ah, but it's just one."

I almost say that smoking one is still smoking, but I just swallow and stare.

"I can stop if I want," she says, "But everybody in Italy smokes cigarettes."

"Yeah, I noticed that," I say. I usually don't like it when girls smoke, but she looks classy as hell, and I don't care. In fact, I'm quite fond of it. She's so beautiful, and those rolling R's when she says *cigarette*, it sounds like she's singing to me.

"You have been to Italy?"

"Yeah, once."

"Where do you go? Roma?"

"Rome and Naples," I say.

"Ah, I'm sorry about that."

"Why, sorry?"

"Is no good there..."

"Where, Naples?"

"*Sì*, is dirty, and too many *Napolitanos*," she says it aloud, but also with her hands.

"That's funny, there was a lot of trash in the streets," I say, still stammering, but somewhat steadier.

"Yes, is no good there. Nobody from Italy wants to go to Napoli."

"Where should I go?"

"You should go to Milano. Is very nice. You will like it."

"That's where you're from?"

"Sì Milano. How bout you?"

"Chicago."

"Ah, Americano."

"Have you been to the US?" I ask.

"No, but one day I will," she looks up at the sky as she says it.

"So, you want to go?" I ask, still as nervous as I've ever been.

"Sì, yes, of course."

"Why?"

"Everybody want to go to America, no? And I want to improve my English."

"Your English seems pretty good," I say.

"No, it's not so good."

"Well, it sounds good to me."

"You only say that because you are a nice person."

"I'm not that nice," I say.

"You seem nice enough," she takes another long drag, closing her eyes as she exhales.

"Why English?" I ask. "Why not French or Spanish?"

"English is everywhere. If you know English, you can go anywhere and talk to anyone."

"Where would you go?"

"Go?" she asks.

"If you could go anywhere, where would you go?"

"I choose America, of course."

"Over anywhere?"

"Sì, it's my number one choice."

"America is pretty big. What would you want to see first?"

"I don't know. Why do you ask?"

"Just curious."

"I don't know... I love mountains. So, I'd pick a place in the mountains, the Rocky Mountains. That would be my first choice."

"That's a good choice," I say.

"Yes, they look so wonderful. You have been?"

"Many times."

"Then, I envy you."

"I'm an American. I think we're all supposed to see them."

"I want to see them so bad," she says.

"Yeah?"

"Yes, of course."

"What's another place you want to see?"

"I pick New York," she says it as quickly as I ask.

"Take your time and think about it for a second," I say sarcastically.

"Everybody in Italy dreams of going to New York. It's everything." She tosses her cigarette and looks into me with a wanting stare, of what, I'm not sure, but it sucks the air from my chest. "I should get back before my family worries."

"Ok," I say; searching for words—something to keep her from fleeing.

"Good night." She turns to walk away.

"It's Raffaella, right?" She looks back at me.

"Yes, how do you know?"

"It's on your nametag there."

"Ah, sì."

"And I was standing behind you in line earlier," I say.

"Yes, I saw you," and she looks down at my nametag. "I saw you, Max."

"Well, it was nice meeting you, Raffaella," I say, unable to come up with anything better.

"It was nice meeting you too, Max." She turns again. I feel my legs weaken, and my heart thumps harder with every step. I don't even know her, but I'm not ready to say goodbye.

"Raffaella," I call out, and she stops and turns.

"Would you, by any chance, want to get together while you're here in town?"

"Ah, I don't know about that. I am with my family, and we leave on Tuesday." I quickly reach for my wallet and pull out an old business card—a souvenir—from some short-lived sales gig I had years ago, but it has my number on it.

✈

"Listen, I'd really like to see you again before you leave. There's a place I'd like to take you. So if you find yourself with a couple free hours and you want to go, please call me or text me, and I'll come pick you up." I hand her the card.

"Ok, I will see what I can do. Maybe it is possible." And with that *maybe*, my heart jumps to my throat. "Have a good night," she says, sliding me a sensationally somber smile, the kind only Europeans seem to possess.

"Good night, Raffaella." And I watch her walk away. I don't follow her, though. I know I can't go back in there.

I stand in the silent breeze, staring into the night sky for some time before I text Natasha: *I'm not feeling well and am heading home.*

She calls me moments after hitting send, but I silence it. What would I say? Then she messages me, but I don't respond. Instead, I take a cab and a couple sleeping pills and pass out.

✈

Part 2:
Her

When I am with you,
the only place I want to be is closer.

— Someone who found her

✈

CHAPTER 14

The Longest Day

IT'S 5:47 a.m. I'm wide-awake; all attempts to fall back asleep have failed. At six, I walk to McDonald's—my vaccine against homesickness. I grab some snacks, a couple bottles of wine, and the latest James Patterson from a mom-and-pop shop with a decent selection of fiction. I don't feel like doing much today.

At a quarter to eight, I get a text from Teddy: *Heard you're sick, mate. Won't ask you to train. I'm heading back to Singapore soon, be back in two weeks. Hope you're still here! Good times, Cheers.*

I know he isn't expecting a response this early, and I can't think of anything to say, so I go back to my book.

Minutes later, I get an email update on my website's weekly Ad-revenue. It's nothing much, a few hundred bucks, far from the Tim Ferriss financial freedom I sought when I spent six months building the damn thing, but still something.

It's nearly nine when I get a text from Anna: *I heard you got sick. Hope you're ok. Teddy leaves in an hour. I was hoping you'd come by when you're feeling better, or I can come to you? Let me know if you need anything.*

I'm not sure what to say, so I say nothing.

Midway through chapter twelve of my James Patterson, I get another message. Raffaella optimistically rushes to mind, but it's Natasha: *Hey Max, as you know, I leave today. I'd really like to see you before I go, or maybe I'll stay another day if you'd like? I hope you're feeling better.*

Again, I don't know what to say, so I say nothing.

Natasha is amazing, there's no doubt about that. She's everything any man would want in a woman, and letting her walk away is undoubtedly foolish. But I don't want to think about that now. So I go back to my book.

✈

After a short nap, I'm flipping through chapter twenty-two when I feel my phone again. Again, it's Natasha: *Max, I guess you're still sleeping. I hope you're ok. I'm about to go to the airport and was hoping to see you before I leave. If not, then hopefully soon.*

I do want to say goodbye, and she doesn't deserve the silent treatment, so I send the address and tell her to text me when she's here.

Ten minutes later, I get that text. She's leaning back against the trunk of a running cab with her arms crossed. She's as beautiful as ever but has a sad smile.

"Max, are you ok?" she asks as I approach.

"Yeah, I'm sorry about last night."

"It's ok, but I've been so worried about you. Are you feeling better?"

"A little," I say. "But it hasn't been a great morning." I feel bad lying to her, but I don't want to hurt her feelings. What am I supposed to say? *I'm sorry, Natasha, but I met someone last night? That I might have fallen in love with them? That I've been sitting up since sunrise hoping they'd write?* Or that; *things between us are moving too fast, that I believe your father to be insane, and that I'm glad we're about to spend some time apart.* I can't say those things to her. She doesn't deserve that, so I stay with the sick bit.

"Oh, that's awful. Is there anything I can do?"

"No, I think I just need to spend the day in bed."

"When am I going to see you again?" she asks.

"I'm not sure. What are you thinking?"

"I'm free next weekend or the one after that. I can fly anywhere, you just have to tell me where you'll be."

"Well, Teddy will be in Singapore next weekend, I'll probably go see him. But we'll figure something out."

"Ok," she says with the same sad smile. "Max, you know you're always welcome to come to Moscow. I have an apartment downtown, it's nice, and you can stay as long as you'd like."

"I appreciate that," I say, "we'll figure it out." Her smile slips away, and she hardens herself. Her customary cool—

calculated confidence is off-kilter. Surely sensing that our short-lived romance is unraveling, she appears worried, and I feel like an asshole.

"Did I do something wrong?"

"No, no, definitely not," I say as I pull her into me and wrap my arms around her.

"You just seem so distant, I don't know how to explain it. I'm sorry I made you meet my father. I now know it was a mistake. I never did that before, and I didn't even think of how you would feel. I'm sorry."

"No, don't be sorry. I promise you did nothing wrong." I pull back to show her my open, uncrossed hands. "I don't know what happened last night; something just came over me. I'm sure I'll be better soon."

"Ok," she says, a hint of happiness returns to her face. "I feel better. I'm sorry if that sounds terrible, but I do. My mind has been going crazy all morning."

"I don't want you to worry about me," I say.

"I hate to admit it, but I sat around all day waiting for you to call me, and now I'm late for my flight."

"Well, I won't keep you. I'm glad you stopped by. I really had an amazing weekend with you, Natasha."

"I did too. I like you, Max... I hope I can see you again soon."

"Then you will," I say.

"You promise?" I cross my heart with one finger, *a lie.* "Goodbye, Max."

"Goodbye," I say. "Text me when you land, so I know you made it safe."

"I will." I give her another hug, and she kisses me.

I open, then close the taxi door, tap the top, and wave. She blows me a kiss as the car disappears into traffic.

I head back upstairs, disappointed in myself, but I can't control my heart or the feelings of anyone who attaches themselves to it. I throw on *Rumble in the Bronx* and open a bottle of malbec before my phone buzzes again. Fingers crossed, I swipe the screen, but it's Lexi: *Hey you! If you're anywhere near Vegas, my friend Ryan is flying us all out to Aspen for my birthday. I'd love for you to come. Miss you.*

Six o'clock comes and goes. My second movie finishes and my second bottle of wine isn't far behind. I think about going out, but my motivation takes me nowhere. Like most in our modern self-serving society, I only talk to God when I want something. And as the day concedes its light, I'm quite talkative.

I still have a few Heinekens, so I run a hot bath, salt a bucket of ice, and climb in. The jets soothe my muscles as I attempt to unwind my mind. But instead of a bubbly bliss, every thought that's recently troubled me comes through. Obviously, Nadja is in the mix, mostly how Anna nailed it. I never did consider moving to New York for her. Not even once. I think about Andrea in St. Louis. She had messaged me the other day about ending it with her fiancé. She's a sweet girl, and I hope she isn't too lonely or sad. I think of Lexi, and how a small part of me wishes I could make it to her birthday party. Not because I want to be with her, but because she's a nice person, and I enjoy seeing her happy. I think about Natasha, and how I hope she doesn't end up hurt or hating me. And of course, I think about Anna. What the hell am I going to do about Anna? This woman I've known for most of my adult life wants nothing from me except me. Sure I care for her, how couldn't I? But I know it can't continue like this; it isn't right anymore. Not that it ever was. I've selfishly allowed the comforts of my circumstance to cloud my conscience for too long. Teddy would do anything for me, literally anything, and I've done nothing but fuck the man over.

But the person I think of the most has only been in my life for a few drags of a cigarette. I hadn't even scratched the surface; but I can't get her face, or her voice, or even her hair out of my mind. I'm fucking spellbound. But I couldn't read her, and still don't know if she was smiling or scared, an unsettling attempt at interpreting the emotions of the Mona Lisa, and the more I question it, the more concerned I grow. *What do I do if she doesn't call? Do I search for her? Do I make a call, find out where she's staying, and go loiter in the lobby? Or should I go to the airport and wait for her to pass by?*

And with that last one, I realize I've been sitting in hot water a tad too long.

I dry my shriveled skin and saunter back into the big white room. My phone is flashing, so I swipe the screen. There are two new messages. I take a breath, savoring the anticipation. The first is from Anna, and the second, my friend Phil. "Fuck!" I shout. *I go fucking days at a time without a single goddamn unsolicited text, but as soon as I'm waiting for one, everybody I fucking know hits me up!* Anna's message reads: *Max, are you ok? Natasha said you were sick, and you haven't answered. I'm worried. Call me!!*

The second message is a link to the *YouTube* video of Andy Samberg's *I Just Had Sex.* Phil typically sends it a few times a year, or whenever he gets laid. It usually gives me a good laugh, but not tonight.

Maybe this is what I deserve after a lifetime of ghosting and a steadfast dismissal of anything stable. Maybe this is how Nadja felt that first year. Hell, I'd go days, even weeks at a time without writing her back. Maybe that's why she tormented me in the end, a strategic retaliation for making her feel this way.

I text Anna to tell her *I'm fine,* and that I'd *come by* in the next few days.

I'm buzzed from the beers, the wine, and the water, but don't feel like doing shit, and I certainly don't feel like worriedly waiting up any longer. So, I swallow some pills with a healthy swig of scotch and turn on *CNN,* planning on depressing myself to sleep—to the sound of pigheaded pundits debating the latest problems on our planet—and it works.

My eyes open some thirteen hours later. I try to go back to sleep, but my well-rested retinas won't stay shut. I don't want to stand, as I refuse to face the fact she hasn't called. I'm angry with myself. *I could've done better.* I've effortlessly seduced so many women in my life, but when it mattered most, I froze. I looked like James fucking Bond in my fancy-ass tuxedo, but I couldn't spit out a goddamn sentence.

✈

I don't even know her, but I know I need to. I need to verify that this isn't some lustful vacation love, a post-dramatic stress rebound, or that I haven't over-hyped her in my head. I need to know if what I felt was real and see if I feel it again. Confirm that she isn't some fantasy, a haze of infatuation, a lucid dream you hate waking up from—but do.

After a while of what-ifs, I calm myself and crawl out from my comforter cocoon. Willowlike, I wander into the living room, where I'm greeted with the flashing green-light of a notification. I say a silent prayer as I swipe the screen. *Fuck!* It's from Natasha: *Hey handsome, I made it home safe. Can't wait to see you again, hopefully soon.*

I throw my phone across the table, knowing I'll never see that Italian goddess again. That *she isn't real*, but rather, the fabled *unicorn*, my *Rosebud*, my *what-if* that will never be. And just as I say it, cursing myself, and sick to my stomach—the son of a bitch buzzes.

I don't even try to believe it; instead, I tell myself that it's Teddy with news from Singapore. I stand there, staring at the locked screen's *"New Message"* notification, both scared and exhilarated. I've been lots of places, and I've seen lots of things, yet the free-falling feeling in my stomach informs me that this is one of the most exciting moments of my life. I swipe the screen. It's an unknown +39 02 country code. I open it: *Hello, this is Raffaella from Saturday night. I can be free today for maybe 2 hours if you still want to meet me?* I jump at least ten feet into the air. Hell, I swear to God I almost attempt a fucking backflip.

I'm not about to play games, so I respond straight away: *Yes, I do. What time?*

And she writes back just as quick: *Can we meet at Dior in IFC mall at 12?*

Sounds good, I reply.

Ok, see you soon.

I'm looking forward to it.

CHAPTER 15
The Monkey Story

I ARRIVE AT THE MALL a few minutes early and sit on a bench in front of Dior. I'm anxious, more than I anticipated, or at least more than I hoped. Just then, everything goes dark when two hands cover my eyes. "I give you two guesses," her sweet Italian voice whispers.

"Hmm, Britney Spears," I say.

"No, you crazy."

"Ok-ok, Celine Dion."

"Ah, you so stupid." I turn and look up at her.

"Dammit, I swear I was gonna say Raffaella next."

"No, you don't remember me."

"Yeah, I'm actually waiting for someone; you're gonna have to go when they show, ok."

"Ahh, I knew it, you are a crazy boy." She sits next to me, and my eyes immediately get stuck in hers. "No, don't look at me. I look terrible," she cries, theatrically covering her face. I'd typically say she's fishing for compliments, but her stained T-shirt, ponytail, and makeup-free face says otherwise. Definitely different from her elegant eveningwear, but I think she's even more beautiful than before.

"I think you look really pretty," I say.

"Ah, you are a good liar—I almost believe you. But I seen myself, so I don't."

"Well, I wouldn't change anything."

"You are very kind. But maybe a little blind," she says, waving her finger in front of my face, an impromptu eye exam. I pretend not to notice. "Ah, yes, you are blind."

"Who said that?" I say, and her eyes smile. "But, I do like that stain on your shirt." I point and smile back.

✈

"I tell you don't look at me... I have a chocolate cookie before you come, and I make a mess."

"Never change," I say.

She looks into me but says nothing.

"So, what do you want to do?" I ask.

"I thought you say you want to take me somewhere, no? That is if you are not too embarrassed to be seen with me and my dirty shirt."

"I do want to take you somewhere, dirty shirt and all, but you said to come to the mall, don't you want to shop?"

"Ah, no, I don't want to shop. I only meet here because mio padre, eh... my parents, they are very protected." Her words occasionally fumbled, but her fluency remarkable.

"Protective?" I question—*why the fuck did I correct her?*

"Ah sì, protective. Grazie." It doesn't bother her.

"So, you want to go somewhere else?"

"Yes, that's what you tell me, no?"

"I did." And glad to hear her say so. "Have you been off the island yet?" I ask.

"No, I don't think so." Her head shakes, and her eyes widen.

"Have you been to Kowloon?"

"No, I don't know a Kowloon."

"What have you been doing since you've been in Hong Kong?"

"Shopping. All-day, every day, I have gone shopping. Please don't make me shop again."

"A girl who doesn't want to shop?"

"Please, I beg you, or I have to kill myself," she says with a cute–crazy look in her eye.

"Ok–ok," I say. "I promise we won't buy a thing. I don't want you dying on me."

"Good, I want for nothing."

"Is that what you did yesterday?" I ask, secretly seeking justification for my torment.

"Yes, all day. I shop with my family. I think maybe we visit every store in Hong Kong. I want to write you, but my

✈

father, my mother, or my kid brother doesn't speak no English, so I have to talk to everybody for them."

It's nice to know that she wasn't playing games; that she actually was busy yesterday. If she only knew what she did to me.

"You said we have two hours, right?"

"Yes, my family is at the pool now. I think they will stay at di hotel today."

"Good," I say. "You aren't by chance afraid of water or animals, are you?"

"What kind of animals?"

"Don't worry about it. Are you afraid of open water or boats?"

"Mmm, a boat will be fine, but I don't want to get killed by a tiger or dragon or something."

"Aw, well, I guess we won't go then," I say.

"No–no, go where?" she asks. "I don't want to ruin the plan."

"I was gonna take you to the dragon cave, but if you're afraid."

"Dragon cave?"

"Yeah, they live in a castle on the hill, they have red eyes, and blow fire from their mouths."

"Ah, you are teasing me, aren't you? You know I mean a lizard, like a crocodile."

"Sure," I say, nodding with an exaggerated pout.

"I did. You a crazy boy."

"It's ok if you believe in dragons," I say.

"No, shut up, I am not a kid... I know there's no fire dragon."

"Ok, I believe you." I shake my head, no.

"*Sei uno stronzo.*"

"What does that mean?"

"It means you're being an asshole," she smiles, so I know she's kidding. "Now, where do we really go?"

"Come on," I say. "You'll see." I lead her out the back exit onto the pier.

Within minutes of receiving her message this morning, I had arranged our day. I called up my old friend Levi. He's a forty-something Australian expatriate I met five years ago when he called me out for drinking his beer at Ned Kelly's. We got into an argument and nearly went toe-to-toe until I realized that I had, in fact, drank his beer. I apologized and picked up his tab. We became friendly and shared a few laughs. He turned out to be a hell of a guy.

It was about a year after that night when I lent Levi seven thousand dollars to start a water-taxi business. With it, he bought a 15ft jet boat and started shuttling tourists across the harbor. It went well, and he paid me back in twelve months with interest. Now he has three boats, and whenever I call him, he treats me to free rides and bottomless beverages.

He's waiting for us at the dock—behind the IFC mall—in his company's T-shirt.

"Levi, good to see you, bud."

"Ay mate, good to see ya, old friend." We exchange handshakes and backslapping hugs, then turn our attention to the reason for our reunion.

"Levi, this is Raffaella. Raffaella, this is Levi."

"Hello, nice to meet you," says Raffaella.

"It's quite a pleasure, miss. I knew it had to be a special occasion, ole Max here never rings me anymore."

"I told you I've been away," I say.

"And it's damn good to have ya back, mate. We're gonna have to catch up over a proper pint. But today, we enjoy this beautiful winter weather, ay."

"It couldn't be a better day," I say as we climb aboard.

"You've got that one right, mate, and it's been a mighty profitable week, I'd say."

"Glad to hear it."

"Have you been out on the harbor yet, Raffaella?" he asks.

"No, is my first time."

"Well, you two picked a fine day to go on your little adventure. It's like I always say; it's a great day for a great day." He hops aboard, lifts the ladder, and fires the engine. "Now, I'm gonna need you two to put on your lifejackets, strap yourselves down, and hold on to one another nice and tight because you're in for one hell of a ride."

We buckle ourselves into that yellow-checkered jet boat before rocketing off. On a small craft like this, it feels as though you're almost flying atop the water. There's a lot of wake from the heavy harbor traffic, she squeezes my hand, laughing—nearly crying—every time we hit a stomach-sinking wave.

I'm taking her to Kam Shan Country Park, which sits just above Kowloon proper. It probably takes about a half-hour to get there by car, but we can get close by boat in ten minutes, and then it's just a short taxi ride. It's really not much of a time-saver, but you can sit in a cab anytime. How often do you find yourself on a jet boat in East Asia?

I curiously watch her eyes as she peers back at the Pearl of the Orient for her virgin view. And, like anyone seeing Hong Kong from the water for the first time, she appears to be both enchanted and impossibly impressed. Exactly what I had hoped for when I arranged this ride.

Levi is typically a big talker, but today he stays silent. Letting us enjoy the sunshine, the skyline, the smell of the sea, and the cool mist as he whips us around a tad more than his typical tourists. He drops us at the dock and says he'll see us soon.

The taxi is on time, and with the promise of a substantially generous tip, he assures me he'd be back in forty-five minutes.

Upon arriving at the park, a Jurassic rainforest with giant tree-covered hills. It doesn't take long for the main attraction to come through.

"Oh my God is so cute," Raffaella cries as a small light brown long-tailed monkey comes running towards us. "He's so cute, oh my God." The monkey stops and sits a few feet in front of us—knowing we're here to feed him.

"Can I pet him?" she asks.

"You can, but I wouldn't."

"Why not?"

"He may be a biter."

"No, he wouldn't bite me. He's too cute to bite."

"Ok, go ahead. If he bites your finger, I'll try my best to grab it before he runs off with it."

"Ok, maybe I don't pet him, but he's so small and cute. I just want to squeeze him. What kind of monkey is he?"

"It's called a macaques," I say.

"Ah, you little mak–ees. I call you, Marco. Marco, the Mak–ees, he's so cute, oh my God."

"Why, Marco?"

"Because Marco is a fighter. A tough little fighting—biting monkey."

"Of course," I say, laughing. "Hey, Marco, how's life?"

The tiny monkey curiously tilts its head to the side as it waits patiently to be fed.

"He doesn't like you talking to him, because he is my monkey."

"Maybe Marco can give you a ride back to the city."

"We are fine, you can go. I'll stay here with Marco."

"Ok, see ya later." I turn and pretend to walk away.

"Wait," she cries out on my fifth or sixth step.

"What is it?" I ask, turning back, smiling.

"Before you go, could you take a photo of little Marco and me?"

"Sure," I say. She hands me her iPhone and sits in the grass next to the monkey. But almost as soon as she does, Marco reaches for her ponytail and pulls—hard. I capture the moment perfectly: her mouth open, the monkey's eyes wide, smiling a devilish full-toothed terrifying smile. She's scared and jumps to her feet.

As soon as I stop laughing, I show her the picture.

"Oh my God, it's my favorite photo. You are a scary little monkey, Marco. But I love you."

"Love? So soon?"

"Yes, Marco knows how to treat a lady."

"Ah, pull her hair and bite her. I'll try that sometime."

"Yes, you can learn a lot from little Marco. He's very smooth." Determined not to be jealous of the primates' ability to make her smile, I opt to befriend him.

"You want to see something?" I ask.

"Maybe, will Marco like it?"

"Oh, I don't doubt he will." I reach into my pocket and pull out a stash of dried mangoes. Marco knows what's coming and pulls on my pant leg. I hand a mango to Raffaella, but she gets scared when he approaches, so she throws it, and before it hits the ground, a dozen more monkeys come running out from the trees.

"Ah, it's so crazy. Are they gonna hurt us?"

"No. Maybe." I laugh, looking down at the frenzied panhandlers, fighting and biting each other.

She steps to the side and takes pictures as I pass out the sweet treats.

"Don't you want to feed them?"

"No, I good over here, they all crazy. You crazy too."

As my mango supply runs dry, they lose interest and return to the trees, but the smile never leaves her face.

We have a while until the taxi is to return. So, we sit in the grass on a small hill. We're still close enough to see the monkeys playing, hollering at one another, but far enough away so she can relax.

"Max, that was amazing, thank you for bringing me here."

"You're welcome."

"Do you bring all your girls here?"

"What? No."

"You can tell me—is ok. It's a nice place."

"I've never brought anyone here. I haven't been here in years myself."

"So, you don't bring your blonde girlfriend here?" She studies my face with the eye of an artist.

"Blonde girlfriend?" I ask.

"Blonde girl from di party. I think she is a Polacca, or perhaps, maybe a Russian girl."

"Ah, you saw us."

"Yes, you look like Ken and Barbie doll; everybody see you."

"She's not my girlfriend."

"I'm not mad—don't worry."

"I know. I'm just telling you, so you know."

"I tell you, don't worry. I already know she's not your girlfriend."

"And how is that?"

"Because... I saw her looking for you after we spoke. Why did you leave her?"

I shake my head. "I don't know. I just wanted to go home, I guess."

"That wasn't very nice. She looked so sad. I felt bad for her."

"It just didn't feel right," I say.

"What's that?"

"Nothing."

"No, tell me."

"Really, it's nothing," I say.

"No, tell me... please," she begs.

"Well, to be honest, I—well. After I talked to you, I just knew I couldn't go back inside."

"So, you really didn't bring her here?"

"I really didn't."

"Good," she says and leaves it at that. "I like it here so much, and I love Marco, even though he's a crazy little monkey and pull my pony."

"Your pony?"

"Yes, my pony—in my hair. I thought he gonna kill me."

"No, you didn't."

"Ok, not kill. But I thought he gonna bite me. Don't tell anybody I was afraid, ok?"

"I won't."

"You promise?"

"Who am I gonna tell?"

"You're right." She smiles. "Is too bad I can't tell my brother about this place, and about Marco. Because he'd think it's very funny."

"Why can't you?"

"Because he's a bad brother, and he will tell my parents I come here."

"You won't tell your parents you were here?"

"No, no way. They kill me if they know."

"Because of me or the monkey?"

"Both... but mostly you."

"Do you want to hear a monkey story that I've never told anyone?" I ask.

"Yes, tell me."

"Nah, never mind."

"Stop it, tell me."

"It's kind of embarrassing."

"I don't believe you—tell me."

"So, we're back to that?"

"Yes, if you don't tell me we are."

"I changed my mind."

"No, you can't do that. You have to tell me right now," she demands.

"It's really not that great of a story—and now it's too over-hyped."

"No, no, it's not. Now tell me, or I'm gonna go crazy. And I may bite you—like little Marco." She shows me her teeth. "Don't doubt me."

"Ok, ok, but only because I didn't get my rabies shots," I say, and she hisses. "But it's a secret, so you can't tell anyone."

"Who am I gonna tell?"

"True." I nod. "Well, it goes like this. When I was just a little boy, not much bigger than Marco, my parents told me that I wasn't actually their child."

"You are adopted?"

"Well, no, but they told me I was."

"Why would they say such a thing?"

"They told me they got me from the zoo as a baby, and that I was really a monkey."

"No, they didn't."

"They did. They also said they shaved my body and had my tail removed by a doctor so that I'd look like a regular boy."

"No, come on. This is a story of Pinocchio."

"I swear I'm not making anything up. They said my real name is Bobo, and that my monkey mom died just after I was born."

"And you believed them?"

"Sure. I was a little kid, and they're my parents."

"But nobody tells their kid that."

"Well, they did, and I believed them. In fact, I believed them so much that when I would play with other kids at school, I would tell them I was really a monkey named Bobo."

"No, come on. So all di kids think you crazy?"

"Probably. I mean, I was one hundred percent sure that I was a monkey. That's why I thought I was always faster and stronger than all the other kids in my class. I would jump off the highest things at the park and climb trees all the way to the top, and whenever I would play tag, or wrestle, or whatever, I would always win. All the other kids would ask me how I was so fast and tough? And I would say it's because I'm a monkey."

"Did they beat you?"

"No, I think they believed it too. Because I believed it."

"Why did your parents do that to you?"

"I don't know, I never asked."

"Is—crazy. When did you find out it wasn't true?"

"It wasn't until I was eleven years old."

"Eleven!" She erupts with laughter.

"Yes, I was eleven. I was at school—and I bit a boy in my class. The teacher called my mom after I told her *I'm a monkey*. So, my parents, they sat me down and told me the truth."

"No way. That's not a real story."

"I swear."

"Why did you bite the boy?" she asks.

"Because he stole my banana."

"Now you're lying to me." She pushes me, and I pause, soaking her in, her full-tooth laugh, and all her particularities.

"Ok, that part's not true. I don't remember why. But the rest is definitely true."

"Everybody at school thinks you are crazy, no?"

"Oh yeah, for sure. After that, I had almost no friends. I was a total freak."

"They probably still make fun of you."

"I don't doubt it. I remember wishing my mom would move, so I could go to a different school. Because my only friend, until I was fourteen, was from the town over, and he was a little weirdo kid named Phillip."

"No, you were the weirdo kid. You were fortunate little Phillip was your friend. I can't believe your parents did that to you."

"I think it kinda messed me up," I say, smiling.

"Yes, of course it did. You never asked them why they do it?"

"No, I didn't. But I can't wait until I have a kid."

"Why is that?"

"So I can tell him the same story."

"No way. You can't do that to your kid. All the kids will beat him."

"Maybe."

"You are crazy." She smiles. "Is it a true story?"

"It is."

"That makes sense then, why you so crazy. You are a crazy little monkey, just like little Marco. You are a crazy little,

Bobo." She slips me a soft, heartwarming smile. "Max, can I ask you something?"

"Anything."

"When you came outside to talk to me the other night, did you know you would bring me here?"

"No... I didn't."

"But, you said you want to take me somewhere."

"I know, but I didn't know where."

"Then why did you say it?"

"I don't know. I just knew I wanted to see you again, that's all."

"I'm glad you were so nervous," she says.

"I didn't say I was nervous. Why do you think I was?"

"Oh, come on."

"Did I look nervous?"

"Yes, of course. And it was sweet."

"Well... maybe I was a little, but I tried to hide it."

"Yes, I know, and you did a terrible job."

"Terrible?" I laugh.

"Yes, you were shaking like you were cold, and you couldn't talk much."

"I was not shaking."

"It's ok, Max, I think it's sweet. I know you probably talk to many girls, and likely have many girlfriends. So, it's nice to know that I made you nervous."

"I never get like that," I say.

"Yes, I don't imagine so. I think you are maybe an expert with girls, no?"

"No, definitely not."

"I don't know, I feel you never worry too much to get a girl."

"I'm no expert. I promise you that."

"But you are not nervous with girls, no?"

"No, not usually."

"That makes me happy."

"Why?" I question.

"Because if you are not nervous with me, then I am like every girl to you."

"You're not like anyone."

"And I know you think that, but only because you were so nervous."

"Well—then I'm glad I was." And I was glad. The truth is, I'm still nervous around her. She's the most beautiful girl I've ever spoken to, that I've ever seen, and every second I spend with her, the more beautiful she becomes.

The cab approaches, telling us it's time to go.

"You ready?" I ask, knowing I'm not.

"Ok, but hold on. I can't be rude, I have to say goodbye to little Marco." And she runs into the trees and talks to the little ponytail-puller in Italian, shaking her finger at him a few times, before waving goodbye.

"How bout it, mate. Were you able to find the monkeys?" asks Levi upon our return.

"Oh, we found them," I say. "And you were right about the mangoes, they were a hit."

"Glad to hear it, mate." And we all hop aboard. "What d'you think, Raffaella?" he asks.

"It was so wonderful... I still can't believe it."

"It's quite the sight, all right."

The small boat smells of gasoline and rumbles as we pull away from the pier.

"Where can I take you two next?"

"We've been gone about an hour and a half. Can you stay any longer?" I ask her.

"I want to so much, you know that I do. But I must get back, or my father, he will worry about me. My parents, they think I am shopping for souvenirs—for *mia nonna*."

"Hey bud, I think we're just gonna head back to the mall."

"Aye, mate."

The water is calmer than earlier, and the sky is clear. It's a perfect December day, but I'm suddenly miserable. I can't

✈

believe I'm about to say goodbye to this girl, to this beautiful woman, who I now believe was put here for me. I know I need more time with her.

Levi gets us back to the dock behind the mall, and we wave goodbye to my Aussie counterpart.

"I don't want to go," she tells me, taking ahold of my hand.

"I don't want you to go either. I could have stayed out there all day," I tell her.

"Me too."

"Listen, I'm just down the street, like five minutes from here. If... by any chance, you somehow become free later, or tonight, or anytime, even if it's just for ten minutes... text me... and I'll come back. I don't care what we do, we can just sit on a bench and talk, or we can go somewhere, it doesn't matter. I just want to see you again. If I can."

"I'll see what I can do," she says, smiling.

"And if not, then I guess this is goodbye," I say, and she wraps her arms around me. My chest tingles, heavy and hollow, and my heart hurts—knowing I'll likely never see her again.

"I really hope this is not goodbye," she whispers, then kisses my cheek.

"Me too," I say. I turn and walk away. I don't look back, I can't. I'm sad, overwhelmingly so, and though she was in my arms moments earlier, I already miss her.

It's Like Magic

I DON'T FEEL LIKE MOPING back at the apartment, so I walk over to the M Bar, a chic cocktail lounge with a boat-shaped bar on the 25th floor of the Mandarin Oriental, and order a beer. The place is half-empty. I play Scrabble on my phone, chew on some cherries, and avoid eye contact with any-one who isn't pouring.

Raffaella had mentioned her brother being mean, and it gets me thinking about my own brother, and that one time in seventh grade when he nearly killed Andy Anderson after the kid threw a small stone at me. My brother's eyes glassed over, and he lost himself. He grabbed Andy by the back of his hair and buried his face into the hood of that rusty Ford at least five times, because when Andy looked up, his nose was as flat, and you couldn't find a spot above his waist that wasn't covered in blood.

Andy's parents pressed charges, and damn, my dad was pissed. My brother got grounded that entire summer, and not the typical type. No, my dad turned his room into a cell. He removed everything: leaving only a pillow, a sheet, and a stack of *National Geographic* magazines. He could only leave his room to shit or cut the grass. He even ate all his meals up there.

I believe my brother was twelve at the time. You only get so many summers as a kid, and he gave one up for me. I'm pretty sure I never thanked him for it.

A couple hours and a few beers later, I'm barely able to think of anything but her. Staring out the window at the late afternoon skyline, I tell myself that *she isn't that great*, but I know it's bullshit because I'm fucking mesmerized. My phone buzzes. *Holy shit.* I say a silent prayer as I swipe the screen. *Holy shit*, it's her: *Hello, I will eat with my family now. But I can be free for two more hours at 17,00 if you still want to meet?*

I promptly respond: *Yes, can I pick you up?*

Ok, please meet me at the main entrance of IFC.

Sounds good... I'll see you soon.

I throw down another quick one to celebrate, but mostly to calm my nerves.

I stop for wine at a nearby bottle shop. It's a little mom-and-pop place that sells dried fish, dehydrated squid, and other cured marine creatures out of bulk barrels. As if you're buying trail mix from Whole Foods back in the states. The store stinks of rotten seafood, so pungent, you'd think something died and is now decaying between your teeth. Concerned about the odor's absorbent abilities; I jog over to the Starbucks to give myself a swift whore's bath, before hitting a knockoff fragrance-boutique to douche myself in imitation Tom Ford.

I arrive at the mall a few minutes early, but she's already there. She looks at Ricky but doesn't see me, so I flash his lights and run around for the door.

She's showered and looks spectacular in her baby-blue sundress. The pony is down, her hair now long and straight and thick as hell.

"Did you miss me?" she asks.

"Eh, maybe," I say, teetering my hand.

"I knew it. If I don't write you, you never remember me." She says it with her hands. "But I won't let you forget me that easy."

"Ah, you're the one from the boat today," I say, smiling as I close her door.

"You're not too good at acting cool." She smirks. "Is this your car?"

"No, it's not."

"Then how do you get a Ferrari?"

"Is that what this is?" I ask, strapping myself in.

"Yes, everybody know Ferrari—don't be stupid."

174 J Gatz

"It's not mine," I say, and we pull away.

"Yes, you already say so—but whose is it?"

"It's my friends."

"Ah, di blonde girl."

"No, not the blonde girl." I laugh.

"Then, who?"

"The guy I was with the other night, not sure if you saw him. He's older."

"Ah, yes, I see you drinking with him. Same person?"

"Yeah, that's him."

"Ok, I believe you."

"You think I'd lie to you?"

"No, but I don't really know you."

Her words shake me for a second. And perhaps to make her forget the fact that she doesn't really know me—I floor the accelerator. The engine roars like an African lion as we launch into traffic on Lung Wo. I only have a couple hours with this incredible thing next to me, and I can only think of one spot I want her to see. But it's nowhere near the city.

"You know that driving fast in a Ferrari don't impress me, right?"

"I was gonna pick you up in a city bus, but I didn't think it'd get us back on time."

"Ok, I'm just making sure you know, because I prefer Lamborghini." Her lips pout smugly, and she lifts her chin. "But it's ok, I know you tried."

Damn. I grin, and a couple seconds of silence slide by.

"You know I kid you, right?"

"I know." I smile.

"I've never been in a Ferrari or Lamborghini before."

"No?"

"Never," she confirms. So I downshift and gun it again. The engine screams almost as loud as her—as the g-forces bury us into our seats, rocketing us past a 150kph while merging onto Highway One. I glance over to see she's scared.

"You are a big jerk, never do that again!" she yells, and slaps my arm, and for a second, it seems serious, until she smiles.

✈

"You want to go faster?" I ask.

"No, you're a fucking crazy man."

"And you're fucking gorgeous."

She looks at me—smiling with her eyes, then casually turns to watch the city shrink behind us.

"Where are you taking me?"

"It's another secret spot. And no, I've never brought another girl here before."

"You think I think that?" She's smirking.

"I just wanted you to know."

She puts her arm out the window, letting her hand ride the waves of the wind. "I'm wondering why you were at di party the other night? You are not banker—no?"

"No, I'm not a banker."

"Then, you are a timeshare salesman?"

"No," I laugh. "Why would you think that?" *Ah, yes,* suddenly realizing why.

"It was on your business card, the one you give me for your number. I looked it up. You sell vacation properties, no?"

"No, well, I did, it was a long time ago."

"So... you are not a banker, and you are not a vacation-salesman. So, you are a socialite?"

"No, definitely not." I smile.

"Then why be at a fancy party for bankers if you're not a banker?"

"I went with my friends."

"Ah, yes, di blonde girl. I almost forget."

"No, well, yes. I was with her too, but I was invited by the older guy, the guy whose car we're in."

"Yes, he look important. How you know him?"

"He's my friend, and I work for him. That's why I'm here in Hong Kong."

"How you work for him?"

"I train him. A fitness trainer."

"Ah, I know it. But don't they have trainers for fitness here?"

"They do, but he prefers me."

"He must really like you. To have you come so far from America to train for fitness."

"Yeah, I think he does," I say.

"So you are special?"

"No, not special. I promise you that."

"No, I think that maybe you are. Maybe you don't even know it yet. But I believe it's true."

"Well, thanks, I think you're special too."

"I'm ok, nothing too special. But I think I am more sporty than you." She flexes her long skinny arm.

"Oh, definitely. You're huge."

"No, not huge, but sporty."

It takes a little over thirty minutes of fancy Schumacher-style driving to make it to South Bay Beach, whereupon arrival: I lay a towel, open the wine, and pour it into a couple plastic cups.

"Max, it's so beautiful here."

"It's my favorite place to see the sunset in Hong Kong."

"Look at the little islands, those are islands—no?"

"They are," I say.

"They look like little mountaintops shooting out of the water."

"Well, that's kinda what they are." I sip the wine. "But they look like camel humps to me."

"What is a camel?"

"A camel, an animal in the desert with humps on its back."

"Ah, sì, cammello."

"Yes, a camelo," I echo.

"No, not camelo, it's cam—mello," she emphasizes the *mello* with her hands.

"Camello," I say, slowing the *eello*.

"No, but better." She smiles.

The sun is falling behind the islands scattered in the sea, some close, some on the horizon. Other than a few wispy corona-colored clouds, the scarlet sky is clear, and the water—

✈

nearly black as that giant-flexing-oval-of-fire gloriously buries itself into the end of the earth.

Sitting in the cool sand, I can feel her heat, our arms nearly touching. She's staring into the horizon, and I at her. "Max, it's like magic here. I never seen a sunset like this in my life." She turns to me, biting her bottom lip, her eyes holding mine. She's looking into my soul, a subtle, unspoken invitation to kiss her. So I do. Her lips taste of grape bubblegum, and her touch seems to say *never let go*. The kiss is soft and wet, slow and sinless, yet somehow I know—*I'll never be the same.*

"I wish I didn't have to leave tomorrow," her breath heavy through her whisper as the sun slides below the sea.

"You have no idea," I say.

"I already know I will miss you."

"Yeah?"

"Yes, of course. You are my Bobo." We laugh. I'm nervous again, perspiring even, but her smile soothes me.

She pulls out her phone. "I want a picture," she says as she snaps a candid selfie of us. I don't even have time to smile, but when she shows it to me, I look the happiest I've ever seen myself.

We flip through the photos she took of me feeding the monkeys. "This one is my favorite," she says. It's of me looking down at the Marco, the monkey, his arms reaching out for the mango.

"I look angry. Like I want to bite him."

"That's your monkey face."

I growl my teeth and show her my monkey face, she laughs, and I kiss her again.

I could sit there in that cold sand forever. I could sit there saying nothing, blithesome silence, just staring at her, but with the sun absent, the sky navy, and the sea black; I know I have to get Cinderella back before curfew.

Pulling back onto the highway, she asks me how old I am. She's so much younger than me—I nearly lie. "I'm thirty-two."

"I'm twenty-one," she says hastily.

"Oh," I murmur to myself, thinking she's about to back away.

"But I turn twenty-two this week." Seeming unfazed by the decade difference.

"Well then, happy birthday. When is it?"

"Is on Saturday, the 16th."

"That's exciting."

"No, not too exciting."

"Why not?"

"Because... I like twenty-one."

"Maybe you'll like twenty-two better."

"Maybe, I guess I will see."

"Are you doing anything special?"

"I don't have any plan yet, but my birthday is the same day as my graduation from university, so I am sure I will do something."

"Congratulations," I say.

"I still must take two exams this week, so maybe not."

"I'm sure you'll be fine, have you studied?"

"Yes, of course."

"What are you going to school for?" I ask, and she looks at me strangely. "What are you studying?"

"Ah, business—I study business."

"And how are your grades?"

"Mmm, I have good scores, but my attendance is, um— not so good."

"Why's that?"

"Because business is boring. I don't like it too much, I only go to please my father."

Sounds familiar, I say to myself. "So you study, but you don't go to class?"

"I go enough to get good scores so that my father won't be disappointed."

"So, you're sharp?" I say.

"Like a knife?" she asks, dead serious.

"No," I laugh. "Sharp... like smart, or intelligent."

"Ah, no, not so smart. I think maybe it's just easy."

✈

"Easy? What's the name of your school?"

"Is di Università degli Studi di Milano."

"That doesn't sound too easy to me."

"It's the major University of Milan. It's big, but not too difficult. I think maybe American school is more difficult."

"I'm sure it's still not easy. I doubt everyone else who skips class has good scores."

"Maybe—maybe not."

"What are you gonna do when you graduate?"

"I don't know, what do you mean?"

"I mean, are you going to get a job?"

"Ah, I have job."

"What is it?" I ask, going against my own disdain for basic questions. But I'm genuinely curious in a way I've never been. Just talking with her, learning about her, I'm as happy as a kid hearing the ice cream truck on a steamy summer day. I don't run any of my regular tricks—no scripted stories or self-deprecation. I want to learn everything about her. I want to study her, with perfect attendance, and ace every test.

"I am a waitress."

"That's a good job," I say, knowing I could never do it. "What kind of place?"

"Place?"

"Your job, is it a nightclub, or a bar, or a restaurant?"

"Ah, no, no club, it's a ristorante Italiano."

"Is the food good?"

"Yes, the food is very nice. Is sort of a tourist place, in Milano. That's how I learn English."

"You learned English from waitressing?"

"Yes, from talking to the customers."

"Well, it worked."

"Yes, I guess, but I need much practice."

"Maybe another day or two," I say, smiling. "How long have you been there?"

"I've been waitress for two years."

"And how was your English before you started?"

"No, no English. I don't speak no English before."

✈

"Nothing?"

"Almost nothing. I guess I could say hello, goodbye, I'm hungry, and maybe a couple more things, but not too much. Oh, and I know American music."

"What do you mean?"

"You know, songs. I know them, but I don't know the words meaning."

"That's a real thing?"

"Yes, of course. It's normal. I mean, I know the music, and could sing them, but I didn't really know what they're about. I think many Italian people do the same. It's funny to me now, some of the songs, because I now know the meaning. But it's common not to know."

"And what type of songs would you sing and not know what you're saying?" I smile.

"All types." Her head turns to the window, so I switch strings.

"So, if you don't like business, what do you like?"

"I don't know." She sighs as she says it, like it's some sort of secret.

"When you skip class, what do you do instead?"

"It depends... sometimes I go sit at a café and read—"

"And other times?"

"I don't know, maybe I see a movie, sit at the park, or paint a picture."

"So, you're an artist?"

"Maybe, but not so much. But I do really like it." She says it as though she isn't supposed to talk about it.

"What do you paint?" I ask, and her eyes perk up.

"Everything," she says. "I could paint you. You would make a nice picture."

"I'd like that."

"Yes, I make you the most beautiful Bobo, and I give you a banana, so you don't bite me."

I growl my teeth at her. *I'm fucking fascinated by this girl.* She's fun and funny, an intoxicating blend of beauty and brains.

"Do you want to be a professional artist?"

✈

"Maybe, but I think there are too many good painters in Milano, and in Italy. Is nearly impossible to get famous for painting. And I am not so good."

"I'm sure you're good, maybe you just need to sell your stuff somewhere else, like America. Italian painters could easily become popular in America."

"Yes?"

"Sure, American's love Italians. Hell, I think a bunch of them wish they were Italian."

"Going to America would be incredible."

"Well, why don't you?"

"You think my father would let me go to America? You really are a crazy boy."

"But you're almost twenty-two, and a soon to be college graduate. They can't really stop you."

"True, but they won't support it, they want me to stay in Milano."

"Moneywise, they won't, or you want their blessing?" I know I'm prying now, but I can't stop myself.

"I think both. I just want them to be proud of me. But it is a dream, so maybe one day I go. And the people will buy my pictures—because I am Italian girl." She's smiling.

"Hell, I'd buy that monkey one."

"And I'd give you a good price." She leans over and kisses me on the cheek.

We're more than halfway to her hotel. I want to slow down and drive around as I value every breath in her presence, but I don't want to get her in trouble.

"What do you like to read?" I ask.

"Huh?"

"You said that when you skip class, you sometimes read. What do you read?"

"Ah, ok, I understand. I like Fabio Volo. Do you know of him?"

"No, I don't."

"He is Italian author. He's very good."

"I'll check him out," I say. "Who else?"

"I also like Dacia Maraini, she has very much talent. Do you know her?"

"No, I don't think I know any Italian authors."

"None?"

"I don't think so, besides maybe Dante or Casanova."

"Ah, of course you know Casanova. Because you are a Playboy."

"I think everybody knows Casanova."

"Ah, I don't know about that." She slips me a playful stink eye.

"Do you like any American writers?" I ask.

"Yes, of course."

"Who do you like?"

"Oh, I don't know, maybe Stefano King."

I feel as though I'm unfairly quizzing her, and perhaps America's top contemporary is the only name she could come up with, but I want to know everything. "Ah, Steve King. I like him too. What is your favorite book?"

"Mmm, I think maybe... *Rita Hayworth and* di *Shawshank Redemption*."

"Yes, that's a good one. Did you like the movie or the book better?"

"They have a movie?" she questions.

"Yeah... it's like one of the most popular movies ever made. You've never seen it?"

"No, I don't know it."

"It's probably on TV every other day."

"I don't know, I never hear of it. But I like the story, so now I want to see it."

"Do you like anything else of his?"

"Yes, I like *The Green Mile*, and the one with the plan to save di President Kennedy."

"Ah, *11/22/63*," I say.

"Yes, that's the one. It's very good, No?"

"I liked it," I say. "What about *The Stand*?"

"No, I don't like a scary story. I don't read it."

"Why not?" I ask.

"Who wants to be scared?"

"I think a lot of people want to be scared."

"Well, I don't get it."

"What don't you get?" I ask, surely smirking.

"Why pay to read a book or go see a movie that's gonna make you scared? Giving away your money to have a bad dream—is like paying someone to punch you in di face."

"I never thought of it like that." I slide her a sinister eye and hold up my fist. "Is it easier for you to read English or speak it?"

"Read it, no doubt."

"Why?"

"I don't know. I think there is too many similar words that mean different things. It's easier to see it than to say it."

Pulling into the mall's parking lot, it's been more than two hours since we pulled away, so I know my time is up. Apparently, she could never tell her parents she's with a guy. So again, I have to say goodbye. I pull behind a line of taxis and turn off the engine.

"I'm gonna miss you," she blurts out.

"Yeah?"

"Yes, of course."

"I'll miss you too," I say. "I've never met anyone like you."

"You never meet Italian girl before?"

"No, I've met Italian girls, just not like you."

"How many Italian girls you meet before?" She squints suspiciously. "I kid you, come on."

I smile back, but I'm sad inside. "Listen, Raffaella, I know that we just met, and I don't want you to think I'm weird or anything, but I know I'm gonna see you again. I don't know how or when, but I know I will."

"You are weird, but I hope it is true." And I kiss her, or she kisses me, I'm not sure, our lips just come together. Hers are soft, slippery, and slightly trembling. The kiss is wet but wonderful, and as we pull apart, I brush a stray hair from her face and run my knuckles down her cheek. She stares at me, my hand squeezed between her head and shoulder. I want to say something, something to seal the moment, something truly memorable, but her smile has my mind a mess. "I think you're extraordinary," I mumble.

"Thank you." She blushes and bites her bottom lip. "I think you are too."

She leans over and gives me another small kiss before closing the door and walking away.

She's flying thousands of miles from me tomorrow, and as she turns for one last wave, I know she's likely walking out of my life forever.

✈

CHAPTER 17

To Be With You, I Would

THE DAYS FOLLOWING Raffaella's departure are not my finest, not even close. I find myself in a self-diagnosed state of depression, fueled by strong drinks and solitude. Bourbon for breakfast and stumbling through sketchy back-alley bottle shops by lunch. The sort of bender that makes any and all previous benders seem responsible. But no amount of booze or blacking out would budge her from my mind.

She text me a couple times, saying she *misses me* and *wishes we were watching the sunset*. She even sent me a picture of a painting she made of South Bay. It's good, it's really good, in fact. It reminds me of Monet's *Sunset in Venice*, the one Pierce Brosnan stole in *The Thomas Crown Affair*, except with scattered islands "cammello humps" instead of a tower.

Because of her, I obsessively hold my phone; phantom rings have me compulsive. I'm well aware of the ease of writing sweet things from afar, no matter how much or little they mean, but her words give me hope. Hope that maybe she misses me as I miss her.

Natasha has been texting me too. Attempting to secure plans to meet up. I respond and am pleasant, but stay distant, and keep my excuses vague.

I've avoided Anna's calls all week, but I asked her to meet me today for a late lunch. I have something to tell her, something that needs to be said before I sober up.

The restaurant is busy, but I snagged a small table towards the back, and am already a few whiskeys in when I get a text from my friend Phil in Chicago: *Hey, Nadja was just at the bar looking for you. She saw me and asked where you were. I told her I hadn't seen you in weeks. Just thought you should know.* With Anna walking in, I don't respond.

"Max, darlin', so good of you to give your old friend Anna a call." I hear the contempt in her voice as she plops in her seat. "Thought I had seen the last of you. Thought maybe you had run off to Russia on me. I pictured you all bundled up in a fancy fur coat, taking a winter tour of the Red Square with your new girl."

Obviously, she's behind on my current affairs, and I don't feel like filling her in, but I also don't want to run out on her without saying goodbye. I contemplate if I should wait a while, enjoy her for ten more minutes, or jump right to it.

"Anna, I don't know how to say this, but I don't want you to find out after the fact."

"What's going on, Max?" Her eyes search mine.

"I'm leaving Hong Kong."

"When?"

"Tonight."

"Are you kidding me?"

"No."

"For how long?"

"I don't know. A while."

"Are you drunk?"

"No... well, sure... a little. But I'm still going."

"So, that's how it's gonna be? You're really gonna do this to me right now, huh? After all we've been through, after everything. You meet this girl—what—a week ago? And now, you're just gonna run out on me, like I'm nothing. Like I'm trash. A piece of trash you can toss to the side, again. A woman who's always loved you. A woman who's never stopped loving you since the moment we met. And now what? What are you gonna do? You're gonna run off, and what, get married? Go live in some giant castle somewhere in the mountains, happily ever after with your fairy-tale Russian girl." I say nothing. I don't even know what to say. "You're gonna forget all about me. I knew it, I did. I saw it coming, I swear to God I did. I just don't understand it, Max. What the hell did I do to you?" her voice cracks to a cry. "Why do you hate me so much?"

"You know I don't hate you," I say calmly. "And you didn't do anything." *Fuck, I hate this.*

"Then why can't you love me, Max? You know I've loved you since the moment I saw you. I've said it a million times, and I'll say it a million more. I've never stopped loving you, not for a second, and I never will. You know that. You know it's true. You gotta know it's true."

"I know," I say.

"You just fall for this girl over a weekend, a goddamn weekend. And now you're just gonna drop me all over again and run away. Why, because she's younger than me? Has more money? What is it? She's more beautiful? What is it, Max? Why am I not good enough for you?"

"I'm not going to see Natasha. She's got nothing to do with this."

"Then what did I do to you? What did I do wrong? I just don't understand. Tell me what the hell is going on."

"You didn't do anything wrong. This isn't because of you. I'm not mad at you or upset with you in any way. I can't explain it, I just have to go."

"It's because of Teddy, isn't it? Max, I know you're a good person, and that you hate this whole thing. You know I love Teddy, but I love you more. I'll leave him, I will. I'll leave him tonight. I'll leave him right now. We can go anywhere you want, anywhere. We can go to the mountains like you always talk about, or go live on an island somewhere. We'll do anything you want, you'll never have to worry about anything ever again. And you know I'll love you forever... until the day I die. Max, I swear to God, I will."

"I know you would, Anna, I truly do. But I don't want you to leave Teddy."

"You don't know how I feel, because you've never loved anyone the way I love you. I would do anything for you, anything. Just name it, and I'll do it, I swear to God I'll do it."

"I know you would, and I'll never forget it, believe me. But you can't leave Teddy. He loves you like crazy. He does, and you know it."

"I would do it, Max. I would. To be with you, I would. Whatever you want, whatever it takes, don't leave me, not like this. Not again."

"I'm sorry, I am. I truly am. But I have to go. And it has to be tonight."

"You gotta go right now? Right this second?"

I didn't really plan on it going like this. I don't know what I expected, but not this. "Yeah, I'm gonna go," I say as I slide my chair back.

"Stay and have a drink at least. You can't just leave like this, you can't leave without at least havin a drink."

"I've got to go, I'm so sorry." I stand and toss five hundred Hong Kong down for my drinks.

"Why d'you even have me come down here then? Make me sit here and cry in front of all these people if you're just gonna rip my heart out?" Her tears turn to hysteria, and her lips shake. "Why are you being so mean to me?"

"Anna, I don't want to make you sad. I just wanted to say goodbye to you. I'm gonna miss you so much."

"Come on, shugah, please don't go like this, don't do this to me. Not now, not in front of all these people. You just came back, goddammit!" And she slams her fist on the table.

I bend down to kiss her forehead and whisper, "You'll always have a piece of my heart. Thank you for everything." A tear collects in the corner of my eye, but I wipe it before it falls.

"Does that mean you're leavin foreva?"

"No, but for a while."

"Max, no, come on, shugah. Just stay and have a drink. Just one drink."

"Goodbye, Anna." And I turn and walk straight out of the restaurant. I can't stand to see her in that much pain. I wish it went differently, but it didn't, and I can't do anything about it now.

And though I know we could never be, she's always been my best friend, my big sister, my mother, and my lover all rolled into one, and I know I'll miss the hell out of her.

The walk back to the apartment is long and lonely. The streets are quieter than usual, and I feel like I'm the last person leaving a great party.

I stop at an ATM to confirm my funds, ensuring I have enough to follow through with the plan I concocted all of seven-beers ago.

Thanks to the Macau money, I have $129,143 in my checking account, barely enough for a new BMW in my savings, and Teddy's *if you want to win like a king, you must bet like a king*, kicking around in my mind.

I had written out and planned on giving Anna a check for the remainder of my month, but seeing her so upset, I knew she'd never take it.

During my shower, I sip a San Miguel and slip into a state of self-reflection. Always imagining a more interesting life for myself. I spent mine in pursuit of superficial pleasures, burying myself in a surplus of short-lived affairs—to subdue the brutal backhand of loneliness. Fueled by an unfaltering fear of missing out, I led a purposeless existence, never looking further than my next pint, my next flight, or my next fuck. An abundance of lovers and lust, but never love, until now.

I've never been too sure of myself, but I know without a doubt that this is no, *maybe I like her—maybe I don't—Hallmark Channel horseshit*. This is an *I have to have her or I'll go fucking crazy* kind of reckless love. And I know if I play it safe for even a second longer, I might as well be dead.

After a shave, another beer, and that dreaded call to my dad, I head downstairs and hail a cab for my 12:40 a.m. non-stop Cathay Pacific flight to Milan.

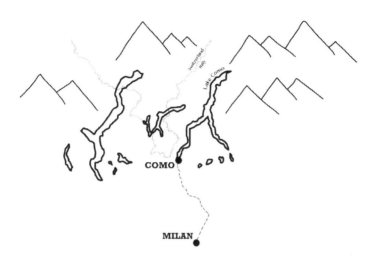

Don't wait for the right opportunity: create it.

— George Bernard Shaw

✈

CHAPTER 18

Buon Auguri

IT'S EARLY MORNING IN MILAN. I'm hanging hard as I check into my hotel. I had been second-guessing my decision to arrive unannounced, so I bellied-up at the bar pre-flight. It was a combination of Fireball, and that fortuneteller's *fear is temporary but love is forever* that got me off the ground.

I'm staying at the Uptown Palace, a modern four-star hotel I picked for its proximity to the university and its free breakfast.

Admittedly, this isn't a very well thought out plan, but I have the big picture down, and figure five nights is enough to see where I stand.

After a shower and a quick bite, I throw on my new cashmere bomber and Burberry scarf. It's cold outside, not kick you in the teeth cold, but definitely different than the mild mid-December mornings of Hong Kong.

I part a sea of filthy pigeons as I arrive at Duomo di Milano, a six-hundred-year-old gothic cathedral with scads of skyward shooting spires. And after a few minutes of awe-inspired stares, I do as most tourists do; I pull out my phone and snap a selfie. I give it a quick once-over, before texting it to Raffaella, with the words: *I met some Italian girl who told me I would like Milan. Eh, it's ok so far.* I take a big breath before hitting send, praying she won't think I'm completely fucking crazy for coming here.

With my phone firmly in hand, I search for somewhere warmer to wait. I find a nearby gelateria with a considerable selection. Sure it's cold, but the store is warm, and I can't pass on Italian ice cream from the source.

I'm barely two-bites into my creamy vanilla bean before my phone buzzes. It's her.

✈

Are you really in Milan? She writes, and I waste no time sending a photo of my gelato atop a napkin that reads, Vanilla Gelati Italiani.

She responds instantly: *The one near Duomo di Milano?*

Yes, I reply.

Don't move! I'll be there in ten minutes! My stomach sinks as my smile stretches.

I spot her through the window; she's in big boots and bigger hair. And as she opens the door and sees me rising to my feet, an unsubtle skepticism slides over her dumbstruck demeanor. She stops in the doorway, staring at me—appearing somewhat scared, and for a half-second, I feel stupid, like I shouldn't be here. Then, after what feels like forever, she snaps to and runs towards me. She leaps into my arms, our lips meet, and everything that's ever mattered in my life suddenly seems less significant. She stiffens herself, grabs ahold of my face with both hands, and forcefully pulls me away. Staring into me, a perceptible fright overtakes her. Her breath is frantic, choppy, and her lips are quivering. "I can't believe how happy you just made me," she whispers. "How did you do this? How are you here?"

"I had to see you," I say, and she pulls my face in for another kiss. It's deep and seems almost dangerous how good it feels.

"I don't even believe this is true. I am sure that I am dreaming, and if I am, I hope that I never wake up."

"If you're happy, I'll do everything I can so that you never do."

"Max, my whole body is numb, and I'm shaking. Look at me, I'm shaking."

"I'm shaking too."

"*Questo non può essere reale*," she whispers to herself.

"It's real," I say, and kiss her again.

"How did you get here?"

"I didn't run."

"No, stronzo, I mean, when did you get here?"

"A few hours ago."

"This is di most amazing surprise I ever receive. I swear to God, I will never forget this moment."

"I won't either," I say.

"Where do you stay?"

"I'm just down the street."

"But where?"

"It's a hotel, Uptown Palace."

"Ah, yes, I know it. Are you alone?"

"No, I came with my girlfriend." She pulls me in and kisses me harder.

"I'm glad you are still a jerk to me. I missed you so much. I thought you forget about me."

"How could I forget about you?"

"I don't know, you don't write me much. I think you forget."

"Not even close. I haven't stopped thinking about you since you left."

"Me too, Max, me too. I was going crazy without you."

"You were?"

"Yes, of course," she says it as though I should know.

"Well, I'm here now."

"Why do you come here? Why are you in Milano?"

"I wanted to try the gelato," I say.

"Stop it, I hate you." She punches me in the chest. "I'm too excited for good English now. I mean, how did you do it. How can you come to Milano? Nobody do that."

"I just wanted to wish you a happy birthday."

"Oh, my God, it's the best birthday I ever have. I never want another birthday in my life. I don't care."

"Hold on," I say, reaching into my coat pocket and pulling out a cell-phone-sized plush-monkey wearing an *I Love Hong Kong* T-shirt. "It's nothing much, but happy birthday."

"Oh, God." She squeezes the monkey and kisses me. "Is perfect. It's di best present I ever get; a little monkey, from my little monkey."

"Sorry, it's nothing great," I say.

"Shut up, it's perfect."

"Good." I smile.

"How long are you here?" she asks.

"As long as you want me to be."

"Oh, Max." She kisses me again.

I can't believe it. She's happier to see me than I thought. I mean, I assumed she'd be excited, or at least I hoped, but I didn't expect anywhere near this level of elation, and because of it, I'm the happiest I've probably ever been. In fact, I know I am. This girl in front of me, with barely any makeup, is the most beautiful thing I've ever seen. And standing here, in this small Italian ice cream shop, on a cold Milan morning, I've reached a level of acute clarity to which I've never experienced. At this moment, I have absolutely no doubt in my mind, my heart, my blood, my cells, or my soul, that I love this girl. And because of her, I know my life will never be the same. I'm as sure of this as I'm sure the sun will set tonight and rise again tomorrow.

"How do you know that I wanted you to come here?" she asks.

"I didn't, but I knew I had to." A single tear drips down her face. "Don't cry," I say, and thumb it away.

"I'm just so happy, I had a terrible week. I thought I'd never see you again."

"But I'm here now."

"I know," she says, and another tear follows the first. I reach for it. "Leave it," she says, "it's a good tear."

"Come here," I say, engulfing her in my arms.

"I got here as quickly as I could," she mumbles into my chest.

"It was fast. Do you live that close?"

"No, I live in Sesto San Giovanni. It's maybe thirty minutes from here by car."

"Then how did you get here so quick?"

"Mia nonna, um, my grandmother; she lives close to here. My graduation is today, I tell you. So, my family, they will all meet me there soon."

"What time is that?"

"Is at two."

I glance down at my wrist. "That's just a few hours from now."

"Yes, I know, my family has maybe already arrived."

"And that's where you stayed last night?"

"No, I stay with my boyfriend."

"Oh?"

"No, stupid, I kid you too." She shakes her head. "Yes, of course I stay with her."

"Well, that's nice."

"I tell you I stay with her sometimes, no?"

"No, I don't think you did."

"Yes, she gets lonely, so I stay with her. It makes her happy."

"I'm sure it does."

"Oh no," she says to herself.

"What is it?"

"Nothing. I just realized something."

"What?"

"When I got your message, I run screaming out of the house. She probably thinks I'm crazy, or maybe that something is wrong."

"What are you gonna tell her?"

"I don't know, I will think of something. She don't hear so good, so maybe she doesn't hear me."

"Let's hope so," I say, staring at her, wondering what would happen if I confessed how I feel. "Listen, I know I need to get going, graduation and all, and I don't want to keep you."

"I don't want to go anymore. I don't care about it."

"Well, you have to. It's kind of a big deal. And it'll make your family happy."

"Yes, I know you are right. I wish you could come, but it's in the theater, and I have no more tickets."

"It's ok, I'm sure I'll see you again before I leave town."

"Shut up, don't be crazy. Please see me tonight."

"But it's your birthday, I'm sure you have plans. I can just see you tomorrow if you're free, it's not a big deal."

✈

"No, that's no good for me."

"You can't see me tomorrow?"

"No, I have to see you tonight."

"Then, you will."

"I'm to eat dinner with my family, but later, my friends, they have a party for me. Can you please come?"

"I don't want to ruin your party."

"No, it will only be ruined if you don't come. Please, it's nothing too big, just a few people, and maybe some drinking."

"Where is it?"

"Is at the Luca e Andrea café on Via Fillippo Argelati, *alle ventuno*, ahh—nine O'clock."

"Ok, Luca and Andrea at nine. Got it."

"Is maybe two or three kilometers from here, maybe too far to walk in the cold. But if you take a taxi, tell them to drop you off at the Porta Ticinese, and just walk the two minutes to the café. Otherwise, they will drive you around."

"Because I'm an American?"

"Maybe that too, but even if I go, it's easier. It can take a long time with the canal, is quicker this way."

"Ok, I'll do that. The Porta Ticinese to get to Luca and Andrea."

"What will you do till then?" she asks.

"Not sure, probably walk around. Any suggestions?"

"Mmm... you already seen Duomo Di Milano. So, then there's the Castello Sforzesco, which is close to the Arco Della Pace. If you want to see paintings, you can go to Pinacoteca di Brera or Santa Maria delle Grazie. And if you want to go for shopping or café, you can go to the Galleria Vittorio Emanuele. And there are many more things. Tell me what you want to see?"

"I think I'll just walk around."

"You don't want to see sights?"

"I came to see you."

"And I can't wait to see you tonight. Honestly, I can't tell you how much it means that you are here, and I hope you know that I hate to leave you."

✈

"I know," I say, and she gives me another soft kiss.

I haven't been to Milan, and wouldn't mind catching *The Last Supper*, but I'm not up for much sightseeing, so instead, I spend my afternoon in a small café close to the cathedral, re-reading *A Farewell to Arms*. I have risotto for lunch and some sort of super crispy cookie. And before Catherine Barkley goes into labor, I make my way to Maruzzella for a margherita pizza, a cup of Chianti, and a few bottles of Moretti. When I'm too full to drink, I walk to the hotel for a short nap and a long shower.

It's cold and windy as I stubbornly walk instead of the suggested cab. Thankfully, I'm in my gray jacket and black hoodie.

The café is an unpretentious watering hole. The room is dark, with antique checkered floors and an old wooden bar holding about a hundred bottles of booze. My first impression is *yes*. It's definitely the kind of place I'd pick myself. The bar isn't big, but it's busy. I order a beer and search for the birthday girl, but she finds me first.

"Max, you made it." She hugs me hard and appears surprised. I am a little late, but she doesn't mention it. Instead, she stares into me, like she's memorizing each piece of parted hair or wrinkle in my smile.

She's enchanting in her form-fitting strapless dress. Her thick-shiny hair is down, and other than a light lip stain, she's makeup-free. But she doesn't need it though; she's so unique, it would only hide her beauty.

"I want to introduce you to my friends," she says, taking my hand. "But, I'm sorry, because only one of them speaks any English. I'm sure it won't be too fun for you."

I kiss her again and tell her not to worry, then follow her to her friends.

Greeted by a variety of kisses, handshakes, and genuine hugs, she proudly introduces me to everyone. There's Abrianna, Elisa, Francesca, Sofia, Bria, Regina, Elizabetta, Carolina, and Antonio. They're all nicely dressed and friendly in demeanor.

✈

But she was right. They don't speak a lick of English, so I scope out what everyone's drinking and excuse myself.

I return a few minutes later with two bottles of wine, one white, one red, and a Peroni for Antonio. *Grazie, grazie, grazie.* They all thank me as I refresh their glasses. I learned a long time ago that winning over friends is nearly as important as getting the girl herself. If they like you, they'll go to battle for you, but if they don't, they'll constantly be whispering worries in her ear.

Staring at me, I can see she appreciates my attempt to connect with her crew; she's not smiling, but rather eying me with an exceptionally endearing glow.

I can't understand anyone, nothing, and they certainly can't understand me, even the one who's supposed to, but it doesn't matter, we're all having a nice time. Raffaella translates the important stuff, to keep me in the conversation, or at least on topic.

I come to understand that some are her friends from home, some from work, and others from school. They're all very nice and appear to genuinely care about her.

After the wine, they bring out a cupcake with a candle, and all sing happy birthday, or at least what I assume is happy birthday, as it's in the same melody. "*Tanti auguri a te, tanti auguri a te, tanti auguri a Raffaella, tanti auguri a te.*" Her face flushes red, but she's happy as hell, and so am I.

I order two bottles of Asti, and the celebration continues without wants.

It's around midnight when she asks me to take her home. Obviously, I agree, and we say our goodbyes.

The wind had died. And though it's cold, it's quite pleasant, so we walk.

"I know you don't have fun tonight because my friends don't speak no English, but I'm so glad you came to be with me."

"What are you talking about? I had a great time," I say.

✈

"No, that is a lie. I know it's hard when nobody speaks your language."

"Listen, I got to hang out, drink beer, and stare at you all night. Believe me, I had a blast."

"You did stare at me di whole night."

"I'm sorry," I say.

"No, don't be. I loved it."

"Good, cause more is coming." I squeeze her hand.

"Max, you are so sweet to me. Just for you to be here is so incredible."

"I just wanted to wish you *tanti auguri a Raffaella*."

"Ahh, you do speak Italian. And you a good singer too." She smiles and kisses me. "Tell me something else in Italiano."

"No, I've got nothing," I say.

"C'mon, you spent the whole day in Milano. You are smart. I know you pick something up."

"Really, I've got nothing."

"Please, say something. Anything, I am sure you know something."

"Ok, maybe I've got one."

"Yes—yes, please," she pushes.

So in the deepest, manliest attempt at an Italian accent, I let out a low and loud, "Chowww."

"Ahhhhh, you were right, you got nothing." She laughs. "That was terrible."

"Terrible?"

"Yes, is no good. You a crazy man."

"That's how they said it to me all day," I say.

"No, nobody says like that. I promise you, you just crazy."

"Chowww," I try again.

"No, is not like that, where do you hear that?"

"That's how they were saying it."

"Who?"

"Everyone," I say.

"Then they were making fun of you. You didn't say like that to anyone today, do you?"

✈

"No."

"Good, now say it again, but not like that. It's *ciao*."

"Chowww."

"No, no, no... is not chowww. Where you hear that? Is ciao or ciao-bella. Nobody says chowww."

"But that's how they said it."

"No, you just imagine it. Now say ciao."

"Chow."

"No, is not chow, is ciao."

"Ciao," I say.

"Yes, that's better. Say it like that."

"Ciao."

"Yes, good... now come here and kiss me, you crazy little monkey." I pull her into me. It's intense at first and softens as we sink into it. I press her up against an old brick building, and we lose ourselves for a second until she pushes me away.

"Oh, Max, you driving me crazy, I don't want to stop."

"Then don't," I whisper.

"I wouldn't. Believe me—I wouldn't, but this is mia nonna's building, and I don't think she like it very much if she see me kissing you like this." I shoot up straight, step back, and quickly search the scene.

"It's ok, I don't think she's awake this late." She's smiling, and I relax.

"Can I take you out for a birthday dinner tomorrow?"

"How about I take you somewhere?" she says.

"Sure... where do you want to go?"

"Do you like the Italian mountains?"

"I've never been."

"Good, I take you to Como tomorrow."

"I'm in," I say. "How will we get there?"

"We take the train. It's less than one hour. I can be at your hotel at twelve. Is that ok for you?"

"Sounds perfect."

"Oh, it's gonna be wonderful."

"I'm already looking forward to it," I say.

"How long are you really staying?"

✈

"We'll talk about it tomorrow."

"No, tell me now."

"I'm gonna go," I say.

"No, don't go yet. You don't even know where you are."

I step back, look up at the sky, and point into the stars, pretending to navigate. "I'll find my way."

"Ah, you are so crazy."

"I know." And I turn to walk away, but she grabs my jacket and pulls me in.

"Don't go yet—stay with me five-more minutes."

I kiss her; it's deep and effortless. I want to stay, but everything about this day, this night, this moment, has surpassed expectations, and I don't want to get greedy. So, I cut the kiss short, turn, and strut down that cold cobblestone street.

"Good night, Raffaella, happy birthday," I say over my shoulder.

"In Italiano," she calls back.

"*Tanti auguri.*"

"Thank you, Max, I had a wonderful night."

"See you tomorrow," I say, before disappearing into the dark Northern Italian night.

CHAPTER 19

So Crazy

I WAKE AROUND NINE to a text from Natasha: *Can I see you next weekend? I can come to HK, or I can get you a ticket to Moscow. I miss you.* I don't know how to respond, so I don't. I eat breakfast and shower.

Raffaella messages me that she's downstairs and greets me with a kiss. We grab a cab to the Milan Central Station, where she refuses to let me pay for our tickets, saying she *won't talk to me the rest of the day* if I do, so I don't.

We board a red and gray SBB Express, which takes just thirty-six minutes from Milan to Como. Our half-empty car is clean and quiet, and our conversation quickly gets serious.

"Max, I still can't believe you are here. It doesn't feel like it can be real, but it is real, isn't it?"

"I'm really here," I say.

"Yes, of course you are here, but it just seems so unreal to me. Do you understand what I am saying?"

"I think so."

"No, you can't know, because it is your plan. You know you are coming, so it's different for you. But for me, it's like a fairy-tale. Like something from a movie, a story that would never happen in real life, but when you see it, you cry because you are so happy. You try to imagine what it must be like, and then, oh, I don't know, I don't even know what I'm saying."

"Well, it happened... I'm here... and it's real." My eyes effortlessly sink into hers.

"Why did it happen? Why did you come here? And if you say the gelato, I will cut you."

"You know why I'm here."

✈

"No, I don't understand it. Please, tell me what would make a man like you fly around the world to see me? Really, I'm flattered, don't think that I'm not, but I don't get it is all."

"I can't put it into words."

"Please, just tell me so that I can try to understand."

I think for a half-second, then turn and point to her reflection in the frosty window. "Do you see what I see?"

"I see you... and a girl with a big pony and a puffy coat." I laugh. "What do you see, Max? Tell me."

I have nothing scripted, but words spew. "Well, I've been walking around this world for thirty-two years, right?"

"Yes, you are old, I know that already." I laugh again, but I also begin trembling.

"Ok, well, in all that time—of getting old. I've never met anyone like you, not even close. You're the most strangely exciting person I've ever met in my life, and the thing is, I know you're even so much more than what I've seen so far, and I want to know it all. I want to learn everything there is to know about you."

"You think I'm strange?" Her eyes on mine, her bottom lip bit.

"Yes, I do. But you're also gorgeous, and graceful, and playful, and glamorous, and authentic, and that's not even it. I don't know how to describe it. I'm sure I sound stupid, but when I saw you that night—I just knew. And after that first day with you—I knew, I knew. I don't even know what I knew, but I did. If that even makes sense. And then after you left, I thought about you a ten-times more—maybe a million times more than anyone I've ever thought of in my life. I would dream about you while I was awake, and look forward to sleeping so that I could dream about you again. I don't know why I came exactly, but I knew I had to, I had to see you, I just had to be with you." In saying that, I realize it's the most honest I've ever been with anyone, and it's the most honest I've ever been with myself.

"Max, that is the sweetest thing I ever hear." She stares into me, straight into my soul. "I have to tell you something."

✈

"What is it?" I ask, scared she'll say I'm stupid, that I've been living in some inflated self-prophesying fantasyland, that I must be a fucking idiot to have flown here for some far-fetched fairy-tale that will never fly.

"I know what it is that you cannot say." Her eyes lock on mine.

"Oh?"

"Yes, I know precisely what it is that you mean. Max, you are handsome, there's no doubt about that, but there are good-looking guys everywhere, especially here in Italy."

"That's good to know." I shrink a bit.

"No, listen... it's like you say, there is something about you, but I cannot say it. I know you are strong, but I only feel gentleness. I know you are a man, but I only see a shy little boy. I know you are confident, but I see uncertainty and distrust in your eyes—like you don't believe in anything. But you are here, so I think that maybe you do."

"Maybe I do what?" I ask, and she pauses for a second, or several—it feels like forever.

"Maybe you felt it too."

"Felt what?" I ask anxiously.

"Max, I have to confession something."

"What's that?" I don't correct her.

"When I first saw you walk into that ballroom with that blonde girl, I feel so strange inside. I never met you, but I was so jealous of her. I wished it was me that was on your arm, and I knew I had to talk to you."

"I didn't know that; I mean, I didn't see you till... you know."

"Yes, I know. But I saw you, and I watch you. And I saw you when you were going to the nametag table."

"You did?" I ask.

"Yes, I tell you I see you with your friend, no?"

"You did," I say, recalling our conversation in the car.

"The truth is. I saw you walking from your table, so I walk to meet you. But then you stopped at the bar to have shots. I tried to wait for you, but I was standing in the middle of the room looking silly, and you seemed worried—like you could drink forever. So, after maybe five minutes, I decided to go to the check-in table. Standing there, in the line, I didn't have any idea that you were behind me, not until I turned around. When I saw you, and you were looking at me, I don't even know what happened, but my heart—oh. I couldn't say anything to you. I couldn't even smile when I walked by you."

"Is this real?" That same strange feeling from the first time I saw her overtakes me.

"Yes, really, it's true." She sighs. "And I have another confession."

"Tell me."

She bites her lip as she looks up at me. "Um, well... the truth is... that I don't even smoke cigarettes."

Confused, my head tilts. "What does that even mean?"

"Well, that night, after you see me at the nametag table, I watched you. I was far away, but I could see you. You were looking all around the room, and I kept imagining that you were looking for me, but I couldn't believe it. So, after I can't take it anymore, wondering if you were. I tell my kid brother to give me a cigarette, and then I go outside, hoping that you would come for me, and you did. You came for me, Max. I couldn't believe it, but you did. You came for me."

"Of course I came for you."

"When I see you, I knew then that it was me you were looking for the whole time, and my heart, oh it beat so fast—like a baby bird. I was so nervous as you walked to me. It felt like forever for you to reach me, but when you did, and I see that you were nervous too, I was ok. You didn't even know it, but your nervousness calmed me, so that I could speak to you."

"I don't believe this," I say.

"You don't believe me?"

"No—I mean yes, of course I believe you. It's just this. I can't believe this." I search her eyes, almost scared I'm still back in the hotel, asleep, and that this all a dream.

"I never feel like that in my whole life," she whispers.

"Neither have I."

"Do you think it's possible?"

"What's that?" I ask.

"Do you think it's possible for two people who never meet before to fall crazy for each other?"

"I don't know... I don't think I did... but I do now."

"I don't want to sound like a... like a psycho girl... but, I feel like meeting you that night, it somehow changed me."

"Yeah?"

"It did. I know it did," she says, her eyes penetrating. "But then I had to say goodbye to you, and I thought for sure I'd never see you again."

"And how do you feel now?" I ask.

"Like you say, I can't even say it. It's just inside me. It's here, and here, and here." She points to her throat, her chest, and her stomach.

"Come here." I pull her in and kiss her. I've never been so elated in my life. I don't say I love you, and neither does she, but I have no doubt I do. I don't know that much about love, but I know this is it.

The train slows as we slide into the station.

"Come on," she says, taking my hand—tugging me off the train and onto the platform. The air is colder up here: it's wet, smells of the mountains, and sort of slaps you in the face. But before I can catch my bearings, or even zip my coat, she pulls me into her—and kisses me. It's a kiss, unlike any before it. It's almost too effortless, and I'm almost too happy. And with our lips pressed, I purposely pay attention to every push, pull, taste, and texture, hoping to never forget even a second of this sensation.

From the San Giovanni station, she tells me it's about a ten-minute walk to the lake, and it probably is if we didn't stop and make out on every corner.

Most of the narrow roads are brick or stone. The buildings are either high-rise apartments with tons of terraces or older Italian style homes—painted in pale yellows, light pinks, and various tints of tan, all with wooden shutters and wrought-iron Juliet balconies. Faded cloth awnings cover most of the cafés and small shops. And every block has its own distinct smell: cured meats, fresh-baked bread, pungent cheeses, fragrant flowers, or fresh fish. There's a cold fog, snow in the streets, and church bells singing in the distance.

"We're almost there," she says, and I can smell the lake, but I'm craving her lips, this time against the baby-blue wall of a small bakery before we continue our quest.

She gasps when she sees it. "There it is." We cross the street that hugs the shore and stare out at that icy body of fresh water, surrounded by snow-covered foothills dotted by distinguished estates.

"Isn't it wonderful?"

"It's breathtaking," I say, but I'm looking down at her. I mean sure, the lake is fine, but she's all I see.

"When I was young, my father would drive us up here on the weekends. We would sit here in this same spot. He would smoke cigarettes, and I would have café, and we'd talk for hours. My time here, in these mountains, is maybe my most favorite memory, and now I'm here with you, my most favorite person." I say nothing, just smile. "Do you know that I am so happy right now?" She says.

"Sure," I murmur, my mind adrift, searching for what I want to say.

I wasn't planning on bringing this up until tonight, but after her confession on the train, and seeing how happy she is at this moment, in these mountains, I can't think of a better time to say what I came all the way here to say. "Raffaella"

"Yes?"

"What if I told you we could spend this winter together in the mountains, what would you say?"

"I would say... what are you talking about?"

"You love the mountains, right?"

"Yes, you know I do."

"Have you ever heard of Jackson, Wyoming?"

"No, I don't know a Jackson, who is he?"

"It's not a person, it's a place," I say, nearly stuttering.

"Ah, then no, I don't know it."

"Have you ever heard of the Grand Tetons?"

"No, I don't know a Teton."

"How about Yellowstone National Park?"

"Yes, it's famous for the geyser."

"That's right, and well, the Grand Tetons, well, they're famous for being these big beautiful mountains. They're a part of the Rocky Mountains in the state of Wyoming, and they're right by Yellowstone."

"Ok," she says, likely looking for a meaning behind my random geography lesson.

"Well, Jackson is the town that's near these mountains. It's a nice town, small and quiet like this one." I hear myself stammer, so I start rambling at an auctioneer's pace. "Listen, I've been to lots of places, and these mountains I'm talking about are as good as mountains get. I mean, they're really something. And well, my dad, he has a house there. But he doesn't really use it; it's just sitting there, empty. And well, I was hoping you would come with me, and we could go spend the winter together. The house is big. It has a great big fireplace, and it sits right there on the side of those mountains. I'm telling you they're really something special, and you'd see them every day. We'd be right there—in the middle of everything. I think you would be happy there. In fact, I know you would. We would. What do you say?"

"Max, I don't understand everything you just say to me, but I am sure that you are a crazy boy. What are you talking about?"

"I'm talking about you coming with me to America and spending the winter with me in the mountains."

"Ah, I was right... you are crazy."

"I'm serious," I say. "I swear, I've never been more serious about anything in my life."

"Truly?"

"Yes, truly."

✈

"Oh, Max, you really are so crazy. Of course, it sounds wonderful, it's like a dream, and I'm so happy that you even say that to me, but I can't just run away with you to America. It's not real. It can't make sense."

"It doesn't have to make sense; if it's a dream, and if you want it to happen, then what's holding you back? This is real. It's why I'm here. It's what I came here to ask you. I want you to come with me, no, I need you to come with me. I need you to take a chance on me, and to be a part of my life."

"Oh Max, you are so crazy, and I want to so bad, you must know that I do. But my parents, they will never let me go to America. You know that."

"I'm not gonna pretend like I know your parents, but I know they'd want you to be happy. And if you want this, if you want to see the world, see America, live in the mountains, then I'm sure they'd support you. Wouldn't they?" I mean they'd have to, right?

"It's not that easy. And I tell you, I can't afford it. Even if they say yes—I can't pay to go."

"You don't have to pay for anything, I'll get the tickets, and I'll take care of you. I promise you won't have to worry about a thing, and you'll love it there. I know you will, I just know it."

"I can't ask you to pay for me, it's not right."

"But you're not asking, I'm offering, because I want you there, I want you to be with me. I don't care about the money. Whatever it costs, it's worth it. It's worth it to me. You're worth it to me."

"But my job, and my grandmother, I mean I cannot just leave them. How long are you talking about?"

This response knocks me back within myself. Maybe she doesn't want to come. I don't want to talk her into anything, have to persuade her, or pressure her into something she doesn't want. I just want her. And I want her to want it too. "I don't know, maybe three months, but you could come back whenever you want: if you miss your grandmother, or your friends, or your parents, or anything, you can always come back. I'm only asking that you give it a shot. I mean, what do you have to lose, really?" My shoulders sink as my plan appears to be falling apart.

"Three months? How can I do that? I need a visa and money, and I don't know, there are so many things. I mean, it's nice to think about. It really is, but it's impossible. It's just not real, Max."

"If you want it to happen, it's real. I've already looked into everything; you just have to apply for an ESTA, and you could be ready to leave in just two or three days."

"Two or three days? What about Christmas? And what about my job? I mean, I can't just leave my job in three days."

"I don't mean that you have to leave in three days, I only mean that you could. And I understand if you want to be with your family for Christmas. I'm not saying that you can't, we can go after, it doesn't matter. We can go whenever you want. If you want to come with me, I'll go whenever you're ready." *I've failed. I know it.* My body feels heavy and faint. She's not ready for this. Listening to my heart over my head, I moved too far, too fast, and now I've scared her. She's trying to be polite, but I'm sure she's searching for a way out.

"Actually, my family is gonna do their Christmas in France this year, and I probably not gonna go anyway, but it's still crazy. You are so crazy, Max. What am I gonna say? Oh papà, I'm going to run away to America with a man I met last week. I don't think you understand; he will kill me, and if he don't kill me—then my mamma gonna kill me, and then they gonna kill you."

"Again, I don't know your family, but I'm sure if you told them in the right way, they'd support you. And as for your friends, they'll still be your friends when you get back, and your job will still be here, nothing will change except for you. The only question is, do you want to come with me? Do you want to be with me?"

"Oh Max, please don't think I don't, because I do, I do. It sounds incredible, it's like nothing I ever imagined, but I cannot go to America in a few days. Maybe in six months or a year, but a few days, it's impossible. It's not even close to reality. And I don't even know how you think of these things."

"Why not? Why not now? Why not with me? This is your time. No, this is our time. Believe me, what we have doesn't happen every day. This right here doesn't happen every day. So when it does, you have to grab ahold of the moment. Well, this is me grabbing ahold of this moment—with everything I have; because I want you. I want you to come with me. No, I need you to come with me. I want to learn everything about you. I want to risk it all, right here, right now. Because, if it goes anything like I know it will, then for the rest of our lives, we'll be able to tell our friends and our family, and maybe even our children someday, how crazy we were, and how we spent that one incredible winter together in the mountains of America, and how it changed us forever."

"Ok," she sighs.

My throat tightens, and my stomach sinks. "Ok? As in you'll come with me, ok?" I ask, desperately wide-eyed.

"Yes, I will come with you, but hurry and kiss me before I come to my senses." I don't hesitate. I wrap my arms around her waist and pull her lips to mine. Cold tears of joy collect in the corners of my eyes as my chest warms to a temperature it's never touched. I'm not much for pictures, but I impulsively pull out my phone and snap the scene—as raw and real as it is—so that one day, when I'm old and senile, and my memory has gone to shit, I can look back on this moment and see how crazy happy I am.

We walk to the Ristorante Imbarcadero, a sophisticated Italian eatery just off the lake. I get the risotto and prawns, and she gets a salad. Then I tell her all about the cabin, the Tetons, and the town of Jackson. The more I tell, the more emotionally invested she appears.

We talk about what she's to tell her parents. It's obvious she doesn't care to lie to them, but determines a fib—a stretch on the truth—to be the only way. She decides on a story of an American classmate—who invited her to come back to America at the last second, and how it'd help her English. I can see she takes no joy in lying to her parents, but determines the cause worthy and is willing to wiggle on a few details.

We decide to leave on Thursday, only four days from now. This is enough time to get her visa waiver, get her shifts covered at work, and give her parents time with her before taking off. She plans to tell them tonight after dinner, but she isn't looking forward to it.

After lunch, we cut the trip short and catch the next train back to Milan. I kiss her goodbye and wish her luck. She tells me, "I'll call you the moment my father stops strangling me."

Upon returning to my room, I book the airline tickets, crossing my fingers they won't go to waste.

She texts me at 7:15: *Max, I'm with my parents so I can't talk, but I'm coming with you to America! My father thinks it's a good idea and is glad about me studying English. I can't even believe it! I'm so happy!*

That's Great! I say, my fingers trembling as I type.

She writes me right back: *I have already changed my work for Thursday and Friday, but have now promised to work a double tomorrow and a dinner shift on Tuesday. So will you please come to see me at my job tomorrow?*

Yes, definitely. Where is it? I ask.

It's La Locanda del Gatto Rosso in Galleria Vittorio Emanuele. Any time is ok, she writes.

Ok, I'll see you tomorrow. I already booked our tickets. Send me your email, and I'll send them to you.

Raffaella-Bellini143@gmail.com, I can't wait. I'm so happy. I already know that I won't sleep tonight.

Same here! Call me if you can't. See you tomorrow.

Ok, good night Max.

Good night, Raffaella.

✈

CHAPTER 20

La Galleria

I WAKE LATE—the deepest sleep I can recall. Missing the free breakfast, I order a prosciutto sandwich, shower, and turn on some Italian television, determined to impress Raffaella with a few new words. I'd received a few random texts from friends asking *where I am* and *what am I up to?* But I still have one message hanging over me. I want to pretend she never happened, but she did, and she doesn't deserve to be ghosted.

Hey Natasha, I'm not in Hong Kong anymore. I'm heading back to the US and can't meet up anytime soon. Please know this has nothing to do with you. You did nothing wrong. I hope you can understand.

Not wanting to deal with a potential response, I power off my phone the second I hit send. I'm completely aware this is the coward's way out, and I don't really feel good about it. But the alternative wasn't any better.

I make my way to Raffaella's restaurant in the Galleria Vittorio Emanuele, one of the world's oldest malls. With its glamorous gothic architecture and grandiose glass arcade, it feels as though you may stumble past Napoleon coming out of Gucci.

Upon arrival at the restaurant, I ask the hostess to *please put me in Raffaella's section.* She seems to be expecting me, studies me with an approving eye, and seats me.

"Ah, you came," Raffaella calls out.

"Did you think I wouldn't?"

"Hurry and give me a kiss." She bends and plants a quick one on me.

She's in a white-collared shirt, black apron, matching tie, hair pulled into a ponytail, and somehow—she's the most beautiful I've ever seen her.

"How's your day been?" I ask.

"Oh, it's been a terrible day."

"Terrible? Why?"

"Because I was so excited last night, I didn't sleep."

"Not at all?"

"No, I don't think so."

"I told you to text me if you couldn't."

"I know, but I don't want to bother you. I want you to be fresh and happy when you come to see me."

"I'm sorry that you're tired. But at least you look good."

"Stop it! I look terrible, and you know it," her hand races to her necktie.

"No, don't hide it, I like that tie. You should wear it the next time we go out."

"You are a jerk to me, and I hate you. No, no, I don't. I take it back."

"At least you'll sleep good tonight," I say.

"Maybe, but I changed my shift again, and now I work tomorrow morning too, so we'll see."

"Why did you do that?"

"The girl, the one who switched me for Friday, she asked me to cover her, so I have to do it."

"Are you gonna be alright? Do you need some help?"

"Yes, please go take my tables, and I go take a nap."

"I'll do it."

"I know you would because you are a sweet man," I smile. "Max, do we really go to New York as the ticket says?"

"For two nights. If that's ok?"

"Yes, of course, I can't even believe it. I'm so excited. I don't know what to say, it's like a dream."

"Well, you have to go to sleep before you can dream."

"I won't sleep for the rest of the week, I know it."

"I'm sure you will," I say. A table signals her.

"Ok, I have to go check on them, do you want a drink?"

"I'll take a beer."

"Moretti?"

"Please."

✈

Sitting there, watching her work her tables, is way more satisfying than any cross-country cruise or Peak view, and I feel beyond blessed as she returns with my beer.

"Gees, that took long enough. The service here is pretty slow," I say.

"Shut up, or I spit in your food." She scans to see that nobody heard her.

"I see how you learned English in this place."

"Yes, I tell you, many tourist customers."

"You didn't tell me you speak Chinese?" I say, glancing over at the six-top of Chinese customers.

"I wish. I think it's a very interesting culture, but it's too difficult to learn."

"Do you speak any other languages?"

"I tell you my mother is Moroccan, no?"

"No, you didn't. But that explains it."

"Explains what?"

"Why you're so beautiful."

"No, I'm not," she says, squishing her face and pulling on her ponytail.

"You know that you are, especially with that tie."

"I'm gonna kill you." Her eyes lift high.

"Then I'd die happy."

"Don't talk like that." She slaps my arm. "But I have a question."

"What's that?"

"Do you know where is Morocco?"

"Sure," I say, recalling that trip I never took to Tangier.

"Where is it?" she asks as if she doesn't believe me. So I make the shape of Africa with my flattened hand.

"This is Africa, this is north, this is south, this is the Sahara, and this is Morocco. You think I don't know?"

"I know you know, I was just testing you. I only ask because I think many American people don't know it. They always ask me *where am I from?* And I tell them that my momma is Moroccan, and they say, *ahh South America, or cool the Middle East.*"

✈

"Well, I'm not as dumb as I look," I say, smirking.

"No, I know you are a sharp little monkey. And not like a knife." She winks.

"So, you speak Arabic?"

"Yes, of course."

"Fluently?"

"Sì."

"Say something."

"What should I say?"

"Whatever you want. Whatever comes to your mind first, I just want to hear something."

"Ok, how about, *aarifu ana Allaha arsalaka ilay*."

"Yes, that's great. What did you say?"

"Don't worry about it."

"No, come on."

"I tell you another time, I promise."

"You better." I squint. "Are there any other languages you're keeping from me?"

"I know French, and Spanish, and some Tedesca, is ah German."

"Fluently?"

"Yes, but not so much German."

"Do you speak French and Spanish as good as you do English?"

"My French is good, it's better than my English, but my Spanish is maybe about the same."

"Damn," I say, so damn impressed I don't even know what to say.

"What, you like that I speak other languages?"

"It's just that most people don't, or can't."

"I think American people cannot, but most European people know more than one language. It's not so special."

"Sure, but not five. You're like Cleopatra."

"No, I am not." A blush flushes her face. "It's only because of my family, that I must know them."

"I want to learn everything about you, Raffaella."

"And you will. That's why we go to America together, no? We will learn everything about each other."

"I can't wait," I say.

"Me either. Even right now, the customers give me their orders, but I just keep thinking: America, America, mountains, Bobo, America."

"Stop it." I smile.

"Is true, I don't lie to you. But now I must go check my tables. What do you want to eat?"

"I'm good, I don't need anything."

"No, I bring you something."

"Then, you pick."

I've been around the world several times, yet I've never met anyone like her, not even close, and now, she's about to spend the winter with me. I started this journey on a whim. An idea that came to me in a daydream, a daydream within a hangover. A hangover brought on by an attempt to drink away any memory of her. And now she's coming with me. I'm about to spend every day with this unbelievable beauty, making new memories, unforgettable memories that will never fade. I feel like the luckiest guy in the world. And to think, this could have easily never happened if I hadn't gotten on that flight, or that ferry that afternoon, or gone to Hong Kong when I did, or even if I never left that bar with Anna ten years ago. If even one of those things hadn't happened, I'd never be sitting here now, blissfully happy and overwhelmingly optimistic about my future. And then suddenly, my free-flowing serotonin-secretion ceases, and seemingly out of nowhere, like an IED, doubt hits me, and it hits hard. Not about the level to which I care for her, there's no doubt there, I'm sure of that. Instead, my sudden influx of fear is of her herself and what she could do to me. What if she grows tired of me? What if she wakes up one day and realizes I'm nothing special? She may be my savior, or perhaps a seductive Siren's song, my salvation, or my undoing, and she doesn't even know it.

She turns towards me with a tray full of food.

"That was quick," my voice unsteady.

✈

"Yes, you distract me, so I accidentally put in this order two times, so now it is yours."

"That works."

"I'm not sure what you like, but this is a grilled octopus, with cherry tomatoes and balsamic vinegar. And this is a fillet of sea bass: with mussels, and clams, and shrimps, and calamari in a nice red sauce. And I know you like a Moretti."

"Thank you, it all looks great, but I don't think I can eat all this."

"It's for two people, but you are a big boy, so I think you can do it. But hurry, and give me a kiss before you smell of fish breath." She leans down, and I do. "Let me know if you need anything else ok, Bobo."

Everything is excellent. The fish melts in my mouth like pats of fresh butter. The clams are just right, and the shrimp are large and fresh. And though I'm not typically a big balsamic fan, it's mild, and the slight bitterness perfectly complements the chewy cephalopod.

My beer doesn't last long, so I switch to water and try not to think about the doubt that had just flashed through my thoughts. But as I watch her work, and smile, and laugh with complete strangers, I almost become afraid of her. She's been on my mind since the moment I saw her. And if she did this to me in a week, what could she do to me over a winter? And somewhere deep inside of me, a small selfish spot within myself, I contemplate making a run for it, calling it all off, jetting home, and shielding my heart from any potential suffering. But as she turns to me, and I get another look at those unselfish eyes, that ponytail, and terrible tie, I immediately suffocate the spark of insecure silliness that had just soured my soul. That's what she does to me, though. She makes me forget about reality, about consequences, or anything other than how much I want her close to me.

Walking my way, her tray holds a bottle of beer, and what looks like a small wineglass filled with a pale wine.

"Here, I got you another beer, and you know grappa?"

"I don't think so," I say.

"Is like brandy, but made from grapes. It's popular here, I think you will like it." She hands it to me, and I sip it.

"It's good."

"I promise, I don't do you wrong, Bobo. This is Grappa Po di Poli, is my favorite one, but be careful, is very strong."

"Sure," I say.

"How's the food?"

"Everything's delicious."

"I'm glad you like it. I wanted to leave you alone, so you could enjoy, but I missed you. And I can't concentrate. My mind is everywhere. I'm making a mess of many things."

"I'll get out of your hair soon," I say.

"No, don't be silly, it's not you. Well, it is you, but it's everything. It's the flight and New York, and the mountains. I'm so excited, I'm going crazy inside."

"Me too."

"I just can't believe it's real. I know I keep saying it, but I'm just waiting for you to tell me you are kidding, or that you change your mind or something. I keep thinking that maybe you come to your senses and run away, but you don't. It's just so incredible, and I feel that I am so lucky."

Impossible, I think. Questioning if maybe our minds are attuned to the same subtle frequency. And somehow she sensed that selfish second that ambushed my thoughts, and that it hurt her.

"I haven't changed my mind," I say, taking ahold of her hand. "And believe me, I'm the lucky one here."

"Oh, Max, what are we going to do in New York?"

"We can do anything. Anything you want."

"Yes, but what?"

"Anything: we can go to a Broadway play, or go see the Rockettes, or visit the Statue of Liberty, or the top of the Empire State Building, whatever you want to do. You tell me, and we'll do it."

"I just want to see it, and be in it, be a part of it. And I want to try American food."

"We can always stay longer, I can change the tickets."

"No, two nights is perfect, but tell me what we will do?"

"Anything. We can go see a show or eat at a famous restaurant like Gramercy Tavern, or we can go to a nightclub, you tell me, we'll do whatever you want. Just name it."

"Can we go to see the Rockefeller's Christmas tree?"

"Yes, anything."

"And can we go to The Met? I want to go so bad."

"Then we will."

"Yes?"

"Anything you want," I say again.

"Can we go for a walk in Central Park and go watch people in Times Square?"

"Yes, we'll do it all."

"And will you take me to try popular American food?"

"Anything."

"But not fancy, I want to try what real American people eat, something cheap."

"I'll take you to the cheapest place we can find."

"And can I get a picture of di bull on Wall Street for my father? He will love it."

"Yes, anything."

"Oh my God, Max, I cannot wait. I'm so happy, I just want to leave right now."

A guy two tables over signals her with a stiff hand.

"It looks like he can't wait either," I say.

She sneers back at him. "He can wait. They are Italian, they not gonna tip me anyway." I laugh. "Max, can I tell you something?"

"Anything."

"If we are in the mountains, and, I don't know, if you change your mind or something, about me being there, please, I want you to be honest with me, and tell me, so I can leave you alone."

"Only if you do the same," I say.

"It's never gonna happen, I know it." She leans down and gives me a quick kiss, and whispers, "I'm gonna bring you dessert, don't go anywhere."

✈

"And bring the check," I say, as she darts away.

I finish the remaining few pieces on my plate and the grappa before she returns.

"Do you like tiramisu?" she asks, sliding me a healthy slice.

"I do."

"Good, this one is very nice, and another grappa, but I tell you, be careful." She watches me as I take a bite of the rich cake, smiling as it slides into my mouth, waiting for my reaction.

"Mmm, it's very good." And the corners of her perfect lips peak skyward.

"I'm glad you like it, I just want you to be happy."

"You make me happy. I honestly can't remember being this happy... since... I don't even know, since I was a little kid."

"You mean since you were a little monkey." I smile.

"When am I going to see you again?"

"I'm not sure. I will be so busy this week."

"I know," I say. "When will you take care of your visa?"

"I tell you, I can't sleep last night. I already did it, I do everything, I even start packing."

"Well, that's one less thing to worry about. Our flight is at 3:40 on Thursday."

"Yes, I know, I study the ticket you send me. You know it's my first time to fly Emirates. I hear it's so nice. I'm so much looking forward to it."

"It's my first time on Emirates too."

"Yes?"

"Yeah, and we're on the Airbus. The A380, it's the big double-decker jumbo jet."

"Yes, I know, I googled it. It's my first time on a plane like that too."

"Well, I'm glad I'll be there for your first time."

Her eyes linger on mine. "Me too," she murmurs, then shiver-shakes from a chill.

"You ok?"

"Yes," she says as her face softens. "Have you been on a big plane like that before?"

"I have."

"Of course you have, you've done everything."

"That's not true."

"Oh?"

"I've never flown Emirates."

"Good," she says. "I'm glad we do it first together."

"I'm sorry it's only coach, but first-class was full."

"No, don't be crazy. I expect nothing. I'm so grateful you are even taking me and making my dreams come true."

"I'll always try to," I say.

"Try to what?"

"Make your dreams come true."

"I know you will, I know it the moment I get the picture of you at Duomo di Milano. And believe me, I will never forget it."

"I hope I can continue to surprise you."

"You don't need to surprise me to make me happy. Just be you. Yes, I'm happy to go to America, but I would be just as happy if you stayed here and be with me."

"But I'm selfish, and I want you all to myself," I say.

"And I love that you want that. Thank you."

"For what?"

"For not forgetting about me, and for not letting me slip away."

"No way," I whisper.

"When I left Hong Kong, I was sure I would never see you again."

"I couldn't live with myself if that happened."

"I know that," she says. "But only because you came for me."

"Listen, I know you have a lot to do this week, so how about we just meet at the airport on Thursday. That way, you can get everything done, and you won't have to stress."

"No, I will stress if I don't see you before then."

"But it's only a few days from now."

"I don't care, I can't be this close to you and not see you," she insists.

✈

"I could come back for your shift tomorrow?"

"Yes, you could, and you can. But I think my parents will come. I've worked here for two years now. My last shift... is a kind of big deal, no?"

"Yeah, it is. And I won't then."

"Is just that you are too handsome. I'm sure they would recognize you."

"I'm sure they wouldn't," I say. "But, you're right."

"Max, you know I'd love for you to meet them, but my father, he will lock me in a closet if he even thinks I am going to America with you."

"I don't want that," I say.

"How about I come and have a café with you tomorrow afternoon after I am finished here? Then it will only be one day where I don't see you. Is that ok for you?"

"Sounds good," I say.

"Ok, I see you tomorrow, Bobo. I'll message you when I'm finished." She leans down and quickly kisses me goodbye.

"Hold on, you didn't give me the bill."

"Finish your grappa, and don't worry about it."

"No, I'll pay for my food and drinks."

"It's already taken care of." She blows me a kiss over her shoulder. "I see you tomorrow."

I spend the rest of my evening in a small bar down the street from my hotel. It gets crowded late, but I keep to myself, in my own merry little bubble, sticking with a steady intake of two beers for every grappa—till I eventually lose track.

I wake with the taste of vomit in my mouth and a stabbing-ache between my eyes. After a shower and several doses of ineffective worms, I meet Raffaella at the cafe. She's eager to hear stories of Wyoming and all the animals we'll likely come across. I tell her of adventures I've had there over the years, and that if she's up for it, I'd take her deep into the wild and show her how to live and survive in the snow. She never stops smiling.

✈

    She can only stay an hour, so once again, I get shit-faced. I'm not sure why I drink so much those last few nights in Milan. Maybe it's to stay consistent. Maybe it's to say goodbye to an old friend. Either way, it's the happiest I'd ever been in my life, and every time I take a sip, I'd raise a glass and toast to my own bliss.

One belongs to New York instantly, one belongs to it as much in five minutes as in five years.

— Tom Wolfe

✈

CHAPTER 21
New York, New York

THE DAY OF DEPARTURE HAS COME. I shake off the harsh grip of the grappa with the regular remedies and arrive early. I'm sitting at the gate when I spot her strutting towards me. She's in a DOPE sweatshirt, ponytail, and a puffy coat. Her spandex wrapped legs appear as long skinny sticks falling from her marshmallow torso. And though she's well overdressed for the comfortable terminal temperatures, she's fresh and very beautiful.

"Oh, Max, I missed you." I stand to hug her.

"Same here," I say. She attacks me with kisses.

"You look so handsome. I like it when you wear a cap."

"You better put a hat on yourself, I think it will be cold on the plane."

"Shut up, you're a jerk. The coat is for the mountains. I didn't have no more room in my suitcase."

"Sure, whatever... but just let me know if you get a chill and need some gloves or something."

"You can tease me, but you won't be laughing when I am warmer than you in my puffy coat."

"Are you excited?" I ask.

"Are you kidding me? I don't sleep last night. I hope I can sleep on di plane."

"Did you see it yet?"

"See what?"

"The plane."

"No, which one is it?"

"It's just over there," I say, and she turns.

"Oh my God, is so big, I can't even believe it. I never see a plane like that."

✈

The first sight of an Airbus A380 is something special. And outside of anything made by Elon Musk, it's probably the most impressive piece of modern engineering I can think of. Every time I'm on one, I always doubt it will get off the ground, but it always does.

We board on time, and the superjumbo's interior is spacious, especially for economy.

With my hands on her and her lips on mine, our fellow passengers probably think we're newlyweds—who could have used another week on our honeymoon.

We toast sparkling wine upon takeoff and order more with dinner. She falls asleep just after we eat, and I don't last much longer.

New York is cold and rainy—that miserable kind that's two-degrees shy of snow—and makes you curse yourself as you step outside.

We catch a cab. As I want her to experience that virgin voyage across Brooklyn and over the bridge, that hundred-and-fifty-year-old span into the center of the universe where everything you've ever seen—suddenly seems less significant.

At nine hundred a night, 1 Hotel Central Park is definitely more than I'd spend on myself, but I want it to be perfect. I picked this place for two reasons. First, I want to make her happy, and second, because online, it looked so different from any other spot in the city. Most hotels on this trillion-dollar island pretty much play the same tune of sophisticated and stuffy. I was looking for something special, something unconventional.

Its uniqueness is apparent the second we reach the front door, which is constructed of a thousand intertwined tree branches, and opens to an industrial urban oasis: a lobby of exposed brick, steel beams, and an artful assortment of hanging plants— a far cry from the sleepy old-world elegance that goes hand-in-hand with high-end New York hotels.

And I'd have paid anything to see her smile like that.

✈

"You can't be serious, this is where we are staying?"

"For the next two nights."

"Tell me you are joking."

"You don't like it?"

"What can you mean like it? I don't even know a place like this exists, it's the most beautiful hotel I've ever seen."

Our room doesn't suck either.

"Oh my God, Max, it's perfect. I've never seen a more perfect hotel room. Can we live here?"

"If I could afford it, we would."

"I will do the dishes, I don't care," she cries.

"How do you think we're paying for this place? You start at seven."

"I would do it," she quips.

"I know you would. And we can stay longer if you want. Just let me know."

"No, I kid you. I want to go to di mountains, but this room. I can't even believe it."

"What do you think of the view?" The sun is down, so you can't see much from our corner suite, except for a massive squared-off black space surrounded by city lights.

"Is it Central Park?" she asks.

"It is."

"Oh jeez, come here, kiss me before I pass out from excitement." I wrap my arms around her and lower my lips to hers. "It's perfect, Max, thank you so much, this is so amazing."

"*Sei il benvenuto bello*," I whisper.

"Ah sì, I know you speak Italian." And she kisses me again.

The Park View Suite is significantly more per-night than the standard, but that smile on her face is worth every cent. The room is exceptional: hardwood floors, white brick walls, a chic couch, and raw-steel furniture. A luxurious glass shower and cement sink make up the minimalist bathroom.

"Max, what shall we do first?" she says, sprawling herself on the king-sized bed. Strangely, it's at this moment I realize that I've yet to be alone with her. Every time we've been together was in a bar, on a boat, a beach, or somewhere in between. She hadn't come up to my room in Milan, and she wasn't even close to seeing the apartment in Hong Kong. I've been having such a great time holding her hand and kissing her, I hadn't even thought about anything else.

"It's nearly nine, we should probably go do something," I say, swallowing hard.

"Will you come lay with me first?"

"I can do that," I say, kicking off my shoes and crawling next to her, as anxious as I've ever been, my eyes surrendering to hers. We're both smiling, the kind where the lips are pouted and pressed, but the face is full of warmth and want. A stray hair falls to her face. I brush it behind her ear, tracing my fingertips—featherlike—across her cheek, to her chin, to her neck, and along her collarbone. She's biting her lip, her eyes begging me to kiss her. I hear her swallowing, and every breath becomes an event—slow and substantial. I lift her chin, my wet lips lingering over hers before her tongue tickles mine. My fingers fall down her arm, over her hip, to the top of her thigh. Her body weakens, melting into mine, her lips quiver, her heart pounds. I pull her in tighter, her breath flutters, but her kiss strays, and her face turns.

"Max, I have to tell you something."

"What is it?"

"I don't want you to be upset." She's suddenly stressed, or maybe even scared.

"How could I be upset?"

"Please, promise you won't be mad at me."

"Of course I won't. You can tell me anything."

"Ok, well... I... well... I have never been touched by a man before."

"You're a virgin?"

"I am." I feel the back of my jaw bite, and I swallow slowly. "But I'm not just virgin," she continues. "I don't know how else to say it, but nobody ever touch me before. You know... down there."

"Never?"

"Not ever." She's flushed with fright, for what, I only imagine, I may say.

"You're extraordinary." I lean in and kiss her forehead.

"You're not disappointed?"

"No, definitely not. Why would I be disappointed?"

"Because I know you've had many girls, and I know nothing."

"I'm not disappointed at all."

"But I want you to touch me. I'm just, I don't know."

"It's ok, don't worry about it."

"You're really not upset?"

"Not even a little," I say, her eyes on mine.

"You are a perfect man."

"No, I'm not," I say softly. "I promise you that."

"Yes, you are. You are perfect for me."

I lean in, kiss the side of her head, and whisper, "Let's get out of here."

"Where do we go?"

"Let's go see New York."

It's cold, about thirty degrees, the air is wet, and the streets are shiny. I've never lived in this city, but I know it well.

We're dressed warm, so we walk. Steam geysers erupt from salty manholes, and like most of Manhattan, it smells of Christmas, as rows of fresh-cut Douglas-firs—sold by hipsters in Santa hats—line the sidewalks.

"Where are we going?" she asks.

"Just for a walk," I say, but she's too smart for me.

"No, I know-you-know."

"We're just gonna walk this way and see what we see."

"Ok, I like that," she says. "Max?"

"Yes?"

"Can I ask you something?"

"Anything."

"Do you think it is strange that I'm still virgin?"

"No, I think it's wonderful."

"Do you really mean it?"

"I really do." I squeeze her hand. "But can I ask you something?"

"Anything."

"You're beautiful—" She cuts me off.

"That's not a question, but thank you, Bobo."

I growl at her before I go on. "What I'm saying is that I'm sure lots of guys have tied to... you know. How is it that you've never... you know, been with anyone—or whatever?"

"Mmm, it is not that they have not tried... I just never really like any of them."

"So, you just haven't wanted to?"

"No, is not that exactly. Because I have, I know I have. I just never find the right person, the right connection. Until I meet you."

"You think I'm the right person?"

"I don't think it. I know it to be true. I know it since I first speak to you, and I confirm it when you first kiss me."

"But how do you know?" I ask.

"I can't say it."

"Please do."

"You really want to know?" She looks into me, her eyes squinting as though she's staring at the sun.

"Yes," I whisper.

"Ok, I tell you... I know it because... because whenever I see you, or just think about you, I'm happy and comfortable, and I feel as though I have no worries. And then when you touch me, or you touch my hand, or my face, or anywhere, it feels like there is a big beautiful butterfly in my stomach. And when I kiss you, it feels as though I am floating, like nothing else matters. I know it probably sounds silly to you like I'm some teenage girl, but that's how it is. And I'm sorry if it scares you, or is strange for you, but that's how I know."

"It isn't strange, and it doesn't scare me," I say, lifting her lips to mine, making sure she knows I am hers.

Most of the next six blocks go this way, missing *walk* signals to make out, and getting in people's way—until.

✈

"Max, what is a Radio City?"

"It's a concert hall. It's where they have the Rockette dancers."

"Ah, yes, I hear of them."

"Do you want to see them?" I ask, but her head shakes indifferently.

"Maybe if we have time tomorrow, but it's not on my list of buckets."

"You mean your bucket list?"

"Ah, yes, my bucket list. Grazie."

Radio City means we're close, but it also means we're on 50th street, the same as Nadja's apartment, which is four blocks west of us. But I'm not worried about running into her. She never sets foot in Central Park, despises Times Square, and unless there's some fashion show, we won't find her at The Met.

"Max, I see it. I knew you know. You brought me to de Rockefeller's Christmas tree." She kisses me and yanks my arm towards that massive Midtown monument.

The crowd is thick, huddled together, and full of enthusiasm as that Norway spruce sparkles spectacularly above.

"It's pretty great, huh?"

"Oh, it is even more beautiful than I picture it. How high is it?"

"I don't know, maybe a hundred feet," I say.

"But how many meters?"

"I think about thirty."

"You think is only thirty?" Disappointed that I didn't say a thousand. "It seems much higher to me."

"I think I read somewhere that this is one of the tallest ever."

"Then we are very fortunate, no? I mean... that we get to see the biggest one."

"Yeah, I think we are..." And then, as if God himself stepped in, the low city-lit clouds give way to a swift avalanche of snow. Some of the largest flakes I've ever seen.

✈

"Is snowing, Max, it's snowing, oh my God, it's snowing so good. Hurry and kiss me and make a wish." I pull her in and kiss her hard. It's powerful and passionate, and she mumbles to herself as our lips part.

"What did you wish for?" she asks.

"I can't tell you, or it won't come true."

"Ah, mia nonna say the same thing, it's bullshit, you know. A wish is a wish. It won't change anything. Now tell me what you wished for."

"Ok," I say. "I wished that I could come back to this same spot again with you next year."

"Oh yes, I like that wish very much. You are so sweet. Gimme another kiss."

"What did you wish for?" I ask.

"I wished that whenever I'm sad, I can remember this moment, and it will make me as happy as I am right now."

I wrap my arms around her and squeeze. I want to tell her *I love her* and that *I know I'll never be the same without her*, but it won't leave my lips. Then, like something out of an old black-and-white Bing Crosby film, a street entertainer turns up his stereo, and Michael Bublé's *Let it Snow* sings loud. Saying nothing, I spin her. And under the bright shade of that sparkling spruce, in a downpour of snow, we sway our smiling selves to the sounds of that spirited song.

"Max, did you plan this?"

"Plan what?"

"This."

"How could I plan this?"

"I don't know, I'm trying to figure it out, it's just too perfect. The tree, the snow, the music, it feels like magic."

"It is magic," I whisper. "Welcome to New York."

It's nearly ten when she tells me she's hungry, and my mind searches for late-night options. Wanting to save Times Square for tomorrow, I flag a taxi to take us to the Murray Hill Shake Shack.

"What we gonna eat?"

✈

"You want American food, right?" I say, as our Arijit Singh jam session concludes when our Lysol saturated cab stops on the corner of 40th and 3rd.

"Yes, I tell you."

"Well, here you go."

I pull open the door to that well-lit wood-walled American chain.

"Is the food nice here?"

"Yeah, it's pretty good."

"But is it popular?"

"You tell me." It's ten-thirty, and the place is packed.

"Yes, it's very busy. What do we eat?"

"Burgers and fries," I say.

"Like a McDonald's?"

"Kind of, but different. You'll see."

We're fifth in line, but it moves fast. I order a double cheeseburger and a large beer. And for her, a single and a mini bottle of sparkling wine. She asks for mayonnaise for her fries, and I make a disgusted face.

She secures us a seat, and our food is ready right away. And though we have a large table to ourselves, she insists I sit next to her. Says *she'd miss me* if I don't, so I do.

"How are the fries?" I ask.

"Is very delicious."

"Here, dip them in the ketchup," I say.

"No thank you, I like di mayo."

"You said you wanted American food, right? Well, no American would ever eat fries with mayo."

"Nobody?"

"No, nobody. Maybe crazy people." I cross my eyes.

"Ok, I do it."

"Here, try mine."

"But you put so much salt on them."

"It's because I'm American, we put salt on everything."

"Ok, I try it, but I feel it's gonna be gross."

She takes a fry and lightly dips it in the ketchup.

✈

"It needs more," I insist. "The more ketchup, the more American."

"Shut up, that's not true." She puts it in her mouth.

"What do you think?" I ask.

"Mmm, it's ok." But her face says otherwise. "I prefer di mayo."

"How's your burger?" I ask.

"I like it very much. Is true, it's much different from a McDonald's. But is too much meat for me."

"What do you mean, too much meat?"

"Look, is too much."

"What are you talking about? It's a thin burger. Look at mine, I have two patties."

"Yes, and yours looks terrible." She grimaces.

"So, you want less meat?"

"It's good, I enjoy the flavor. It's just a little too much meat."

"Never in my life have I heard someone say they want less meat, most people want more." I laugh. "Do you want to order something else?"

"No, I tell you, it's a nice flavor. But next time, I'll tell them to smush it more." She sees that I'm laughing. "What, you think I am strange? Maybe I'm not like those people who want a big fat burger."

"Believe me, you're not like anybody," I say.

"And neither are you." She kisses me, dips another fry in my ketchup, and feeds it to me. "You know Max, I think they have this in Hong Kong."

"What's that?" I ask.

"This place. It's called a Shake Shack, right?"

"I don't think so," I say confidently.

"Maybe, but I'm sure I have seen it before."

"I'm pretty sure it's an American thing." But she refuses to take my word for it and pulls out her phone.

"Max, can you please google it for me? My phone don't have any gigas."

"Any what?"

236
J Gatz

"Any gigas." I tilt my head, birdlike, and stare blankly. "You know, internet connection," she says.

"Ah, gigs. You don't have any gigs."

"Yes, gigas, I say that."

"Say it one more time." I smile.

"What, it's gigas, no? Do I say it funny?"

"No, you say it just fine."

I pull out my phone and google: Shake Shack in Hong Kong. *Son of a bitch.* They have one location, and it's in the damn mall.

"You're right," I say.

"I tell you, it's downtown, no?"

"Yeah, it's in the IFC mall."

"Ahh, yes, that's where I see it. I think my brother ate there, but I didn't try it."

"I don't know how I didn't know that."

"I tell you, you should listen to me. I don't lie to you, Bobo."

I shrug in surrender. "I'll never doubt you again."

"Good, now let me try your beer." I hand it to her, and she takes a sip. "It's very nice."

"I didn't know you like beer."

"I like it sometimes, and I tell you, I want to experience everything." She takes another sip.

"Do you want to try my favorite little bar in the city?"

"Yes, of course. Why do you not mention it before?"

"Because it's not that nice of a place, they only have beer. And, I didn't think about it till just now."

"Is it a popular American place?"

"No, not really. It's different, and it's too small to be too popular. It is pretty old, though. I think it's been there for over a hundred and fifty years."

"Yes, please, take me."

After the food, we walk through the snow, over to 2nd Avenue and flag a cab.

✈

McSorley's sits a block below the East Village's unofficial Little Tokyo. There's sawdust on the floor, a thousand rusty and dusty trinkets on the walls, and authentic Irish bartenders to serve up the suds. They say Abraham Lincoln once stopped in. I don't know if it's true, but it somehow makes the beer taste better.

"Do you want light or dark?" I ask her.

"I want both."

With two mugs each in hand, one light, one dark, we settle in a seat near the coal-fired furnace. The place is alive and loud, not from music, but from the natural noise of conversation. The last men's only saloon in the city is now filled with an eclectic set of diverse characters. There's a table of dads in flannel shirts flirting with smiling Spanish girls. Scottish soccer fans huddled around the TV in the back—singing songs and slapping each other. Across from us, hipsters in tight jeans and long beards toast businessmen in long coats and slicked-back hair. Next to us sits a big-shouldered black guy in a Hawaiian shirt with his arms around a pair of leather-bound blondes; the place is so damn original, it almost feels artificial.

I sit there, sipping as I watch her eyes dance around the room. I'm the happiest I remember being. She does that to me, though. She does it with her delicacy and the sincerity in her smile. I'm not attracted to her, I'm addicted to her. I haven't had her physically, yet I know I couldn't function without her.

I get up to use the restroom and grab us another round. When I return, there's a tall, dark man in a suede camel coat talking to her. I stand back and watch. I'm not jealous, or at least I tell myself I'm not as I'm sure she deals with thirsty dudes daily, but this guy handsome as hell. He looks like goddamn Mariano Di Vaio, and I doubt he hears *no* very often. After a few seconds, she waves him off and searches the room, so I move in. He says something to her in Italian, eyes me up-and-down, and disappears into the crowd. "New friend," I say, smirking.

"He's a pig."

"Hell of a handsome pig."

"Yes, he thinks so too."

"He's Italian?" I ask, handing her a fresh beer.

"He's a *Napolitano*, and a disgusting disgrace of a man."

"Why? What did he say to you?"

"Believe me, you don't want to know." She sips her beer and sits back.

"Well, now I do."

"Don't worry about it." But I stare at her, waiting for her to spill it.

"Ok, I tell you, but don't do anything. He's not worth di fuss."

"I won't," I say.

"He tells me that he could pleasure me better than the pretty boy pussy I am with and that I should leave with him."

"He's got confidence," I say.

"He is disgusting." She shakes her head. "I tell him, the only pleasure he can give me is when I see him walk away."

"Ouch."

"Then, he call me a bitch."

My eyes shoot to the back of the room, but I don't see him. "You want me to say something?" But what I mean is, *do you want me to go slap the shit out of him?*

"No, I tell you, he's not worth it. I forget about him already."

She raises her glass to signal that it's over, and we toast to "New York."

"Max, you know when I first saw you, I think maybe you are Italian."

"Were you disappointed when I wasn't?"

"No, I was relieved." She squeezes my hand. "You are Czech, no?"

"How did you know that?"

"Don't think I'm crazy, but the night you send me the tickets, I googled your surname. It's similar to a town in Czech Republic, so I imagine it must be Czech."

"It is," I say.

"Why is it like the town? Did they change it when your family came through Ellis Island?"

"Good guess."

"So, they changed it?"

"Yeah, but not at Ellis Island."

"How then?"

"You want to hear about it?"

"Yes, I want to know everything."

"Ok, well… from what I've been told, is that my great-great-grandparents came here in 1906. My grandfather didn't speak any English, but he got a job through a fellow passenger working on The Virginian Railway, it connected the coalmines to the Atlantic. The railway was a special project of Henry Rogers, who was best friends with Mark Twain. Anyway, whoever processed his employment paperwork accidentally put his birthplace as his last name. He didn't want to make a fuss about it, being happy to have a job and all, so he said nothing. But eventually, when they went to buy a house some years later, it was just easier—paperwork wise—to keep using that same name. At least that's the story my Grandfather told me. So who really knows."

"That's a nice story. But, what was the original name? Do you know it?"

"I do, it's my middle name, and my dad's too."

"What is it?"

"It's Procházka."

"Ah, I love it. What does it mean?"

"I actually just looked it up a few months ago. It means *wander*. It was a name given to traveling tradesmen."

"It makes sense why you are a traveler then. It's in your blood."

"I guess it is."

"Possibly, I am wrong, but wasn't the Czech Republic named The Kingdom of Bohemia, at the time your great-great-grandfather came here?"

"That's right, it was," I say, surprised anyone would know such a thing.

"So, if that's the case, doesn't it mean your true real name is, Bobo the Bohemian?"

✈

"You're an ass."

"And you're a cute little Bohemian." She kisses me, and we both sip our beers.

"Can I ask you something?"

"Anything for my Bohemian."

"What's a Napolitano?"

"Ah, good pronunciation."

"I've been practicing." I wink. "But what is it?"

"Mmm... I think in America, it's most similar to your hillbilly." I laugh again. "Do I say it incorrectly? Is hillbilly, no?"

"Yeah, you got it. And I get it now. But why don't you like them?"

"It's not that I don't. They don't like us. They don't like people from the north, so we don't trust them."

We order another round, and I list off insignificant facts I know about New York, from the microscopic shrimp in the water to the mass graves on Hart's Island. I'm not sure if she enjoys the trivia, but she listens actively, not just waiting for her turn to talk. And she never stops smiling, but neither do I.

Stepping outside, the snow has stopped, maybe an inch or two of accumulation. We cab it back uptown and make it to our room just as the jetlag kicks in.

"Thank you so much for tonight, Max. I can't wait to wake up."

"I can't either."

✈

CHAPTER 22

It's For You, Or It Isn't

WE WAKE EARLY. I'm well-rested and in good spirits. The comforter is warm and cozy, and we're as carefree as a couple cats. I don't want to get up, and neither does she, so we don't. Instead, I roll over and order us room service to share. I get an egg-white omelet with feta and a smoked salmon bagel with whipped cream cheese and scallions. It's promptly delivered and delicious, although I sense she's disappointed after she asks, and I tell her it isn't *a typical American meal*, though she'd never say.

We decide she's to shower first, her hair being long and thick, and needs time to dry. She selects some clothes from her oversize suitcase and pulls the large sliding door shut. I hear the water run as I fetch the *New York Times* and sit back in bed. I'm barely through the first page when the bathroom door opens again. She's standing there, hands on her hips, in her birthday suit, and a wanting stare in her eyes. "Max, if you don't mind, could you please come wash my back?" Tossing the paper over my head, I spring to my feet.

"I could probably do that," I say.

"Then take off your clothes and join me," she smiles.

Hurriedly, I peel off my shirt and nearly jump out of my drawers as I shadow her into the shower. Her lips meet mine, and my soul celebrates as I embrace the entirety of her naked-ness. Our kiss quickly escalates as she eagerly guides my hand over her breasts, across her body, and between her legs. She trembles as I touch her. Hell, I'm trembling. My mouth moves to her neck, where I whisper, "You're driving me crazy." She pulls back on my hair as my fingers slide across her clit. The heat of the shower—or maybe just the heat of us—steams the room. She's dripping. It's a distinctly different wetness than the water, and I want to bathe in it. My touch intensifies until she's on her toes—ballerina style—her breath is shallow, faint, and frantic. I'm harder than I've ever been. I want her, I want her badly, so badly—my visions blurred and I'm barely breathing, but it's not about me. Everything at this moment is about her. Everything I have is hers. She flushes chili red as my fingers find her spot. Her head snaps as she screams out a rapturous roar of satisfaction, "Oh, Max!" Crippling convulsions seize her core. Her nails slice into my skin. "*Vengo, vengo*, I'm cumming, oh God I'm cumming!" My fingers fervently caress her clit. I want it to feel better than she's ever imagined. I want my fingers to make her cum so hard that she craves them every time I touch her, every time I squeeze her hand, or hold a door for her. "Ahh, ahh!" Her screams convert to cries, her eyes slam shut, and her body spasms in fits of painful-looking pleasure. "Oh, Max, *sto venendo*. Oh, I can't take it!" she screams, so I steady my hand, and she collapses in my arms.

I hold her, breathing her in as I kiss her forehead. Her lips tremble as her owl eyes peer up into mine—searching my face—for what, I'm unsure. She's beautiful, soaking wet but beautiful, and I want to tell her I love her, I want to say cheesy shit like *you complete me*, but nothing comes. "Max, look at me, I'm shaking. Look. I think I cum maybe a whole minute, maybe two. I don't even know," she sputters under her heavy breath. "I'm sorry I couldn't take it anymore, I wanted to, it feels so good, oh God it feels so good, but I just couldn't."

"You don't need to be sorry," I say, holding her under the hot water, knowing I never want to let her go.

Minutes later, she grabs the soap and starts washing me: first my chest, then my stomach, then more. I'm still hard as hell when she takes ahold of me. "Can I?" she asks.

"You don't have to."

"But I want to make you feel good." I nod, and she drops to her knees.

My dick is rigid as she runs her tongue along the side. I watch her inspect it as though she'd never seen one up close because apparently she never has. She wraps her lips around the head and goes down as far as she can. It's only a few inches, maybe halfway back, but the way she sloshes her tongue is sensational. I could easily cum straight away, but want to savor it.

"Do you like that?" she asks, looking up at me.

"It's wonderful."

"How do you want me to do it?"

"Just as you are." And again, she pulls me into her. Her eyes stay on mine, which makes it even hotter. She's attempting to go deep, a personal challenge to take it all. I brush her wet hair from her face as she takes more of me with every gag. It hasn't been long, but looking down at this beautiful woman with my manhood in her mouth, I feel the pressure of an impending orgasm. I hold my breath, my body involuntarily convulsing, my abs clinch, and my cock throbs. The pleasure passes the point of return. So, with one last deepthroat attempt and a slight push on the back of her head, I pull myself from her mouth and shoot everything inside of me onto the glass. "Goddamn!" I yell as the second contraction kicks. She looks up at me through the steam, a proud smile upon her face.

"How was it?" she asks. I pull her up to me. My legs are weak.

"It was perfect."

"You are sure?"

"So sure," I say.

"Good... because I enjoy doing it. But next time, I want to taste you."

We stroll over to Columbus Circle and take the train downtown to Tribeca. Our car smells of bleached vomit and is standing room only—shoulder-to-shoulder. We're sandwiched between a group of Hasidic Jews in furry shtreimel hats, curly hair, and long coats. And a pale head-banger in tats and torn everything, Skullcandy in his ears, who's shouting Slipknot songs to himself.

After the show, we walk to the 9/11 Memorial, then down to Wall Street to get the bull picture for her dad. We share a bag of

✈

Tajín mangoes on our way to Battery Park for a peek at Lady Liberty from afar.

I tell her we can take a tour or hop on the Staten Island Ferry for a closer look if she wants, but she doesn't. Instead, she admits that she's *terrified* of open water, but had said nothing, as she didn't want to ruin my plans in Hong Kong.

"Did you know that di Statue of Liberty was originally designed to be an Arab woman?"

"I thought it was, what's his name, Bartholdi's mother."

"No, it's not true. Frédéric Auguste Bartholdi originally designed it to be a peasant woman holding a lamp, destined to stand at the Suez Canal in Egypt. It was only after his plan failed that he came to America and petitioned it to be in New York."

"But it's his mother's face, right?"

"No, the face is meant to be unspecific. So, the people arriving to America could imagine it as they wished."

"Hmm," I murmur. "I do know it's a gift from France, and the guy who built the Eiffel Tower designed the frame."

"Yes, that is all true, but the French, they did not create the pedestal."

"The big star it stands on?" Realizing I know nearly nothing about America's most iconic symbol.

"No, not the star. That is from an old army fort. It was here long before the statue. I'm talking of the pedestal, the big block below it. That part was built here in America. And because of its high cost, New York nearly didn't get the statue."

"No?"

"No, because New York, it run out of money. And the American government decided not to give them anymore. So the leaders of Boston and Philadelphia offered to pay to have it built in their city. It was only because of the famous publisher, Joseph Pulitzer, who offered to print in his newspaper—the names of any person who donates to the pedestal, even if they give just one cent. Because of this, they were able to raise the money, and it's the reason why the statue stands where it does today."

✈

"I didn't know any of that."

"Now you do. And you can add it to your list of New York trivia," she winks. Letting me know the—*did you know*—part of my personality I typically suppress is not only acceptable but now has an amiable adversary.

It's cold, the shiny streets are just a few degrees shy of ice, and the skies are granite. But besides the occasional gust, it's pleasant, so we set out on foot up Broadway.

Walking in lower Manhattan is like walking nowhere on the planet. Two incomparable worlds living as one, an axis of diverse prosperity, where twenty-five-year-olds making two hundred thousand a year, are low man on the totem pole pikers, grinding to gain access. And the privileged—who have already paid their dues—impulsively dismiss helpless peasants pleading for hope. In all of my trips to this city they named twice, I've only ever met two types that thrive here: the hyper-competitive go-getter and the self-destructive degenerate.

The people we pass are so damn peculiar, the city itself, a concentration of unique characters. We see little children on leashes and little dogs in strollers. On Chambers Street, we pass skateboarders in Supreme everything chatting with a couple black cops eating kimchi. There's a gray-haired man hand-in-hand with a big-lipped opportunist, a Caribbean woman caring for blue-eyed children in Brooks Brothers, and fashion-forward feminists in faux-fur coats. We pass a couple old Chinese men playing dominoes, quietly cheered on by a considerable crowd of heavy smokers. We walk behind an Indian gentleman in a well-tailored suit, bragging how much he lost in the *last split* to a colleague who's so stoned—he's probably lost himself. We watch haughty homemakers in haute couture passing strong-willed businesswomen in slate-pantsuits. And where Broadway crosses Canal, we walk by a boisterous bachelorette party, piling into a Barbie-pink limousine, sporting *Thank You For Being A Slut* sweatshirts and chugging bottles of White Girl Rosé.

I keep a secret survey of her eyes as she soaks it all in. I study the curve of her lips as she stops to pet every bodega cat we pass—the fat ones that keep away the rats. I smile at how selfless she is when needy strangers solicit us for change, and though she doesn't yet possess any US currency, she promises to pay me back when she does.

She reminds me of how magical those first moments in Manhattan can be. How a casual stroll downtown can make you feel as though anything is possible. Or how that first cab ride is a rite of passage and never forgotten. "Look," I whisper, eyeing a dark-haired woman in black-tights and Yeezy boots barreling towards us.

"She's beautiful, who is it?" she whispers as the woman passes.

"It's Kim Kardashian."

"Ah, no way." Her eyes follow Kim as she bolts down Bleecker. "She's even prettier in person."

I had mentioned tacos for lunch, and she looked at me like I was speaking Shanghainese. She's never had tacos before, and I've never heard anyone say that. So, I take her to Chelsea Market, a gentrified industrial dining extravaganza across from Google's New York headquarters.

I discovered Los Tacos No.1 some years back, after an extra late night at 1OAK. It's a small walk-up taco shop, with the best tasting carne stuffed tortillas I've come across on this coast.

"How many tacos do you want?" I ask her.

"I don't know, taco, you decide."

"I'm gonna have four," I say.

"Ok, then I want two."

"What kind of meat?"

"Whatever you get, anything but pork or shrimp."

"Steak and chicken, all right?"

"Yes."

"Everything on it?"

"However you take it, Bobo."

I order six with everything and a side of chips and salsa. We find a table and dig in.

✈

"How do you like it?" I ask.

"Is so good. It has many nice flavors."

"It's one of my favorite foods."

"This is a taco, right?" She scrutinizes it.

"Yep, and those are chips."

"Shut up, I know that." She smiles. In fact, she hasn't stopped smiling since the shower. "Max, I'm wondering if di taco is an American food or a Mexican food?"

"It's Mexican, but it's really popular in America."

"So... typical American people eat this?"

"Everyone eats tacos," I say. "Especially on Tuesdays."

"Why Tuesday?"

"LeBron James," I say, which draws a blank stare.

"I don't understand."

"Don't worry about it," I say, unsure how to explain it.

She takes another approving bite. "I wonder why they don't have this in Italy."

"I'd imagine it's because Italy doesn't share a border with Mexico."

"Yes, I guess that's so."

"But I'm sure they have Mexican places in Italy," I say.

"Now that we here, I think I see a place before, but I'm not sure if they have a taco. It's very good, I will tell my friends about it."

"I'm glad you like it. We'll have more in Wyoming."

She sits there, eating, and smiling, and whenever her head isn't on a swivel, absorbing the sights and sounds of the world around us, she looks at me.

"What do you think about America so far?" I ask.

"It's nice."

"Nice, that's good. I can see it now. *How was your trip to America, Raffaella? Oh, it was nice.*"

"Don't make fun of me, it is nice... I love it. You know that I do, I love every part of it."

"What stands out to you, something that's different from other places you've been?"

"Well..." there's a brief pause, then nonchalantly, as if she's ordering a Coke, she says, "There are many black guys here." I almost spit out my food.

"Yeah, I suppose there is," I say, laughing and sort of looking around to see if anyone heard her.

"Why so funny?"

"Nothing, I just never heard anybody say that before."

"What, black guy? Is no good?" She questions, her eyes absent of prejudice.

"No, it's good, or at least it's ok. It's just funny."

"In Italy, we don't have many black guys. I only get to see them on TV and in the movies."

"So, it's a good thing?"

"Yes, of course. Black guys are so cool."

"And why is that?" I ask, still trying not to laugh.

"You know, because they make hip-hop, and they have a good style, and your president, he was a black guy."

"Those are all true," I say, taking a big bite of taco and mumbling with my mouth full. "But I'm pretty sure black guys got more going for them than songs and swag," I chew.

"Yes, I know that. But it's still true."

"You like hip-hop?"

"Yes, everybody in Italy likes hip-hop. It's not the same here?"

"No, it is... it's probably about as popular as it gets."

"Do you like it?"

"Yeah, sure."

"I want to learn the black guy accent. Do you know it?"

"What do you mean?" I laugh.

"You know—how they talk. Like *yo-G* and *my-man*. You know—smooth—gangster style."

"Ah, I got ya." I scan the room again.

"Let me hear your black guy accent," she says.

"No, I don't think so." I shake my head, wondering how someone in our hypersensitive-society would interpret her obviously innocent inquisitiveness.

"Come on, I know you know it, please, Bobo."

✈

"Nah, I'm not gonna do it."

"But, you know it, right?"

"Sure."

"Then do it for me. Please."

"Maybe another time."

"Oh, come on," she insists.

I looked around the room, thinking about it. "Nah, I'm not gonna do it here."

"Don't worry of what people think."

"Some other time," I say.

"Come on, do it for me, please. You know I work at di restaurant, and I see people every day, from Japan to Jordan, all trying to imitate black American people, because their culture, it is so special. Nobody cares if you do accent, it's not racism."

"Ok," I say, leaning in and speaking softly, "Yeah, I guess you make a good point, baby-girl. How you feelin?"

"Oh my God, you do it so good. You sound just like a rapper. Do it again."

"Damn, girl, you gotta chill."

"Oh my God, is just like a video. You have practiced this many times, no?"

"No, I promise, I never practiced it before."

"You could be famous if you want to," she teases, "like Kendrick Lamar, or Kim's husband—Kanye. I know it."

"You never know," I say, sitting back in my seat, my smirk nearly permanent.

"But if you do, I want to be in your video. Ok?"

I lean forward, my eyes on hers. "Sounds good, baby-girl," I say in the same mellow accent. "But before I do, what if we take that fine ass of yours over to The Met?"

"Yes, can we do it? I'm so excited."

The twenty-minute taxi ride uptown and across the park is a relaxing way to see the west side. And the park itself, a two-and-a-half mile stretch of tranquility that keeps the citizens of this concrete island sane.

✈

You can't help but stand in awe as you admire the Great Hall of The Met and the grandeur of one of Gotham's great treasures.

I grab a guide, but before I get past the royal-red cover, Raffaella takes ahold of my hand, pulling me ahead with purpose. She whisks us through the crowds, past six-hundred-year-old sculptures and countless of pieces of world-renowned art, until we reach the Impressionists wing.

She stops at the gold-framed *Bain à la Grenouillère*, by Claude Monet. She stands tall, her arms crossed, her jaw rigid, an enchanted expression brightens her face in a way I've yet to witness.

"This is what I came to see," she says.

"No kidding."

"*È magnifico,*" she murmurs.

"It's pretty great."

"You know, I've wanted to see this picture for so long."

"How long?"

"Many years."

"Years? How many years?" I step back and attempt to soak in the chaotic 19th-century day-party, with pretty water.

"I don't know, maybe ten years."

"You've wanted to see this painting right here for nearly half your life?"

"Yes," she says, her eyes immersed in the scene.

"And why is that?"

"There are many reasons," she says, shifting her weight from one leg to the other.

"Such as?"

"One, it is beautiful. Look at it."

"It is good," I say.

"You're not seeing it correctly," she says. "Here, step back." So I do. "Monet himself, he call this one 'a bad sketch,' but it is considered one of the first true impressionist paintings. It was created before they even call it impressionism. When they considered this style 'unfinished,' compared to the more refined contemporaries shown at the Salon. Notice how, when you look at it from here, the water, it so much looks like a photograph, one that successfully captures all the beauty of the movement and the light. It's only when you get close, when you carefully study it, and spend time with it, that you're able to see its many flaws, its thick paint, its quick strokes, its beautiful imperfections, and that is when its personality comes to be true. It's because of this, I believe this picture to be very much like a person, and that it's either for you or it isn't."

"I think it's for me," I say, now staring at her, somewhat stupefied. "And the second reason?"

"Second?"

"You said many, so I assume there's at least two."

"Ah, sì. Two, I like di story... and three, I have been there."

"Tell me about it. Where is it?" I ask, now significantly more interested.

"Is outside of Paris, on the Seine, close to the town of Bougival. Is a wonderful little town; it's where my brother lives."

"That's where your family is going for Christmas?"

"Yes, that's right. They there today. I don't tell you, but my brother, he is French."

"And how is that?"

"He is the child from my father's first marriage. He is much older than me. He's your age." She smirks.

"I've been to the Seine," I say. "But only in Paris."

"Yes, Paris is nice, but I prefer it here at Bougival. I have been to this exact place many times, and I have painted many pictures here."

"And where are those paintings?"

"Like all my pictures, they are at mia nonna's house."

"And the story? The one you like?"

"You want to hear it?"

"I do."

"Ok, I tell you."

She speaks with so much passion and raw enthusiasm that I quickly become rapt in her tale. "Is a story of Claude Monet and Pierre-Auguste Renoir, and a dream to paint the bathes of la Grenouillère. They were best of friends, and both very poor. This was long before the critics and the dealers come to appreciate their style. Napoleon di third, who was then the emperor of France, he went and visited this town of Bougival with his family, so it becomes sort of famous for its time. So, Monet and Renoir, they go there, and they work side-by-side as partners, challenging one another to bring out the best in each other and to bring out the best in themselves. It is believed that they each created three paintings there. And because I am here today, I have now seen them all. Except for the tableau, the large Monet, which was lost and cannot be found."

"Where are the others?" I ask.

"The Monet is at The National Gallery in London, and the Renoirs, they are spread throughout Europe: in Stockholm, Switzerland, and Moscow."

"I've been to The National Gallery," I say.

"Ah, then you have seen the Monet."

I stare at her, engrossed in her beauty, her eyes steady on the canvas.

"Are you happy?" I ask.

"Yes, I am so happy." Her smile confirms it. "I believe this picture to be the most beautiful of them all. Because of the water, it is the most fine in this one."

I glance back at the picture. "It does look pretty real."

"Yes, it is extraordinary."

"So, what do you like about the story?"

"What do you mean?" she asks.

"I mean, you just told me the story, but you didn't say what you like about it."

"Ah sí, I understand. Well... it was just a year before Monet painted this picture that he tried to kill himself. He do it by drowning in that same river, di Seine. But, because of the love of his friends and his persistence, he never gives up again. This painting was created four years before they even call them *Impressionists*, and they only do so because they were criticizing him. And... well... despite their criticism, Monet soon became one of the most famous painters in all of Paris, maybe even di world."

"That's a nice story," I say.

"Yes, is one of my favorites, and I'm very happy I get to see this picture with you. Can I please have a kiss?"

"Sure," I say. "But we're in a museum, so I can only give you a little one."

"Ok, kiss me, hurry," she says.

"No, not a quick kiss... a little kiss."

"What is a little kiss?"

"Here, make a kiss face with your lips," I instruct.

"Like this?"

"No, smaller, less pucker. Just a normal kiss face."

"Like this?"

"Yeah, just like that. Now hold it." With her lips slightly pursed and her eyes open. I move in slowly with a matching pursed-pucker until we're only millimeters apart. We can feel each other's breath, but our lips are yet to touch, almost, but they aren't. I move a hair closer, so they barely meet, barely if at all, a feather's tickle, a peach's fuzz. She's smiling through her pouted pucker as I make an over-the-top exaggerated kissing noise, *mmmrrrrrrup*, and pull back.

"Ahhh, you so crazy. Give me another."

"Nope, we're in a museum, only one."

"No, come on, give me another little kisses."

"Sorry," I say.

"Don't be a stingy little monkey, give me another little kisses, please."

"Maybe later."

"Ah, you are so mean to me, I hate you," she says, looking deep into me. I sense she wants something. Something to mark this moment forever, but I remain silent. As if saying *I love you* would somehow wake me from this dream, and that by shying from that sacred phrase, my totem continues spinning, and my dream stays my reality.

We continue our tour, and she tells me everything there is to know about Monet and his significance to the movement and points out some of her favorite artists throughout the museum:

Albert Bierstadt, Max Beckmann, Jacques-Louis David, and she tells me stories of them and their work. She's never been here before, yet her knowledge is unparalleled.

Unlike me, who's referenced Picasso's Blue Period, but couldn't name a single piece; she's no pseudo-intellectual. This is her passion, and though I'm only seeing it for the first time, it's painted on her face.

"Raffaella, you obviously love art. Why didn't you go to art school?"

"My father, he says, it is a waste of time."

"But you don't like business, right?"

"No, but he says if I get a business degree, I can do anything I want. Even go into the art world."

"That's kinda true, I guess."

"It is, I know. And I was able to get my education in both schools, anyway."

"How's that?" I ask.

"I tell you I have terrible attendance, yes?"

"You did."

"Well, when I would skip my business classes, I would typically go sit in art history, or painting, or appreciation class instead."

"And the teachers would let you?"

"Yes, I tell them about my father, and they say if my grades stay good in business, it's no problem. I just had to bring my own supplies. That's one reason why I don't save so much money."

"Hmm, so you got an education in art but a diploma in business."

"And everybody's happy," she says with a smile.

Wow, I whisper to myself. "Are you gonna paint when we get to Jackson?"

"I would like to, but I don't bring any of my brushes or my paints."

"Now, I'm no artist or anything, but I'm pretty sure they sell art supplies in Wyoming. And we can get you whatever you need."

✈

"Yes?" Her smile creases her young skin. I shake my head. "That makes me very happy, give me another kiss." I lean down to kiss her. "No, you crazy man, what are you thinking? We are in a museum, you have to give me a little kisses." So I do, and it's even smaller this time.

We leave the museum at half-past six. It's dark and snowing again. And as I go to flag a cab, I spot a horse-drawn carriage and jog over. It's a handsome and obviously well fed, well cared for horse. All white with brown spots, pulling a fire-engine-red carriage. So I hire him.

The driver has a top hat, handlebar mustache, and a deep baritone voice. He tells us everything one would want to know about the park: how the city's marathon started here, how it's larger than Monaco, and how it cost more to build than to buy the entire state of Alaska.

She gets excited when she sees a sign for the zoo.

"Can we please go and see your monkey family?"

"I think they're closed now, but I'll bring you back to meet mother in the spring."

"Yes?"

"I promise," I say as the driver serenades us in a cappella of *White Christmas*.

The somber night is silent. With its curved paths, rolling hills, and giant rock formations, the park has you forget you're in the middle of a massive city. And snuggled next to me, she makes me forget that anything else matters.

The ride ends at a wall of buildings on 59th as the sirens of the city abruptly return. A storm is blowing in, the winds intensify, and the snow heavies. Despite this, we're warm and decide to walk the ten or so blocks to Times Square.

As we pass Carnegie Hall, I point it out and ask her if she knows "how to get to Carnegie Hall?"

She looks at me, confused, and says, "It's there, no?"

I turn to her and say, "Lots of practice." She shakes her head, signaling a total fail, and I fall apart laughing.

"Is it supposed to be a joke?" she asks.

"Yeah," I say. "A pretty bad one."

"Is good that you can laugh at your own jokes. That means they're really funny."

"Ha-ha, you think you're funny, huh?"

"No, I know that I am funny. But not in English."

"Oh, you know?"

"Yes, it's true. Is too difficult for me in English, because I must translate it first in my head. But all my friends and family thinks I'm funny. They laugh at all my jokes and always say to me that I'm *so funny*."

"Maybe they're just laughing at you," I say.

"Yes, because unlike you, my jokes are actually funny." She kisses me.

The weather worsens by the block, the howling wind smacking our uncovered faces as we cross 52nd. Because of the storm, the crowds in Times Square are sparse, and the blowing snow dulls the brilliance of its billion-dollar billboards, but she doesn't care. She has a smile that'd make you think it's seventy-five and sunny.

She pulls out a disposable camera from her bag and starts winding and snapping sporadically.

"Sweet camera," I say. "How many megapixels does that thing have?"

"Don't be jealous that I'm using something from your time. I take all my photos on a film camera. I suppose I just like old things." She mouths me a kiss.

"All of your photos?" I don't know why I feel the need to question her, especially over something so silly. I suppose it's some suppressed insecurity that keeps me searching for flaws, inconsistencies in character, meaningless white lies that would someday work themselves into big lies.

"Yes, all of them."

"Why didn't you use that camera this morning on Wall Street?"

"Because those pictures were for my father, and these are for me," she says it as though I should know.

✈

"Why didn't you use a film camera in Hong Kong, for the monkeys... and the sunset?"

"I tell you already, my kid brother is no good. He take my camera that night I meet you and use all my film for photos of his butt. Now tell me—do you have any more questions of my camera? Or can I take my photos without you being jealous?"

Though the masses have sought shelter from the heavy snow and stiff winds, we still manage to find a few characters—one, in particular, stands above all. A tall man in a peacoat—attempting to shield himself—finds trouble when his oversized red-umbrella catches the wrong side of a gust. This bright-red parachute on a pole pulls the dumb bastard down the street in the fight of his life while shouting *Shit! Shit! Shit! Motherfucker! Shit! Shit! Shit!* Until the umbrella folds—snaps, and he falls flat on his ass. This gets her laughing, hell, close to crying as she *snorts* and collapses to her knees. She's hysterical and struggling to breathe, so I snatch her camera and snap the poor bastard's photo.

After she gains her composure and brushes the slush from her puffy coat, she tells me she's *hungry*. I tell her I'd take her anywhere she wants to go, the best of New York: Nusr-Et Steakhouse, Gotham Bar and Grill, the Rainbow Room, or any fancy feature in *Time Out New York*. I don't give a damn about cost, or even reservations. I'd hand the hostess or maître d' a hundred dollars for a table, hell, a thousand dollars if that's what it'd take, anything to make her happy. But she doesn't want it. No, she still insists on popular no-frills local fare. Something *a typical American would eat*. So, I take her to the most typical American treasure I can think of.

The Buffalo Wild Wings on 47th Street, with its high ceilings and contemporary brick and steel build, is likely the granddaddy of all wing joints. The place is packed, not a seat in sight, yet we scrounge up a couple stools at the bar. The fifty flat-screen televisions stream some meaningless bowl game, and pouring beer, is a cute blonde with big teeth. I order a pint, and she picks a gin and tonic with two limes.

J Gatz

✈

"Max, I noticed that you only have beer while we're here in America. Why you not drink whiskey, like with your friend?"

"Do you want me to order some shots?"

"I want you to do what you want. I'm only curious."

"Maybe you're intoxicating enough for me."

"Ah, you are full of cheese."

"What?"

"You are full of cheese," she says again.

"You mean I'm cheesy?"

"Ah, yes, that's what I mean. You are cheesy."

"Maybe I am," I say. "Where'd you hear that?"

"I don't know, I think maybe a movie. But I am curious. What kind of cheese is it?"

"I don't believe it's any particular type."

"Well... if I had to pick a cheese for you... you would be a mozzarella."

"Oh yeah? And why is that?" I ask.

"Because... is my favorite cheese."

"Ah, I see you're pretty full of cheese yourself."

"Yes, it was a joke."

"You think you're pretty funny, huh?"

"I tell you, I know I am funny. But also because we are at the Buffalo Wild Wings, so it's funny. No?"

"What do you mean?" I ask, "What does Buffalo Wild Wings have to do with anything?"

"Because, the mozzarella, it's made from a buffalo's milk."

"I didn't know that it was."

"Yes, everybody knows that."

"I guess I'm a dummy," I say. Her head shakes no, but her eyes say *maybe*. "Don't mean to burst your bubble, but I'm pretty sure the cheese here isn't made from buffalo's milk."

"Of course it is," she says. "Di place, they name it for a buffalo."

"Yeah, but I'm pretty sure it's because of the wings."

✈

"Maybe, but the cheese, it has to be from a buffalo. It only makes sense."

"Maybe... but what do I know."

But she's not satisfied with my maybe, and signals to the bartender. "*Scusami*, the mozzarella cheese sticks on your menu, are they made with milk from a buffalo?" She says it with a dead straight face. The bartender obviously doesn't know what to say and looks over at me; I'd imagine she's gauging if we're fucking with her or not.

"I'm not sure. I'll ask my manager," she says sheepishly, suppressing her smile, and turns towards the back.

She returns moments later—her face flushed from a fresh laugh—and confirms that their mozzarella is "not made from buffalo's milk." Raffaella squints in disbelief, almost as if she doubts the girl even asked.

"I don't get it," she says, then wonders aloud. "Why is this placed called a buffalo wings?"

"Now, I've never been, but I'm pretty sure it's because Buffalo wings originated in Buffalo, New York. I know they have them in Europe, but I'm pretty sure they just call them chicken wings."

I see she's genuinely disappointed in herself for getting that wrong, so I don't bust her chops. Instead, I ask her what she wants. Being the easygoing tourist that she is, she says, "whatever you're having." So I order a bit of everything: the Bourbon Honey, the Parmesan Garlic, Traditional Buffalo, Hot, and Asian Zing. I request a refill on my beer and tell her to kiss me before I get sauce all over my face.

"Raffaella, you know so much about art, why don't you sell your paintings?"

"Maybe one day, I will."

"Have you tried?"

"No, but I will someday. When I make a truly beautiful painting, I will try to sell it."

"That sunset you sent me, that was great. Why don't you sell that?"

"It was ok, but it wasn't, how you say... *magnifica*."

"It was pretty damn good. Even magnificent."

"Thank you. I agree that it was maybe my best sunset. But it wasn't... magnificent."

"How do you know if something's magnificent?"

"You just know."

"But how?"

"You just do."

"Ok, but how?" I press.

"You really want to know?"

"I wouldn't have asked if I didn't."

"Don't get snooty with me, Bobo." She kisses my cheek. "If you want to know, I tell you."

"Please."

"My favorite teacher, he show me a way to know if a painting is magnificent or not. It's very simple."

"I like simple," I say.

She takes ahold of my hand, massaging it as she speaks. "First, I need you to put in your mind a very beautiful painting."

"Ok," I say.

"You got one?"

"Yes."

"Ok, now hold it there, and now try to imagine many more beautiful paintings, even better than the first... and stop."

"I don't think I got many," I say.

"But you did get some, yes?"

"I think so."

"Good, now tell me all the paintings you saw, but don't count di Mona Lisa or any pictures we saw today."

How did she know? "Why do you think I was gonna say the Mona Lisa?" I ask.

"Because everybody say di Mona Lisa, that's why is the most famous painting in the world. Now tell me what you got."

"Ok, then I got two."

"And?"

"I can't remember the name of it, but it's the one where the tigers are jumping at the girl—"

✈

"*A Dream Caused by the Flight of a Bee Around a Pomegranate a Second Before Awakening* by Salvador Dali, yes, this is very much a magnificent picture. I knew you were a crazy man. Now tell me di second."

"It's called *The Genius of America* by—"

"Adolphe Yvon." She cuts me off again.

"You know this painting?" I ask.

"Yes, it's fantastic. And Adolphe Yvon is a wonderful painter. He is a Frenchman, you know? He painted pictures for Napoleon himself." I could see her face light with excitement. "You have seen this painting?"

"I've seen it many times," I say.

"Where?"

"In St. Louis."

"Ah, then you have seen di small one."

"What do you mean, the small one?"

"Adolphe, he paint this picture two times. First di small one you see in St. Louis, it's the original; then they commission him to paint a big one, a mural of the same picture, but much larger, nearly ten meters wide. It's here in New York, but in a different city called Albany."

"I didn't know that," I say. "And I've been to Albany, that's crazy."

"What is crazy?"

"That's one of my favorite paintings, I look forward to seeing it nearly every time I'm in St. Louis, but I didn't know it had a twin, and that's crazy that you did."

"I know it only because it is maybe my favorite period in painting, and I have much interest in Napoleon. Adolphe Yvon is a fine painter of that time, and I think it's wonderful that you know of his work. You are a wonderful man, and so intelligent."

"Thanks." I smile. "But you still didn't say how your little quiz determines a painting to be magnificent or not."

"But I did." She leans over and kisses me. "If you can see something in a seconds time, a picture, and love the way it makes you feel, appreciate it, and know you want to see it again

262

and again and can recall it in just a glimpse of time. Then it is magnificent. Some pictures are magnificent to some but not to others. You can only know when you see it, and when you do, you know if it is for you, or it isn't." This has me thinking of her, and how I knew she was magnificent the moment I saw her.

Our buffet of wings is placed before us, and we continue chatting about art and everything in the world that interests her. I can't get enough. She's so damn intelligent and sincere in everything she says, wowing me more every moment. Our only interruption in conversation comes when she pauses to ask what flavor wing she's grabbing. Then gives me a number *one to ten* on how delicious it is. First, an *eight* for the Bourbon Honey, then a *nine* for the Buffalo, and finally a *ten,* and a huge smile for the Asian Zing, only to drop back down to a *seven* for the Hot, as it hurts her tongue.

"Try the Parmesan Garlic. I got those for you."

"I don't really care for too much garlic," she says.

"But you're Italian. All Italians like garlic."

"That's not true."

"No?"

"At my restaurant, many American tourists ask if we are an authentic Italiano ristorante. I tell them *yes, of course.* And ask them *why?* And they say that they 'expected the food to be more garlicky.' "

"And it's not garlicky?"

"No, Italian people don't like so much intensity of the garlic flavor. We use it, but not so much that it overpowers the dish. Did you taste much garlic in Milan?"

"I'm not sure, I guess I wasn't paying attention to how garlicky the food was or wasn't."

"But many Americans do because I hear it maybe every week. If not more."

"That is weird. I'd bet if you asked a hundred people, ninety-nine of them would say *Italian food is garlicky.* Why do you think that is?"

"I don't know, but it is only American people. I think maybe it's from the mafia movies." I laugh at her insight.

✈

"We should write an article and submit it to the *New York Times*, we'll title it *Mafia Movies Caused Garlic Stink in America.*"

"Yes, can we do it?"

"Maybe, we'll see how bored we get this winter."

"You know there's another thing that American people always get wrong about Italian food."

"What's that?"

"At the restaurant, American people always ask me for a 'spaghetti and meatballs,' but Italian people don't eat pasta with meatballs."

"No?"

"No, meatballs don't go in a pasta, is crazy. It must be an American thing."

"Fucking mafia movies."

"Yes, and all the people at the restaurant makes fun of them when they order it."

"Probably like when Europeans come to New York and order mayonnaise with their fries."

"Shut up. You can't be a smart-ass with sauce all over your face." She leans in to wipe it, but I pull away and attack her face with mine. "You are disgusting. You're getting your smelly garlic breath all over me like a bad little monkey."

We have to be up in five hours, so we catch a cab and crash— our final New York dream before heading west.

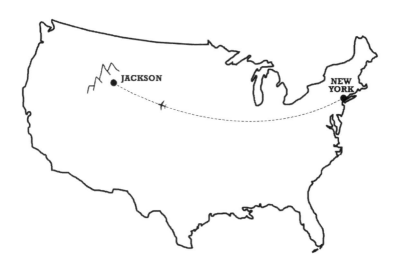

The two most important days in your life
are the day you are born and the day
you find out why.

— Mark Twain

✈

CHAPTER 23

Jackson

WE MAKE IT TO JFK ON TIME, and despite several inches of snow throughout the night, Delta flight 2793 is set to depart as scheduled.

As the stewardess mimes the seatbelt routine, I squeeze Raffaella's hand and whisper, "It's been exactly two weeks since we first saw each other."

"Oh my God, we are both so crazy. What time is it now in Hong Kong?"

"I'm pretty sure it's ten-after-eight on Saturday."

"Yes, it was nearly nine when I went to smoke."

"I almost forgot that you smoke."

"Stop it," she slaps my arm. "Max"

"Yes?"

"Thank you for always thinking of ways to make me smile. Please give me a kiss." So I lean in. "Hey, what are you thinking? We are on an airplane. You know I can take only the little kisses."

We land in Jackson to light snow and high winds. The sky is gray and gloomy, and the mountains aren't visible. I checked the radar before we left. The local forecast is calling for heavy snow, but it appears we beat the bad stuff.

Exiting the plane, the all-timber log cabin airport is a fitting welcome to this American arcadia called Wyoming.

And as we step outside to catch our ride, the cold, wet air smells of sawdust and the refreshing scent of nothingness.

266   J Gatz

And as our hired ride turns down the long remote road, which leads to the house, I watch her eyes grow wide. "Is this really where we will stay?"

"It is."

"Oh my God, is so perfect," she whispers to herself, a serendipitous smile on her face.

Seven years ago, my dad was preparing to retire when he built this place. *The ultimate man cave*, he called it. But since then, he's maybe spent six months here. I told him to rent it out, but he *doesn't want anyone messing it up*. So, I've taken it upon myself to make sure this two-bedroom, three-bathroom, 2,200 square-foot, stone and timber ranch doesn't go unused. I try to spend a few months a year here, sometimes more. The place is paradise, just twenty minutes north of Jackson, and only one neighbor in sight.

We unload our bags, and I carry my queen inside.

"Max, this is more amazing than I ever imagined. I can't even believe this is it."

The inside is quite imposing. Upon entering, you walk into a tall timber room featuring a dramatic, locally sourced, all-stone fireplace. Nearly the entire back wall is a window, with French doors opening to a large patio, a Jacuzzi tub, and epic views of the Teton peaks. A granite island separates the great room from the all Viking chefs' kitchen. On opposite sides of the home area are two identical master bedrooms, both with high ceilings, California Kings, and copper soaking tubs. The only difference being that one holds a stirring array of mounted and stuffed animals: an elk's head, three deer, a full bore, pheasants, a sad-looking fox, and trophy fish of all types. After I give her the tour, I ask, "what room do you want?"

With her eyes full of fright, "Please don't make me sleep in there."

"But that's your room," I say, straight-faced.

"No, please, no."

"But that room has the best bed."

"I don't need to sleep." Her chin high, her eyes beady.

"I'm only kidding."

"I know. Another bad joke," she frowns. "Who killed them?"

"My dad."

"Good."

"Why good?" I ask.

"I'm glad it wasn't you."

"Why's that?"

"Because, if you did, they would be mad at you, and I'm sure they would haunt us in our sleep."

I remember my dad telling me why he had to put all the *dead animals* in that one room. It was just after he built the place. They had invited a couple out for a weekend. A guy he worked with and his wife. And unbeknownst until arrival, the woman was a hard-core vegan and a prominent PETA member. When she walked in and saw the elk's head above the fireplace, she *shrieked* and ran out of the house. She said that she *wouldn't stay there* if she had to look at another dead animal.

I remember my dad telling me how pissed he was that weekend. How they were all sitting on the back patio—having a few laughs when the *biggest goddamn bull* he'd ever seen happen to stroll across the backyard, and that it stopped and stared at him. Said it was *taunting* him. It was hunting season. His rifle was ten-steps away, and he had an unused elk-tag in the truck. He didn't do it though, said that woman *would have burned the place down.*

"The snow is really picking up. We should probably get some food and stuff for the house before it gets any worse," I say.

"Ok, let me get my hat." She runs back to the bedroom, I blink, and she's back, but I can't move. I try, but I can't. I don't even know what it is. I guess, just seeing her in this house, having her here, in the mountains, in the west, all to myself. All winter, just me and her, her and me. I sort of lose myself. She's so damn beautiful, so damn perfect, perfect for me, at least.

"Max, are you ok?"

"Yeah," I snap to, struggling to remember what the hell we're even doing.

"Why are you looking at me like that?"

"Don't worry about it. Let's go," I say.

"Not until you give me a kiss." So I do. And for the next ten seconds, I fall back into that daydream. My two-week long daydream of this girl, this goddess, who doesn't even know where we are, but doesn't want to be anywhere else.

"What if it snows so much this winter that we get stuck in the house, and we can't leave?"

"That's never gonna happen," I say.

"But what if it does? And what if you go crazy, and you try to kill me?"

I smile at her, a toothy psychotic kind, and in a killer's voice, I whisper, "darling, I'm not gonna hurt ya."

"Stop it, stronzo!"

"I thought you didn't like scary stories?"

"I don't, I tell you. But I know of it, so don't do that."

"Ok, but I promise that no matter how much it snows, I won't go crazy... or will I?" I hiss, dark and raspy.

"Stop it, don't try to scare me."

"I'm just kidding," I say, "or am I?"

"I'm gonna punch you in di face." She folds her hand to a fist and holds it to my chin. "And I don't want to hurt my little monkey."

"Come on, tough guy." I take her into the garage. "This is how I know we won't get stuck." I flip on the fluorescent lights to reveal my 94' Oxford White, Ford F-150 pickup truck, with the extra-large tires.

"This is yours?"

"You like it?"

"Yes, is so cool."

"It's no Ferrari." I open her door and help her up.

"Is better than Ferrari. We have no big trucks like this in Italy."

As the garage door crawls open, I can see the storm has already dumped a few inches. But I'm not worried. This truck can get through anything. My only concern is for her.

"Raffaella."

"Yes?"

"Can you do me a favor?"

"Anything for you, Bobo."

"Can you please put on your seatbelt?"

"But in Italy, nobody wears a seatbelt. And we are in a big truck."

"I know. And I didn't say anything in Hong Kong, but I would feel better if you wore it... please."

"Ok, I do it for you."

"Thanks."

The old truck rumbles down the long snow-covered street, past our only neighbor, and turns southbound onto the I-191, which runs parallel to the Teton Range.

The wind is whipping, and there's only a few-hundred-feet of visibility, but this truck has seen worse. I feel my phone buzz. I ignore it at first—focusing on the road—but it buzzes again. Raffaella is staring out the window, and there's nobody in sight. So, I dig deep into my front pocket to fetch it. I glance down for a second to swipe the password, and down again, to see a text from my mom. I look up, the snowy road is empty, so I open it.

Max, I saw that French girl outside the house last night. It was dark, but I'm sure it was her. Are you in town? Love You. ERRRR! ERRRR! My head snaps up to the chilling scream of a semi's horn.

"Jesus!" I shout, seeing I'm few feet in the wrong lane, jerking the wheel—I true the truck. And though we weren't that close, a couple of seconds later and it could have been bad.

"Oh my God, you almost hit that truck! What are you doing?" she cries.

"Are you ok?"

"Yes, I'm fine, but we almost died."

"We did not." I turn to her with a bottom-tooth smile. "But I'm sorry."

"Just try not to kill us... I am so happy right now. I don't wanna die."

✈

"I don't want you to die either." I squeeze her leg. "That'll wake you up though, huh?"

"Yes, or make you sleep forever," she says sharply.

"Ah, come on, we weren't that close."

"We were close enough."

"I'll pay better attention."

"I'm just glad I have my seatbelt on." She winks.

My blood pressure levels off by the time we pull into downtown Jackson. A small mountain town, with a uniform log and timber look.

"I know you can't see much with the snow, but what do you think?"

"I think it is wonderful, is a beautiful town. It reminds me of Val-d'Isère. Is a ski town in France."

"Well, just up there is a ski mountain. With all the snow tonight, it should be good tomorrow if you want to go?"

"Can we do it?"

"I told you... we can do anything you want. I didn't even know you skied."

"Yes, I'm sporty... I tell you."

"Sorry, I didn't know sporty meant skiing."

"It doesn't, it means good at sport and fitness. But I can ski."

"Then let's go tomorrow."

"But tomorrow is Christmas Eve. Are they to open?"

"I think so. I think it's actually one of their busier days."

"So it will be a nice snow and many American people. I cannot wait."

"We don't have to go there, there's another mountain that's a bit bigger, a lot bigger actually. It's called Jackson Hole, and in my opinion, it's probably the best places to ski in the entire country."

"Whatever one you prefer," she says.

"No, it's whatever one you prefer. Can you ride the big one?"

"Max, I live my whole life close to the mountains. If you want to, I'm sure I can do the big one."

"Then that's what we're doing," I say, happy to know I have a ski partner this season; never motivated enough to go more than once on my own.

"Oh, I'm so excited. Give me a kiss, but keep your eyes on the road."

"Yes, mam."

"What is a mam?"

"It's just what you call a woman, the polite way, like *mademoiselle*."

"Ah, yes, I know it. And... since you are a polite little monkey. When we get to the grocery market, I will get us many nice meats and make us some delicious sandwiches for the mountain tomorrow. What do you think?"

"I think that's a good idea."

"And I am to pay," she says.

"Not a chance."

"Please, I want to," she insists.

"I got this one. You can get it another time."

"You are such a stubborn little monkey." She leans over and kisses my cheek. "I can't wait for tomorrow... is gonna be such a nice Christmas Eve."

"Hopefully this storm stops by then, and they can clean the roads."

"Yes, is very dangerous, but it's gonna be such beautiful snow."

"Beautiful," I echo.

"Max, I'm wondering something."

"What's that?"

"I don't have my ski's, what will I do?"

"We can rent them. Or, if they fit you, you can use my stepmom's. They're basically brand new."

"She won't mind?"

"No, she'll never even know."

"But if she does know, would she mind?"

"No, she wouldn't care at all."

"Does she have a 38' foot like mine?"

"I have no idea. You can try them on when we get home."

"Home," she echoes warmly.

I squeeze her hand and smile. "Home."

"I'm sure they will fit, I cannot wait."

We pull into Hungry Jack's. Sure, there's a bigger store down the street, but this place has that unique small-town feel I'm looking for. We load up on fresh fruits, veggies, eggs, French bread, roast beef, and turkey for our sandwiches, cheeses from the deli, fish and fresh cranberries for Christmas dinner, dried fruit, and a few other ingredients so she can make a *panettone*— an Italian style fruitcake—for Santa, or *Babbo Natale* as she calls him.

"No cookies?" I ask.

"No, we give cookies only to *La Befana*. But that's not for a couple of weeks."

"In America, we give cookies to Santa."

"Ok, then we make him some cookies too."

I also pick up a six-pack of Melvin beer and a bottle of malbec. She mentions champagne, so I grab a bottle of Moët.

"What should we have tonight," I ask. "The champagne or the wine? Or both?"

"No, let's celebrate with champagne tonight, and save di wine for Christmas. It will be like a present to ourselves, and we will look forward to opening it."

"That sounds like a nice little present," I say.

"Yes, and it's gonna be such a wonderful Christmas."

It's near-blizzard conditions on the drive home; I keep my eyes off my phone and on the road.

As we pull down our street, I see our one and only neighbor, Mark Parazader, a retired schoolteacher who lives a few football fields from us. He's bundled tight as he attempts to shovel his driveway. I pull up to his curb and crack the window.

"Hey, what are you doing out here?" I shout through the wind. He shields his face and hollers towards the truck.

"Max, is that you?"

"Yes, sir," I say, and he moves towards us, mindful of every slippery step.

"I was hoping those tire tracks were yours. It's good to see ya, boy."

"Good to see you too, sir. But what in the hell are you doing out here?"

"Figured I'd clear a few inches before it gets too nasty."

"I'd say it's past that point."

"You know me, I'm tired of sitting inside. Besides, how many good storms does an old man have left?"

Now I can't recall exactly where in North Florida Mr. Parazader is from, but wherever it is, it's where they have a strong southern accent.

"Augh boy, you know I live for this. I was watching the television, The Weather Channel says it'll go on like this till two-three in the morning."

"I wouldn't mess with it till then," I say. "How about I come back at sunup and give you a hand?"

"Oh, no. No need for that. I'll probably call it quits here in a few," he says, stretching his neck. "And I'm serious, I know how you are, don't you worry about it. I'm just gonna hit it with the blower in the morning. It'll be easy-peasy, I promise. But I do appreciate the offer."

"All right," I say. "But give me a ring if you change your mind."

"Will do."

"Oh, and this is Raffaella, and Raffaella, this is Mark Parazader."

"Hello, sweetheart," he greets her through the window, a friendly wave and a warm smile.

"Good evening," she says. Another strong gust blows.

"Whoo-baby," he hollers into the wind.

"We're gonna try to ski tomorrow. How's the snow?"

"Heavy as hell, but should be nice up top. What a great way to spend Christmas Eve," he says.

"Yeah, it looks to be a good one."

"I don't wanna keep ya. Why don't you go on and get that beauty inside and get a nice fire going." The sideways snow whistles through the cracked window.

"That's probably what we're gonna do."

"You kids have a good night. It's good to see you, Max, and it was nice to meet you, sweetheart."

"You too," she says.

He taps the hood of the truck and turns back towards his house.

"Mister Parazader," I shout through the wind. "If you don't have any plans, how about you come by on Christmas day around four o'clock, and join us for dinner?"

"Oh, I don't wanna intrude."

"Nonsense, we'd love to have you."

His frozen face wrinkles to a full Arnold Palmer smile. "All right then, I'll be there."

"Glad to hear it."

"Can I bring anything?" he calls back.

"There's no need, but you're welcome to bring anything you'd like."

"How about candied yams and some beer?"

"That'd be great. We'll see you then. Be safe out here, fight her another day."

"I think I might do that. Y'all enjoy your night now."

And with that, I roll up the window and pull away.

"That was so nice of you," she says to me.

"You don't mind, do you?"

"No, of course not. He seems like a nice old man."

"A nice and lonely old man."

"Why so lonely?"

"He's all by himself."

"Where is his family?"

"They're all dead."

"Oh no, what happened?"

"His wife died a few years back. He said they were married forever, since high school, I think. He told me how they had saved their entire lives to come out here and build that house. But she got cancer and died just after they did."

"Oh my God, that's so terrible. I feel so bad for him."

"Me too."

"Do you know how many years they were married?"

"I think he said it was just shy of fifty. That she went a few weeks before their anniversary."

"Oh, that's so sad. Don't they have any children?"

"They do, or they did. They had a boy, but he died too. He was just a kid."

"I can't even believe it, I just want to give him a hug."

"Well, you can, the day after tomorrow."

"That was so nice of you to invite him, you are such a thoughtful man."

"I know he's just gonna sit at home and drink beers by himself, so he might as well come drink them with us, right."

"Give me a kiss," she demands. "What am I gonna do when you die?"

"What do you mean—when I die?"

"You are much older than me. You gonna die before me, Bobo."

"I don't know... my grandfather was pretty old when he went."

"How old?"

"Ninety-five."

"So... I will only be eighty-five, I think I can make it."

She changes while I start a fire, and then she starts dinner. Pasta without meatballs lightly tossed in olive oil, black pepper, and a healthy heap of Parmesan. For the side, a juicy slice of tomato topped with buffalo-milk mozzarella and more olive oil.

She's wearing a long gray T-shirt that's past her knees, high pink socks, and her hair is up. I'm not sure if it's the fire reflecting off of her eyes, the warm glow of her skin, or the fact she's making me a meal, but she's even more beautiful than the last time I thought she was the most beautiful, and I didn't think anything could get better than that.

I pop the champagne, but as I go to pour it, she insists on a coupe, saying, "champagne never goes in a flute."

The cold and creamy caprese is a perfect complement to the pasta. But after only a half glass of bubbly and a few bites, I can't take it anymore. "Raffaella, there's something I want," I say, hungrily staring into her.

"What is it? I'll make you anything."

"I want dessert," I say, standing, wiping my mouth. I pull her into me, grab the back of her neck, and kiss her with purpose. I want her to feel how badly I burn to please her. How badly I crave to make her moan. I pick her up and toss her onto the counter. I don't waste any time, I know where I want to go, so I go there. I know what I want to do, so I do it. I don't want to play games with her. I only want to make her cum. I want her to cum so hard that every time she walks into this kitchen, into this house, she gets a little wet from the memory of this moment.

Her eyes say *yes* as I peel away her panties. My mouth is watering, my breath hot, my touch soft. She's as sweet as a late summer peach; her delicious juices drip down my chin as my tongue attacks her clit. "Don't stop," she cries. Savoring every second, I want nothing for myself; her pleasure is my only purpose. I want her to experience something she never knew was possible. I want the texture of my tongue to make her mind melt in a moment of immobilizing ecstasy.

Her legs shake as she succumbs to the sensation—her stomach contracts, spasms, as she begs for more. I bury my face between her legs, my tongue on a mission, a determined hunger for her pleasure, her moans, her madness. "Oh, Max!" she screams. She's soaking wet and gushing with gratification. "*Sto venendo!*" Her legs kick, her stomach trembles, her screams echo. "*Vengo! vengo!*" Her eyes slam shut, her body locks. "I cumming, I cumming, oh God!" Her face flushes with fright as if she's afraid of the pleasure—twitching and terrified until she falls limp—gasping for breath.

I collapse on top of her, my face to her stomach, blissful at my feat. I lay there, riding the rhythmic rise and fall of her post-orgasmic serenity, already looking forward to the next time I get to taste her.

"Can I get you anything?" I ask.

"No, I need nothing. Nothing ever again."

"Never?"

"No, I can die right now."

"Please don't," I say. "Who would make the cookies for Santa?"

"Santa don't need no cookies, I'm gonna make 'em for you, baby. Santa's never given me a present like that."

After a while, we collect ourselves. She mixes the batter for her cake and cuts the cookie dough while I attend to the fire.

I bring the champagne to the couch, and she snuggles up next to me. Outside, the wind slams against the house, but inside, it's quiet, only the fire's crackle and the bursting bubbles of our brut.

"Max, I still can't believe this will be our home for the next three months."

"I'm glad you're happy."

"This is a fairy-tale. Is like a movie, but it's better than a movie. It's like we are the two luckiest people in the world, and nobody will ever be as happy as us."

"Nobody," I smile.

"Max, this is the best day of my life."

"Yeah?"

"Yes, and before today, yesterday was the best."

"I hope tomorrow doesn't suck," I say.

"You make jokes, but I'm serious. I'm crazy about you, I hope you know that."

"I know."

"Sometimes, I'm afraid to blink because I'm afraid to wake up from this dream."

"It's all real," I whisper. "This is your life and my life, and for at least the next few months, it's our life together."

✈

"Is our story," she says.

"Yeah, it's our story."

"Is gonna be the most incredible story ever told. I know it... it's already so wonderful."

"It is pretty wonderful, isn't it?"

"So wonderful." She bites her bottom lip. "Maybe a story like my parents."

"What do you mean?" I ask.

"Nothing... never mind."

"No, tell me," I press.

"Is nothing, is just a story of a long, happy life."

"Tell me the short version."

"Are you sure you want to hear it?"

"Obviously."

"Ok... I tell you, but I don't want you to feel any, how do you say, any pressures."

"Pressure?"

"Yes, no pressure. To make a story like theirs."

"Our story is ours. Nothing's gonna change that," I say. "Now, tell me."

"Ok, is a story of a long time ago. My father, he go to Morocco for work. He is Italian you know, and at that time, he only speak Italian and French, no Arabic. But he was the best in his company, so they send him. He stay a short time in Marakesh but mostly in Casablanca. That's where my mother lived. He stay for six months. And on his very last day, just as he was about to leave for di airport and go back to Italy, he stopped in for a bocadillo. It's a type of Moroccan sandwich. And this is how he meet my mother. She was working there, at her father's restaurant as a waitress. He say he fall in love with her the moment he see her, before she even say a word. And she say that she fell in love with him di second he said hello to her."

"So, it was love at first sight?"

"Precisely. He tell her that if he wasn't leaving today, he would ask her for a date. But my mother, she only speak Arabic, so she couldn't understand him. But my father, since he had been there now six months, he speak a little Arabic, just enough

✈

to ask my mother for her telephone number. But she tell him *no* because she cannot have a man calling her house. So he asked for her *address* because he wants to write her a letter when he get back to Italy."

"And she gave it to him?"

"Hold on, Bobo, I get there."

"Sorry, go on."

"So my father, he return home, and he write my mother a letter, and before she could even respond, he write her another. He writes her many letters every week, and she writes him too. He even takes a class in Milano to study Arabic, so he could write her in good Arabic." She's looking into my eyes, and I can see how much this story means to her. "After one year of this, and fifty letters, my father, he goes back to Casablanca to see my mother, and to ask her to marry him. But, my mother's parents, they tell my mamma that she is not to see my father, or talk to him anymore because he is a Catholic. And that if she marries him, then they will never speak to her again."

"So, what happened?"

"My father, he returned to Italy alone, but they keep writing each other. My father tell my mother that he love her so much, that he'd do anything to be with her. He tells her he would convert to Islam so he could marry her. But my mamma knows that her family would never accept him. So one night, she ran away. She take a boat to Spain, then take three different busses to get to Italy, and her and my father, they get married six months later." She stops and stares at me.

"That's a great story," I say. "What happened to your mother's parents? Do they still talk to your mom?"

"No, they never speak to her again."

"Never?"

"My mother says that when I was born, her parents, they tell her auntie that they want to come see their grandchild. But my mother, she tell my auntie, *if they cannot accept her husband, then they cannot see the child who he has created.*"

"So, you never met your mom's parents?"

"No, never."

"That's really something."

"Yes, I tell you."

"Did your father ever convert to Islam?"

"No, my mother, she loves God very much, but she don't want my father to change his custom for her. He tell her he don't need to get married in a church, but she convert to a Catholic for him anyway because she loves him so much."

"Is that why you don't eat pork?"

"Yes, it's the one custom my mother never change. She doesn't eat pork, and so I never eat pork."

"You never tried it?"

"No, never."

"I bet that's tough in Italy."

"Maybe yes, everybody eats pork in Italy. But I never try it, so I don't miss it."

"I guess I could see that," I say. "But in New York, why did you say no 'pork or shrimp' for the tacos? Why no shrimp?"

"It's silly, don't worry."

"No, tell me."

"I don't know, I always feel that if I eat beef or even a chicken, then only one animal must die to feed many people. But if I eat shrimps, then many shrimps must die just to feed me. It doesn't seem fair."

"Of course it doesn't," I say, wiping the hair out of her sleepy eyes.

I can see she's fading. With the jetlag and the shitty airplane sleep, I'm surprised either of us lasted this long. I pull her into me and hold her in my arms. She takes a few placid breaths as her eyes fall heavy. "Max."

"Yes?"

"I love the way you are with me," she whispers. Her face twitches as she slips to sleep. I kiss the top of her head.

"So do I," I whisper. Then carry her into the bedroom and tuck her in.

✈

CHAPTER 24
I Believe in You

I WAKE EARLY to help Mr. Parazader with his driveway. Upon returning, I'm greeted with a kiss. I can tell she made and sampled our sandwiches as the combination of cheese, meat, and morning breath still lingers. I let her know in the sweetest way I can think of; I hug her around her arms, so they're stuck to her sides, and sniff her face like a dog. *Mff Mff Mff Mff Mff* "Mmm... your breath doesn't even smell like onions," I say, forcing a kiss on my squirming, clinched-lip Italian queen.

"Shut up, stronzo," she mumbles through her tightly butted lips, but I don't let go.

"Come here, I just want a little kiss. I like your onion breath."

"Stop it! You're being a bad monkey." I know she isn't mad; she's smiling under her pout. "Let me go, I have to brush my teeth."

"No, don't brush them. Not until I get another kiss." I pull her into me and peck her twenty-something times all over her twisting—turning face.

Aside from the sandwiches, she made breakfast. Fluffy eggs with melted feta, served on a toast, with sliced cherry tomatoes. It's 7:05 a.m., and the sun is about to rise. After she brushes, and I grab a few bites, I tell her to follow me to the back window where I flip the switch that slides the curtain, and I watch her eyes light up.

"Oh, God, Max, it's magnificent." The storm has long passed, and the sky is clear. The sharp peaks of the Tetons tear from the valley floor like giant jagged shark's teeth. The top-half is a mirror of the sun itself—as bright as anything found in nature, while the icy bottom remains shadowed in cold blues and muted grays. This early morning sight is the reason my dad built here. It's why the house faces the direction it does, and why the back windows reach from the floor to the frame. Sunrises like this are usually only seen a few times in one's life, and they always make for the best days.

After breakfast, I help her unpack. With her bag being overweight, she had paid extra on the plane. However, I had yet to lift it, as she'd always snatch it before I could. And when I'd go to help, she'd tell me *don't worry, I'm sporty*, and then stubbornly struggle.

So, with her legs bent and her back straight, she lifts a large canvas sack—stuffed full of fiction—out of her suitcase. "Max, where should I put my books?" she asks, pulling them out two at a time. I see *The Birth of Venus, Don Quixote, The Count of Monte Cristo,* and *Gone Girl*.

"Are you planning to disappear on me?" I ask.

"Don't tell me about that one. I don't read it yet."

Then there's *Walden* by Henry David Thoreau, *Cat's Eye*, and Holly Bourne's *Am I Normal Yet?*

I point to the title and shake my head, "No chance."

"Speak for yourself, monkey boy," says the apparently full-blown bibliophile. She has Orwell, Balzac, Matthew Quick, and *The Adventures of Tom Sawyer*. "You remind me of him."

I always imagined my younger self more the Holden Caulfield type, but I don't contest. Instead, I fetch a random piece of lint from my pocket, and in the slangiest backwoods-twang, I can spit out—I say, "I'll trade you this here witches eyebrow, and a daddy long-leg spider I saw in the kitchen fur a kiss."

She pauses, pressing a single finger to her pouting lips. "Hmm… I don't know about it, let me see this spider first."

"Ah, you are the stronzo," I say, stealing a kiss anyway.

She pulls out: Dumas, Oscar Wilde, Graham Hancock, John Green, Tarryn Fisher, Steven Pinker, and *The Nightingale*. I see some Italian authors. Dante's *Divine Comedy*, Italo Calvino,

Fabio Volo's *One More Day*, and *The Letters of Vincent Van Gogh*. "You like this too?" I ask.

"Yes, it's so much inspirational, but it's so sad."

She has: *Catching Big Fish*, *The Goldfinch*, Neil Gaiman's *Stardust*, *Into The Wild*, *Revolutionary Road*, and F. Scott Fitzgerald's *The Beautiful and Damned*. At the bottom of the bag, she pulls out: Sandra Brown, Veronica Roth, *The Road*, Norman Mailer, and *Wilderness and the American Mind* by Nash.

"Are you planning on doing anything while we're here? Or are you just gonna sit inside and read all day?"

"Shut up, don't make fun of me."

I stack her thirty-four books on a shelf by the fireplace before we rummage through my stepmom's closet. We find a pair of snow pants and gloves that fit, and so do the ski boots, or at least she says they do. I pack the truck, and we head out.

It's a glorious day. Overnight the mountain received a reported two feet of fresh powder, and we arrive early enough to ride those first tracks. On her request, we head straight to the Rendezvous Bowl, a black diamond that doesn't dissuade her. She's a much better skier than she had been letting on. Gracefully, she slices her way down that high un-touched backcountry run before bombing the piste trails at bone-chilling speeds. But I guess I shouldn't have expected anything less; she's exceeded expectations in every possible way.

She's remarkable, so much so that she doesn't seem real. But she is real, real as the sun, the sky, and the snow below me. And she wants me. She actually wants me. She's here to be with me. She doesn't care about the things I have or the things I don't. She doesn't care about the clout I carry, what clothes I wear, or what social clubs I belong to. She doesn't care about what I can do for her, or what I can give to her, and for that, I want to give her everything. I'm crazy about her. She consumes my every thought, my head, and my heart. She's my person, my panacea.

She's waiting for me down at the tram station, and in no time, we're heading back up in that big red box.

"You weren't kidding. You're not too bad," I say.

"Yes, it's a lovely mountain. The snow is like a pillow. But I'm how do you say, something of a rust. It's my first time skiing this winter."

"I didn't want to say anything," I smile.

"Oh, I didn't know that you could see me from that far behind." She winks.

"Stronzo," I bark back. "Who the hell taught you to ski like that?"

"My father. He was a champion when he was my same age."

"I suppose that makes sense. But why didn't you tell me you were so good? You could've brought your own skis and your own stuff."

"I didn't know. You speak of di mountains, but you said nothing of skiing, so I don't mention it. And anyhow, skiing, it's so expensive. And I tell you, I don't save so much money."

"That's because you spent it all on books."

"Shut up," she says.

"Will you do me a favor?" I ask.

"What is it?"

"Will you not worry about money this winter. I mean, I'm not rich by any means. But don't worry about it so much. We're staying in that house for free, and you really don't eat that much. We can come skiing whenever you want, or do whatever it is you want to do. Just say it, and we'll do it."

"I want to say *yes, ok*, but I cannot. I know how expensive it is, and I cannot have you pay so much for me every time we come. I tell you, my father, he gives me some money before I leave, but he's very conservative with money, so it's only enough for food, and maybe to ski a couple more times." I shake my head at her stubbornness. "And you have to let me pay our groceries while we here, or I will hate you." She gives me a fake-serious stare. "I only kid. I could never hate you. But I mean it of the groceries." And she kisses me.

✈

I smile inside at how lucky I am. "How are the skis?"

"They are nice. I have Rossignol back in Italy, and they ride very similar. But are you sure it is ok that I use them?"

"I'm positive."

We reach the top, and again, I watch her attack the trails from behind, far behind. She's so much better than me, my superior in every possible way. But it doesn't bother me; instead, it inspires me to push harder, past my comfort zone, and touch speeds I've never seen.

After several hours on the slopes, and with our sandwiches long gone, I'm looking forward to warming up with a hot meal. We ski over to The Handle Bar, a modern wood-walled beer hall with a stone fireplace.

It's packed, so we squeeze into a community table. I sit on the same side as her and order a couple cups of hot cocoa. She has the Handle burger with blue cheese and truffle aioli. And I have the Bison burger with roasted peppers and BBQ sauce. The food is brilliant, and the conversation even better.

Her hair is messy, her cheeks windburnt, and her face makeup-free, but she's still the most exciting thing I've ever seen. And for the first time in forever, I know exactly what I want.

"I love you, Raffaella," I blurt it out. "I know this isn't how it's supposed to go, or how it usually goes, or I don't know. I know we've only known each other for a short time, and I'm probably moving too fast. I mean, this whole thing is moving so fast, but I don't want to play games with you. I don't want to waste a second longer without you knowing that I do. I'm sure this isn't how you wanted to hear it or if you even wanted to hear it at all. I don't know, I just want to—"

"Max, shut up." I stop rambling, catch my breath, and stare into her, terrified of what she may say. "I love you too."

"You do?"

"Of course I do."

I kiss her, and a hot flush of merriment overtakes me. "You're sure?" I ask, as though I don't believe her.

✈

"Yes, I have no doubt."

"Good... because I love you. I really truly love you. I love you so much it hurts." She's smiling at me as I say it. "I love you, Raffaella." I can't stop myself. I don't want to. I've wanted to say this since the second I saw her and feel better every time I do. "I love you."

"I love you too, Max."

"I want to tell other people, can I tell other people?"

"Sì, sure. Who do you want to tell?"

She probably imagines I mean friends or family until I lean towards the couple across from us. "I don't mean to bother you two, but I just want you to know that I love this girl right here."

"Aw, that's so sweet," says the woman.

Then I lose it. Maybe it's the altitude, the clean-crisp air, my mild hypothermia, the smell of the wild, the wide-open nothingness, the tall trees, or the towering peaks. Or maybe it's just her and how wonderful she is, but I lose myself in a moment of madness. And I think nothing of it as I lean back to the table behind us. "I don't mean to bother you folks, but I just want you to know that I'm madly in love with this girl right here." After the initial surprise, a guy in a gray sweater reaches back and gives me a high-five, which only fuels the fool inside of me.

"Max, what are you doing? You so crazy." Her hands race to her face as I stand.

Flush with a feeling I've never felt, I climb up onto my seat. I can't stop—I couldn't if I tried. Loudly tapping a nearly empty cup of hot-cocoa with my spoon, *Dink! Dink! Dink!* I get the attention of the entire room. Some hundred or so people, all in scarves and snowcaps, muffle to silence. Every hushed face turns their attention to me. I glance down at her, her hands on her head and her face beet-red. But she's smiling, so I continue.

"Excuse me," I say loud and proud, standing tall where I sat seconds earlier. "I'm sorry to interrupt, I promise I'll be brief." I see phones lifting to record me. "First, I want to wish everyone here a Merry Christmas and a Happy New Year. And second, I just want you all to know about this woman right here, and how I think she's the most beautiful, most intelligent, most interesting person I've ever met in my entire life, and that I love her like crazy."

As soon as I say it, that first couple across from of us burst into applause, and their cheers swiftly spread, several stand and some shout, *way to go man*, and *she's beautiful*. Sure, it's a bit *Notebook*-esque, but it's spontaneous and sincere, and I know I'm not scared anymore.

I look down at her, and her daiquiri-red cheeks, and I hold out my hand. She takes ahold of it, so I pull her up to me, and in front of those smiling strangers, I give her one of those over-the-top fairy-tale type of kisses. The kind where she bends backwards, and you instantly believe that anything is possible. Applause rip through the room as our lips seal our now spoken bond of adoration. I take a quick bow, and we both sit, staring into one another.

"Max, you are so crazy."

"I'm crazy about you, I know that."

"No, you are really, really crazy, but I love it, and I love you."

"I love you too."

The manager ends up comping our tab and even throws in a chocolate cheesecake with an Oreo crust, so I throw the waitress a hundred dollar tip before we take off.

On the drive home, she spots something in the distance most Americans have only seen in the movies, but here, bison are commonplace. They're a football field from us, but we stop. "A zoo without bars," she says in awe, and tells me how she wants "to paint them," and that she feels bad because I "probably just ate their cousin in my burger."

Back at the house, she grabs the malbec, saying she "can't wait till Christmas," and tells me to meet her in the Jacuzzi. I snatch a couple glasses and strip down to my Calvin Klein briefs. The patio's snow is knee-deep, but the water is hot as hell. I grab

✈

some towels, quickly shovel a path, pour the wine, sit back in the bubbles, and stare up to about a billion stars.

She appears from the house tightly bundled in a white robe and tiptoes across the frozen deck. She takes an enormous breath as she steps out of the robe and into the steam. Her suit is black, her stomach tight, her hair down, and I'm hard as hell—concealing my swollen self beneath the bubbles—as I hand her the wine.

"Is very nice," she says, stepping in.

"What do you want to do tomorrow?" I ask.

"I don't know. I'm not yet thinking of tomorrow." She swims towards me, her eyes on mine. "Today was too perfect, and it's not over yet."

She kisses me under those stars, and I lose myself in her, and I believe she loses herself in me because she isn't interested in the sky, the moon-kissed mountains, or the wine. She wants something else tonight, something she's never had. Staring into my eyes, she slides her hips into me, eager and anxious. Her lips tremble as I trace her face with my fingertips. I can't believe how lucky I am, lucky to share this moment with her, this memory that will never fade. But as perfect as it is, I want her out of this water. I want to hear every breath, feel every touch, twitch, and tremble. I don't want a single sensation dulled by the heat or curtailed by the cold artic air. So, I pick her out of that steaming bath and carry through the frigid winter night, into the house, into the bedroom, and lay her soaking body on that big soft bed.

I stare at her in disbelief; *how did I get so lucky?* I want her more than I've ever wanted anything.

I lean in and kiss her lips before moving my mouth to her breasts. I could spend a lifetime tracing her with my tongue, but she wants it too bad, moaning as she pulls me out of my shorts, and our wet bodies become one. I press my weight into her. "Yes," she sighs, my throbbing self slides inside, my eyes on hers, my movement meaningful, my breath sporadic. She's dripping wet, tight as hell, and pulling me deeper.

✈

I don't fuck her, at least not at first. Instead, I press my weight into her and rhythmically roll my hips, so that every rock-hard, blood-enriched inch of mine stimulates every need she never knew she had. Her twitches of pleasure are plentiful and easily perceived as a climatic euphoria builds in her breath. She digs her nails deep into my back, and I watch her eyes fall high into her head. "Oh, Max." She pants and her legs kick.

"God damn," I swallow, struggling to hold back the pleasure, slipping so dangerously close to the edge. "Oh, shit!" I shout, rolling deeper into her, harder, filling her, giving her everything I have. Her face buries into me, her body locks, and her legs lose control as a waterfall of wet-heat flush between us. "Ahh! vengo! vengo!" she screams as violent contractions attack her core.

I collapse on top of her, a grin of satisfaction slides over her eyes. "Max," she's panting. "That was so incredible. I can't believe it."

I cover our warm, wet bodies with the comforter and pull her in close. I hold her tight, tight enough that she knows I'll never hurt her.

"What did you really think about it?" I ask.

"I tell you... it was incredible."

"No. I mean the malbec. What did you think?"

"Ah, you are so crazy. Don't joke with me. I don't even know my name."

We lay there holding one another, drifting in and out of dreams. Or maybe I wasn't dreaming. Maybe it's just my life now. Having never been this happy, it could easily be so.

Ding-Dong! The doorbell startles her. *Ding-Dong!* My first thought is Christmas carolers, but not likely way out here. Then, I think of Mr. Parazader, but he usually calls first. I jump to my feet and peek out the window in time to spot the ass-end of a van pulling away, and it clicks. "Why don't you go see who it is?" I say, crawling back into bed. She looks at me strangely but doesn't contest. Tossing a T-shirt over her head, she hurries out of the room.

290   J Gatz

✈

"It's nobody... is only a package," she yells through the house.

"Bring it in here," I holler back.

"It's very big."

"You're sporty. I believe in you."

She returns moments later, awkwardly lugging a large cardboard box. A box I'd all but forgot about. It's late, but Amazon's guaranteed Christmas Eve delivery came through.

"What is it?" she asks.

"I don't know—open it up."

"Right now?"

"No, in ten minutes."

"Stronzo."

As excited as a pet store puppy, she peels away the black and blue tape and tears through the box. Her eyes close, and her lips quiver. "I can't believe it."

"What did you get?" Pretending like I don't know. But she says nothing, not until that first teardrop falls to the floor.

"You are so incredible to me."

"Don't cry."

"I'm so happy. It's unbelievable. You are unbelievable."

"Bring it over here. Let's see what you got."

Out of the big brown box, she pulls the Deluxe Artist Paint Set, and a couple hundred dollars in extras I had ordered from my phone in New York, once I saw how much she truly loves art. The box comes complete with easels, several canvases, sketchpads, a variety of brushes, and more colors than a dozen rainbows.

"I know it's not art-school level stuff. But is it enough to get you started?"

"It's perfect," she says, and another tear traces her chin. "Is the best gift I ever receive. Thank you so much for always thinking of me. I love you."

I lay a sheet on the living room floor and set up the easel so that it looks out to the mountains when she paints. I carry in a small cabinet from the garage to store her supplics.

✈

We finish the wine and set out the cookies and cake for Santa.

It's late, and I'm spent, so I stretch out on the couch. She sits at my feet with my legs on her lap and calls her parents. It's Christmas morning in France. And as I lay there—fading fast—I hear her switching languages, as I assume the phone is being passed amongst the various members of her family. *"Buon Natale, Papà."* I catch a word or two but understand nothing.

"Mamma, el djibālou houna djamīlatoun jiddan." But I do notice a slight hint of an Italian accent whenever she speaks Arabic or French. *"J'ai vu le tableau di Monet à New York."*

CHAPTER 25
The Next John Cheever

I WAKE REFRESHED. I'm still on the couch, and she's on top of me. Part of me wants to get the day started, get the bird in the oven, and tackle a few chores. Instead, I spend the next hour running my fingers through her hair, watching her, until her sleepy eyes fall open.

"Merry Christmas," I whisper.

"Merry Christmas." She stretches to kiss me. "Can I have the little kisses?" So I kiss her again. "No di little kind, you know the ones I want." So I give her the smallest, softest kiss you can give someone. "Yes, those are my little kisses. I love you so much."

"I love you too."

She climbs to her feet and runs back to the bedroom. Seconds later, she returns with a decoratively wrapped package that looks to be a book. "Here, it's not much, but is for you."

I tear the paper. It's a gold-framed photo, the one I took of her in Hong Kong. "It's me and little Marco. Is it ok?"

"It's perfect," I say, studying the photo, my face filled with smiles, knowing everything from that day eventually lead to this.

"I'm sorry it's not as good as the painting supplies you get me, but I don't know what you want."

"I want you," I whisper. "And I love it. Thank you. It's the best gift I ever got. And you look beautiful as hell."

"And little Marco, he looks so handsome. He's my second favorite monkey, you know."

"Second?"

"Yes, of course. You are my first favorite. You know that." And I kiss her again.

"Hold on," I say, standing, then jog into the kitchen. I return with a cookie in my mouth and a rose-colored envelope in my hand.

"What is it?"

"Open it."

She pulls out a folded piece of paper and reads it. "Max, this is too much, I cannot accept this."

"Well, they're already paid for. So if we don't use them, they'll go to waste."

"You are a crazy man, this is too much."

"The way I see it... now we don't have an excuse not to go," I say, about the printout good for two seasons passes to the Jackson Hole Ski Resort.

"You are so incredible to me. I can't even believe you."

"You're happy?"

"Of course I'm happy. I don't even know what to say... I will never forget your kindness."

"And I'll never stop loving you."

At $1,800 apiece, it's the most expensive gift I'd ever given anyone by far. But after seeing her on the slopes, and that smile across her face, I would've given everything I had. She makes me feel as though I'm the wealthiest man in the world, yet I want for nothing except to make her smile. I purchased them when I pretended to use the bathroom after we ate. The money doesn't matter because I know whenever we're on that mountain, it will remind me of the first time she said she loved me.

She makes us breakfast: poached eggs, avocado toast, a slice of fruitcake, and a few of Santa's cookies.

She wants to help prepare dinner, but I tell her to relax. So, she spends her day painting the mountains while I prep the food, call my parents, and soothe my sore ski muscles in the tub.

While soaking, I scroll through my phone. I'd received *Merry Christmas* texts from Anna, Natasha, Lexi, and two other girls I'd been with since Nadja. I don't respond to any of them.

In fact, I promptly delete them, knowing that part of my life is over.

I'm juicing the bird when she asks what I think. "It's great," I say, "it's really great." *And it is great.* A near-perfect rendering of the mountain peaks violently tearing through the calm, snow-covered valley. With realistic trees and a true to life contrast between the snow, the clouds, and the sharp stones.

"How about we hang it above the fireplace?" I say.

"We can, but I was thinking maybe, that we could give it to your neighbor for a Christmas gift. If it's ok with you?"

"Sure, that's a nice idea."

"I don't know him like you do. Will he like it?"

"There's no doubt he will," I say, glancing down at my watch. "Actually, he'll be here soon. How about you hop in the shower."

It's not a second past four when the doorbell rings. She runs out of the room in an oversized sweater, leggings, and candy cane socks.

"Ho, ho, ho, Merry Christmas," says Mr. Parazader, in a red Santa hat, a dusting of snow on his shoulders, and a heavy-looking box in his hands.

"Merry Christmas," I say. "Come on in."

"Happy Christmas," she says before her eyes move past him. "I didn't know it was snowing. Max, look, it's snowing on Christmas."

"It just started up a few minutes ago," he says, in his slow southern drawl.

"Here, let me take that from you," I say.

"Thank you, young man."

"Where's the truck?" I ask.

"Traveled by foot."

"Damn, you carried this heavy-ass box all the way here?" I say, setting down the thirty-plus pound package. "What the hell you got in here, coal? I haven't been that bad."

"Oh, you know I ain't good at deciding these things, so I brought a little of everything. We got some candied yams, some fresh cranberry sauce, and I made my famous deviled eggs. We had them a few years back, and I remembered you ate almost all of them.

"You carried this all the way here?"

"I did," he says, standing straight, puffing his chest, making his old man's body look bigger. "Not gonna lie to ya though, I took a couple breaks along the way. That's how I know the snow just kicked up. Because it sure as heck wasn't snowing when I left."

"Why didn't you just drive over?"

"Well, boy, I like my truck. And I don't always leave here as sober as I came in."

"I could've come and picked you up," I say.

"Nonsense. I made it, didn't I? So what are we even talking about it for? Most of the weight came from that beer in there anyhow. I picked us up a dozen of those fancy pottery bottled Belgium brews you like, that Delirium Tremens, or however the hell you say it."

"You didn't have to do that."

"Nonsense, my boy, you're kind enough to invite me over, and well, hell, you're my favorite drinking buddy. If we're gonna drink, we're gonna drink the good stuff. And I wasn't sure what you like, sweetheart. I noticed you have a nice accent, I'm guessing Swiss or Italian?"

"Yes, I'm Italian," she replies.

"That's what I thought." He reaches into the box. "I know you're accustomed to good wine over there, so I picked up a couple bottles of our finest American stuff for you to try. I got a chardonnay from California, and what the liquor store lady told me to be, a very nice pinot noir from Oregon. Do you like any of those?"

"I'm sure I will. Thank you very much. It's very kind of you."

"Make yourself at home," I say. "That bird's got about twenty minutes left in her."

✈

I open the pinot and pour us a couple cold ones. He's looking out the back window, going on about how he wishes he'd gotten this lot, so he'd have that view.

Then he tells us how he comes over every few weeks to rake the leaves or pick up sticks, hoping I'd be here.

We've always have had good times together, him and me. Both being from different eras—different worlds really—we'd bond by building a fire, getting blitzed, and bullshitting. He's a nice old man, so I'd always find a night or two to throw back a few whenever I'm in town.

"How you like the brew boy?" he asks.

"Hits the spot. I've actually been craving one of these."

"It is a damn fine beer, I'll give you that. But it's about as strong as an alligator's scute, and it ain't too easy to find."

"I think they've got it over at Jack's," I say.

"Yeah, that's where I got it."

"You didn't have to go to any trouble."

"Nonsense, it's Christmas goddammit, and I ain't seen ya in a while. Besides, this pink elephant piss is awfully tasty."

"Well, cheers, and Merry Christmas," I say, and we all raise a glass.

"How's that wine, sweetheart?"

"It's a very nice wine. Thank you again."

"Hey, that paint set over there is new. What are you working on, Max?"

"It's hers," I thumb.

"Whatchya painting over their sweetheart?"

She looks at me, asking with her eyes if it's a good time. I nod, and without a word, she jogs across the room, grabs the painting, and presents it to him. "Here, this is a gift for you. Merry Christmas."

"Gee golly, look at that. That there is really something special. Who painted this?"

"I did," she says.

"Oh, I'll be damned. There's no way you painted this. I reckon you're jerking my chain." She glances over at me for translation. "You really painted this sweetheart?"

"Yes, I did it today. Careful, it's still wet."

"Now that there sure is a purdy picture."

"Thank you," she replies.

He holds it up with straight arms and admires it as though he's seeing color for the first time. "Look at those details, it's like I'm looking out that there window. Look here, boy, now I've got the same million-dollar view y'all got over here. Hell, it's a perfect picture, save me a fortune."

"I'm glad you like it," she says.

"Like it, hell, I'll tell you what. I don't doubt this to be the best damn Christmas gift I ever received, and I'm one hell of an old man. Well, that is besides my son."

"Your son was a Christmas gift?" she asks.

"Born on Christmas morning, he was. I wanted to call him Jesus, but my wife wouldn't have it. Said we'd sound like a bunch of bible thumping hillbillies. I suppose she was right on that one, so we called him David instead."

"David is a nice name," she says.

"It sure was a nice name, and he was a nice boy." He pauses momentarily, closes his eyes, and instinctively makes a quick four-point cross with his fingers. "I don't know if Max told you or not, but my son... he died."

"I'm sorry to hear it."

"Oh, it's ok, sweetheart. It was a long-long time ago. I hate to even bring it up. But I will tell ya one thing about death, something I went my entire life without knowing until after he passed."

"What is it?" she asks.

"Oh, I don't wanna bring down the evening with such grim conversation, you just handing me this lovely picture and all, maybe some other time."

"No, I want to hear it," she says. He smiles and settles back into his thought.

"Ok, well... the thing about death is just how forever it is. I lost my parents at a young age, but that just seemed like a part of life. Losing my boy was so different. For ten years after he died, I swear, I'd wake up every morning expecting to find

298   J Gatz

him at the breakfast table—eating his Cap'n Crunch—reading his Dick Tracy comic books. That boy was as smart as a damn dolphin, coulda grew up to be anything. It's a goddamn shame it is."

"I'm so sorry," she says.

"Oh, it's alright. Like I said, it was a long time ago. Sure, I think about him every day, and how he could've been. But that's life, we're all gonna die someday. When my wife went, God rest her soul, I didn't wake up expecting to see her. I knew she was gone, and I'm sure if I haven't messed it up too bad with the man upstairs, I'll be with her soon enough." He mumbles another prayer to himself, and silence fills the air...

"Well, I hope you enjoy the painting," she says.

"Oh, I will. This here is a real gem. It's gonna go right on my wall. I want to look at it every day when I wake up and every night before I go to bed. Only, there's something missing, though."

"What is it?" she asks.

"Well, I don't see your autograph. With talent like this, I have no doubt you're gonna be a famous painter someday, that's if you aren't already. This thing's either gonna make me a bundle or be hanging in a museum somewhere. And I'd sure as hell like to have your name on it, so when I tell people that you painted it and that I met you, they'll actually believe me."

"You want my autograph?"

"Well, hell yeah, I do. Otherwise, folks are gonna think I just snuck over here and took a photo out that there window."

She blushes, then hurries over to her paints, pulls out a brush, and dips it in some black that's still on her palate. I can see how proud she is as she signs her name, *Raffaella Bellini*, in the bottom corner.

"Who knew such a good-looking couple like yourselves would have so much artistic talent between the two of you," says the old man.

"What does it mean, between the two of you?" she asks.

"Well, with you being such a fantastic painter, and Max being a writer."

✈

"Max is a writer?" She turns to me.

"Hell yeah, he is. He hadn't shown you any of his stuff yet?"

She buries her eyes into mine. "No, he never mentioned it."

"Hell, the boy's the next John Cheever, I swear he is. Hell of a good storyteller, this one. What have I read, what, five-six of your stories? You got anything new since I seen you last?"

"No, didn't write much this year," I say, looking into her, imagining she's vexed for me not mentioning this. And though I never lied to her, I sense my omission hurts her, believing I didn't trust her with this information. But outside of this old man, I've barely told anybody about writing, or even my interest in the subject, not my parents, not my friends, not my lovers, nearly nobody.

"Well, that's a damn shame. I really like that last one, the one with the guy who travels all over the country, helping people along the way. And then it turns out he's a goddamn murder, who's actually testing people to see if they're good or not, and if they aren't, they get the knife. I mean that one was something; I'd like to read it again if I could. Hell, I should be able to check it out at the library—a story like that."

"Maybe one day," I say.

"How can I see it?" she asks.

"Well, ya see, sweetheart, that's the boy's only problem. He doesn't share his work with anyone worth sharing it with. I mean, I've been telling him for years to send his stuff out for publication, but he doesn't listen to me."

"They're not finished yet," I say.

"Hell, they ain't. Raffaella dear, now I know I'm just some old decrepit schoolteacher, who probably couldn't write squat about nothing outside of the animal kingdom, but I tell you what, that's some damn good reading those stories are. Max, how about that one with that guy chasing women over in the Pacific islands? Hell, that'd be a best seller the day you released it. Or the one with those man-eating cougars in the hills of Hollywood, man, they'd make movies out of that one."

"Did you ever try to publish them?" she asks me.

"No, I just wrote them for fun. I wrote them all here when I had nothing else to do."

"Oh sweetheart, I'm sure they're sitting around in a drawer somewhere, just gathering up dust. That's if he hasn't burned 'em all. I swear, I seen him do it. I seen him burn a stack of pages as thick as a beer can is round. All because he got it into his head that it wasn't any good. Remember that night, boy? We got all juiced up on that maple Crown, and you kept going on about how you wasted months of your life, and then without warning, you stormed in and out of the house holding that manuscript and not saying a word—you just tossed it in the fire. And then I swear he just sat back in his chair like nothing happened, and poured us another whiskey. We toasted to something about moral or immoral shenanigans, or something like that. I'm telling you—it was like watching a crazy man, calm and crazy at the same time, a full-blown psychopath sitting next to me.

You know, I still tell that story to the boys down at Eleanor's. What was that, Max—what—two summers ago?"

"Yeah, I didn't like that one much."

"I don't know why you're so down on yourself, son. I may not be a fancy New York book editor, and in your eyes, I'm probably just some old hillbilly, but I know a good story when I read one. You gotta remember, I grew up in a time when we didn't have all these fancy electronic gadgets and distractions you kids have today. If you wanted entertainment, you either rode a bike, read a book, or got drunk. And well, I wasn't such a rummy back then. So believe me when I say that I know a thing or two about a good story."

The oven timer dings and I plate the food. We have enough for ten people: turkey, salmon, stuffing, yams, mashed potatoes, cranberry sauce, cubed cheddar cheese, green olives, fresh peppers with ranch, and deviled-eggs.

None of us go wanting for anything, nor do we eat so much that we don't drink. I have three Deliriums with the meal, and Mr. Parazader keeps pace.

"Max, did I ever tell you about the time I lit a cigarette for Frank Sinatra?"

"I think you have," I say, having heard it a dozen times, "but Raffaella hasn't."

"Do you know who Frank Sinatra is, sweetheart?" he asks.

"Yes, he's famous for singing."

"That's right, famous for singing. And in 1968, he was the most famous there is. Now I was in Miami for a teacher's convention. It was as hot as Satan's breath that day, so I popped in this little spot called Duffy's for a cold one. And just as I had finished my beer and was about to leave, some guy signals the bartender. 'Jack with a splash of water and a light if you got it,' he said. Now, I had just lit my own cigarette, so I instinctively held up my lighter. He turned to me and took a draw. And as he stood straight and puffed on that smoke, I realized it was ole blue eyes himself. 'Thank you, friend,' he said to me, then took his drink down in one smooth swig, tossed a ten on the till, and hit the door."

"That's a nice story," she says.

"Greatest moment of my life, besides marrying my wife, and the birth of my boy." He goes on to tell us a few more, less sensational stories.

We all sit at that table for a few hours, eating cookies, cracking jokes, listening to the old man's tales, and when we get drunk enough, we even sing a couple Christmas songs.

After the beer and wine run dry, I dig into the liquor cabinet. He and I have a couple Captain Cokes and toss back a few Jacks. She's in good spirits and seems to enjoy the night, the songs, the stories I've heard so many times, but unlike the old man and me, she doesn't drink much.

It turns out to be a great Christmas, the nostalgic kind you remember as a kid: with sugary smells, fresh snow, and *Charlie Brown* in the background.

It's late when Mr. Parazader stumbles to the door, his painting tucked tight under his arm, refusing a ride home. I shake his hand and tell him we'd *get together soon.*

Closing the door, I turn to her; she's staring at me, her arms crossed, her face serious.

"Hello, beautiful," I slur, squinting, so the two of her returns to one. I smile to myself, realizing she's never seen me this skunked.

"Can I please read your stories?" she asks.

"And why would you want to do that?"

"Because I love you, and I want to know everything about you."

"They're nothing special." I'm shitfaced and slurring.

"How do you get the ideas to make them?"

"I don't know. How do we do anything? They just came to me, mostly while I was here. You'll see... there's really not too much to do here. Especially when you're alone. Lots of time to think."

"But five stories, that's not nothing," she says.

"Well, there's act—*Hick!*" I hiccup. "Actually, there's only four. I burned the last one too."

"But why?"

"It was fu—*Hick!* It was fuk-*nnn* garbage."

"I'm sure it wasn't."

"Well, it's long gone... and not coming back."

"You don't have them saved on your computer?"

"Nah, I can't write anything on a goddamn com—*Hick!* Computer."

"How do you write them?"

"I use a pen and a yellow paper. And when I'm done, I type it out on this old electric typewriter I've had since I was a kid. It works juss... fine."

"And you make fun of my film camera."

"I'm fuckin old babe. *Shhhhhhh.*" I shush her for some reason, then whisper, "and I'm really-really drunk."

"Yes, you are drunk, but not too old." She pulls me in and kisses me.

"I am. I'm old. I'm an old—old guy."

She cups my face in her hand. "I remember a magazine article I read about Danielle Steel, the famous writer. It said that she uses a typewriter too. You are the same."

"No, I'm nothing like her. Not even close. She's written like a hundred—*Hick*—thousand books. You know how many— *Hick*, how many books I've written? Zero. That's how many... but I got you—*Hick*. And that's all I need."

"You do have me, but you also have four stories. And that's really good."

"Four, fuck—*Hick!* I wrote seven. Seven shitty stories, but I burned those sons-a-bitches too." I swallow hard, holding my breath, an attempt to suppress my spasming diaphragm.

"Do you still have them?"

"Sure, I do."

"Can I please read them?" She looks scared as she asks. As though I'd say no.

"Babe, they're shit," I mumble.

"Please."

"You really want to?"

"Please, I really-really do."

"Sure, why the hell not. But do me a favor—*Hick!*"

"Anything."

"Once you see that they're shit, just put it back in the drawer and forget all about 'em, ok."

"Ok," she says.

And so I stumble into the second bedroom, the one with the heads, and return carrying four manuscripts, all typed on plain white paper, a few-hundred pages apiece, and bound by twine. I drop the stack on the kitchen counter and mumble my way through them. "This one here is the one Mark was talking about, with the guy who travels around America murdering 'the morally weak,' as the killer calls them. It's alright—*Hick!* But the ending sucks. This one is called *Cats in the Hills*. It's, well, it's about this group of cougars in the hills of Los Angles. But they're actually ancestors of this old tribe. During the—*Hick!* During the day, they fight global warming, and then at night, they turn into big cats, and they kill people with power, people who they see as destroying the earth. It's a kind of teenager story—*Hick!* And I promise it's not too scary." I'm stumbling, mumbling, and barely holding my shit together, but she's smiling, so I keep slurring on. "And this one right here is called *A Life of Ten Men,* but it might as well be called *What A Fucking Waste of Time.* It's about some guy who moves to Hawaii and gets into a bunch of shit. I don't think there's really a point to it; it's not really about anything. I guess it's just a story for the sake of reading a story. And then there's this one. It's called *The Squirrels of Central Park.* It's about a guy who moves to New York on his thirtieth birthday. And he—*Hick!* He struggles for many years as a busboy and then a bartender, before he eventually opens his own restaurant on his 40th birthday—*Hick!* Anyway, there's a bunch of stuff that happens to him along the way, but no matter what happens, he always feels better when he sits on his favorite bench and feeds the squirrels. It's kind of literary, and probably my best."

"Which one can I read tonight?"

"You want to read tonight?" My eyes are falling as I brace myself with the table.

"I do."

"Have at it—*Hick!* Read whatever you want. But baby, I think I'm gonna go to bed, ok?"

"Yes, go to sleep, you need your rest," she says. "Merry Christmas, give me a kiss." So I do. Then I stumble into our room, spinning as I crawl into the bed.

I wake alone, my head throbbing, my eyes sore, and my shoes on. *Fuck.* It takes a good twenty minutes of self-speak before I coax myself into standing. I walk heavy-headed into the living room. "When did you get up?" I mumble.

She's flat on the couch, reading one of my manuscripts. *Fuck.* I forgot I gave her those.

"I didn't sleep."

"You've been up all night?"

"Yes, I've been reading your stories," she says.

"Which one?"

"I finished *Ten Men*, and now nearly halfway through *Vagabond Scourge*."

"Great," I mutter to myself.

"Baby, I think they are so good, I really enjoy them. But I have questions for you."

"Sure," I say, filling a glass of water from the faucet. *My head feels like it's on fucking fire.* After a few nauseating sips, I aim my bodyweight back towards the bedroom, hoping momentum will carry me.

"Wait," she cries out. "Please... come lay on the couch with me, so I can see you."

I stumble to a stop and turn to her, my eyes sore, my brain possibly bleeding. I pitifully teeter towards her and sprawl out on the oversized sofa.

It's silent for the first few minutes, and I'm almost back to sleep when. "Is *Life of Ten Men* about you?" she asks. *Fuck!*

"No," I reflexively mutter. But it is. Or at least it was.

"Are you sure?" she presses. "Is very sexual."

"I know."

"And the main character, he is very much like you. I think it is you, no?"

"He's like me because I created him."

"Yes, I know, because in the *Vagabond*, he is like you too. He's very gentle and kind, but he is a murderer. You're not a murderer, right?"

"Maybe I am," I sputter, my eyes struggling in the sunlight. "They're just characters," I mumble. *Fuck.* In reality, the whole goddamn story is pretty much about me. Even Anna is in there. But I can't tell her that. I love this girl, and never want doubt to enter her mind.

"There are many sex scenes, some with more than one girl. Is it a real story?"

Fuck! I say nothing. I don't want to lie to her, but my dehydrated—likely damaged—brain can't think of a goddamn thing to say. So, I painfully stare up into her curious eyes, my mind numb, my mouth immobile.

✈

I've been a scoundrel, there's no doubt about it, but how can I say this to her? A woman I truly love. A woman whose virginity I took two nights ago, who just read a story I wrote five fucking years ago, about fucking every goddamn girl I talked to. *And why the fuck did I even give that to her anyway? How fucking stupid-drunk was I last night? Fuck!* But I can't lie to her. I won't. And I never will. Ever. I'd rather hurt her feelings than keep something from her. "Babe, I need to tell you something, something that—" but she cuts me off.

"Stop... I don't want to know. I don't care about it. I don't care about what you did before you meet me. I love you, and I know that you love me. And that's all that matters from this moment forward."

"You're incredible," I murmur.

"No, what we have is incredible." I pull her lips to mine. "But I have to say something." She pulls back, looking almost scared.

"What is it?"

"The story."

"What about it?"

"I'm not sure how to say, but it makes me whoreish."

"Whoreish?"

"Yes, like I feel so sexy."

"You mean horny?"

"Ah, sì, horny. It makes me horny." Her body presses against mine.

My crippling hangover dissolves into desire as I spread her legs and slide between them. Her screams echo off the high ceiling, and after she cums and can't take anymore, I walk her over to the window and deposit my manhood into her mouth. Looking out at that million-dollar mountain view, I cum harder than I ever have.

"You weren't kidding... you were whoreish."

"That was so perfect." I pull her up to me. "I still can't believe this is real."

"Me either."

✈

I hold her on the couch and watch her heavy eyes struggle as her sleepless night catches up.

     I carry her into the bedroom and cover her with a sheet.

"We really are in love, aren't we?" she whispers.

"So in love."

"Max," she says listlessly.

"Yes, darling?"

"Have you ever loved anyone else?"

I don't even think about it. "No"

"Never?"

"No. I once thought I did, but no."

"What happened?"

"Nothing. It just wasn't love."

"What was it?" her eyes strain to stay open.

"It was nothing like this."

"Did she hurt you?"

"It doesn't matter."

"Max."

"Yes?"

"I'll never let anyone hurt you."

"I know," I whisper, and her eyes fall.

J Gatz

CHAPTER 26
I'd Die For You

I SPEND MOST OF MY DAY DOING CHORES. I change the oil in the truck, fill the birdfeeder, and shovel the deck. I drive into town to pick up a few things, and then chop firewood that's been drying in the shed.

After an eventful day of pondering, I pull out *A Life Of Ten Men*. I hadn't read it since I wrote it. So, with my tired wood-chopping arms and a neck that stiffens by the second, I sit in the Jacuzzi and dig in.

She wakes just before sunset; I'm slouched over in the steam, about sixty pages in. Sliding beside me, she tells me, "it's good," and that I "should publish it." She's not totally wrong; it's not half bad. Sure, it's sexual, but it's entertaining. I tell her *I'll think about it*, and she says she "can't wait to read the others."

After a while, I whip us up some dinner: grilled chicken sautéed in Irish butter and fresh herbs. I slice it over a bed of baby spinach, dried fruit, walnuts, and creamy goat cheese. We wash it down with a bottle of Martini & Rossi Asti and vanilla bean ice cream.

As we digest, I read *The Squirrels of Central Park* aloud to her as she paints a photo she took in Times Square. We make love. Then curl up on the couch to watch *The Neverending Story*.

Our next few days go pretty much like this. We wake early, ski, soak in the hot tub, eat dinner, and make love. Or make love and then dinner. I read to her while she paints in front of the fire, and then we watch a movie before bed.

We eat Sno-caps and watch all the classic American films she'd never seen: *Shawshank*, *Turner and Hooch*, *Dumb and Dumber*, and *The Notebook*. She cries after all of them.

I tell her I love her as her eyes open every morning and countless times throughout the day.

I've had good times in my life, wild times, but nothing like this, not even close. Our love comes as easy as a country song—effortless and free of doubts. I selflessly give myself to her, and she responds by giving herself back to me. We simply enjoy being together. I tell her how *I don't even like driving into town without her*, and she tells me *I need to get better at skiing because she misses me when I'm so far behind.*

New Year comes quickly. We decide to keep it simple, dinner and some drinks. I'm in khaki pants and a collared shirt, and her, a turtleneck dress.

I pick a small downtown spot called The Kitchen that could compete with any fine-dining experience in the state. I order wine, we both decide on the striped bass, and she tells me how *wonderful everything has been.*

"I'll drink to that," I say, and we tap glasses.

"Max, can I ask you something. It's something I've been wondering?"

"You can ask me anything."

"Well, I don't want to be nosy, and I know it's your father's house, so it's not too expensive, but the skiing, and the dinners, and the flights, and the presents, are you ok with money?"

"I told you, don't worry about that. We're fine."

"But you've been spending—"

"We're fine."

"But we—"

"We're fine. I promise. And besides, we're not really spending that much at all. You eat like a dollar's worth of pasta a day. And all we do is ski, and have sex, and sit in the hot tub. "

"Yes, and it's wonderful. But eventually, don't we need to get a job?" I laugh.

"I don't want to get a job," I say. "I've gone way too long now without a normal job; I couldn't do it now if I tried. I don't want one. Do you?"

"Is not a problem for me... I don't have a visa, but I'm sure I can find something."

"No, I don't want you to get a job either," I say. "But I do expect you to start making us some money."

"What do I do? You tell me what to do, and I do it."

"Listen, you're too damn talented to work as a waitress. I think it's time you start selling your paintings. In fact, I know it is."

"What do you mean?"

"Just what I said. You're ready. Your stuff is good. No, your stuff is great. No, your stuff is magnificent. You and your paintings are magnificent, and you're gonna start selling them."

"But who will buy them?"

"People."

"Yes, people—but who?"

"Raffaella, you don't need to doubt yourself anymore. You don't need to be afraid. You're ready to be seen by the world. Your work is incredible, and people will want what you're creating. You just have to put it out there. Like that one you did of the guy, the one with the umbrella in Times Square, it's amazing." *And it is.* "Raffaella Bellini, you're just as talented as any of those famous painters you showed me, like that guy who paints the dripping honey, Mike um... Mike Dargas, or that Reisha Perlmutter, or however you say her name. You just have to believe in yourself as much as I do."

"Don't be silly. I'm not as good as them."

"Yes, you are. You just have a different style, that's all. Like you said, 'cooler cools, brighter brights, pink when possible, and multiple focal points, a mix between hyperrealism and impressionism.' That's what you said, right? And it's your own style, and that's a good thing. People want something different. Something nobody else is doing."

"How do we sell them?"

"Promise me you won't be mad?"

"Yes, of course—I promise."

"Well, I took some pictures of your paintings the other night, and I emailed them to this guy I know in Chicago. He has

✈

a gallery in the building where I used to live. It was just below me, and I'd always talk to him. It's a nice gallery. And well, he's agreed to show your pictures at an event next month. Both *The Red Umbrella* and the *Tooth of God*." Her mouth falls. "He said that if they sell—which I know they will—then he'd gladly take more of your stuff."

"You really did that?"

"I did."

"I can't believe it." Her smile stretches ear-to-ear. "You really believe in me, don't you?"

"Of course I do."

"And you really think someone will buy them?"

"I have no doubt about it."

"Why are you so good to me?"

"Because I love you."

She pulls my palm up to her face and exhales deeply. "What do I do next?"

"Nothing. We'll mail it out the day after tomorrow, and you just have to keep painting. Every day."

"I can do that." Her eyes are full of hope and happiness.

"We'll have to pick up some more canvases too. We'll get a dozen in all different sizes."

"But canvases are so expensive."

"I told you not to worry about it. Besides, they're an investment. Those canvases will pay us back fifty-times what we pay for them. I know they will."

"I love you so much, Max, and I love that you want to see me be success." I don't correct her as she reaches across the table to kiss me. "Wait." She stops.

"What is it?"

"We can only send di pictures if you promise me one thing."

"What's that?" I ask.

"You have to promise me you gonna send your stories to a publisher."

"But they're not ready yet," I say reflexively.

✈

"That's bullshit, you know it. You tell me yourself—that they better than you remember, no?"

"But that doesn't mean they're ready."

"What are you waiting for? Believe me, I know they are good, baby. I promise you. Your writing, it's different, it's not so similar to other writers."

"So I suck?" I smirk.

"No, of course not. It's like you say for me, it is your own style, and because it is so different, is the reason people will like it... like a singer has his own voice."

"And what singer would I be?"

"Bob Dylan." She says unthinkingly as if she's already thought it through.

"You know Bob Dylan?"

"Yes, everybody knows him. He's is much influence in American culture."

"And why would my writing resemble his songs?"

"Because he is not refined."

"Thanks," I smirk.

"No, what I mean is... he is wild... his sound, and the way he sings is so free, his voice, so unrefined, but his words, even the simple ones, they can be so powerful, and the meanings of what he says is often so important. A meaning that is deeper than the surface words." She grabs both of my hands. "And besides, if you do nothing—then nothing will happen. If you don't try, yes, nobody will criticize you, nobody will judge you, or say you suck, but also, nobody will get to learn from your experiences or take joy in the stories and characters you create. And if you do try to publish, what is di worse that can happen? They tell you no? They tell you it's not for them? Fine, then you send it to somebody else, somebody who sees the potential you have."

"Ok," I say, knowing I already have everything I want and nothing to lose.

"That is a yes?"

"If you say they're ready, then they are."

"Thank you, Bobo, you make me so happy, give me a kiss." So I do. And then I sit back and stare at her.

"I've actually thought of another story I want to write," I say.

"What is it of?"

"Well, it's about a girl."

"Who is the girl?"

"I'm not sure yet, but she's smart and beautiful and talented. And I'm pretty sure she's a princess. A princess who saves her prince."

"Is it a story of us?"

"Are you a princess?"

"I am your princess."

"You are..."

"Do you really want to write a story like that?"

"I do."

"But what will it be about?"

"I'm not sure yet, but I know I could write a dozen thick books about nothing except how beautiful you are."

"I love you, Max."

"I know. I love you too..."

"How does it end?" she asks.

"What?"

"The story. The story of us, how will it end?"

"Oh, well... you die."

"Really?"

"No, I'm kidding. It'll have a happy ending. Happy ever after, because it's a fairy-tale."

"Our story is a fairy-tale."

We head over to Town Square Tavern, a typical neighborhood bar, busy, with a first-rate all-girl band belting out hits. I order a pint of Budweiser and her a Titos cranberry.

"What is the name of this song?" she asks.

"I have no idea. Why?"

"Don't you think it's nice?"

"Yeah, it's good."

"Oh, I like it so much. I want to listen to it at home." She pulls out her phone, looking stressed as she studies her screen. "Can you please Shazam it for me? I don't have any gigas here."

"Sure," I say. "But I'm pretty sure it doesn't work like that. I don't think it will recognize a cover band."

"Just try it, please."

So I do. I pull out my phone and open the app.

"Hey, it worked," I say.

"Who is it?"

"It's called *Dream it Possible*."

"Who is di singer?"

"It says it's by Delacey."

"Oh, I will look it up later when we get home. I think it's a wonderful—" She stops speaking; I look over to see her eyes grow as disturbing disbelief flushes to her face.

"What's wrong?" I ask.

"That guy. That guy there, he just grabbed my butt."

"What guy?"

"The one over there. The big one with the white shirt."

"Was it an accident?"

"No, no, he did it on purpose. He squeezed it." It hurts me to hear her say it.

"He grabbed you just now?"

"Yes, just as he walk by."

"You're sure it's him?"

"Yes, I'm sure." She looks terrified as I turn towards the man, a tall cowboy with big shoulders and a buzz cut.

"What you gonna do?" I hear her ask over my shoulder, but don't look back, I don't even put down my beer.

I walk straight up to the guy. I haven't come up with a plan, but I'm boiling. I hate him, and it takes everything inside of me not to hit him, not smash this glass into his face, or rip out his fucking throat. But I don't. I don't want her to see that side of me. He stands tall, his chest puffed, his arms akimbo, and he looks to be clenching his jaw, probably expecting me to swing.

"You got something to say to me, pretty boy?" he says it through a fat-lip full of dip.

"Go fucking apologize to her right now," I demand.

"You can fuck yourself, I ain't doing shit." He squares his shoulders, moving his face towards mine.

"Apologize to her... now," I demand again.

"You don't want any of this, pretty boy. Go on and get on outta here before I whip your ass." I'm not even sure where my reaction comes from. Maybe I saw it in a movie somewhere. I want nothing more than to dig my thumbs into his eyes, but instead, I lift my beer above his head and empty the entire pint. Drowning him in a cold shower of American hops.

I tighten my jaw, expecting a fist, or maybe headbutt, but as the beer dribbles down his shirt, he doesn't do anything. Instead, his face scowls-up sour—almost sad, and he begins to bark like a little bitch. "Oh man, you just fucked with the wrong guy, you don't even know who I am, you fucking faggot!"

I stand there—empty pint in hand—waiting for him to retaliate, but he doesn't. So, I turn and walk nonchalantly back to the bar. I expect security to come kick me out, but they don't. The band keeps playing, and barely anyone outside of his circle seems to notice.

"Max, I can't believe you did that."

"He didn't want to apologize."

"He's soaking wet."

"He grabbed your butt, right?"

"Yes, he did."

"Then he's a jackass, and he deserves—"

"Max, he's coming," she says quickly.

"Stand back," I say.

With a few friends behind him, he gets right back in my face. "I told you you fucked with the wrong guy." He spits as he says it. "I got all my boys here with me, you fucking faggot!"

"Did you come over to apologize?" I ask.

"No, I came here to whip your ass, pussy." He steps closer, now nearly nose-to-nose.

✈

"Are you threatening me?" I breathe, smirking as I lean into him.

"No. I'm telling you I'm gonna whip your ass. And then I'm gonna slap your little skanky girlfriend's ass again, too."

I don't take the time to talk myself in or out of any action as a fearsome McGregor craze overtakes me, and I crack him in his fucking throat with everything I have. It's a quick and powerful closed-knuckle jab, a brutal blow that sends him stumbling back. Both of his hands race to his windpipe and he collapses to his knees—gasping for breath—wheezing and whimpering. I raise my hands, waiting for his friends to jump in, but they don't. So, I turn to Raffaella and casually mention *it's time to go*. She places her half-empty cranberry cocktail atop the bar, and we walk out without looking back.

"That was so crazy. You're a crazy man," she says, speeding across the parking lot.

I turn to her once we reach the truck. "I'm sorry you had to see that. But I can't have anyone treating you like that."

"Is he gonna die?"

"No," I laugh. "But I guarantee he'll think twice before he touches anyone again."

"I love you, Max."

We decide that liquor-store champagne is the best way to ring in the New Year. We watch the fireworks on TV and make love in front of the fire. I can feel her thirst for me intensify with every thrust. And as I'm holding her, wiping the hair from her sweaty face, she looks at me in a way she never has. She already knows I love her, admire her, and believe in her. But after tonight, she knows that I'd fight for her and that I'd die for her.

Planning on skiing all day, we wake early. I make us a stack of blueberry pancakes with locally sourced huckleberry syrup, and we're about to take off when the doorbell rings.

I think nothing as I turn the knob, half expecting to meet the Sherriff. I jump back, startled, hell, fucking scared as I find my own Rosaline standing there. She's in big boots and a pink vest. "Surprise, handsome. Happy New Year," says Nadja, in her hoity-toity French accent.

"What are you doing here?"

"You are not happy to see me?"

"What are you doing here?" I ask again.

"I came for you, of course. I missed you, Max. Didn't you miss me?" I say nothing—total silence. I don't know what to say. "I'm sorry I left," she blurts. "I needed time to think about things. And... well... I have."

"You can't be here," I say. "You have to go."

"Don't be silly, Max. I just arrived." She leans in to hug me or kiss me, but I pull back. "Why be like that? I told you I'm sorry. You know I mean it. And you know I've been looking for you, don't you? I've been to all of your spots: Chicago, California, Kentucky. That doesn't mean anything to you?"

"No. It doesn't. Not anymore. You could have called, and I would've told you this over the phone."

"You don't' miss me?

"No."

"You didn't miss me at all?"

"No. I didn't."

Just then, Raffaella walks to the door. "Max, who is it?"

"Oh, I see." Nadja steps back. Her face narrows.

"Raffaella, this is Nadja," I say, lowering my eyes.

"Hello." Raffaella extends a hand, but Nadja doesn't take it. Instead, she lifts her chin and looks down at her.

"Nadja, I think it's time for you to go," I say.

"I see how it is. I leave for just a short time—what—a couple months? Nothing. And you, you are nothing, so weak, so pathetic, you just go find some slut to come fill my spot." My heart sinks as she says it, but only because I don't want Raffaella to hear.

Raffaella says nothing. She's standing silently, her hands holding her elbows, her bottom lip tucked under her top teeth, appearing perplexed as to what's happening.

✈

"Nadja, your cab is still waiting. I think you should get in it and go home."

"Why? So you can stay here, and play house, and fuck your little tramp? You're such a loser, a pathetic fucking loser." I signal my hand towards the taxi. Thinking, *goddammit, what else can I fucking do!*

"Nadja, there's no need for this. Please, just get back in the car and go home." I say it as calmly as I can.

"This is why we could never work, Max. Because you're just a pathetic fuck-boy. Go ahead, fuck your stupid slut. I don't give a shit anymore. You're not even worth it. You're pathetic. A nothing. Just a fucking looser. A weak, pathetic fucking loser and you're always going to be a—" I see a shadow shoot over my left shoulder. Feel the breeze of a fist as it rockets past my ear. Nadja steps back, or stumbles back, her eyes wide, frightened, and confused. Her hands race to her face, and blood pours from her nose, over her lips, and down her chin. Raffaella had thrown a quick jab—a sucker punch—that hit her square in the schnoz. And as her initial surprise slips away, and the pain perceived and the taste of blood recognized, she screams. "You broke my nose, you fucking bitch!" *I didn't see that coming*, I say to myself. But nobody is more stunned than Nadja, who turns and runs towards the cab.

"Never come here again!" Raffaella yells. I rush inside to grab a roll of paper towel and jog it back. Nadja is sitting in the cab, using her sleeve to stop the blood. I hand her the roll of towels through the halfway-cracked window.

"If your little slut broke my nose, I'm gonna fucking sue your fucking ass, you fucking loser!"

I stay silent as she continues shouting profanities out the window as the car pulls away.

"Where the hell did that come from?" I ask Raffaella.

"I don't know, I swear. I didn't even mean to do it. It just happened." Overwhelmed with fear, anger, and adrenaline, she's shaking and pacing.

"Well, no shit," I smirk. "No more blueberry pancakes for you, Rousey."

"Stop it. Don't joke me now. I'm sorry. I really didn't mean to do it. I never hit anyone before. I just hate how she speaks to you, and I want her to stop."

"I know."

"Are you mad at me?"

"No, I'm not mad. I just didn't expect it is all. And well, I don't think she did either."

"No, I don't imagine so. I don't even intend to do it. It just happened. Why did she say those things to you?"

"I don't know. I guess she was just surprised to see you here."

"Yes, I think it hurt her on the inside."

"And now on the outside too." I smile.

"Stop it, I feel terrible. I shouldn't have hit her."

"It's ok," I say. "I'm sure she'll be alright."

"I hope so," she says, before steering the subject. "Max"

"Yes?"

"How did she know to find you here?"

"Well, just before you came to the door, she said she had been looking for me everywhere. Chicago and California."

"Yes, but how did she know this place? You bring her here before?"

I don't want to lie to her, so I don't. "I did," I say.

And as it leaves my lips, the disappointment heavies her shoulders and dulls her face. "I see."

"But I promise you, it wasn't anything like this. It wasn't anything like what we have here. It was just a stupid weekend of partying with friends, and she knows that I come here. That's all. I promise you..."

"You don't have to promise me, I know. I know what we have. And I know that nobody will ever have it as we do. And I am sorry that I hit her. But I don't take it back, because I think she deserve it—the way she speak to you, I will never allow anyone to speak to you like that. But I am sorry if it brings you trouble."

✈

"I've never wanted to hit anybody either," I say. "But it just happens sometimes. You react, and you lose yourself in that moment, and before you know it, someone is bleeding."

"Yes, it was like that."

"Do you think you broke her nose?"

"I don't know. I tell you, I never hit anyone before. How do I know if I break it?"

"You just feel it. It cracks against your knuckle, and sometimes you feel it go flat."

"I think I hit her in the cheek, and maybe just hit a little in her nose."

"That's good; hopefully that's the case. But she sure did bleed a lot though, huh?"

"Yes, it bleed so much. I don't want her to have a crooked nose. I just want her to stop speaking to you like that. I hated it. I hated her. Why did it bleed so much?"

"I don't think she's been hit in the face all too many times."

"Yes, I don't think so either. She is very pretty. I can see why you liked her. If she calls you, please let me talk to her, and I will apologize." I smile to myself, imagining that conversation.

"I don't think she's gonna call," I say.

"But if she does."

We still spend the day skiing, then make love all over the house. She paints in the evening, and for whatever reason—I start writing again. In fact, I write a lot over the next several weeks of our historically harsh winter. I work on that story, the one I told her about, the one with the princess, the princess who saves her prince. I name her Rochelle and him Braxton, or Brad, I haven't decided.

The words come easy; they pour from my soul and flow through my fingers. I call it *She Made Me This Way*. And I feel like a great man as I pen that story, like Napoleon writing to Josephine, or Beethoven to his beloved. And after a few weeks, it actually shapes into something worth reading. Sure, I make myself a little handsomer than reality, certainly more charming.

And maybe I embellish a bit on how perfect she is, but hell, it's how I see her. It's the story of us, raw and real, from Hong Kong to the high mountains of the west. From strangers to lovers to best friends. From fantasy to finding exactly what I never knew I always wanted. I try to keep it concise, only showing what we saw, only telling what needs to be told. My only real concern is if I truly capture just how crazy Braxton is about Rochelle and if I accurately portray his evolution from selfishly pleasing himself to selflessly pleasing her.

She's so damn easy to love this girl. And the passion and enthusiasm she pours into everything makes me believe that anything is possible. She makes me a better person by just being around her. And in the high wild wilderness that is Western Wyoming, I never doubt my love for her, not for a second. She's my soulmate and my savior, and I wake every morning thankful that she's next to me. And I spend a part of every single day thinking of ways to make hers better.

We do a lot over that great winter. Not only do we ski three or four days a week, but I teach her to shoot, something she's never done. I show her how to use a rifle with a scope to be accurate at a hundred yards. I show her how to steady her shot, align the crosshairs, and time her breathing as she squeezes the trigger. She hits the target on her second shot and rarely misses after that.

I take her deep into the woods, where we listen to the wind, and how it works its way through the tall trees. We listen to the river flow under the ice and watch the elusive otters play in the stubborn stream that refuses to freeze.

We climb a hill to watch the wind roll in like waves for miles, swaying, squeaking, and squealing every Alpine Fur and Lodgepole Pine in its path.

And after that first hike, I have her smell her hands. *They smell like Christmas*, she says, and then asks *how I knew?* I tell her *she always smells*. Then I take a snowball to my face.

After reading *Cats in the Hills,* she tells me she's afraid of mountain lions. So, on one of our hikes, I spend the afternoon throwing rocks and saying, "What was that?" She tells me *she'll cut me in my sleep,* and I tell her *she's banned from scary stories.*

I find out that she's never been fishing, so I show her to fish through the ice: how to use an auger to bore a hole, secure her bait, and set her hook.

I show her how to cut and clean the Lake Trout and Mountain Whitefish we pull through the ice. And though that isn't her favorite part, she makes us mouthwatering meals and insists that fishing becomes part of our weekly routine.

I show her how to survive in the wild and in the snow. We go for long snowshoe hikes through Yellowstone, where I teach her how to build a fire, make camp, and store food—so that scavengers won't steal it.

One afternoon, we spend hours building an igloo deep in the backcountry, packing, shaping, and stacking snow blocks until my mittened hands scream for mercy. We packed enough supplies for the weekend, but on that first night, a storm hits so hard, and so strong, and with winds that could bite any bare skin to the bone. She believes we're *going to die,* she tells me so, and we would have if the igloo failed. But we wake warm and rested, and decide to stay.

On the second night, the storm retreats, revealing a sky saturated by an uncountable number of stars. We make love in that igloo, under Orion's Belt, and she tells me *I'm the most incredible adventure she'll ever have.*

We spend several frigid nights bundled in sleeping bags, counting constellations, smelling of campfires, and enjoying the rustic self-reliant life of the west. But most days we ski, we sit in the Jacuzzi, drink wine, and make love. She takes pictures of me when sleeping, and I make her dance with me whenever that one Bublé song comes on.

She paints a lot, creating some really fantastic stuff: pictures of the mountains, the Bison we'd sneak up on, the town and its variety of eclectic people. She paints and an old abandoned miner's cabin we find deep in the forest. And she even paints me, and in the nude. It's the night of the College Football Championship, Alabama versus somebody, a night I'd typically spend making bad decisions, but I don't miss it for a moment. I gladly sit for her, my arms crossed, my jaw clenched, patiently posing, until she leans back in her chair and asks me to *make love* to her.

I often lose myself in her for hours at a time. Sex with her is something spiritual, a powerful drug that keeps me up all night or makes me sleep like I hadn't slept in a summer.

She sells a painting, and the gallery agrees to take on more of her work. I tell her I'm taking her to Chicago; so that she can see—through her own eyes—strangers enjoying and admiring her talent as I do. That night, she tells me a dozen times that she loves me, and probably makes me cum twice that.

She loves me the way every man wants to be loved. A love that fuels a fire but never shies away from truth. She doesn't laugh at my jokes when they aren't funny and never hesitates to say when something sucks. She doesn't desire to bring me down, but to make me better. And I come to find pleasure in proving myself to her, a zest to dig deep and discover my full potential, though I know she'd love me all the same.

We grow into quite a team, her and me. A team that motivates, encourages, and inspires one another to bring out the best in ourselves, and I become the best man I've ever been, both confident and proud. And for the first time, in a long time, I have a purpose. And I owe it all to her—everything. She made me this way. She saved me from myself, a careless boy, seeking insignificant pleasures—fueled by self-doubt and self-pity—and I love her for it. I love her for who she is, and I love her for who she makes me, and I know I'll cherish her until I take my final breath, because she's my everything.

It's instilled in us that love takes time, that interests, goals, and social standing must align, that you must live in the same place, like the same people, and cheer for the same side. But the truth is, none of that matters. True love can't be reasoned with. It has no logic or limits. It can't be bound, and there are no barriers capable of constraining it. True love is a once in a lifetime alignment of the stars—that strikes suddenly and steals your breath. It's caused and ended wars, dethroned kings, and transformed prisoners into poets. It's the most powerful force on the planet, and if you're lucky enough to experience it—your life will never be the same.

✈

CHAPTER 27
The Luckiest Girl

THE DAY IS FEBRUARY 22nd, and it's unquestionably the happiest day of my life. In fact, it's the happiest I'll ever be, no matter what.

It's sunny outside, terribly cold, but the skies are clear. A welcome sight, in a season filled with so many storms. It's been a few days since Raffaella first came down with stomach flu. She's getting better and has her apatite back, but doesn't feel like doing much. So, we spend our day inside, where I fry us up a couple grilled cheese sandwiches to dip in our tomato soup.

She paints as I sprawl on the couch, thumbing through Ben Franklin's Autobiography, reading my favorite parts to her aloud. And just as I reach the point where he determines himself incapable of achieving perfection, she stands and sprints into the bathroom. "I'll read something else if you don't like it," I joke. But grow concerned when I hear her vomiting again.

"Darling, are you ok?" I try opening the door, but it's locked, so I stand there, telling her, "Everything will be ok."

A couple minutes later, she comes out looking lost. I hug her. "I'll get you some ginger-ale for your stomach," I say.

"I have to tell you something." She sounds scared.

"What is it?" I ask, but her uneasy eyes fall to the floor. "Is everything ok?"

"Please don't be mad at me."

"Of course I won't." I kiss her forehead, then lift her chin and search her eyes. "What is it? What's wrong?"

"Max, I don't have a flu."

"No? What is it then? Are you ok?"

"Max."

"Yes." She's looking into me, her lips quivering as she speaks.

"Max... I'm pregnant." My heart stops, or at least it skips several beats, my stomach sinks, my body numbs.

"Are you sure?" My voice is unsteady, my legs shaking below me.

"Yes, I take a test from di supermarket two times. And it's a plus two times." Her lips pout downward. "Are you mad?"

But I can't think of anything to say, hell, I can't even breathe. My heart is hot, my chest hollow, my head numb, my hands uneasy, but my smile—it feels like the biggest goddamn smile I've ever felt on my face. I stumble forward and fall to my knees. Tears race down my face. I take her hands in mine and say the only thing I can think to say. "Raffaella, I love you so much, so damn much it hurts. You're the best person I know, and I want to hold you every day, every single goddamn day for the rest of my life. Will you marry me? Please?"

A tear falls from her eye. "Of course, I will marry you." She collapses to her knees, and I pull her into me. And on that early afternoon kitchen floor, I kiss her, I kiss her so hard, and with so much purpose, that I imagine someday, when she's old and senile, and I'm long gone, she'll look back at this moment, this unbelievably perfect snapshot in time, and she'll think to herself, *damn, he really loved me.*

We lay there a while, her head on my chest, her eyes on mine. "Can I take you to dinner tonight? To celebrate?" I ask.

"You know I want to, you know that I do. I'm so happy, I don't even know how to be. But, I still don't feel so good. I'd prefer it if we could stay home tonight. If it's ok with you?"

"We can do whatever you want."

"Can I cook for you?" she asks.

"If that's what you want. But I can cook for you if you don't feel good."

"No, I feel good enough to cook. Plus, today is a day for you too, Max. You're gonna be a papà." She's grinning at me, glowing. "I want to make you something special. It's a dish that my mamma make for my papà when she wants him to know how much she loves him."

"What is it?"

"Don't worry about it. It's a surprise to you. But it's a traditional Italian dish. I know you gonna love it."

"What do you need me to do?"

"Nothing, just drive me into town to get some basil. And I need some more ricotta, maybe a nice piece of Parmesan, and of course some fresh tomato."

"Just give me a list. I'll go get everything. You stay here and relax."

"No, I want to go with you. I can't stand to be apart from you. Not today."

"I'm ready whenever you are."

"Give me five minutes, ok? I need to freshen my face. Otherwise, everybody knows I was crying today."

"But those are good tears, so it's ok," I say.

"Ah, they are the best tears. I wish I could save them."

"I love you, Raffaella."

"I love you too, Max."

"When we get back, I want to call my parents," I say.

"Yes, I will call mine too. I can't wait to tell them how much I love you."

Cruising down I-191. *Free Fallin* is on the radio. There's shiny sun-sparkling snow as far as the eyes can see. The road is dry, and the sky is clear. She asks me if we can name the child Max because *it's her favorite name in the entire world.*

"And what if it's a girl?" I ask.

"Then we call her Maxine. Is that a good name?"

"Whatever you want. I love you so damn much, I can't think about anything else right now." I glance over at her. She's smiling and more beautiful than I've ever seen her.

"And I love you too, Max. I truly do. I feel like I'm the luckiest girl in di world, and nobody will ever be as happy as I am right now."

We're coming over the top of a hill when I feel my chest explode. And not with pleasure, but with pain, horrible pain. And everything goes dark.

✈

CHAPTER 28

A True American Love Story

MY EYES OPEN, I can't see anything but brightness. I hear my name being called over and over. *Max, Max, I'm right here, Max, come on honey, come on, Max.* I recognize the voice; it's the voice of my mother. And she's crying. *Max, can you hear me? I'm right here, Max.* Everything is blurry and bright, but I can tell people are surrounding me, frantically whispering. And I can hear the rhythmic beeping of medical equipment. *Beep-Boop Beep-Boop Beep-Boop.*

"Max, are you there? Can you understand me?" asks a man with a deep voice.

"Yes," I murmur.

"Do you know where you are, Max?" asks the voice again. And my vision suddenly becomes clear, crystal clear. So clear that it feels like a dream, a dream where I'm looking down upon myself. It's a sunny day: the room is clean and white with flower baskets lining the windows and *Good Morning America* on the television. I can see that I'm lying in a hospital bed. I have casts on both of my legs and both of my arms—to the shoulder. The deep voice is coming from a dark-haired man, with three-day stubble, wearing a white coat.

"Do you know where you are?" The voice asks again.

"Yes."

"Where are you, Max?"

"I'm in a hospital."

"Yes, that's right. You're in the hospital. Max, do you know why you're in the hospital?" The voice asks.

"No, no, I don't." I look at my mother, her lips are thin, shaking, and her eyes are red.

"Max, you were in an accident."

✈

"Where's Raffaella?" I ask, looking at the man in the white coat, and then back over at my mother. "Where is she?" I ask again. But again, I get no answer. "Where is she?" I yell. Struggling to move, to break free from the restraints of my casts, but I can't. "Where the hell is Raffaella?" I demand.

"Max, please try to relax," says the doctor. "Raffaella isn't here, Max."

"Where is she?" I yell. "Where the fuck is she?"

"Oh, sweetheart," my mom cries, her eyes shiny.

"Max, I'm sorry to have to tell you this, but Raffaella didn't make it through the accident."

Everything around me goes silent. I can see, but I hear nothing. I feel nothing except pain, horrible-horrible pain, and then darkness, total inescapable darkness, the death of my soul, the slaughter of my spirit.

I wake again a day later, and it's explained to me that as we came over the top of that hill, there was an SUV waiting for us in our lane and that we hit each other nearly head-on, and at more than fifty-five miles per hour apiece.

They determined the woman had been texting on her cell phone and had crossed the center divider.

I ask to see Raffaella's body, so I can say goodbye, but they tell me *it's not possible*, that I've been unconscious for almost three weeks, and that her mother and father had already flown in and taken her body back to Italy.

They tell me she was wearing her seatbelt, but that the impact was just too much, and that she died instantly. *I pray to God that she didn't feel any pain.*

I broke thirty bones throughout my body: my nose, collarbone, sternum, and several ribs—that they actually ripped apart. I snapped several others in my legs and arms. I punctured a lung, lacerated my liver, and lost a few teeth. I ruptured my spleen and herniated dozens of discs in my spine. There are more, but with the concussion, I can't remember them.

But none of that matters, the pain in my body is nearly imperceptible compared to that of my broken heart. Without

✈

her, I have nothing. Absolutely nothing. And since I opened my eyes, not a single breath has left my body without wishing I had died that day too.

I spend another nine weeks at that Idaho Falls hospital, where I undergo seven more operations, fourteen in total. My dad had just stepped out when I woke, but had been there since the beginning, and stayed till the end.

After I'm released, I move in with my mom in Palm Springs, California, where four days a week, I endure several grueling hours of intense physical therapy and then cry myself to sleep.

I hate myself, and I know I always will because I know she'd never have died that day if I hadn't convinced her to come with me to America.

Life without her is meaningless, and I know I'll never be the same. She was the best person I ever knew. And after months of uncompromising pain, hate, anger, rage, regret, and ceaseless self-pity, I can't take it anymore. The Valium-vodka-opioid cocktails I consume—no longer numbs my pain or curtails my rage.

In my left hand, I hold that black-and-white flyer from the airport. The one with that Indian guru—and his goddamn grin—that reads: *You Love Me and I Love You.* I found it in my suitcase some months back and still haven't tossed it. It reminds me of her, or at least how lost I was before she saved me.

She showed me how to love someone, how to truly give yourself to them, and how to accept their love when they give themselves back to you. *But what does that fucking matter now?*

Pearl Jam plays in the background while the flyer falls to the floor. In my right hand, I hold a gen-three Glock-17 pistol, and I admire the way the dull-shiny patina glistens under the desert moonlight. It's the one my brother gave me when I graduated college. I've studied it inside and out. Hell, I've disassembled and cleaned the thing a hundred fucking times; it's the cleanest goddamn gun in California. I know precisely how that polymer grip feels in my palm, and the weight of the seventeen 9mm rounds it holds in its magazine.

Today it holds only one and feels light as I lift it to my chin. I know it's selfish, and I know my mom will miss me, but I have no other choice. I can't take it anymore. I'm tired of crying myself to sleep, and I'm tired of missing her so goddamn much. I want to be with her. I have to be with her. I have to be with my Raffaella. So I squeeze the trigger, and once again, I am free.

Boom! Boom! Boom! There's a loud knock at my bedroom door.

"Rick, are you ready to go?"

"Yeah," I murmur, lost in my thought.

—*Boom! Boom! Boom!* "Rick, are you up?"

"Yeah!" *Goddammit.* "I'm up! I'll be right out," I yell.

"Well, if we don't leave in five minutes—you're gonna miss your flight."

"All right... I know... I'm coming." I hurriedly shovel a stack of yellow legal pads into my backpack, throw on my Nikes, and head for the door.

My mom is waiting for me in her car. "Are you sure you have everything?"

"I think so," I say, checking my pockets.

"I put your passport and tickets in the front zipper of your suitcase."

"Thanks," I say.

Without traffic, it takes twenty minutes from her house in Redondo Beach to the airport. And today, the PCH is uncharacteristically clear.

"Rick, are you sure you want to go? Why don't you just stay with me for another month?"

"Ma, I already told you a hundred times, I'll be fine."

"I know, I know, I just worry about you is all," she says. "How's the book coming along?"

"Good," I say. "I think I actually just finished it."

"That's great." She smiles a sad smile. "The love story one, right?"

"Sure," I nod. "Something like that."

"You gonna let me read this one?"

"You want to read it right now?" I smirk.

"No, when you get back silly. After you type it all up the way you do."

"I doubt I'm gonna do anything to this one," I say. "I think I like it how it is, it's sort of raw and real. Definitely different than anything else I've written, and well, it's either gonna be for you, or it isn't, and I don't really want to go and mess that up."

"Same old Ricky," she smiles. "You've been working on that thing forever. Now that you're finished, can you at least tell me what it's called? Please." She looks at me like I'm the saddest man in the world, and I'll never tell.

A trembling smile slides across my face as I stare out at the Pacific, the blue sky, the horizon that takes your breath and never gives it back. "It's called *She Made Me This Way.*"

"Oh, honey. I'm so sorry."

Bags in hand and tears tracing down my mother's cheeks as I hug her goodbye.

"I'll only be gone a couple months," I say.

"I just worry about you is all. You're my whole world. You know that, right?"

"I know."

"Please come back to me in one piece."

"I will."

"And please don't be riding around if you don't need to be."

"I won't."

"I put all your medicines in that big front zipper pocket, the one with your picture."

"Thank you."

"Don't forget to take them."

"I won't."

✈

"Every day."

"I know—I will. I promise." I hug her again, and more tears follow. Then I turn and stagger towards the terminal.

"Ricky," she calls out. I have to turn my entire body to look back. "I love you, sweetheart."

"I love you too, ma."

The automatic door slides open, and I hobble into the Tom Bradley International Terminal for my double-layover Alitalia flight to Milan. Today is February the 22nd. It's been exactly a year since I stopped believing in fairy-tales. I have nothing left, there's nothing to me. I'm just an empty shell of a man moving around in this patched-together body with a barely beating broken heart. They tell me *I'm lucky to be alive*, but as I see it, my life is over, my soul dead, too lost to ever be found. And not a day goes by where I don't think about putting a bullet in my head to stop the sadness. But before I can do anything like that, I have to go say goodbye to my Raffaella.

THE END

Congratulations, you just finished this book.

If you enjoyed it, please consider leaving a review and passing
the word along to others. If you didn't enjoy it, then please
forget you read that last sentence.

★ ★ ★ ★ ★

Also, if you're hurting inside, no matter the reason,
I promise you the pain will pass. Better days are ahead.

Acknowledgements

To the writers I love to read. I couldn't have done this without you. Many of you, dead or alive, are mentioned in these pages.

✈

J Gatz: traveler, wanderer, son, brother, lover, friend.
This is his first novel of many to come.

© Jgatz2.0

Made in the USA
Middletown, DE
12 June 2021